EUXINE
ILLYRIA
THRACE
MACEDONIA
Hellespont
AEGEAN SEA
GREECE
IONIAN SEA
Athens
Corinth
Sparta
LYCIA
PISIDIA
Messana
Syracuse
Pachynum
Heracleum
Rhodes
CYPRUS
CRETE
SYRTIS MAJOR
Alexandria
EGYPT

THE MAN WHO MOVED THE WORLD

by

Sheldon A. Jacobson

Also by Sheldon A. Jacobson

Fleet Surgeon to Pharaoh

THE MAN WHO MOVED THE WORLD

SHELDON A. JACOBSON

THE GALLEY PRESS

GALLEY PRESS
P.O. Box 892
Portland, Oregon 97207

To

GOLDEN APHRODITE

who for two score years has bestowed upon me her love

in the guise of my

ANNETTE

I offer this hecatomb of books

Identification of Ancient with Modern Place names
(Fairly recently, some place names have been changed back toward the classical form.)

Akragas	Agrigento		Lilybaeum	Marsala
Pr. Akrokeraunia	C. Karaburnu		Lycia & Pisidia	S. Coast of Turkey
Aegates Is.	Egadi Is.		Massalia	Marseilles
G. Ambracia	G. Arta		Mediolanum	Milan
Apollonia	Pollona		Melita	Malta
Aptera	Khania		Pr. Mercury	C. Bon
Ariminum	Rimini		Murgantia	Baselice
Brundisium	Brindisi		Naxon (Sicily)	Capo di Schiso
Bruttii	Calabria		Neapolis (Italy)	Naples
Calaris	Cagliari		Neapolis	
Chimaera	Himare		(Sardinia)	Naboli
Corcyra	Corfu		New Carthage	Cartagena
Cyparissia	Blitra		C. Pachynum	C. Passaro
Drepanum	Trapani		Palaiste	Palase
Epidamnos	Durazzo		Panormos	Palermo
Euxine	Black Sea		Rhodanus R.	Rhone R.
Gades	Cadiz		Sequana R.	Seine R.
Gytheion	Githion		Pergamon	Bergama
Heraklion	Iraklion		Portus Veneris	P. Venere
Hydrantum	Otranto		Rhegium	Reggio
Iapygia	Puglia		Syrtis Minor	G. of Gabes
Iodmene	Paleokulia		Tanus R.	Luku R.
Illyria	Dalmatia		Tauromenion	Taormina
C. Lacinium	C. della Colonne		Thyrea	Astro
Lanuvium	Lanuvio		Ticinum	Pavia
Lasion	Lala		Toryne	Parga
Latana	Caetaria		Utica	Bordi Bou Chateur
Liger R.	Loire R.			

List of Historical Characters

Agiatis, Queen of Sparta
Agron, King of Illyria
Antigonos Doson, King of Macedonia
Aratus of Sicyon, General of the Achaean League
Archimedes, mathematician, astronomer, engineer
Catulus, Roman consul
Cleomenes, King of Sparta
Damippus of Lacedaemon, Syracusan envoy
Demetrios, King of Macedonia
Heraclides, pupil, friend and biographer of Archimedes
Hiero, King of Syracuse
Hippomedon, a Spartan exile in Alexandria
Marcus Claudius Marcellus, Roman general
Margos of Caryneia, Champion of the Aetolian League
Otacilius, brother of Marcellus
Philip V, King of Macedonia
Publius, Roman consul
Marcus Claudius, father of Marcellus
Teuta, Queen of Illyria

THE SCIENTIST

I know well I am mortal, and live my fleeting day.
  Yet when I mark the myriad wheeling stars above the air,
My feet touch earth no longer. Beside high Zeus himself
  I dine on sweet ambrosia, the god-sustaining fare.
Claudius Ptolemy

The action may be dated by the battle of Drepanum, 249 B.C., in the fourth year of the 132nd Olympiad, the 504th year after the founding of the city of Rome.

Foreword by Pyrrhon of Massalia

I believe that my grandsire, Pyrrhon of Syracuse, was the foremost seaman of his time; and I am going to recount his exploits for the pride of the family and the interest of others who may have a taste for the annals of the sea.

I could not evoke that time of Titans or my grandsire's role in it without setting forth the tales of three other men. The deeds of two of them, the greatest Greek and the greatest Roman of their time, determined the shape of much of his life between them; the third, a lesser man but still in the public eye, was in the center of certain other events that concerned him very nearly.

Accordingly, I present with my forebear's memoirs parts of Heraclides' biography of his friend and teacher, Archimedes, the correspondence of Marcellus compiled by his freedman Cleanthes, and (the last a purely accidental but richly rewarding find in a dingy shop in Ostium) a manuscript by the comic dramatist Lallos of Syracuse.

Rather than start and finish four parallel but separate narratives, it has seemed best to me to interweave them, so that I might present a single progression of events in chronological succession. And so I begin my history. May Clio guide my pen!

I

Extract From Pyrrhon's Voyages

I never saw my father. Even as my mother lay in the birth-throes, he met his death by an accident. I was born therefore unacknowledged, consequently without family or city. In most households that would have been the end of me too — it is very hard for a slave woman to raise a child, unless it be admittedly her master's, or if he breed her for profit. My father's lawful son and heir, my half-brother Apelles, might have sold us, or at best put us out of house and mind with some hard-driving retainers. My mother often recounted the conference that followed the funeral.

"I suppose," Apelles said to her, "that my father would ultimately have freed you. But since he died so unexpectedly, I'll do what I think he would have wanted. I've thought about you repeatedly during the past few days. I offer you four choices.

"Firstly, I am willing to give you your son and your freedom, and set you up in a small shop of some kind. Secondly, I could free you and send you both back to your old home, Utica. Thirdly, I could free you and try to marry you off to some freedman. Lastly, you can remain here in the protection of my house with complete freedom of your person, and I will raise and educate the boy.

"You need not decide now. Think it over, and make your choice."

"I do not need time to think it over," my mother answered him. "As a foreigner, I would be none too sure of myself in the business world of Syracuse. Back home it would be little better; my parents and brother lost their lives when I was captured, and there is nothing and no one for me in Utica or Carthage. As to the marriage, a freedman is a doubtful master, especially for another man's child.

"So I will accept with gratitude your last offer, and raise my son in his father's house."

From that time forth my brother assumed toward me the

duties of a father (he was 22 years my senior). I was treated in all respects as a member of the family, and he saw to my education with the boys of the best circles of Syracuse; and indeed we were kinsmen of some of them. (Our father had been of the Gamoroi, and these Land-dividers constituted the aristocracy of Syracuse). He showed in short the same affectionate concern as though I were not on the left-hand side of the family.

In early years I took my status for granted, like all children. Only gradually, and gently, was I led to perceive the difference in position between my mother and the ladies of my brother's family and friends. I remember well the time when my mother told me her history.

Her father had been a merchant of Utica. He had embarked with his wife, son, and five-year-old daughter for Malta; the sirocco had caught them, and in a wild night the ship had rammed some piece of flotsam big enough to start her seams. The leak proved uncontrollable, and the ship foundered on the following day. The crew took to the longboat, abandoning the passengers to drowning; at the last minute they permitted the little girl to be put into the boat.

As ill luck would have it, they were picked up by some rovers of Messana. The Messenians hated the people of Carthage (and of course her dependencies), even though it was a hundred years since the Carthaginians had destroyed Messana's colony, Himera, and slaughtered 2000 men to appease the shade of Hamilcar. The boat's crew was thrown overboard to perish, and the child sold as a slave.

She never spoke much of the vicissitudes through which she passed, but I can imagine them. Finally she was bought by my father, who became rather fond of her, and treated her with kindness. And so I was born.

I still remember how I cried at the tale. "How I wish, Mother, that you had never left the Carthaginian land!"

Smiling, she gathered me into her arms. "But then, darling, I should never have had you! There would have been no little Pyrrhon — ever!"

One should be very circumspect about what one tells a child.

My mother had no inkling, then or later, of the agony that her story had brought about. To rejoice henceforward in life and the good things of the world was to approve of my mother's orphanhood and enslavement; to lament them was to desire annihilation, or at least non-existence, for myself. It was a tortuous quandary for a child. That it was a ridiculous one, and that no one can change the past but must make the best of things as they are, was beyond my childish philosophy.

It did not, of course, except at odd moments, darken my days. In time I forgot the incident. I was for the most part a healthy and normally heedless youngster. But when, occasionally, I was blamed for something, at home or abroad, a momentary feeling of unworthiness would darken my mood — whether I were guilty of the charge or not.

I had nevertheless a happy boyhood playing in my brother's great house, and later wandering the hills above town with my fellows. What I liked best was rowing about the harbors of Syracuse in a borrowed shallop; and I never tired of visiting the shipyards to watch the contruction and repair of the noble galleys, and to listen to the sailors' yarns spun in recompense for my lunch.

No sailor ever forgets his first ship or his first woman — even if the latter was merely a waterfront doxy, and the former only an equally disreputable broken-down rowboat.

There was an old four-oared akation, her keel and ribs still sound, but with her fastenings corroded to uselessness and several of her planks split. This my brother bought me in honor of some minor triumph in school. Under the eyes of my friends in a shipyard, I cut replacements for the flawed members; and they showed me how to clamp them in place on the frames. The last two needed some bending, and in the yard's boiler I sofened them till they could be shaped as necessary. It was a long job boring all the holes for complete refastening, clinching all the iron nails (I could not afford the more permanent copper), and, finally, caulking; and labor of love though it was, I was glad enough to finish.

I would have rigged her at once, but my friends insisted on my taking first steps first; so I organized some of my fellows into a boat's crew, and, myself at the tiller, we made many a cruise around the island of Ortygia or across the harbor to the sack of Troy. And when, later, we put in a cut-down boat mast and a scrap of sail, I swaggered ashore as peer to the sworded trierarchs of the king's navy and the merchant skippers with wrinkled brown faces; even though I alone knew that I was of their fellowship.

My friends of the yard and the ships at first encouraged my interest, saying jokingly that I would yet be the best sailor of them all; and some of them dubbed me "Little Ulysses". But as the years passed and my love of salt water and the ships showed no sign of being dissipated by what some would term more mature interests, they began to view it with some concern. More than one took me aside to urge upon me the folly of a seafaring life.

"Look you, Pyrrhon," the proprietor of the shipyard once said earnestly. "Of all manner of callings that a man may choose, the mariner's is the worst. Life at sea isn't a glorious adventure. At best it's brutal, man-killing work, scanty and irregular sleep, poor food and never enough of it. If you remain single, you're a lost, lonely man, with only the bottle and the sluts of the waterfront when you're ashore; and usually poverty in your old age. If you marry, you can't spend the best part of the year with your wife and children, if they are your children — loneliness and neglect can drive even well-intentioned women to do things they regret too late.

"And at worst it's death at sea by drowning or fighting, or maybe capture and sale into slavery. Many poor devils can do no better; but you're a gentleman. You have a choice. Pick the court — the army — a merchant's establishment — anything rather than the sea."

This was, as I knew vaguely even at the time, good advice. Any one who knows the first thing about the nature of a boy can guess at how much impression it made.

As I grew up prosody became one of my greatest delights. In

this field I continually surpassed most of the boys at the school. Without effort I memorized long passages not only of Homer but also of the Athenian tragedians and of many of the lyric poets.

My mother supplemented this education with much from her own background. Not only could I speak Phoenician — something that later was to be invaluable for me as a merchant seaman — but she remembered and taught me much of the poetry of her own people. My paedagogos was a Gaul who often sang and talked of the lays of his nation.

I thus developed at the same time an appreciation of the austere beauty of hexameter and hemistich, the gorgeous imagery of the Semites and the lilt of Celtic song. Small wonder that I began to compose on my own around the age of eight, and continued thereafter. Small wonder, too, that the purists of the Academy (Plato had been to Syracuse, and Syracusans had been among his students in Athens) conceded that I had talent, but were made uneasy at some of its expression. There were occasional snide remarks about the "Phoenician". This was unjust; my writings were not Phoenician; neither, I am bound to say, were they in classical form; but I developed a style that was (as I think) distinctively my own.

I well remember the day on which I first saw Aeschylus' "Persians". Lallos had kept the whole theatre laughing with one of his plays, I forget which; and we were in exactly the right mood to switch to a more serious theme.

When, after the bragging of the chorus, the queen-mother Atossa told of her night terrors, a feeling of the doom that we knew had overcome the Persian host slowly congealed. Then came the messenger, with his hammerstrokes of disaster, the awful evocation of the ghost of Darius, and finally, reeling under the wrath of the gods, the ruined Xerxes.

Then I knew my appointed task. I, too, would glorify the men of old Syracuse, who even so had saved their city from the yoke of foreign tyranny, and flung back to Africa their would-be Punic overlords. I would not attempt a drama, but I should compose an epic in which I would tell of the valor of olden days. And I could make it even more real; for was not I half a Carthaginian, and could I not, therefore, feel for and with both sides in the struggle?

And so, drunken with the rhythm of Aeschylus' choruses, I took my homeward way, the beat of my own measures half-heard in my ear, the homage of Hellas already mine.

As I grew into the teens, I began to realize that I did not wish to spend my life in the house of Apelles. For all my pride in him, and for all the great love between us, I was not willing to be a non-entity in another man's home. I began seriously to consider two things; a career in the world of ships, and fame and happiness as the creator of great poetry that should bring glory to my native city.

Perhaps these would have continued only as daydreams, but when I was sixteen I received somewhat prematurely the terrible blow that everyone has to suffer. My mother — my sweet, gentle mother whom I had taken for granted for so long — sickened and died.

Those who came as comforters were wrong. No one ever recovers from such a loss. But, in time, the unendurable becomes that which is endured. And the lashings of conscience over all the sins of omission and comission — for who of us has done his duty by those who love him? — subside to a milder regret.

Something worse, in a sense, was to follow. A few months after my bereavement, I began frequenting the gymnasium once more. Meeting by chance Alcides, an acquaintance, I challenged him to a bout at the pankration. I suppose it must have been an expression of my still disturbed emotional state, for I excelled neither in boxing nor in wrestling, let alone the combination of the two. He demurred, but I pressed him — to be frank, I shamed him into it.

In the course of the bout, I felled him, then leaped upon him. He uttered a sound of agony, covered his belly with his hands, and lay still. Why he had not turned over, to protect himself, I do not understand.

He died that night.

His parents were, of course, beside themselves. His mother called me a murderer, and added bitterly, "And you stand there, alive and well, in place of a better man! I wish that you had died, instead!"

So did I.

I tell the tale thus briefly; it will be readily understood that it is not something on which I care to dwell. And I tried ever after as best I might to avoid thinking about it.

So, for both these reasons, the old pattern of my life was broken. Five weeks later, with my brother's best wishes in my ears, and a purse of his gift in my hand, I boarded a wheat ship for Massalia as apprentice to her master and owner.

It was a beautiful day in May. King Hiero had established the festival of the Romaia in honor of Rome, and its first observance was about to be held. We left a city bedecked as though to bid us a fond farewell.

My apprenticeship to Eumenes began auspiciously. A flat calm held us harbor-bound all day, during which time we finished stowing some odds and ends of additional cargo, and doing some of the thousand and one things involved in making a vessel ready for sea. Toward sunset a weak land wind sprang up; we made sail, stood slowly out of the harbor and with the wind abeam pointed her for the south. Since it was light and off-shore, it raised no seas, and we ghosted silently through the night.

Harmonia was a ploia, 92 feet overall, with a beam of 32 and a 12 foot depth of hold. In her deck were 3 cargo hatches. The stem came up in the usual swan's neck curve; the bow was rather low. The mast was slightly forward of the middle; its yard and sail overlapped each side of the ship by about 10 feet. In the bulwarks were ports for 10 oars on a side.

The captain and owner was a man of Cos, in middle age, grizzled, muscular, fairly cheerful, and — most important to me — articulate. His mate was his freedman. The boatswain, like several of the crew, was a slave.

There were 21 sailors aboard. A dozen could have handled the ship under sail, standing watch and watch for long runs; a score of men however were all too few adequately to man the oars or fight off the robbers which infested the coasts of the larger islands, particularly.

The captain had a cabin on the afterdeck, where the mate, too, occupied a tiny stateroom. The rest of us slept on deck, unless rain or cold drove us through a small hatch to a space below decks in the bow, left vacant so that her head would have buoyancy enough to rise to the waves. Head seas of any size, of course, we almost never challenged.

With the coming of day we found ourselves becalmed. "Don't we row?" I asked the boatswain after sweep-down.

He raised his head in negation. "A light, slender, heavily manned war galley would. But the best we could do would be perhaps a few stadia an hour; and at the end of a spell of that the men would be too exhausted to take care of an emergency. If we wanted to get into a harbor whose mouth was before us, or make the lee of a cape before an expected storm broke, we would row. As it is, a small distance ahead on a voyage of thousands of stadia would help us little. Meanwhile, a few lessons in marlin-spike seamanship will do you no harm."

"Besides," put in Chrysogonos, the mate, "we'll soon be getting a sea breeze that will help us on our way. That's the beauty of coastwise cruising — you can work both land and sea breezes to get ahead!" And sure enough, it came, and we were around Cape Pachynum before dusk. In the same fashion, for the next two days we made leisurely progress to the northwest.

As it turned out we did not make a cruise of thousands of stadia. It was some months after the Roman defeat at Drepanum; off Lilybaeum one of their cruisers stopped us. Their army besieging the Carthaginians in that city needed grain, and they ordered us into a cove where unloading could take place in good shelter. Our captain protested, but to no purpose. They paid for his cargo in drafts on the treasury of Rome.

I realize now, of course, that that was what he had been expecting all along; a good trader finds ways of dealing with a warring nation in such fashion that its enemy cannot take offense.

I had a further illustration immediately thereafter. Despite a brisk northerly wind, the skipper put out, only to be blown southward toward Africa.

I still retain an evil recollection of my first blue-water run. The breeze was, as I say, fresh, and the ship, riding high in ballast, rolled and pitched as though to toss us all off her deck. It was not long before I was miserably sick. I had been assigned the task of scraping the rust from a lot of marine hardware, preparatory to greasing it. I stuck it out, with frequent trips to the rail in obedience to my rebel stomach, but a more wretched sensation I have never known. With a boy's pride, I would not ask for relief; but when after a few hours the mate suggested that I lie down during the half hour for dinner (of course I wanted no food myself), I gave him no time in which to change his mind.

While I lay still I was not too uncomfortable. But when I was summoned to clean the oily pots and bowls as best I could, my misery returned undiminished.

I have never understood why seasickness is regarded as something funny. But men who will be humanly sympathetic to any other form of suffering will make jokes about this. I have, of course, long since come to terms with the motion of a ship. Nevertheless, I remember this misery as something to which outright pain might well be preferred.

A day and a half sufficed to cross the Straits of Sicily. Off the Promontory of Mercury a Punic scout commandeered the ship and directed us to nearby Utica, where under enforced but lucrative charter we loaded up with horses for the Carthaginian army in Iberia.

The heroic picture of the seafarer I had formed in my boyhood was a composite mental portrait. Men still lived whose grand-sires had pulled an oar at Salamis in the ships of Themistocles; most of the Odyssey I knew by heart; and I was of course familiar with the exploits of Jason, although the epic of Apollonius of Alexandria, later of Rhodes, was not yet available.

There was little resemblance to all this in the duties that fell to me in a horse transport! The cleaning up after the wretched animals in the hold — the distribution of immense quantities of food and straw for bedding — the endless carrying of water — these tasks were allotted me not only as the most junior member of the crew, but as a necessary part of my nautical education.

There were, of course, compensations. I spent time on deck, and learned to hand halyards, sheets, and braces. After I got my sea legs, I learned to accomodate to the motion of the ship, and the infinite play of color overside was a ceaseless delight.

We remained harbor-bound for two days, when a moderate southeaster sprang up; this gave us two days of westing. There followed a single day of calm, during which I was introduced to the oar (our numbers had been reinforced for the purpose lest with a live cargo we run out of water), and then a spanking northeaster found us, and in four days blew us into New Carthage, in Iberia.

I have learned long since that there is no sentence worse than a life at sea, unless it be the mines. I do not complain. Thus far (I began this account eighteen years after the events here described), I have been one of the lucky ones. Beauty and pride walk in the ships, and fortune sometimes. Also death. Heat, cold, and rain; bad food, limited water, lack of comfort; driving, unremitting work, beatings, and above all, omnipresent danger — from storm, from failure of hull or gear, from uncharted reefs, from coastal barbarians, from pirates — take a terrible toll of our young men.

For all that, no sailor ever forgets his first port after a long run, and I have always held New Carthage in affection. There are three things that make a boy realize that hs is coming into manhood; holding the first money of his own making, the first time a small boy salutes him with the forms of respect due an adult, and the first time that Woman invites him to dalliance. They all happened to me when I swaggered ashore in New Carthage early in my seventeenth year.

There were times when I wished that I had shipped in one of the clumsier roundships which could move only under sail. When becalmed off a dangerous coast with safety not impossibly far away, the captain would set us to rowing at our back-breaking speed of a parasang in four hours, and keep us at it for the better part of a day or, with time for rest or sleep, longer. If we found ourselves off a harbor mouth with a light offshore air, we had to pick up the sweeps and drive her wearily in; some-

times the crew of an oarless hulk, on a line from a hired triak-
onter whose thirty oars could tow her to her berth, would jeer at
our labors as they passed.

In that way, however, I learned the problems of the rower; how
much effort he could expend at varying rates, under what conditions of wind and sea he could effectively swing an oar, when he
had one more spurt left in him and when he was finished.

By the end of the second month I was, of course, one of the
greatest living authorities on the art of sail-trimming, and knew
precisely at what angle across the deck a yard could catch the
greatest amount of useful wind on each point of sailing.

It was with considerable surprise that I discovered how large
a part of the seaman's work is not a romantic struggle with
wildly billowing canvas on a raging sea, but the humbler arts
of ship maintenance — what ashore would be called house-
cleaning and repairing. I remember the first time that the shipmaster gave me some tools and a piece of wood and told me to
repair a section of deck rail that had been splintered by a
drunken stevedore. When I had finished, he inspected the job
and fell to cursing me roundly for a fool and a loafer who was out
to destroy him, his ship, and my own life. Only thereafter did the
boatswain draw me apart to explain my sins.

"Ashore, Pyrrhon," he told me, "you can do a job of woodwork-
ing well, less well, or badly; and the result of any deficiency is
inconvenience and perhaps some damage from leaky roof or
window. But let there be any point of weakness in your ship, be
sure that the sea will search it out; and worry it, and rend it, and,
if possible, use it as a point of attack to break up your ship and
drown you. Everything must be perfect. Your joints must be
square, without spaces; any little working in them is completely
unacceptable."

I don't thing any sailor ever forgets his first lesson in steers-
manship, if he ever gets that far. I found that it's not nearly as
easy as it looks to hold a course in a following sea. Each wave
seizes your ship's stern and makes her yaw — her bow falls off
and points in a new direction. As the wave passes under her
middle, she rolls as though in precarious balance, which is

exactly the case. And as it passes away under the bow, she yaws again in the reverse direction.

A moment's clumsiness or inattention, and the ship may broach to, roll over in the trough of the wave, and perish with her feckless helmsman.

I spent three years as a deck hand.

Metagonium is probably the worst hole in Mauretania, which is saying a great deal. Yet here of all places our boatswain had to lose his heart to a dockside slut.

There was some excuse for him. A slave is often severely restricted in his access to women; and service even under Eumenes, no cruel master, could not make up for the sex starvation inherent in passages at sea. Nevertheless, I cannot think what possessed him to let her know (as I assume) that he carried on him the better part of the price of his freedom. Of course, she doctored his drink; and when he staggered out, retching and vomiting, the bravo was waiting for him. We gave him a decent burial.

The captain promoted me to boatswain in his place. I was to hold the position for two years.

We finished loading our cargo of hides and started for home. After three days' waiting we caught a westerly that carried us beyond Utica; then a sirocco, almost too much of a good thing with its haze of dust, pushed us back to Syracuse. The ship was laid up for the winter months, and I repaired to the house of my brother.

I had not, in these three years, forgotten my dreams of literary fame. I did but little composing at sea; the hard-driving skipper exacted a long day's work, though there was time enough — but no more — for as much sleep as health demanded. In port, when we were not discharging or loading cargo, there was always something new to be seen, or an old shipmate to greet, or a girl to be persuaded, and, of course, the unavoidable duty of evaluating the wines of this country and of that.

And when an hour's leisure presented, I would steal time for my minute but growing traveling library, or write a letter to my brother, if some ship were bound his way.

But in the winter months, when gales raged outside, Harmonia was laid up for the season and our lives assumed some semblance of those of normal human beings. There were of course the eternal carpentering and painting, the chipping of rust preparatory to regreasing the anchors and what little chain cable we carried (most of the cable, of course, was hemp), the overhauling of the lines of papyrus and linen, the caulking and rendering of the seams with pitch. But evenings were free, and not a few of the days; and there was plenty of time for visiting friends, making use of their fathers' libraries, partying and writing.

The winters also afforded me opportunity to use the gymnasium. There is, of course, no lack of physical activity in the working of a ship; but that it is very confining can not be denied, and it was particularly of the sports of track and field that I availed myself when I could.

I also made a point of training myself in military exercises; I would join a group of ephebes for practice with spear, javelin, sword and shield, or, weather permitting, take part in a practice scout or military problem in the field.

There was an eruption of Mt. Aetna one year. It inspired a hymn to Hephaistos which the seamen honored me by singing at his shrine.

> *Shall I not sing you your mountain, its terrible aspect and breath?*
> *Hail to thee, god and destroyer! Maker of chaos and death!*
>
> *With the red smoke of your burning you clouded the kindly blue sky.*
> *Rent by the wrath of your writhings the shattered citadels lie.*
>
> *Fiercely you fired the forge in the throes of your terrible mirth.*
> *Rivers of flaming rock you spewed on the face of the earth.*

It went on in the same vein. I should not acknowledge it except that it is unchangeably associated with my name. It hooves a poet, like a woman, to have nothing in his history that may later bring him shame.

With my verses I had come not nearly as far as I had hoped. There was a variety of lyric pieces, including a few to a lass with a roguish smile, but to whom, herself, the adjective turned out to be only too applicable. But with the larger theme, the Carthaginian siege, I had made several false starts without headway.

It was the beginning of autumn. There had been an expensive fire in the skipper's home, and he was nevertheless about to marry off his daughter. Against his better judgement, therefore, he accepted a cargo of wine for Massalia, at the mouth of the Rhodanus in Gaul.

We worked our way slowly up the coast of Italy on a succession of brief easterlies, frequently lying in harbor while an adverse wind blew itself out. I have never liked this coast; its northern portion is poor in really good shelter, and it would be easy to be blown ashore in several stretches. Fortunately, a wind blowing directly onshore is uncommon.

Despite my uneasiness we made Massalia and discharged our amphorae in good time. We picked up some tin; much of it, of course, comes from Britain in Phoenician or Carthaginian bottoms via Gades, but a certain number of enterprising Gauls ship it up the Liger or the Sequana, trans-ship at the headwaters, and bring it down on the Rhodanus.

One can generally count on a Ponente blowing out of the northwest to push one back to Italy and then down her coast. On such we put to sea for what we hoped would be a rapid passage home. The Gulf of Gaul is notoriously boisterous, and we were eager to leave it astern as soon as might be. It was late the same day, however, when the wind first dropped, then began to blow strongly out of the north; and with some gloom we realized that the Mistral was upon us.

There was nothing to do but run before it. So run we did in a rapidly rising sea. We brailed up the middle of the sail so that only its wings caught the wind, and they were quite enough. All night we drove southward, rolling widely from side to side. It would have been bitterly cold had we been rowing into it (which was, of course, impossible), or even lying motionless at an anchorage. As it was, we fetched our woolens from below and even so were none too comfortable.

The next day, though clear and bright, was even wilder. We lowered the yard and bent a tiny trysail; this when set was sufficient to give good steerageway. The helmsmen lasted only two hours each; I took my trick at the tiller, and the steering sweep demanded all my strength and endurance.

There is one good thing about the Mistral: it is almost always lighter at night, which makes, of course, for both comfort and safety. For another thing, it makes capture almost impossible; although, weakened as they are, the Carthaginians no longer drown all Greek sailors caught west of Sardinia.

It was on the third day that a moment's inattention, as I believe, on the part of the helmsman let her yaw so widely that a sea wrenched her stern around and swept the deck. Had we been in ballast, she would have broached to, rolled over, and — finish! But the weight of our cargo of metal in the hold held down her keel and kept her upright. As it was, the forward hatch cover was torn off and swept overside.

It took the mate with it.

To stop or turn the ship was utterly impossible. I am not sure that a boat could have lived, and her recovery after launching would have been even more doubtful. With a volunteer crew I might perhaps have been willing to try — I don't know. But our first duty, of course, was to the ship, in imminent danger of foundering. It was urgently necessary to go below, into the wildly leaping hold, to wrestle out timbers from the dark. We had to keep them in place on the reeling, watery deck while the captain and a boatswain's mate nailed them to the hatch coaming, covered this with sailcloth, and timbered it again. Meanwhile the skipper had ordered me to the tiller to hold the steadiest course possible and try to keep green water off the deck.

Within minutes our poor shipmate, if afloat, was far astern.

The Mistral blew for five days. There followed two days of light airs; whereupon it picked up suddenly from the southwest, and with sinking hearts we knew that a Marin had us. Another storm, blowing us back in the very direction whence we came! But we were on the outer edge of this one, and its full fury passed us by to westward. Well that it did — the ship had been badly strained, and only constant labor kept the bilge water under control.

If any young person has the ridiculous idea that a seaman glories in storm, let him forget it. I own to fear. The fear has never unmanned me to the point at which I cannot carry out whatever duties fall to me, and I am able to put a pretty good face upon it, and not betray my feelings. But the sick misery is there, and I have wondered a hundred times why I let myself in for the ordeal, again and again and again.

Every series of storms blows itself out some time. The normal northwesterly finally re-established itself. Tired out by days of toil, of peril, of sleeplessness, of cold food, of ceaseless, bruising motion, we kept her head wearily before the seas. The skipper's reckoning had been thrown out completely by the alternation of northerly and southerly drift, and he had only the vaguest notion of our position. Eager though we were for surcease, after two days we furled sail during the hours of darkness, lest we come to grief on a lee shore.

It was after five days of this run that we finally made Neapolis, well south on the western side of Sardinia. By good fortune this was not a piratical stronghold, and we were able to unload, beach, and effect repairs at the cost of a mere fourth of our cargo.

Thereafter, still with a favoring wind, we caught the prevailing easterly current to and along the north coast of Sicily. We were home shortly before the onset of winter.

I was now mate of the Harmonia.

Naturally, I had looked forward to promotion, and was proud to be thought worthy of the new dignity. But I found it hard to overcome a feeling of guilt. My office was due to the death of a good and competent man, and it seemed almost wrong to rejoice in it. I knew in my heart that this was silly; I had not been responsible for his death, even though (whispered my inner antagonist) my voice had been heeded in deciding that that luckless helmsman was qualified for the steering sweep. But the captain, after all, had passed upon his competence, and so, for that matter, had the unfortunate mate himself. In all justice, I could not fairly be blamed.

Nevertheless, it was long ere the feeling went away.

Ever since the death of Alexander, his successors had been at one another's throats to win greater empires for their dynasties. This, I have felt, was indefensible, but a merchant seaman cannot direct the policies of kings.

The ambition of Ptolemy the Third made insatiable demands for construction by land and sea; and the weakness of Syria after the death of Antiochus had opened to his rival the lumber ports of the eastern end of the great Middle Sea. Phoenician power, of course, had been broken long since. It did me no harm neverthe-less in the city of Byblos to be able to proclaim my Punic ancestry, and to speak the western Semitic without a trace of foreign intonation — although Greek was fast becoming the general tongue of the eastern seaboard.

It was here that the years finally caught up the the captain and owner. A painful affliction of the joints had long been troubling him; of late months its progress had been rapid, and he now found himself unable to carry on. There was by good fortune a ship of Kalimna in the harbor, loading for home with a cargo of dyed goods. On this he engaged passage, and at twenty-four I became master and part owner of the Harmonia.

The young are ever venturesome. Using not only the working capital but drawing also on the credit of the ship and on what my own name was good for (by now I was known to the merchant community in a number of cities), I loaded the ship with lumber and not only assembled the usual raft for towing, but made up two more. I strung them in series with good hemp hawsers. The wharfside loafers, of course, said that no ship could tow against such a drag. I knew that they were right, but let them laugh. Near the bow of each raft I set up a mast. Once at sea, I put two men on each and hoisted sail on all of them.

I counted on the fairly reliable Etesian wind of summer to blow us straight to Egypt. The rafts, though poor sailers, should have way enough with their makeshift rigs to take most of the drag off the ship, and I hoped to make a fairly rapid passage. If the wind turned southerly for a day or so, I could lie to them as to a sea anchor and ride it out.

In case of dirty weather, I could rescue my sail trimmers, but the rafts would almost certainly break up, and my losses would be ruinous. Contrariwise, given the usual good weather, my profit would correspond.

Today, of course, I should be less daring.

Fortune favored me.

On arrival at Alexandria, therefore, I went to her temple to show my gratitude; and to the goddess Tyche, standing on her orb and holding (what more symbolic for me!) an oar in her hand, I dedicated a golden bracelet.

It was thereafter, while buying some provision for my dinner, that I heard the Doric. It was not unusual, of course; Cretan merchant seamen (some of them little better than pirates), Rhodian Coast Guards, Peloponnesian mercenaries and Asklepiads from Kos, with their scrolls and their packets of drugs and measures, were all over this part of the sea. Nevertheless, something about the stranger took my eye, and I invited him aboard to sup with me. He was Hippomedon of Sparta, obviously a gentleman and one who had fallen upon evil days.

After our bread and fish and onions, washed down with a little of the Egyptian beer that I enjoyed now and again, I asked what had brought him to the Nile.

"Exile," he replied. "I was one of the supporters of Agis, and was lucky to escape with my life."

I nodded sympathetically. "I have heard some fragmentary account of seizure of lands and money. What was the story?"

"A story of virtue betrayed," he answered bitterly. "Of patriotism punished with death."

"Tell me."

"You know what Sparta once was," he began. "A city of ten thousand citizens, all equal, all heroes; no rich or poor among them, but each with his plot of land, all eating their black broth at the common table.

"You know what Sparta has become," he continued. "An oligarchy of a mere seven hundred Spartiates, miserly, selfish and rich; the rest of the Heraklidai landless, debt-ridden, or both. Well, when Agis acceded to one of the dual thrones three years ago, he resolved to restore the city to the stern and purifying law of Lycurgus, and the homonoia of Zeno. To this end he proposed an abolition of debts and mortgages, and a redistribution of the land. He made over to the state his own immense fortune in land and money.

"Leonidas, the other king" — Hippomedon paused to swallow a draught of beer — "tried to prevent this. The people would have killed him, but Agis saved his life and sent him away to Tegea. Leonidas' daughter Chilonis nobly left her husband Cleombrotos to care for her father. But enemies were plotting. Agis was sent on a military expedition; Leonidas invaded with an army of hirelings and seized power; when Agis returned, he refused to inflict a civil war upon his people, and took sanctuary in a temple. They lured him out and slew him. With him perished his mother and grandmother — the first two to share his dream. All died bravely; they asked no mercy, and received none. His wife, lovely, gentle Agiatis, was left a widow."

"What of the rest of his party?"

"Cleombrotos would have shared his fate, but Chilonis successfully begged her husband's life. This time it was he whom she loyally followed into exile. And I was his friend, so I am here."

"A noble dream! And a noble man, to strive to make it true!"

"He was that, indeed. Unhappy city, to lose such a king! Unhappy wife, to lose such a husband!"

I was moved (as who would not be?) by his tale.

Before departing, he asked my routing.

"I have already undertaken to load some fine furniture, some cotton cloth, and some fabrics from the east for Corinth. Wheat, of course, is always a paying cargo in mainland Greece. I have heard of a shortage of papyrus cable in Cretan Kydonia; I'll pick some up, and if I do not delay, I'll be able to get home before the autumn gales."

"Gytheion could use your cable, I think. Could I persuade you to carry it there? If you don't find a market, surely the shipping of Sicily could take it?"

I looked at him and laughed, and after a moment he joined in. The grotto of the cordwainers at Syracuse, with its relatively uniform temperature and moisture, produces the best line in the world. Then I asked, "Why do you want me to go to the port of Sparta?"

"I should like to get a message to Sphaeros, our old tutor. He may be in serious difficulties. I should like to let him know that I have renewed my friendships here, and will shortly be in a position to aid him if he finds it advisable to go abroad. I can give you the name of a reliable messenger to carry the word from Gytheion."

"I will do that."

I did better, I was the messenger. I found an arms factory at Gytheion, which turned out arrow-heads and spearpoints of excellent quality; because of a political upset, a buyer had cancelled a large order, and it was available on advantageous terms. I had never seen Sparta; so I made use of the delay by turning the transporting and loading over to my mate, and taking the road north.

I think that everyone who visits Sparta is impressed anew by the aptness of the quotation to the effect that generations to come will find it difficult to believe in the greatness of Sparta because so little will remain. There she stands on the winding Eurotas, the long hogback of Taygetos to the west, eastward the shorter Parnon; an unimpressive scatter of mostly mean stone houses, a few severely simple temples, and otherwise — nothing.

Sphaeros I found without difficulty, a grave man of middle age. He thanked me for my trouble, but gave me to understand that he felt no danger. "But if you will come with me, there is someone else who would be glad of news of the welfare of Hippomedon."

Hippomedon had not exaggerated. Agiatis was an almost breathtakingly beautiful woman. It was not merely the classic regularity of the feature and the lines of her body — nowhere too full, everywhere fleshed out well enough. She had one of the most musical voices I have ever heard, but that was not it, either. I might simply say "spirit"; perhaps I might best describe the effect by likening it to layers of transparent, delicately tinted, intricately shaped glass.

Afterward, in fact during an interminable afterward, I remained under the spell. Nothing ridiculous, of course — she was a queen, even if a deposed one, and an immensely wealthy woman besides. I was no calf.

But the enchantment remained. Everyone has some unfinished business in his life.

The season was well on. Heavy winds and squalls presaged the gales of winter when we saw Syracuse again.

This voyage marked a triple turning-point in my life.

In the first place, there were my captaincy and the foundation of the financial success which it made possible. For the voyage succeeded; the more so in that I carried my wares at the time of a rapidly rising market.

Secondly, it determined my involvement in the Spartan revolution for eight long years.

The other significant event was that in the theatre at Alexandria I heard Mnesichos give forth three of the last idylls of Theocritos. I was, of course, not unfamiliar with his work; I had picked up a scroll at the Peiraios. But these poems were new to me, and in any case the actor's beautiful rendition gave them a loveliness by which I was at once enraptured and saddened.

For I realized that this was far beyond my powers. I had talent, yes; but this was genius. And I knew definitely what I had not till then let myself believe — that the fellowship of the Muses was not for me. I could write pretty verses, yes; beautiful ones, even. But they were buried in material that was — well — pedestrian. Pegasus might come at my call, but he would never bear me up to the empyrean. My gift was only for the admiration and pleasure of myself and my friends.

The blow was not as bitter as one might think. Half unconsciously, I had long been prepared for it. Neither had I devoted myself utterly to Apollo. I was fundamentally a seaman; and if the gods had made me, even in a small way, something more, I should not repine, but give thanks for their favor.

So I told myself, and it was indeed true. A man should accept his limitations, and within and despite them make of himself the most heroic figure that under the fates he could. Yet often as I reconciled myself, day after day, to that self-appraisal that I knew was the true one, I rebelled against those same fates night by night. A seaman — yes, even a seaman of clouded birth and Punic heritage — might attain to that renown in which he would consort with generals, bankers, merchant princes. But a poet walked with the gods; and a Homer, an Aeschylus, a Pindar, might woo and win a queen, and not demean her bed.

For stubborn, impossible dreams of glorious Agiatis as fair and ardent wife long haunted my pillow.

It was a little more than a year after I assumed command of the Harmonia that I met Archimedes for the second time. Heraclides had invited my brother to a meeting of his club; my brother sent his regrets when he heard that my ship had just made port, whereupon Heraclides at once included me in the invitation.

Most clubs were made up of either citizens or metics; in a few such as this, however, Syracusans mixed with the resident foreigners. At the house of Heraclides we were introduced to Hesychios, Euphranor, Paianios, and of course Archimedes, all of this city; Scyllis, an Argive; Hegasias the Corinthian; Demetrios of Alexandria; Saul ben Menassa, a Judean; Hermagoras (not, of course, his original name), a Carian slave; and the one they always called "the Traveler." These were not all of the eranistai, I was told, but the remaining few were unable to attend.

We washed and reclined on couches arranged in the usual open square. We dined well on bread, onion, greens, a little fish in olive oil, nuts, honey, and cheesecake. Thereafter, wreathed, we received our cups and poured the three libations, to the gods, to the heroes and to Zeus, of the good Cretan wine. After drinking, a few of the guests began to play kottabos. Paianios was particularly skillful in his throw. The wine drops from his cup arched high, hit the mark almost every time, usually striking the little bust of Hermes with a tinkle and occasionally making a second sound as they dropped from it to the saucer in which it stood.

As a young serving maid, both shapely and comely, removed the dishes, our host asked Archimedes to open the symposion by telling us of his newest prospective field of study. The scientist was, as I later learned, a man at that time in his late fifties, but could have passed for less. He had a fine head, with regular, bearded features; he was a man of commanding presence, slightly over middle height, of medium muscular development. I must confess that I was still at that stage of life when I preferred to gaze at the maid, clad only in a skirt, rather than at the famous personage in the seat of honor.

"I have become interested in the measurement of curved bodies," Archimedes began. "The area of a circle, as I will not demonstrate now, because the demonstration is very lengthy, can be expressed by multiplying the radius by the circumference, and halving the product."

Watching the girl, I began to calculate idly. Suppose the diameter were seven — no, it looked like six finger-breadths, then the radius would be three and the circumference about eighteen. The product would be about fifty-four. Divided by two, that gives twenty-seven. But Archimedes was still speaking.

"I would rotate an imaginary polygon within a sphere to estimate its volume."

But I was interested at the moment in hemispheres, not spheres. Now Scyllis was speaking.

"Was it not the perfect beauty of the sphere that fascinated Pythagoras, and induced Parmenides to postulate a spherical world?"

"What does our young friend the sea captain say to that?" Archimedes, the kindest as well as the greatest of men, would see no one neglected.

I tore my attention from the girl with an effort, my mind racing as I did so. "I think the hemisphere or the semicircle more beautiful, sir," I replied. "Is not the promise of the new moon even lovelier than the fulfillment of the full?"

"Well said, young man!" Archimedes rejoined, with a twinkle in his eye. "But," pretending to glance out through the window as the maid, her task done, left the room, "I fear that your moon has set with both hemispheres!"

Now Euphranor, at the great man's left, recited, very beautifully, the last chorus of Oedipus Tyrannos, ending with, "Call no man happy before the day of his death."

Hegesias picked up a lyre and rendered a dithyramb of Bacchylides.

Scyllis set us laughing with a fragment from the comic dramatist Antiphanes.

Hermagoras gave us a love song of his native Lydia.

I was next in order. I plucked up my courage and rendered one of the products of my days at sea.

Sappho's Isle

Have you seen Lesbos?

I have seen Lesbos in the silver dawn
Lift up her head rough-hewn from out the sea
Where to the East sleeps Asia's alien shore.

What did you see on Lesbos?

I saw ravines fall from the craggy tops.
I saw the olive-groves upon the steep
Mantle in decent green the ragged rocks.

Whom did you see on Lesbos?

Hard by the sea I saw the silent town.
Upon an upland slope a village lay,
A stronghold higher; Grecians saw I none.

24

Although I knew that they must have thought it outlandish, they were kind enough to praise it.

Saul ben Menassa favored us with a desert song of the camel caravans.

Demetrios took the floor. "I have a problem to propose," he said. "How may a man know what is the way of virtue?"

"Our law bids us to love our neighbor," Saul offered. "If, therefore, we refrain from giving offense, we do well."

"Do you mean that the wish and welfare of the other party is an adequate criterion of the rightness of an act?"

"I do."

"Suppose, then, that you were a magistrate, about to try someone for a crime. The prisoner would want to be let off, innocent or guilty, would he not?"

"True."

"So, in like case, would you, would you not?"

"Probably."

"Then to do by him as both you and he would want to be done by, would be to fail your duty, would it not?"

Hesychios cut in. "There are various orders of duty. First, we must act according to the wishes of the gods. Then comes duty to the City. Then our families and friends have their claim."

"When the Great King ruled," said Demetrios, "he could, and did, require any Persian to give his own or his son's life at the King's merest whim. If you were in his domains, and he wanted your son killed for no good reason, you would try to escape with the boy, would you not?"

"Certainly."

"But how could the same act be adjudged righteous for one man and wrong for another?"

"Different peoples have different laws."

"And the same people has different laws at different times, does it not?"

"It does, surely."

"Then there is no such thing as right and wrong," exclaimed Demetrios triumphantly. "There is only legal and illegal, which is, after all, a mere convention!"

"I think not, Demetrios," Archimedes put in. "I believe that there are eternal verities, and that right is right, within wide limits, and wrong is wrong — regardless of place and time. You remember the Spartan general who was told by an omen that he must sacrifice a couple of girls if he hoped for victory; he refused to do it, but gained the victory nevertheless. On the other hand, Agamemnon sacrificed his own daughter, Iphigenia, to gain a favorable wind for Troy. Shall we believe that what was right in the time of Agamemnon suddenly became wrong later on? I cannot accept that. Again, it has always been accounted evil among the Hellenes for a man to wed his closest kin; yet in Egypt, where this had long been practiced, the Greek King Ptolemy wedded his sister Arsinoe, and in Persia mother-son marriages have been permitted. Did that which was wrong suddenly become right?"

"What then is the answer?"

"As I said, I think that, in general, right and wrong remain the same, regardless of place and time. But to ascertain the right that is permanent, as against unimportant customs and practices that are ephemeral — this is the great task of philosophy."

The master was so good as to invite me to visit him at any time.

For two years my brother had been suggesting that I marry, and in my twenty-sixth year I let myself be persuaded. I had no overwhelming desire for fatherhood, but felt a reluctance to let my mother's blood run out. I might, I am sure, with my brother's sponsorship and my financial independence, have gotten a bride from one of the better families of Syracuse, despite the shadow of my birth (although the aristocracy, I suppose, would have been closed to me). But a certain loyalty to the past — or perhaps mere stubbornness — drove me to seek a mate from among those who were born of slave mothers, like myself. My brother Apelles, of course, disapproved, and his wife even more so.

There was in Syracuse a small Athenian merchant to whom an Iberian housemaid had borne a daughter, and this was the maiden I selected. And so, between the cold rains of the month of Gamelion, according to Athenian custom, we made sacrifice to the divine sponsor of marriage. Here, after the ritual baths in water from the sacred spring, Praxilla and I, with our friends and relatives, met for the wedding banquet. Her father, I am bound to say, did himself well, and my bride, sitting veiled at the women's table, had no reason to feel ashamed.

I had one moment of sharp sadness. When the white oxen had drawn home the carriage on which Praxilla sat between the Conductor of the Bride and myself, followed by the wedding guests with her mother bearing the torch, my own poor mother was not there to welcome her.

But as the party hurled small fruits and nuts, and Praxilla ate her quince, the cheers and songs dissipated my dark mood of the moment. And when the smiling Nympheutria had led her to the chamber, and left us alone, and the epithalamion was raised outside by the young men in chorus, I was quite myself once more.

When I went to sea again that spring, I gave my steward special charge concerning my bride, for a new life was burgeoning within her.

But she miscarried.

A young husband approaches his home after an absence with very happy anticipations. I must own to being somewhat taken aback when Praxilla greeted me with, "Oh, so you're home again!" and followed this with a stream of complaints in which I seemed to be made responsible for her miscarriage, her "abandonment," and the loss of her girlhood home. In a sense, of course, I was.

Well, we made it up, more or less, by bedtime. It rankled, nevertheless, and continued to do so.

It was mid-winter. In thirty days, in the month of Anthesterion, Syracuse would hold the festival of Kore, the maiden, in honor of the goddesses Demeter and Persephone. The two have always been more devoutly worshipped by us Sicilians, I believe, than anywhere else in the world; and indeed I know of no other lands where the favor of the goddesses results in richer crops. In Attica, in their honor, they celebrate at this time the Lesser Mysteries; but I much prefer the greater festival at Syracuse.

Our club was meeting to consider sponsoring an entry in the lyric poetry competition on the holy day, and I had been asked to submit something for the occasion. Not to be uncooperative, rather than in any real hope of winning, I had looked through my writings for something suitable.

I suppose that what I have just written is a bit disingenuous. My reluctance to give forth with my writings has always, I suppose, been a form of petty hypocrisy; and it must be so. An artist of any kind cannot work in a void. He needs a public — preferably an approving one, but at any rate, a public.

This proposition, of course, recalls the old philosophical question: would there be thunder in a world in which there was no living creature to hear?

At any rate, I came up with an account of the first voyage on which the shipmaster had considered me competent to stand a trick at the helm at night. There was always, of course, half the crew available, but often in good weather all but the helmsman would nap off and on.

Akragas, as is well known, exports delicacies to Africa, and we had loaded up there with fruits and nuts for Kelibia. I have always liked Akragas; her architecture is too much decorated for some tastes, but I like touches like the lion-headed rainspouts of her palaces. Our landfall was to be the Promontory of Mercury. I had written up my impressions of the voyage, as follows:

Sunset and dusk, and the dying of day; and night on the helmsman.
Overhead clustered in brilliance undimmed the clear constellations
Swinging around with the Bear, that ordered their way to the westward!
Forward, astern, and abeam the empty vastness of Ocean
Hailed him as fellow and friend with a lusty blow on the shoulder!
Underfoot felt he the heave and the surge of the black-bosomed vessel
Thrilling with glorious life to the sport and the space and the darkness!
What were her braces and sheets but the stuff of his very own sinews,
Straining their strength to withstand the breath of the driving northeaster?
What was her forefoot awash but his bosom cleaving the waters?
What was her mainmast tall but the spear-straight stance of his backbone?
What were her arching sails but the wraith-like wraps of his spirit,
Lofty and lone and washed with the wide-blowing winds of the heavens?

Presently was he aware that the blackness of sky to the eastward
Now seemed a little less black, and the stars lost some of their brightness;
Then a grayness arose and walked in the waters of heaven,
While that the waters below were yet enwrapped in their darkness;
Then to the middle spaces the gray gleam dropped; and thereafter
Naked lay in the dawn the wan sea's shoreless confusion.

Slowly, after that first swift charge on the powers of darkness,
Over the breadth of the ocean broadened the smile of the morning.
Only into a world that was well bedecked for his coming
Shone after long delay the golden orb of the sunshine;
Crouched for a moment to peer from over the sill of the sea-line,
Rose to his proper round and donned his garments majestic.
Under his gaze fled the ship through the blue and gold of the morning.

And so, on the appointed day, we joined the crowd that marched to the temple of the Mother and the Maiden, singing hymns and bearing gifts which the priests received. The animals were sacrificed, the other offerings placed before the statues. While the bones, fat, and viscera burned, the meat roasted to be devoured in honor of the deities. Later, still in our best, we went to the theatre, where each of the contestants presented his composition. Naturally, I was nervous, but not too much so to acquit myself as well as I am able.

I didn't win; but neither was it the fiasco I had feared. There was much praise for my verses among the seafaring fellowship.

Shouting orders on the deck of a ship in a squall is not conducive to the nurture or preservation of the best singing voice; and my lyre is not the equal of the kithara that is generally used in competition. Nor can my simple Dorian mode rival more complex musical styles. I am not searching for alibis; I confess frankly that I was up against more gifted poets. But even to be admitted to such competition is, I suppose, something.

I have written almost nothing concerning my domestic affairs; my home life was an unhappy one. I could not seem to please Praxilla. I wooed her with fair words, with gifts, with every means that I could think of. All was to no avail.

It was not that she was a selfish woman, or greedy, or light-minded, or lazy. It was simply that I could not do anything that would give her joy.

I finally asked her whether she would like to call it quits. She answered that nothing would please her better.

So, without any recriminations on either side, I divorced her and sent her back to her father with her marriage portion and a good deal more.

She had not the gift of happiness, and no one could help her.

The Epirote cattlemen required large amounts of salt. They needed it in the first place for their livestock, but in very much greater quantity for salting the meat and dressing the hides. My commercial correspondent at Corinth had notified me of a current shortage. The region was a dangerous one, by reason of King Agron's Illyrian pirates. "Sail west of Cape Malea," ran the old Aegean proverb, "and forget home!" But where on the sea could one expect safety? The midsummer following my wedding, therefore, found us at the salt pans of the Lesser Syrtis. The ship had been light and in ballast; we discharged the rock and proceeded to take on a full cargo.

On a moderate westerly, we made our way northeastward to Cape Pachynus, then along the eastern coast of Sicily.

The news at Hydrantum was disquieting. The Roman squadron had been withdrawn, for the time being, to the Tyrrhenian Sea, and the ships of prey were unusually active. There was nothing else to do, however, but stand across the straits toward Oricon, at the head of the bay behind the promontory of Acroceraunia, and hope to elude them.

The hope proved vain.

We started across with a steady beam wind from the north. We had not very long cleared the harbor, when two or three voices at once sang out for a sail broad on the windward bow; and within minutes we were able to identify the stranger as one of those long, lean Illyrian lembi — speedy, crowded with fighters, and implacable. Of course, we turned; but to run was as hopeless as to stand and fight.

My crew was demanding that I abandon the ship with its freight and let them make for the shore in the longboat rather than wait for capture and sale in the slave market. Even the slaves among them feared to risk a worse master and bitterer servitude. But I did not think that we could make the beach in time.

And then came the great idea. And on the heels of it, the greater. While the longboat was being prepared, I called for the sounding lead and hove it. As I hoped — a mere two and thirty fathoms! I hurriedly had a hundred fathom coil of line bent on to the anchor cable, and another — my last — to it. Meanwhile, others opened the seaplugs, swung an axe to cut another hole in the hull, and tossed the anchor overside. Then we took to the longboat, set the boat sail and steered for shore.

As I had expected, the pirate stopped at my ship only long enough to put a few men aboard, then took off after us. We could not hope to outdistance him.

As I likewise expected, he had covered only half the interval when he became aware that my ship was sinking under his companions. Perhaps he had encountered that trick before, and was keeping a sharp eye astern, as I had hoped. At any rate, back he turned to rescue his men, and we made good our way ashore as Harmonia disappeared beneath the sea.

My crew was greatly surprised when I made arrangements for them to sleep in a farmer's outhouse, and sent to town for a week's provisions. They had expected that I would either go about making arrangements for transportation home, or that I would sell the slaves and pay off the freemen. (I had, of course, brought all money and valuables ashore.)

It took a little longer than I had expected. It was about three weeks later that we arose one morning to find Harmonia, as though risen from the dead, riding quietly at anchor. We had lost the cargo, but saved the far more valuable ship.

My men bragged, of course, on our return to Syracuse; and the word got around, and this established the basis for the modest reputation which I came to enjoy. Even Archimedes heard of it, and sent me a renewed and more specific invitation to call on him.

When I did, he asked me, "That the sea water would dissolve your salt, any one would know. But how did you guess that the resultant brine would be heavy enough to flow down and out through the holes in the hull?"

"Wells which are dug at the seashore have to be used sparingly," I told him, "lest they be contaminated by the salt water underneath the fresh. The fresh water floats on top of the salt because, presumably, it is lighter. Metal sinks in water, I suppose, for the same reason. Wood, being lighter, floats. A bladder full of air floats even higher."

"And so your wooden ship, having no ballast in her, floated once the heavy salt had drained out of her, as you figured she would. Well reasoned! You have the makings of a scientist! I should be happy to have you join our discussions of mathematics and geometry, if it please you."

And so I did, in the wintertime, when the ship was laid up. And so progressed my friendship with Archimedes.

It was on a voyage to Pisae, Portus Veneris, and Genua with a cargo of small metalware and ceramics that our luck ran out. We were reaching on a fine westerly when a hemiola was sighted astern. She ran us down rapidly. Her sail and yard were struck, then she lowered her mast till it lay aft along the deck; then oarsmen along her lower, and the forward half of her upper decks, pulled her alongside. Resistance was useless; most of my crew were no fighters, and they were hopelessly outnumbered.

Our feelings can be imagined. I had reason to hope, of course, that my brother would ransom me, given the opportunity; for which I would try later to repay him. But my ship and cargo were lost. For the freemen among my crew, slavery was the only prospect. It was the slaves who were in best case. For them it was a matter merely of exchanging one bondage for another; and while I flatter myself that they would not willingly have changed masters, they alone had no reason to despair.

They brought us ashore at a small harbor somewhat to the westward of Calaris, in Sardinia. We passed through a high stockade and were locked in the barracoon, a stoutly built shed with an earthen floor, unfurnished except with a couple of buckets that served for latrines, another two with drinking wa-ter and a long, narrow table on which, morning and evening, they set our unappetizing meals.

As I remarked, my slaves, I think, had had little to complain of (as slavery goes). It had not been my policy to work them up to the limits of endurance; they ate the same as the free, salaried seamen, and I was never a man for the whip. I nevertheless perceived, I think, a certain grim satisfaction on their part that we now found ourselves in the same unenviable status. They were far from parading the feeling, I am bound to say; except to the enhanced sensitivity of my mixed Greek and Semitic blood it was, I am sure, imperceptible. Perhaps they even deplored the sentiment that they were powerless to control. But such is the stuff of our poor humanity.

A few days passed, during which I had an inconclusive talk with my captor on the subject of ransom. It was not a thing that was very conveniently arranged.

Then, one morning at daybreak, there was the peal of a trumpet, followed by shouts and the noise of men running, and, a few minutes later, by the rhythmic thudding of what proved to be a battering ram against the gate. This broke off repeatedly, as the defenders downed an attacker, but resumed as often. Peering through one of the barred windows, we saw pirates manning the wall in defense.

It took but a moment to organize another battering party in the prison. I wasted no time on the thick, iron-studded, oaken doors. Forming a small human pyramid, we swung the table again and again at the roof just above the eave.

It gave. We wriggled through to see a half-dozen men in armor surmount the wall and turn to the gate, only to be hemmed in by five times their number of pirates, while others of the defense party re-established the continuity of the line of men on the wall above.

We charged down with long knives snatched from the cook shacks, quickly exchanged by some of us for weapons wrenched from the wounded or dead. In a moment I found myself alongside the one who seemed to be the leader of the assailants — I had realized from their shouts that they were Romans — and together with them we cut our way to the gate, struck down those who manned it, and loosed the bar. The legionaries poured in, and it was all over.

The young officer at whose side I had been fighting offered his hand. "I owe you thanks," he said. "I am Marcus Claudius."

"And I am Pyrrhon of Syracuse." This was my first meeting with Marcus Claudius Marcellus.

My ship, with cargo intact, was still moored in the harbor. They let me recover her, with my crew, in recognition of our assistance. Marcus Claudius, having been first over the wall, was crowned with the corona muralis.

Similar assaults and captures, I soon learned, were taking place all over the island.

In such fashion Sardinia was wrested by Rome from the enfeebled hands of Carthage. The African city, so recently defeated in war by her rival and further exhausted by the Numidian revolt, dared make no counterstroke. And since she had been unwilling or unable to keep the island from becoming a lair of pirates, none of us who followed the sea grieved at her loss.

In most quarters, this is regarded as a shameless and unjusti-

fiable conquest by Rome. As far as I am concerned, I find it hard
to quarrel with a decision and a train of consequences that
raised me from capture and potential slavery to freedom. It is
true, however, that if Carthage was unable to police her colony,
it was because her power had been broken by Rome. In an
earlier day, piracy had been kept to a tolerable minimum. Instead of this use of naked power, Rome might have proposed a
joint police project, or at least she might have given Carthage an
ultimatum, with time for its implementation.

But such are the ways of statesmen.

On my return home, I did not forget to make an offering at the
temple of Poseidon, who had sent me Marcus Claudius in my
hour of need.

II

Extracts from the Life and Letters of Marcus Claudius Marcellus, as arranged by his freedman Cleanthes.

Marcus Claudius, later surnamed Marcellus in honor of his prowess on the fields of Mars, was born in the year 485 after the founding of the city.

He was named after his father. Even as a boy young Marcus evinced a seriousness and maturity beyond his years. Not only was he keener even than the generality of Roman boys in every sort of military study and exercise, but on the family farm he was assiduous in labor of all kinds — in order, as he said, to increase his strength for the service of Rome. Under the supervision of his tutors he was never so happy as when the subject at hand was geography or history — both of them, he believed, of prime importance in war.

For the rest, he was ever a dutiful son, and scrupulous in his observances of all that concerned the gods.

The result was a tireless body and a mind that could exclude from consideration everything that did not pertain to success in the field. As might be expected, he soon drew to his achievements in combat the approving attention of his superiors. His blooding at the age of nineteen was in a most unlucky engagement; it is recounted in a letter that by good fortune still survives. I append it not merely for the experience it describes, but even more as an example of how, even so early in his career, Marcus analyzed and tried to draw lessons from every experience.

I was so fortunate as to obtain, and include herewith, a few letters which, although written neither to nor by Marcellus, bear significantly upon his career.

Sextus Lutatius to Marcus Claudius Maior. Before Lilybaeum, Sicily, on the 2nd day before the Nones of August, in the consulships of Claudius and Junius, and in the year after the founding of the City the 504th.

By now you know of the battle of Drepanum. I write to acquaint you with some of the details, as well as to tell you about your son, Marcus. You will be gratified but not surprised to learn that he behaved like a Roman.

On his arrival, I secured a place for him on the flagship Cerb-era, in the praetorian guard. (In the case of a raw eighteen-year-old, this took a bit of doing.) He, of course, had never been aboard a ship before, saving the ferry over the Straits of Messina, and you should have seen those enormous eyes as he climbed aboard and saluted the officer of the deck.

The boy had a hundred questions, naturally. Yes, I told him, the quinquereme was exactly 100 feet long, with an eighteen foot beam at the waterline and 27 on deck. I showed him the fifteen oar ports on a side, each beside its five-man rowers' bench, and the two steering sweeps at the raised poop. I explained the working of the corvus on the high forecastle. He wanted to know her speed; I explained that the sail would drive her up to 150 miles between dawn and sunset, under ideal conditions, if we got them — which we don't except rarely, and then only an hour or two at a time, with a fresh quartering wind off a weather shore. With the oars, I told him, she could make over two miles in a quarter-hour spurt, up to twelve in a fast two-hour run; but for long periods the rowers could not maintain more than two and a half miles per hour. I finally turned him over to a decurion who took him below and showed him where to stow his gear.

It was only a few days later that it was decided to attack at Drepanum, up the coast. Then occurred that unfortunate incident that you may have heard about. The augurs told the consul that the sacred chickens would not eat. He smiled grimly. "Well, then, they will drink!" and with his own hands he flung them over the side.

Between ourselves, cousin, I share his scepticism concerning the auguries; I doubt whether the blessed gods speak through chickens and crows. But his action was a grave flouting of ritual, and had, I believe, a dampening effect on morale throughout the fleet. If there is any one thing in which we excel all other peoples, it is the constancy with which we pay the immortals their due of form and order.

We got under way after nightfall in the hope of surprising the Carthaginian fleet with most of its crew ashore. The veterans took the opportunity of sleep before battle, while the rowers plied the oars; young Marcus, as you may imagine, did nothing of the kind. He cleaned his weapons a dozen times, and looked like a wine bottle about to pop its stopper.

Our attempt at surprise was a failure; as we reached Drepanum at dawn the enemy put out to meet us. I overheard the brief tactical discussion.

"Form a circle well offshore" was Otacilius' advice. "The enemy are our superiors in ship handling. This will cancel out their advantage and force a bow boarding action. Our legionaries outmatch the Africans at this, and one ship can aid another."

"We could not maintain such a formation," was the opinion of the praetor Servilius. "The battle would become a confused melee; too many of our ships would be rammed and sunk by the enemy, maybe by one another. But if we draw up, bows out, in line alongshore, our sterns are protected by the beach, our beams by one another."

"That is what we will do," the consul Publius decided, and a dispatch boat carried the word throughout the fleet.

It was hot work in the Cerbera, I can tell you that. She was the southernmost in our line of 120 ships. The enemy were numerous enough to overlap by five, so we were under continuous attack from the bow and from the port side. Only an exceptionally skillful shipmaster, P. Fabius, and the best oarsmen in the fleet kept us from being rammed and sunk.

The boarders simply poured into her. My sword arm grew mighty weary, my shield arm too.

When I could spare a glance for Marcus, I saw that the boyish excitement was gone. He was fighting like a veteran, self-possessed and sober, his sword darting out just long enough to do its execution, then back and poised. Twice I saw him stand over a downed Roman and receive on his shield the blows that had been meant to finish him. Once, when the hooked corvus at the bow dropped and offered its gangway onto an enemy ship, javelins felled our men as they raced across; the praetor called for volunteers, and Marcus was among those who cleared the enemy deck. It was beautiful to see how well he went about it.

The other ships, though, weren't so lucky. The rowers were weary. They had no room to maneuver; ahead was the enemy, astern the shallows. It was impossible to go along the line to succor a hard-pressed friend. The Carthaginian galleys, on the other hand, had plenty of sea-room. They could back at will, and any luckless Roman who darted ahead was rammed in the side. The Carthaginians generally evaded the corvus, and there was no bridge, therefore, from one deck to another. The soldiers stood helpless while the Punic rams did their work. Some of our ships grounded in the shallows and became easy prey.

When the consul finally sounded the retreat, only thirty vessels fought clear.

It was indeed a melancholy day for Rome. There are many new widows.

Between ourselves, cousin, I think that the senate made a grave error in its choice of an admiral. The consul is a fine administrator, but not much of a field commander. He should have been in the van, where he could have launched an attack on the enemy fleet as it issued from the harbor in disarray; instead he had taken the rear to hustle the stragglers along — which any old centurion could have done for him.

Marcus escaped with scratches. I think that the boy will go far.

Do you think you could send an amphora of Falernian? The army Posca is about the worst I have ever drunk.

If you are well, then so am I.

Marcus Claudius Maior to Marcus Claudius. At Rome, on the first day of the Kalends of September, in the year after the founding of the City the 504th.

Marriage and fatherhood came to you young; young, you must bear their burdens.

With sorrow I write to inform you of tragedy.

There was a piratical descent upon Liternum, upon the occasion of the intended wedding of your cousin to the daughter of Lucius Terentius. The bride and several other women and girls were carried off, including your infant Claudia. Your wife escaped.

We hope, of course, to recover them by ransom, and thereafter to punish the villains. The gods will decide.

Take it like a Roman.

Marcus Claudius, of the 13th Legion, to Otacilius. Written at Ticinum, Northern Italy, on the eve of the Kalends of February, in the year after the founding of the City the 505th.

You ask about the recent action at Cenoni.

According to our orders, four days ago my century went on a punitive expedition against the village of Cenoni. Led by a guide, we proceeded by a little-used trail and escaped observation. Toward dawn, the centurion sent 30 men circuitously downstream, then attacked by the first light. We achieved complete surprise. Resistance was unorganized, and fugitives were despatched by the advance detail as it came back upstream to join us. Flaminius the centurion was cut down by a big Gaul; I killed him in return. We had one other man killed and seven wounded, two seriously. The Gallic males we slew at once; the ranking decurion gave the women to us for an hour and then we finished them off, with the children.

We found no Ligurian plunder. These people were not the ones who had raided over the border. The deterrent effect should, however, be no less for the error.

On a personal note, would you be so kind as to inform my wife that I am well?

Marcus Claudius Marcellus, of the 13th Legion, to Spurius Claudius. Written at Ticinum, Northern Italy, on the second day before the Ides of September, in the year after the founding of the City the 505th.

You will remember our action at Cenoni.

It will please you, I know, to hear that on the recommendation of the centurion Flaccus I have been promoted to decurion.

If you are well, then so am I.

Marcus Claudius to Otacilius, written at Rome, on the 2nd day of the Ides of November in the year after the founding of the City the 507th.

Your supplies will be shipped within 5 days.

It may interest you to know that I have become the father of a son.

Marcus Claudius, Evocatus in the 13th Legion, to Marcus Claudius maior, before Drepanum, Sicily, on the 5th day beore the Kalends of March in the year after the founding of the City the 509th.

Thank you, Father, for your congratulations on the crown of oak leaves. Otacilius has been loud in his expressions of gratitude. To hear him tell it, one would think that I had stood off a whole century of the enemy to save his life.

The siege drags on with little activity. It rains a great deal. Tell mother that her cheeses are a big improvement in my rations. Please tell my wife that the long abolla is fine and warm; one appreciates a good woolen garment, especially when on guard duty at night.

Father, I wish you would throw your influence behind Catulus in the Senate in the matter of the new ships. The talk in the fleet is all about the superiority of the newer Carthaginian design.

It is true that our existent quinqueremes offer the lightest possible hull consistent with their concentration of manpower, 15 oars with 5 rowers each on a side. But they have two serious disadvantages.

They are low. The javelins and slung stones even from a trireme come down with great force; our men, of course, cannot throw upward with the like effectiveness. And it is easy for boarders to leap down onto a lower deck, but harder to climb, especially against resistance.

The second objection is that at any oar there is an optimum position for the rower. At this distance from the thole-pin he can most effectively apply his strength. The men inboard of him have to pull through an arc that is inconveniently long; the men outboard, through one that is too short, and waste strength. It follows, then, that on a five-man oar, only one can pull efficiently. If the men next to him on either hand are handicapped, the ones beyond are even more so.

We should build ships like the captured one that Catulus brought to Rome — deep enough so that each man can pull his own oar. That means five banks of rowers. (Probably the two uppermost oars should be longer, and be pulled by two men each.) These ships will be heavier, it is true; but the enhanced effectiveness of the oars will more than make up for it. And even increase in weight has one advantage — it makes the shock of the ram that much more destructive.

The trireme, of course, offers some of the advantages of the great ship; and both we and our enemies, as you know, have on occasion put two men at each of the oars in the upper 2 banks of a trireme, which converts her into a quinquereme of sorts. But by the same token, we could do the same with a five-banked ship, and get a still greater turn of speed out of her. In any case, the trireme is obviously obsolete.

I was with the squadron of Quintus Fulvius at Messana when a five-banked Carthaginian stood up for the straits. It was the time of full moon; the current was setting through at about 4 miles an hour; there were eddies and whirlpools all over. Our dozen ships (single-banked quinqueremes and a few triremes) were spun helplessly hither and yon. But the Carthaginian pulled grandly through the broken water, ramming and sinking us at will like a dog killing rats in a pit. The half of us who were left were lucky to escape.

I am no defeatist, Father. We'll beat them in any event. But it will be much more costly to do it without the proper ships. So please do what you can for Catulus.

Yes, the siege takes long. But we must take Lilybaeum and Drepanum, which can only be done by having enough ships to interdict their supply by sea.

Who controls Sicily, controls the seas. If we hold it, it is a short jump for an assault on Africa, but a long sail for the enemy from Africa to Italy, and with a hostile force in their rear when they get there! And vice versa.

I have left for the last the news that I know will please you most. Our centurion took an arrow in the recent fighting. I have been appointed centurion in his place.

Please give my duty to my mother.

Spurius Claudius to Marcus Claudius. At Rome, 3rd day before the Ides of May, in the year after the founding of the City the 509th.

We were happy as always to hear from you, and know that you are well.

We have done as you request in the matter of the ships. You must bear in mind, however, that it is only with the greatest of difficulty that a new fleet could be built. Metellus tells us that the treasury is empty.

Even at the start of the war, the maintenance of a trireme in operation ran to over 20 talents a year — the price of 10,000 measures of wheat, or 1,000 days of labor for 70 men. To say nothing of construction. True, the 6-to-1 devaluation of the as has made things easier in some ways, although the price of imported wheat and bronze has shot way up.

The senate is now trying to persuade our wealthiest citizens to lend the money for construction. When we win the war they will be reimbursed from the Carthaginian indemnity. The attempt, I am gratified to report, is meeting with considerable success, and I am confident that new ships will be on the ways before midsummer.

Your brother-in-law has been posted to the north with the Ninth — the Gauls are restless.

Your mother sends her love, and bids me tell you to be sure and keep your feet warm and dry. Your wife also sends love; she is working on a woolen hood.

Marcus Claudius to Publius Metellus. At sea, under way from Drepanum for Panormus; the day before the Ides of July, in the year after the founding of the City the 511th.

The consul has written an official account of the battle of the Aegates Islands. You will, however, want an evaluation of the new ships in comparison with the old. Your efforts procured them; read then.

Upon the arrival of the ships at Drepanum, the Consul Catulus immediately began a vigorous training program. The soldiers who had been told off as rowers practised every day. The captains were given problems in ship handling and maneuvers. The sailors made sail and took it in under all conditions of wind and sea, and on all points of sailing. No members of the fleet were exposed to the chances of siege operations at the walls.

The Carthaginians must have known that we had a fleet at sea, and its size. They nevertheless loaded their own undermanned ships with supplies for Drepanum. The intention was obviously to evade our forces, slip into the city's harbor, discharge cargo, embark soldiers, then come out and destroy our fleet. A foolhardy plan!

Nevertheless, Neptune favored the foe. Hanno put to sea from the Islands with a fresh wind and rising seas at his back.

The consul had a hard choice. To row into the teeth of wind and sea against an enemy fleet has always been a doubtful expedient. It is difficult for the ships to maintain formation. The rowers are exhausted by the effort — when they can balance well enough to row at all. On the other hand, to let the enemy carry out his plans was also dangerous.

Catulus decided to attack. He sacrificed a black ram to appease the adverse westerly, and we got under way.

The action was a dramatic demonstration of the value of training. Our rowers kept the beat beautifully despite the waves. The helmsmen formed and kept line of battle. That is to say, the newer quinqueremes did; the older, five-man-to-an-oar ships did less well, and so did the few triremes; the dispatch boats and pentekonters had great difficulties. The light hulls were tossed helplessly about; they had not an adequate grip of the water for such a seaway.

As the two fleets approached one another, our men suffered a little from missiles — ships under sail make steadier platforms for archers and slingers. For some of their ships remained under sail and tried to evade our galleys. A few at the wings succeeded. Most, however, hauled down their sails, took to the oars, and tried to fight it out.

They were heavy and sluggish with cargo; we were light and handy. The difference in maneuverability was so marked that our captains were able to use the ram — for us an unaccustomed tactic. As to the rest, we flung over our grapnels on light chains and boarded. This was tricky in that sea; we lost a number of men who fell and drowned in their armor, and a few who were actually crushed between the hulls.

The enemy ships were badly undermanned. To force one's way aboard one of them, clear the deck, and take command of the ship and of any foes who surrendered was not difficult. Our losses in combat were surprisingly light as compared with other boarding actions. Only on a few ships was there hot fighting.

I led half a century aboard a Carthaginian, whereupon for some reason the ships drifted apart, and we had to fight for our lives against three times our number. We had boarded not far from the bow, and the smaller number of foes was in that direction, fighting us hand to hand and stinging us badly with arrows and javelins from the fore castle. I joined a holding line across the deck and shouted for those behind us to take that fighting turret. Two dozen of our men pressed desperately forward, cutting down or throwing overside all their opponents, and a half dozen assailed the castle; they could not at once overcome the opposition, but the close grapple put an end to the missiles. Fortunately, the enemy were, for the most part, green troops, and we were driving them aft when our ship laid alongside once more and her people came to our support.

We sank fifty ships of the enemy and took seventy. Hanno made his escape with the rest.

When our new ships were first delivered, a few of our captains had had misgivings on account of the windage of the higher hulls. These proved in the event to be completely unfounded.

Particularly in the struggle to get the ships back to port with tired crews, in the face of a now adverse wind, was the greater power of the new ships vindicated.

On thinking over the battle, I find the greatest lesson is the value of unremitting training. The Carthaginian oarsmen were observed again and again to catch a crab or to plunge an oar too deeply. They were obviously more or less green.

The second point is the demonstration once more that the battle belongs to the bold. The consul's decision to attack despite adverse weather conditions found favor with the gods.

As to Hanno, one cannot criticize his tactics. He attempted to obey orders, ill-advised though they were. He failed, for reasons beyond his power to control. We hear that they crucified him for it nevertheless. The third lesson, then, is that a commander should not be expected to perform miracles.

The Carthaginians, we are sure, will now sue for peace. Let the senate insist that they evacuate Sicily once and for all!

Please greet my father for me.

If you are well, then so am I.

Sextus Claudius to Marcus Claudius maior. At Rome, on the third day before the Ides of March, the year after the founding of the City the 513th.

It is with pleasure that I inform you, cousin, of the honor that has befallen our family.

As you know, two offices of fleet quaestor have recently been created. When it came to filling them, your son's name was mentioned. It was objected that he is very young — he just barely meets the age requirement. But the record of his outstanding military performance was brought up, and especially his formidable prowess in single combat.

And so, to be brief, your son Marcus is one of the first pair of fleet quaestors in Rome! Congratulations!

The weather here has been vile. I envy you the snugness of your farm.

Greet your spouse for me!

Marcus Claudius, quaestor classis, to Rufus Scaevola. At Ostia, 5th day before the Nones of June, in the year after the founding of the City the 513th.

Wheat Rations Report

On hand, 5th day before the Kalends of April	CCIƆƆ	CCIƆƆ	CCIƆƆ	CC	LX	I
Received from C. Metellus, 3rd day before the Nones of May		CIƆCIƆ		CCC	XX	VII
Received from ship Hamadryad, 4th day before the Kalends of June		CIƆCIƆ			LXX	IX
Received from ship Fidelitas, 2nd day before the Kalends of June		CIƆCIƆ CIƆ		CC	XC	VI
Total	CCIƆƆ CCIƆƆ CCIƆƆ IƆƆ CIƆ CIƆ			C	X	I
Expended to ship Vulpes, 3rd day before the Ides of June		CIƆ CIƆ		C	XC	VI
Balance on hand, 5th day before the Nones of June	CCIƆƆ CCIƆƆ CCIƆƆ CIƆ CIƆ CIƆ CIƆ DCCCC				X	V

Respectfully submitted.

In consideration of your prowess on the field, and the probity of your conduct, and the grave dignity of your bearing in all places and at all times, the eight surviving brethren of the Sacred College have elected you to fill the vacancy among them created by the death of the late Titus Sallustius.

Not only as an old friend of your father's, but also as a lover of
Rome, I rejoice to learn that on the Ides of March you assume
the office of curule aedile. The people have chosen well. Good
fortune attend you!
If you are well, then so am I.

You may well imagine my joy at the Senate's consultus to occupy Sardinia. We should have wiped out that nest of vipers years ago. Too many Romans have the same cause as myself to hate the pirates who infest those shores. To say nothing about their preying on our commerce for these many years.

You can guess that I pressed as hard as I could for orders to the expeditionary force, and got them.

I was assigned to a quinquereme, originally of Aetolia. She had three banks of oars, each of the upper two with oars longer and pulled by a pair of oarsmen. (If you call that a quinquereme. So, at any rate, she was listed in the fleet.)

On the morning of our departure, the praetor ordered me to take the auspices, in my capacity of Augur. I faced the south. I announced the foreshore as far as the first house for my eastern sector, an anchored hulk as my western border, and certain ships of the fleet, moored nearer and further off, for my northern and southern areas. As I raised my head to scan the skies, my conical augur's hat slipped and almost fell off!

The entire ship's company groaned in dread. The praetor postponed our departure for a day; he transferred me to another ship of the fleet, with another destination.

On the following morning I was ordered to take the auguries once more. Again I chose my boundaries.

There was a boy fishing from a pierhead off the beach. While I watched, a cat seized a still wriggling fish that he had caught, and made off with it.

I hailed the good omen. The Italian animal was eating the dweller in the sea! A clear indication from the gods that Rome would devour the pirates! And to make it more sure, it was in the lucky eastern sector! I gave thanks, doffed my hat, and went to report to the praetor. He sacrificed a white lamb to the favoring wind, invoked its assistance, and gave the signal to put out to sea.

Our object, of course, was to surprise the pirates in their various strongholds before a warning could enable them to get clear. The fleet therefore dispersed on the moderate norther for the harbors all along both coasts. The largest detachment, of course, made for Caralis, the main harbor, at the southern end of the island. Let its Carthaginian master like it or not, we would end the menace for all time.

The ship on which I was embarked was to have been attached to the main group. At the last minute the praetor detached her and ordered us to assault a smaller harbor some fifteen miles west of Caralis.

I am going to close this letter in haste. The battle is over, and we were successful, and are now in the captured town. I have just learned that we are ordered hence, I don't yet know to what place.

I am sending this letter by Pyrrhon, a ship captain of Syracuse. He was a prisoner of the pirates, but broke free and gave us considerable assistance in the fighting. In fact, he probably saved my life.

III

Extract from the Notes of the Comedian Lallos

These notes I made originally for my own use, but I think now that I will probably give them to my friend Thesetidion of Rome.

When King Hiero first established the Romaia at Syracuse, I came up from my farm to see whether I might manage to have one of my comic dramas performed at the festival. Naturally I stayed at the home of my friend, the goldsmith Archias, bringing a saddle of mutton as a gift.

He was in an expansive mood. "The King," he told me, "is going to present a large crown of electrum to the temple of Demeter and Persephone. I have been commissioned to execute it. It will be in the form of a wreath of oak leaves and acorns. The commission carries with it considerable prestige; from the amount of gold and silver which I have received for the crown, there should be a pretty profit — a very pretty profit." He had the bearing of a man who was well pleased with himself.

When we retired he turned over to me for the night Oppia, a kitchen maid, one of nine Roman slave girls whose misadventures she began to recount to me while we waited for sleep.

As she spoke, it suddenly occurred to me that the story had dramatic possibilities. It could be worked up as a modern version of the Trojan Women. I am not the man for that, nor do I know anyone who is. Next I thought of using it for its comic value. Lately, though, I have come to realize that you'd have to make it very broad, and the Syracusan public won't go for it. The Romans, among whom I lived for a while, have cruder tastes, and perhaps Thesetidion and his mimes may make something of this. And if he does, perhaps he'll remember where he got it.

I know the names of those girls and will give them, but they must not, of course, be mentioned at Rome. They can be represented as Ionians or Gauls.

It appears that a Sardinian sea-rover made a well-timed descent upon the coast of Latium at Liternum. Lucius Terentius was about to marry off his daughter to her second cousin, De-

56

cimus Flavius, and many guests had come from the city. By a skillful feint, the men were drawn off; and before they realized the trick the villa had been plundered, and with the women and slaves aboard, the villains were away.

Their captain seems, for a pirate, to have enforced more than the usual discipline; hoping to realize on the ransom or sale value of his freeborn captives, all of the senatorial and cavalier classes, he forbade his crew to tamper with the better trade-goods. With the captured slaves, of course, it was another matter, and the boys and girls of Terentius' household staff were relished by the captain and his ruffians.

Arrived at Sardinia, however, he seems to have received a rude jolt. His conversation with the agent who handled these transactions must have gone something like this:

"Here I am, back with a shipful of prosperity! I have taken eight marriageable Roman girls and the mothers of six of them, also a dozen odd of famuli, including an expert cook. Tomorrow we'll bring a few chests of silver, bronze and sundries."

"Excellent, my dear fellow! I'll set about arranging for ransoms, of course with the usual commission. Bring the ladies to the detention house, and the slaves to the barracoon. What are the names?" The agent was smiling and rubbing his hands.

"The wife and daughter of Lucius Terentius. The wife and daughter of Decimus Fulvius. The daughter of Sextus Julius." The agent looked reflective.

"The wife and two daughters of Gnaeus Livius. The wife and daughter of Titus Cornelius." The agent was frowning.

"The wife and daughter of Publius Aemilius. The wife and daughter of Gaius Oppius. The daughter of Marcus Claudius. But what's the matter?" Because the agent's face was dark between anger and alarm.

"Matter? You fool! You've pushed your luck to the point of madness. Seven of the most powerful families of Rome! Do you think we want a Roman fleet here? Let the word get out that we've been connected with this in any way, and we'll all end on crosses!"

"What do you suggest? How do I get my ransom?"

"You don't! Triple ass! Are you tired of living?"

A sigh. "Well, if I must, I must. Buy them, then, as your slaves. Some of the girls are pretty — one is beautiful."

"Has the wine pickled your wits? Don't you understand? Neither I nor anyone else in town will touch your girls. My advice is that you drown them at sea, and forget you ever had them."

One could get some comic effect out of the disappointment of the pirate. He could be shown taking out his anger on one of the mothers, for instance. If cleverly written and produced, the spectacle of the old hag being kicked, half-stripped, and thrashed, and using her nails in turn should be good for a belly-laugh.

Well, he didn't drown them. But he decided to dispose of them reasonably far from Rome. And so, a week later, when a squall drove him in to Tauromenion, in Sicily, opportunity rid him of the older women and slaves — minus naturally one or two who had already succumbed to the overly robust lovemaking of his crew. The girls he kept for the higher prices of the sophisticates of Syracuse, largest and richest of the Sicilian cities.

My informant told me that they there twice made an effort to have their purchaser send to Rome for ransom money. Apparently he did, but without results. Perhaps a ship was wrecked; perhaps a messenger was untrustworthy At any rate, after two months of silence, their new owner refused to wait longer. On the bulletin board of Adeimantos, the slave-dealer, appeared the following notice:

> *Auction of slaves, male and female, on the 14th day of Skiropho-*
> *rion. On the day following, nine maidens will be disposed of by*
> *private sale. They may be inspected at the establishment of*
> *Adeimantos.*

It might be well to write the comedy in two versions — one for the general stage and another, bluer, for select audiences. In the latter, one could have a scene in which prospective buyers examine the merchandise.

After a few of these episodes, Oppia told me, there was some talk of suicide among the girls, but it remained only talk.

They were all sold on the same day.

The Roman Terentia was not particularly beautiful. She was knocked down for five minae to a freedman of Epirote parentage who had been given by his master for some special service a small but adequate farm some distance from town. He was on the look-out for a wife for his son, an only child. More, I think, to avert the possibility of a venereal infection than to delight the boy, he was willing to pay a premium price for a virgin.

The youngster was well pleased with his gift, and Terentia settled down with her husband, her wifely duties, and the labors of the field.

For the comic stage, one might work up an increasing interest in the girl on the part of her father-in-law. Her perplexity, the doubt as to whether her interest lay with the old man who controlled the purse strings or the young one who controlled the future, could introduce some complications into the plot; and a suspicious and hostile mother-in-law could bring in all sorts of possibilities of robust humor.

In point of fact, Terentia seems to have accepted the burdens of farm work without too much resistance or even reluctance; the more so, in that she quickly became quite the devoted wife. Young Phares was not by any means a bad fellow or a tyrannical husband. More and more, Rome receded into the background of her thoughts; and when within fifteen months she bore him a son, they seem to have been deeply happy.

The Livia sisters, both strikingly good-looking girls, had been raised to expect only the best of everything. Sisters, of course, were rather the exception in Rome as in Greece; the fact that both had been raised suggests wealth and a certain indulgence on the part of their father. They had been prepared to marry very well indeed.

The elder — the beauty of the lot — caught the eye of Kallimachos, one of the wealthiest men in Syracuse. He actually paid 18 minae for her! It's rather ridiculous, the spectacle of a man well past his prime trying to renew his youth by means of a slave girl. There is nothing I condemn so bitterly as the vices I have not the funds to practice!

Imagine, then, this highborn, beautiful girl who, a few months ago, had looked to be the wife some day of a son of one of the greatest houses in Rome, now following her purchaser forlornly to his villa. Perforce, as I suppose, she put the best face possible on the business; perhaps he supped with her that first evening, and she drank enough wine to help her through the transition from girlhood to concubinage.

At any rate, Kallimachos seems never to have tired of his purchase, but to have enjoyed the girl immensely, despite the sneers of his wife. (Comic effect — jealous wife trying to make her faded looks of middle-age rival a teen-age girl's freshness and beauty — you could have a scene in which she is being groomed and painted, and her hair is being dressed by her slave girls; she slaps one, scolds a second, and deprives the third of food for the rest of the day. Also, old Kallimachos dodging around to keep his girl out of the eyes of the old beldame, perhaps being kicked in the shins by the old woman, with a sharp, heavy shoe, etc., etc.)

Xenophanes, although a lesser member of the Gamoroi, was nevertheless moderately well off. The sudden death of his wife had left him with two young children, one of them a mere babe, to care for as best he might. For some months he had made shift with the services of his wife's aging maid and the houseman; and his considerably older half-sister had looked in as she could.

Noticing the slave dealer's auction, he suddenly determined to buy a woman young enough to cope more adequately with two healthy, noisy youngsters; and whether or not he went with any other purpose in mind I cannot say. At any rate, when Julia was on the block, he found himself sufficiently attracted by her pretty face and fairly good figure to outbid the other prospective buyers.

Julia was a girl with a very strong conscious maternal instinct. She took at once to the motherless children, and they clung to her from the first. Xenophanes had been fasting for a long time; Julia, although as moral as the next girl of her nation (which, to do them justice, is saying a good deal), was nevertheless fatalist enough to accept what she must; so after a few tears she gave her master reason to be well satisfied on both counts with his bargain.

One might, in a skit, have the girl dupe her master by carrying on an affair with a houseboy behind his back, though I dare be sworn that no such episode actually took place.

Fulvia, decidedly on the pretty side, had been brought up by a doting father and mother who, nevertheless, had strength of character enough to demand of their daughter a marked devotion to duty. At sixteen she was the most idealistic of the group. She would agonize over a horse or a slave who was being flogged, and could always be counted upon for an inconvenient or unpleasant service. She had a grave, sweet face which was short of beautiful, but which one remembered with mounting pleasure.

The younger of the Livia sisters, pretty, flighty, precocious at fourteen and boy-crazy, caught the eye of Pataikos as soon as he entered the slave-dealer's hall. He was a Lybian from Cyrene who kept a brothel in town, and he knew at once that this piece of goods was for his business.

At ten, Aemilia had the sort of elfin beauty that degenerates into coarseness after puberty. There was a section of the wretch's clientele whose lubricity was aroused by immature girls.

He bought the three.

When they suddenly realized the character of the establishment into which they had been sold, the two older girls made a concerted dash for the door. The slaves of the place had, of course, expected this usual reaction, and blocked their flight. Despite their sobbing and frantic pleading (in which the little one joined in uncomprehending fear), they were locked in a room. In due course one of Pataikos' older harridans instructed them in their duties.

Pataikos advertised his wares.

Aemilia, of course, suffered from her initiation, but less than might have been expected. The brothel keeper had no wish to have his property badly damaged, even temporarily, while still new; and he used the arts of his kind to prepare her as much as might be for her role thenceforward. And since she did not fully realize what had befallen her, she underwent no spiritual distress. She accepted her job as purveyor to some strange silliness of men; and if she had to act thereby as her parents, she knew, would consider outrageous, she was beyond their power to punish.

Livia, to use a time-worn analogy, reacted to prostitution like the swimmer who plunges into a cold river. Once over the initial shock, she found in herself no great reluctance to participate with her customers in the joys of the embrace. Sensuous and self-indulgent, with clothes, cosmetics, jewelry and maid service, she quickly became one of the most enthusiastic and cooperative numbers in Pataikos' stable.

One could write in some amusing brothel scenes in which young fops and old fools are mulcted and deceived. But I do not think that Aemilia's experiences are material for humor.

It was Fulvia on whom the full blow descended. When the foul-mouthed elderly lecher fell upon her, she defended herself so vigorously that he was sent, in fury and chagrin, one eye blackening, to sputter his indignation to Pataikos. So when Fulvia, bound and spread eagled, was delivered to him, he had the double ecstasy of voluptuousness and revenge.

Immediately after his grinning departure, the brothel keeper turned the girl over to three of his slaves — a Syrian whom the public executioner somewhere had deprived of nose, ears and lips; a giant of a Gaul whose customary cruelty had caused his enslavement, but who was all the more useful to Pataikos for that reason; and a tiny, swarthy, outlandish bit of what could scarcely be called humanity from some land beyond the frontiers of Persia.

"Little Lady Lilybottom," Pataikos said, "thinks that she is too nice to be a whore. Take her and teach her different. See that you do a good job."

They did a good job.

It was that evening that Livia, entering her friend's cubicle for mutual condolence, found swinging by her girdle the hideous, lifeless thing that had once been a lovely girl.

Cornelia (my Oppia tells me) had never expected too much of life. A big, raw-boned, ill-favored, graceless girl, she had grown up aware of her deficiencies and how they affected others. Inwardly sensitive, she presented to the world a false picture of indifference; with her booming voice and mannish laughter she would repulse with disbelief even those few gestures of liking that came her way. In short, she was one of those women whom the Graces had passed unfeelingly by.

Even so, she could hardly have anticipated at the worst the fate that came upon her. Polyaenos had been buying labor for a little iron mine, and had attended Adeimantos' private sale, mostly out of curiosity. Cornelia's complete lack of charm turned away the buyers who were looking for a girl qua girl. Her size and strength (she was the oldest of the group — eighteen) made her eligible for heavy labor. He bought her.

The comic dramatist might turn to some account the drunken party at which that evening Polyaenos, in the presence of his guffawing fellow roisterers, took her innocence by way of a bit of clowning. "Is that a she-ass or a sow that Polyaenos is mounting?" "It can't be an ass — any self-respecting she-ass who had foaled her would have kicked her to death as soon as she got a look at that face!" "It can't be a sow either; have you ever seen a rump that wide even on the fattest porker of a drove?" "Well, whatever it is, it's female, and that's an improvement on the louts Polyaenos usually favors." "Is it? I'm not so sure." "Ah — he's struck gold! Listen to her squeal!"

Two days later Cornelia was in the hell of the mines, where even a strong man might, if he was unlucky enough, live for as much as two years.

It seems very unfair that a comedian should be called a heartless rogue merely because he sees the humorous possibilities of a situation. All men make the most of the material of their trades. What does a farmer or a grainseller do but exploit the hunger of others for gain? What does a ruler do but exploit the docility of the mass? What does an apothecary do but exploit the sufferings of the sick? Why, then, should a comedian be considered unfeeling if he perceives the humorous aspects of a wretched situation, and uses them to lighten the cares of an audience by making it laugh? That what I am writing is essentially tragic, I know; but I am not responsible for the tragedy. I do not order the world, nor, like the Fates, apportion the good and the evil to each. It might well be maintained that humanity is essentially tragic — "The best thing is never to be born; the next best, to die young." Only the possibility of laughter at our miseries makes them endurable.

Sometimes I think that each man makes of his fellow a Pharmakos, a scapegoat to bear the burden of his own misery and guilt.

Claudia, in contrast to Cornelia, was but a barely (and decidedly prematurely) weaned babe at the time of the piratical descent on Latium. Her mother, as it chanced, was out of the house for some reason, and Claudia was found in the arms of one of the girls, who the pirates assumed was her mother. An infant is of no trade value, but experience had shown that the mother of a murdered child was likely to throw herself into the sea. The rascal refrained therefore from braining the baby, and the girls, with some difficulty, kept her alive. When the pirates discovered their error, they shrugged their shoulders and did nothing about it.

A few hours before the sale (which naturally would have been the end of her) the coppersmith Kimon stopped by with his wife in tow to pick up a slave for his smithy. The couple was past their first youth. To their bitter disappointment, the marriage had been barren.

The child, lying in a corner of the floor, caught Eratho's eye, and with the hunger of the childless woman, she picked it up in her arms. There was something about the woebegone creature that went straight to her empty heart. Naturally, she made inquiry, and learned that there was no mother — or none available.

"Kimon," she exclaimed, "this is of the gods! This will be our daughter!"

He was easily persuaded. The slave dealer, scenting a future large profit, made out a bill of sale for the token price of a half an obol, and the new mother carried her baby happily homeward.

When she proposed that he execute a freedom paper for the child, her husband shook his head.

"It would be unwise. We have bought her; we have a bill of sale for her; she is ours by the law of Syracuse, and no one can do anything about it. But if we free her, and then, six years hence, a true or pretended mother crops up, even a foreigner, she might be able to claim her and either take her away from us or extort everything that we have by the way of settlement. When she is grown, and ready for marriage, we will free her before we give her to her husband." And so the matter rested.

My proffer of a comic play for the festival had been well received. I wrote at prodigious speed to produce an original work in honor of the occasion. It was thus that I composed my Olympidion, which, as all the world knows, is a satire on the pretensions of the late Syracusan physician Menekrates. As a foreigner I would not have dared so to attack a citizen in his lifetime, but the departed, a man of no important family, was fair game.

When I went up to town to submit the manuscript, it was a worried and unhappy Archias who received me.

"I told you about the votive wreath for Poseidon," he reminded me.

"I remember. Did you finish it?"

"I did. And Hiero was loud in his praises of my workmanship. But some rascal put into his head the idea that I misappropriated some of his gold and substituted a like weight of silver."

"Which you, of course, denied."

"Of course. Whereupon Hiero sent the chaplet to his kinsman, Archimedes the scientist, for an opinion. And there it still is, and I have not been paid. Outrageous! Trying to blast the fortune and reputation of a defenseless man! What that fool of an Archimedes will make of it, there's no telling."

"How will he go about it?" I asked.

"He can't. It is possible, of course, to run an assay; but to do that one would have to destroy the chaplet. He could make a series of wreaths similar to this, but of varying composition, and make comparisons — bending strength, color, musical note when struck, I know not what — but it would be prohibitively expensive."

I knew Archias fairly well. "Then you have nothing to worry about," I told him.

I must say that his troubles, then or later, made no difference in my reception. He dined me, gave me a bed, again with the kitchen maid for entertainment.

My little Oppia was, truth to tell, decidedly on the plain side. (I was, in fact, somewhat annoyed at my friend for not providing better for my comfort). She had not aroused any erotic interests among Adeimantos' clientele, and had been knocked down to my friend's majordomo, who had been commissioned to buy a kitchen slavey, for only 3 minae.

Oppia's story was that of the ill-favored daughter of a wealthy family who as a child tries hard to believe in the praises and compliments of loving parents and self-seeking slaves against the ever stronger testimony of her mirror. In time, the occasional taunt of a schoolmate and, later, the obvious indifference of adolescent boys left no room for doubt.

She had nevertheless been a not unhappy child, goodnatured, and secure in the knowledge that her family and estate would bring her a husband at the proper time.

Enter the Sardinian pirate.

The young Roman lady thenceforth, instead of being the darling of her parents and the junior mistress of a household, learned to get up in the dark and have a fire going for the cook, and to scrub, scour pots, chop and carry in the firewood, and receive a box on the ears when the cook was dissatisfied or had been cudgelled by the majordomo. As many and many a woman lived before her.

Her new master, after seeing her, took no further interest, and later when one of his house boys asked for a favor, shrugged his shoulders. Here again one might get a comic effect: an exceptionally ill-favored wench could be struggling with a crude type wearing one of the large artificial phalluses of stock comedy, and it could be particularly funny if she were screaming about her virtue at the same time that he bedded her down in a heap of garbage in the scullery. Of course, as I say, it takes a Roman taste to enjoy it.

The first festival of the Romaia was well conceived and executed, and presumably most gratifying to the city in whose honor it had been instituted and named. The Dionysiacs presented a drama by Sophron (with its witchcraft and its hauntings not at all to my taste).

My Olympidion was a tremendous success. The old quack trying to woo at once a wealthy widow and her pretty page boy was a smashing hit, and at first sight of the chorus of victims of his charlatanry the entire theatre roared. His god-like pretensions I satirized, I think, rather well. I found myself the recipient of many gifts and invitations to dine, as well as invitations of a nature which modesty forbids my disclosing. I could have transferred my luggage to any one of several of the finest mansions in town, but naturally refrained lest I hurt the feelings of my friend Archias. Particularly at that time.

For Archias was a ruined man.

It was the matter of the wreath of electrum. Archimedes, commissioned by Hiero to find out the composition of the wreath, had racked his brains to no avail.

On a day which we hold sacred to Apollo according to the custom of our mother-city of Corinth, he had attended the sacrifice at the temple to the god on the island Ortygia. It was a warm day; he stopped to drink at the fountain of Arethusa near its western side. His reflection showed him that he was still wearing a chaplet, and that turned his thoughts to his problem.

Meditating thereon, he walked across the bridge to the agora, passed on his left the smaller temple to the god as well as the Great Altar of King Hiero and proceeded toward what some of us think the most beautiful section of the upper city, the Hill of the Achradina, where he had his home. Here he encountered a man leading an ass up the steep street. The animal's burden was a small one, yet it climbed with obvious difficulty. Marveling, the scientist asked what it was that was so heavy although of such very little bulk. "Pig lead," the man answered. "Little as it seems, it weighs as much as you."

Later that day, as Archimedes settled in his bath, the water overflowed. He reflected that the equally heavy but smaller mass of lead would not have raised the water level as much; and in a flash he had the answer to the king's dilemma.

It seems (I know nothing of such matters) that the scientist realized that if he measured the water displaced from a vessel by a weight of gold equal to that of the wreath, and the larger amount displaced by a like weight of the much lighter and therefore much more voluminous silver, and then that by the wreath itself, he could use the method of proportions to determine its composition, or something like that.

It was not true (I learned later) that, as the bitterly jeering Archias described, the scientist at once ran naked through the streets of Syracuse shouting, "I have it!" But he told the tale so widely that it has already acquired a foothold in Syracusan folklore.

At any rate, he tested the wreath, and it was found wanting.

Archias laid the whole blame for his downfall on Archimedes. Few of us have the toughness of mind to take the responsibility for our troubles upon ourselves, but he developed an almost insane hatred for the scientist. He was fined to the extent of all of his possessions, the king guessing (probably correctly) that Archias' peculations had been going on for a long time. He was publicly flogged, and his goods were sold at auction. The wise do not measure their wits with kings.

I was an idle spectator at the scene when Oppia was put up for sale. I had enjoyed the girl despite her plainness, and on a sudden impulse I bought her, for two and three-quarter minae. Besides, I reflected, the girl had dramatic value; through her I could, perhaps, view the further unfoldings of her multiple tale.

The elder Livia learned fairly soon, through the underground communication network that exists among slaves in every community in the world, of the fate and whereabouts of her sister. Once she felt secure (or as secure as a bought concubine can be) in Kallimachos' favor, she tried to avail herself of it by inducing him to buy her sister out of her shameful bondage. In this, however, she encountered unexpected resistance.

Kallimachos' wife got wind of the matter. Powerless to prevent her husband's purchase of a playfellow younger than herself and more beautiful than she had ever been, she could yet assert her right to prevent the squandering of her son's patrimony in uncalled-for charity. So, at least, she maintained, and for a long time successfully, although I am certain that nothing more than jealous hatred of the other woman was at the bottom of it.

It was well over a year before he was prepared to defy her. By then, however, the girl was no longer in Pataikos' establishment. In one of the frequent exchanges of personnel characteristic of such operations, she had been sent to a house in another city, and a new face replaced hers in Syracuse. Kallimachos was no doubt relieved to learn of it.

Julia had been living in the house of Xenocrates, caring for his motherless children and, as he might require, for himself. Apparently she was decently treated, and, so far as I could determine, she lived there not too unhappily — which, over a long period of time, is perhaps the best that can be said of the human condition.

Xenocrates' sister had a dream in which she was bidden to journey to Katana, there to worship in a certain famous temple of Demeter which may be entered only by women. Her husband being partly crippled from an old riding accident, she requested the escort of her brother.

It was an ill-omened venture. On the journey home he was seized very suddenly with an attack of cramps, then vomiting and diarrhea; after which fever ensued, and he died within three days.

His sister took the children, and Julia to continue her care of them.

Julia, I believe, was sorry for his death, but felt no great grief; and since the sister, like her brother, was a decent sort, the change made little difference to the girl. She carried on her domestic duties as the children grew up, and quite doted on them. I suppose she had her love affairs like any other housemaid, but on the whole (to get ahead of myself a little) she had and enjoyed a fairly placid existence.

Cornelia, of course, was doomed. Even had he been inclined to do so (as was nowhere the case), a Sicilian mine owner could not have have provided decently for his slaves; the iron ores of the island were low-grade, and their operation was a marginal enterprise in the best of times. Even the crude systems of ventilation in the form of sail-like wind catchers and short air ducts were minimal, and the slaves slowly gasped out their lives at the heads of hot and airless shafts.

For the long hours of almost intolerably hard labor the cooks provided a niggardly amount of the coarsest bread. There was little supervision in the refectory, and in a grim, continual struggle the stronger took more than their share.

In addition, Cornelia found it impossible to enjoy all of her few hours of permitted sleep. Charmless as she was, she was still female, one of the few in the barracks. While most of the men were too utterly weary to care, among the newer slaves being cycled through the mountain workings to their graves, there were some in whom nature still made her imperious demands. These regarded the few women as common property, and as such they were used to exhaustion and beyond.

It surprised me no whit, therefore, that on inquiring for Cornelia about a year after the beginning of her labors, I learned that she had succumbed.

Nor did it surprise me to learn, a few months later, that the workings had been abandoned.

I suppose that I have been wrong, after all. This story is not really the stuff of comic theatre. Neither is it fit material for classic tragedy in the "Trojan Women" manner. They were no kings and heroes by whom these hapless maidens were undone. Their conquerors were effete voluptuaries, slaves, and greedy little tradesmen.

Some sort of tale may nevertheless be stitched together from these threads, by that much perhaps the closer to our common wretched humanity; so using Oppia as my intermediary I shall follow their adventures.

At four years, Claudia was exactly the sunny, happy little creature of which her adoptive parents had dreamed. She was pretty and healthy; she loved and was loved. Although living on a lower economic scale than would have been her lot in Rome, in other respects she seemed not to have suffered by the mischance which had cost her her freedom and her country.

Aemilia, on the other hand, had arrived at her puberty already well skilled in the arts of harlotry. Having as a woman known nothing else, she took her profession quite as a matter of course, and professed to be genuinely puzzled by the opprobrium with which, as she could not help knowing, her way of life was associated.

"I live by being a woman, just as married women do," she said, when I took Oppia to see how she was getting along. "The young blades who visit me have all been out with girls of the town, and they've lain with them, or say they have. (I'm not talking about maidens of the aristocracy). When a man visits me, there are no pretenses about why he has come. Elsewhere, he has to woo and coax, and even then be uncertain; and a pregnancy or discovery by an angry husband, father or brother can have serious consequences. Here he knows that he'll get what he needs, and there'll be no complications."

Oppia shook her head and sighed, but was, of course, in no position to argue.

Kallimachos was dead.

There had been the sudden onset of an abdominal pain, followed by a fever, and almost before he realized the seriousness of his illness, he was sinking into the final coma.

Almost his last words were an injunction to his wife to free Livia. Gladly would she have disobeyed; but his physician had heard, and a friend and neighbor who had come to inquire about him, and both his sons. She dared not ignore the order.

But that did not mean she would forfeit her revenge.

Livia joined the other women of the household in the ritual wailing about the body. They were led by an experienced conductress of funeral lamentations. On the next morning a choir came and sang a dirge which had been composed specifically for the dead man. In the afternoon the funeral procession carried the deceased, now clad in white, to the family tomb outside the town. He was placed on a pyre and burned. The ashes were put in the tomb with a sword and a barleycake.

"Your master said to free you," the widow said to Livia after the funeral rites, "so free you I must. But I can require you to remain here, even as a freedwoman, to serve me until I die, and so you shall. And if you want your daughter's freedom, you must pay me for it."

"But Kallimachos surely intended her to be free with me!" Livia exclaimed in horror.

"Did he? He didn't say so."

"Only because he was dying, and could hardly speak! He certainly meant to free his own daughter!"

"Was she his daughter? How do I know that? I can persuade a few men to swear that they shared your bed." The old witch smiled. "If you want her, you'll have to buy her. Otherwise, she takes your place when I am ready."

"But how can I get money?"

"Don't you know? After being your master's leman for so long, you can hardly pose as the spirit of chastity!" And the older woman picked up a whip which no doubt she had planted there, and drew it, as it were idly, through her fingers.

Livia felt that whip many times during the years that followed. Nominally a freedwoman, she was flogged for any real or invented fault, and was frequently in fetters.

But the worry about her child was the worst. It had to be fed and cared for; public opinion would have been outraged if the freedwoman's child had been allowed to die. But a slave it was to be nevertheless.

Kallimachos had given her some jewelry, and she sold it. But it was not enough.

There came a day when the dead man's brother-in-law, an oily, dandified fellow, whispered again into her ear; and she bowed her head hopelessly and nodded. And then the neighbor. And then the foreman of her late master's estate.

Eventually, she bought out her daughter. And eventually, her mistress died. But by then, of course, all hope of a better life had vanished.

It's a pity, of course, that Kallimachos did not attend to the enfranchisement while he was still living. It may have been just procrastination. No one really expects to die — certainly not for years and years. But I think that he just couldn't face the possibility that this young and beautiful woman, given freedom of choice, would turn in disgust from her aging lover. He didn't think that she would. But he didn't dare find out.

A message from Archias brought me to the squalid quarter where he now lived. Although free, he had never recovered anything approximating his erstwhile status. That I knew; but I was shocked to behold the evidences of his poverty, and was to be even more shocked at the degradation to which he had succumbed.

There was no reason for it. Granted that he could not, perhaps, assume his former position of prosperous and fashionable goldsmith, he might still have set up a more modest shop to cater to the small merchant and artisan class, or at worst have hired himself out (for the man was able, despite the weakness of his character) as journeyman in the workshop of one of his former competitors. But there are people whose characters, once flawed, go on to a progressive and uncontrollable degeneration, like an amphora which, once cracked, develops further and further extensions of the separation until it is utterly shattered.

I had first to listen to his fulminations against Archimedes. Thereafter, his news was that Croesion, a Lydian and one of the wealthiest of the resident foreigners, was considering the production of a comic play at some one of the festivals. He was giving a banquet on the following day, and my former acquaintance — I hesitate still to call him friend in view of his new commission — was recruiting women for the occasion.

Gross as I knew Croesion to be — and he turned out to be even worse than rumored — there was no reason why I should not persuade him, if I could, to produce my "Akrostetai", my satire on those merchants who were making a good thing out of balancing between assistance to the Roman and to the Carthaginian causes in the war. I felt constrained to accept his invitation for the following day, although with no enthusiasm.

His associates I found to have been cut out of the same cloth as himself. The climax of the party came when a few of the hirelings put on the sort of exhibition I had seen only once, and then by accident, and not among Greeks.

Usually one protects himself emotionally when beholding any nasty occupation by not thinking of those concerned as human beings. But in this case I had perceived a Roman accent on the lips of one of the girls; and when a companion called her Livia, I realized that the sister of Kallimachos' favorite had reappeared. This made it entirely too personal; it too closely associated the obscene spectacle with my own Oppia.

I looked with pity upon the hideous thing that once had been a lovely girl.

Terentia continued to live happily, so far as Oppia could tell, with her husband. The birth of their son was followed two years later by the appearance of a little girl. They had their difficulties; after a dry season they found themselves on short commons, and grasshoppers and other stealers of crops were a constant threat. But they survived, and for the most part lived not too badly.

Sorrow came to her when, early one year, a second daughter was born. Despite her pleas, her husband refused to rear it.

"This is a small farm," he said. "It supports one family well enough. When we are gone, it will be our son's. And we must make something of a portion for the one daughter. With another, how will they live?"

So, like many another father, with a heavy heart he took the child into a distant field and abandoned it. Perhaps it died of hunger, thirst, or exposure; perhaps a fox killed and ate it; perhaps some speculator found it and raised it as a slave. They never knew.

It was at this time that, knowing Terentia's time to be upon her, Oppia asked me to take her to her. As we approached the cottage where the young mother lay, we saw her family at the olive harvest. Her husband and a hired slave boy were in the trees, beating the branches with rods; the olives fell, and were being gathered by Terentia's mother-in-law and another woman. Nearby, her father-in-law was hanging his weight on a lever that crushed the fruit in a stone press. The oil was running into a jug.

Oppia entered the house. Terentia wept on her bosom. But she knew that her husband was right. In the histories of most families this is a recurrent tragedy.

I too had sired a daughter. Oppia made a good mother. The cares and expenses of fatherhood had certainly been far from my mind when I bought her; but when nature took its course and she bore the child, I succumbed to a certain weakness of my character of which I am well aware, gave in to her pleading and refrained from exposing the babe. For which I thank the gods!

For my own affairs too had prospered. I was in constant demand as an actor, and several of my plays had been produced; I had even gone to Athens to oversee a production of my farce, the "Sicels".

Claudia grew into a charming girl of thirteen. She was obviously happy in her home, and brought happiness to her foster parents. As well she might; at that age a girl is all sweetness, her only desire to please. It is shortly thereafter that the change comes.

Kimon had done well. His copper works had been enlarged, and the quality of his goods enjoyed the highest rating. With his prosperity, he had been generous to his wife and daughter. He did something that was unusual for his class, even among us of the Doric dialect: he sent the girl to school, and she learned reading, writing, and poetry. She was naturally bright, and made the most of her opportunity.

She seemed to have no regrets whatsoever that she was growing up in the house of Kimon, instead of that of her natural father, the Roman Marcus Claudius.

With some difficulty, we kept track of the younger of the Livia sisters, long back in Syracuse. As debauchery, disease, wine-bibbing and time took their inevitable toll, she had lost first her freshness, then her beauty. From establishments like that of Pataikos, who catered to gentlemen of means and of at least superficial refinement, she was sold to the second-rate brothels, then to those for the workingmen; and now, aged before her time and drunk whenever possible, she was an inmate of a noisome den on the waterfront where, for a few coppers, she serviced slaves and the dregs of the ships' crews.

IV

Extract from Heraclides' "Life of Archimedes"

It was long before I got to know him that I first heard of Archimedes. I was a boy of 14 — this was in the 21st year of the reign of Hiero — and my father had had some business to transact at the shipyard of Nabis, and had taken me with him (what boy can resist the lure of a shipyard?). While we were there a big merchantman from Argos, her deck almost awash, stood into the harbor and made for the yard. It was nip and tuck as to whether she'd make it — but the rowers finally managed to beach her there. Her skipper came ashore and was met by Nabis', "You seem in a bad way, stranger", to which the other answered, "You may well say so — we ran onto a reef and strained her, and have been bailing for our lives ever since," and Nabis replied, "You should have had one of Archimedes' cochliai."

"Who is Archimedes and what is a cochlias?" asked the captain, to which Nabis replied, "Archimedes is a scientist who lives here in Syracuse. He is a cousin of the King, Hiero, and is, I

76

should judge, close to 40 (he was 38, as I figure); he devised the cochlias, an instrument for raising water. It is essentially a metal ribbon in the shape of a helix, lying within a metal tube and designed so that the ribbon at every level extends from the center of the tube to its wall. When this instrument is slanted and its lower end immersed in water, and the helix is then rotated, water is carried upward in the tube against its lower side by the rotating helical ribbon. Recently two of them were used to clear a ship of water, which they did very quickly."

"If what you say is true," remarked the stranger, "this invention is worth a chestful of money."

"Archimedes does not value it," my father put in. "He considers anything of practical usefulness to be a degradation of his science."

In the second year of the 133rd Olympiad, seventeen years before King Hiero ascended the throne, Archimedes was born to the mathematician and astronomer Phidias in Syracuse, then at the zenith of her wealth and power as the greatest western city of the Greeks.

The lad, exceptionally precocious even for that eminent family, was the most assiduous and gifted pupil of his sire; he took to numbers with great eagerness, and needed little encouragement to study. At a tender age he was deeply involved in higher mathematics, and he lived in its serene, passionless atmosphere, where reason must dominate the field, and emotion did not even attempt to intrude. Two plus two equalled four, there and everywhere, then and forever, and no amount of longing could make a difference; for not the power of the king — not Zeus himself — could change it; mathematics was part of that great Anangke — that necessity — that compelled both gods and men. This, his father taught him, was at the basis of the cosmos, this was the purest and most absolute form of knowledge. Man might aspire to live a life of reason and order; in the science of the mathematicians, and only there, could he attain it.

Otherwise too, the boy moved in a world that was largely one of predictability and order; under his father's direction, his mother administered the modest household and its pair of house slaves smoothly, and the lad thought, if he thought about it at all, that such was the ordering of the world.

And so it remained, until the day when the father found it necessary to visit a small landholding. Up and over the hill to the valley beyond led the road, and for quite a long way the one-horse chariot carried them along it, so that it was early afternoon when they reached the farm. They spent the night under the porch roof, and started home after a coarse breakfast.

The horse went lame before they had gone more than a quarter of the way. Time was wasted in leading it, slowly and painfully, to a farm where it could be left; more time went in going along side roads, trying in vain to hire a replacement; and when they finally took up the journey on foot, it was so late that they were benighted on the mountain.

As the man and the weary eight-year-old boy plodded upward, a turn around the shoulder of the height brought to their ears, through the darkness, distant cries of a kind that the lad had never heard before. The man stopped, and the boy sensed rather than saw that he grew anxious.

"What is it, Father?" he asked.

"I had forgotten. This is the season of the worship of the god Dionysos-Bacchus. Every second year his devotees roam the hills at night, clad (if they can get them) in fawn skins, carrying thyrses — staves bound with vine leaves at the tips, and call upon the god."

"Is something wrong, Father?"

The parent forced a laugh. "Of course not." But he was hesitant, obviously uncertain of what to do.

Then from nearer at hand erupted song, mingled with shrill cries of "Evohe Dionysos!". And there were flutes and tambours, and again that strange shout from another quarter, "Evohe Dionysos!". And soon there were torches, and approaching figures, throwing themselves about.

Phidias pushed his son under a clump of bushes. "Stay here!" he hissed, "and be silent!"

Suddenly the air was full of menace. Wildly dancing women,

and a few men, drew near. In the light of their torches the boy
saw that some of the women carried wine skins, and he shud-
dered as he perceived writhing serpents in their hair. One or two
carried small animals — a lamb, a suckling pig — which they
occasionally nursed at their breasts.

Someone spied his father. There was a rush, and wild voices
cried, "Who is this?" and "Are you of the Initiate?"

"Evohe Dionysos!" from Phidias. A wineskin was pressed into
his mouth. Then, "Bromios! The god!" a woman exclaimed.

"Hail to the God!" others cried.

Before the lad's horrified gaze, two of them grasped a puppy
by its fore and hind legs and attempted to tear it apart, but the
screaming animal was not so easily disjointed; a knife did the
work, finally, and the wretched beast was still. "Evohe! Bromios!
Bromios!" the boy heard again, and several dabbled their hands
in blood.

Wine was being drunk; a woman leaped at a man, and they
coupled on the ground. More wine was forced upon his father.
Then the celebrants rushed on, the songs and cries diminishing
behind them. Phidias accompanied them, but in a few minutes
came quietly back, alone.

"You have seen the Bacchae," he said, "the worshippers of the
mad god. They are possessed by him — or so it is said. They are
completely irresponsible and unpredictable while under the
spell. We had better not travel tonight. Sleep, if you can, under
that shrub. I'll stay with you."

"I don't understand it, Father. Why do they kill little animals?
Why the blood? The snakes?"

"I don't know whether I can make you understand. For all that
you are more advanced in your studies than most young men,
you are still a child, with a child's feelings and knowledge of the
world.

"We worship, of course, the blessed Olympians; and particularly, those of us in the arts and sciences, worship glorious
Apollo — master of the Muses, patron of the beautiful, giver of
knowledge, god of light and enlightenment, guide and teacher of
all that is Reason. (Although more and more of us of recent years

suspect that there is really only one god, and that the divine members of the Olympic council are but his various manifestations.)

"But, as you know, to Hellas from Asia came this new god, Dionysos, the winegiver, in a chariot drawn by panthers, with the god-intoxicated Bacchantes in his train. He is the god of the wild and irrational in man. He stands for all that we scientists and philosophers condemn. But woe unto the human who gives him not his due of honor! He is a dread and merciless god, and terrible is his wrath."

Of course the lad did not understand. But he remembered.

As he grew, he of course received the whole range of training in musica and gymnastica — the general cultural and physical education that was standard for boys of good family throughout the Greek world. He felt himself drawn at times to the cosmological and ethical speculations of the philosophers, at times to problems of government or the military life (like all boys, he was trained for war, and he had a good physique and could, when necessary, bear hardship well), at times to music which was a joy to him (throughout his life his lyre was to be a constant companion, his rest in weariness, his consolation in sorrow.)

The boy had an orderly mind, and was inclined to question doctrines not susceptible of proof; but to question did not mean automatically to disbelieve, and tentatively he went along with what he was taught.

To his seeking intellect, Euclid's geometry burst like a brilliant light. On the basis of only some half dozen axioms (such as that if to two equal quantities two other equal quantities be added, the results will be equal) which had to be taken as self-evident, a series of propositions was erected. Each of these had to be established by the most rigorous logic, within strict limitations of allowable method, each proof being based on axioms and antecedent propositions — a series constructed like a column of bricks each resting upon another previously laid.

"Heracleitos of Ephesus," his father said to him, "taught that wisdom lay in understanding the essential — the formula — that underlies all things. Only in mathematics is there perfect and always reproducible truth. Therein lies its beauty. The theorem of Pythagoras, that the square of the hypotenuse is equal to the sum of the squares of the legs on a right triangle, is true not only of the triangle of which you demonstrate it, but of all right triangles — it is, in fact, part of the essence of right triangularity, everywhere and forever. Two and two make four, not only here and now, but throughout time and even in the halls of the blessed gods themselves!

"In all else there may be doubt, but in mathematics we are on firm ground. The laws of mathematics, best illustrated in geometry, are the prototype of logic. Prior belief, love, hate can have no effect. It follows of necessity, therefore, that the mathematician obeys the laws of logic. To the extent that he observes them, he is dealing in pure reason. By their use, man could solve all his problems — providing he has the necessary basic facts!"

With this key to the world of matter one could march onward from the limit to which Euclid's explorations had carried him, and there was no barrier, in earth or high heaven, to stay one's path! For the first time he realized the truth of Pythagoras' proud boast that if one could fully understand numbers, he could control the world! And the boy had a dazzling view of his mission as a mathematician — to carry the frontiers of knowledge on through the cosmos!

If it be true that the greatest hope of a parent is that his offspring may surpass him, few fathers have been so blessed as Phidias — he was doubly blessed, in fact; for to a father who is happy in his lifework, it is a gift of the gods when his son elects a similar career, since he not only rejoices in the prospect that the son may find the same happiness, but it gives him hope that the boy has found the father worthy of emulation.

Quite early a great friendship developed between Archimedes and his kinsman Hiero, the son of a nobleman by one of the female attendants in the house. It is unusual for a youth and a man seventeen years his elder to have much in common when there does not seem to have been in their relationship anything of the erotic, which might have explained it in so many others; nevertheless they maintained a deep and sincere attachment.

Hiero, as is well known, elected a military career in which he was extraordinarily successful. He became a general while still in his early twenties and gained in his leadership such popularity and fame that when the throne became vacant he was acclaimed ruler.

He sent for Archimedes.

"Cousin," he said, "my good fortune is yours. Come to the palace. Any post you want in the government is at your disposal."

The other laughed to himself. He was to soar dizzily through the rarefied heights of the eternal verities. What to him were the ephemeral considerations of wealth or statecraft?

"I thank you, cousin, and most sincerely. But the relationships of numbers are the same in my cottage as in your palace. Were I to take up any task in your service, it would just be time lost from my calculations."

"Then join me here as my permanent guest! There will be no demands upon your time; you may spend the days as you will."

"I am truly grateful, Hiero. But I know that in the palace there would be many distractions. My work will proceed better at home."

"Is there nothing, then, that I can do for you?"

"Yes, I can think of one favor I should like — a big one."

"It is yours — what is it?"

"In a year or two, I should like to spend some time in the Museum at Alexandria. My father has told me much about it; I am eager to study in the hall that Euclid once knew."

"The money will be ready when you are."

Hiero did more than that for his old comrade. He gave him estates, so that his friend's modest circumstances changed to a moderate affluence.

Outside of his father, the teacher who made the most profound and lasting effect upon young Archimedes was a man who had studied in Athens under Zeno. The stoic philosophy was in all ways suited to the nature of the youth. To enjoy the good things of life in moderation, scorning not pleasure but luxury; to follow sternly the way of virtue, doing evil to none, not through fear of punishment, but to be in accord with the plan of the universe; to recognize the divine inherent in all things; to honor the humanity of every human regardless of station; to love the search for scientific truth; equably to accept what comes, knowing that we turn it into good or evil — all this became the lasting code of the young mathematician.

The scientific ambience of the Museum at Alexandria affected Archimedes like a bath in a vivifying fluid. His knowledge grew fast and far. He made friends — Conon of Samos, Eratosthenes of Cyrene, and others — who became his lifelong correspondents. To Conon, in fact, as long as the Samian was alive (and thereafter to Dositheos), he subsequently sent his works before publishing them for the scientific world; and to Eratosthenes he was to dedicate his Method of Mechanical Theorems.

The young man had grown up, then, in an ivory tower. He was, and continued to be, so devoted to pure science that he was reluctant to turn his talents to practical purposes. The way of science is like a priesthood, and the jealous god demands the complete surrender of his devotee in thought and act alike if he is to bestow his rewards. Only exceptionally could the Master be persuaded to lend himself to the world of practical men. A few of these exceptions took place in Egypt.

Out of Alexandria, he was traveling with a companion on an unusually hot day. He pointed to an agricultural laborer.

"What is he doing?"

"He is raising irrigation water to a higher level. This is a heavy and continuous task in Egyptian agriculture — it is a characteristic feature of the landscape."

"He seems to be in trouble."

"So he does! Sick, I daresay. He has collapsed!"

"One of his fellows has come to his aid. Poor devil! He does seem in a bad way."

"It is a grueling and relentless job. Well, nothing can be done about it."

For the rest of the day Archimedes asked many questions about the field workers, their incessant labor and meager rewards. Then in the Museum workshop he made a cylindrical object.

"I call this my cochlias", he explained. "In this is a flat helical ribbon of copper which completely fills the lumen. It rotates upon an axial rod. If you dip it into a basin of water — so — and rotate it, it raises the water to a higher level."

The cochlias of Archimedes proved a tremendous success. Its use quickly spread through the fields of the country. It later proved useful, as every one knows, in emptying the bilges of ships, and for other purposes. The inventor, once having produced the tool, took no further interest in it. He never wrote a description of the product of his genius on this or any other occasion on which he applied his talents to practical matters, but forgot it as quickly as possible, as though ashamed of having degraded his science to make it a servant.

On a later occasion, learning of the deaths of some of a party of laborers in an attempt to cross a large branch of the river, he examined the area and produced a drawing of a type of bridge adapted to this particular purpose; and many such were built. So, too, with his dykes and other devices to control the flow of the river in its unruly stages. He did the needful, and thereafter removed himself from the scene.

Archimedes spent three years in Egypt.

There has been a persistent story that Archimedes made a voyage to Spain for the purpose of introducing the use of his cochlias to control flooding in the silver mines. This is not correct.

What happened was the following. A request came to him, by very roundabout channels, to consider whether his device might be so used; and if he thought it worthwhile, to permit its introduction for the purpose. He never considered visiting that land, nor was it necessary. At one time he did give some thought to sending a representative to investigate the local conditions in the mines. The mate of a certain ship, whose captain had been consulted regarding possible passage for one of the Master's student associates, visited to discuss the matter. It soon became evident, however, that he was considerably the worse for drink, and we dismissed him.

On the following day another ship captain presented himself.

He had gotten wind of the plan, and came to offer his services. There was considerable rivalry for the assignment — it might lead to a lucrative "in" on the tin trade. The newcomer stated that he had in his crew a bright young fellow who not only could speak Phoenician, but was actually half Carthaginian by his mother. He produced the seaman — a prepossessing eighteen-year-old who proved to be a lad of considerable education as well. It seemed likely that this young man could act for us in the matter, and it was so agreed.

There was an unpleasant sequel. The hard-drinking mate lost his position, and his doxy came while we were in discussion with the young sailor — Pyrrhon was his name, I remember — and made quite a scene. At first he maintained a dignified silence; but when she accused him of holding a place in lieu and at the expense of a better man, he started as though remembering something, and wilted visibly. It was so striking that the picture has remained in my mind's eye until this day. I cannot imagine why he reacted in this fashion — he was really quite blameless in the matter. It almost seemed as though he would abandon the project, captain or no captain. But ultimately, his ship sailed to Spain; he returned with the information we sought; and some of Archimedes' pumps were shipped to the mines. They operated, as it seems, very effectively.

This was our first encounter with Pyrrhon, who was to become the friend and associate of Archimedes.

When first I had the privilege of being the student and associate of Archimedes, he was interested in the problem of numerical notation.

He was thoughtful enough to introduce me to the five who were with him, most of whom I knew.

I was naturally quite nervous lest I play the fool, and indeed it became speedily obvious that my fellows were conversant, as I was not, with Conon and Aristarchos (although with the works of Pythagoras I was naturally familiar), but the exquisite courtesy of Archimedes soon made it obvious that I might be at ease. Let me hasten to explain that this betokened neither indifference nor lack of a decent consciousness of his own worth on the part of the Master. As I was to discover, he did not suffer fools gladly, and had little use for those who could not follow his lucid explanations; I have in fact seen him break out into rather cutting sarcasm, but seldom toward any whose self-conceit did not deserve it and never, even under provocation, toward a slave.

They had been discussing, as it seemed, the number of living things in the world, and Hesychios resumed with an objection.

"It would seem, Master, that we cannot become involved in any such considerations as these. There is no way of expressing or writing quantities nearly large enough for our purpose. We have only 24 letters in the alphabet. The highest number which we can write is ten thousand."

"It should be possible to go much higher," replied Archimedes. "The scientist should admit no problems to be beyond consideration, and, yes, solution."

"How, then, can one deal with quantities for which there is not even a method of notation?"

"What is the most numerous kind of thing you can think of?"

"The sands of the sea, I suppose. They are infinite in number."

"Infinite means without end. But is there not a border to the sea and its sands? Is not the upper border, the air, and the lateral border, the rocks and soil of earth?"

"The latter is indefinite in places, Archimedes. Even the former; for in places the sands are cast up into dunes, appreciably higher than the surface of the sea."

"That is true, Hesychios. But if we can establish a definite border, then the number of grains of sand, though very large, would be finite, would it not?"

"True. But sometimes we come upon patches of sand even in the hills. To be certain of including all of it one would have to assume a sphere of sand whose diameter is the diameter of the earth, prolonged to earth's highest mountains."

"We will do better than that. What is the cosmos?"

"The cosmos is the spere whose center is the center of the earth, and whose circumference is described by the sun as it circles around the earth."

"Essentially, that is correct. Aristarchos of Samos, however, supposes that it is the earth which revolves around the sun, and not, as generally believed, the reverse. At any rate, the size of the sphere is the same, regardless of which be at the center and which at the periphery. Now the stars he places on an outer sphere of the universe, the ratio of whose diameter to that of the cosmos is the same as the ratio of that of the cosmos to that of the earth. And what is the circumference of the earth?"

"According to Dikaiarchos of Samos," Euphranor put in, "it is 30 myriai of stadia."

Archimedes nodded. "Thirty times ten thousand stadia, or, as the Romans would say, 36,000 miles. Let us accept that. Now let us compute that of the cosmos."

The Master then calculated that the diameter of the cosmos measured less than ten billion stadia. I shall not give the method here; any of my readers who are conversant with the works of Euclid of Alexandria will understand it.

"But we will not be content merely with the cosmos," the Master threw out. "We will calculate, and find means to express, the number of grains of sand if they filled not merely the cosmos, but the sphere of the fixed stars."

He then assumed the volume of a grain of sand to be a ten thousandth that of a poppy-seed and the latter 1/40th of a finger breadth. The succeeding calculation brought out his system of notation for higher numbers as follows.

"Since we have a symbol for myriai, or ten thousand, we can already write myriai myriades, ten thousand times ten thousand. Values up to this point let us call First Numbers. Taking this value as a new unity, let us now go up similarly to myriai myriades, through the Second Numbers. Beginning again with this as a newer unity, we can go up through the Third Numbers to myriai myriades again.

"There is, of course, no limit to this process. When this series is exhausted one can begin with a new unity in numbers of the Second Period, until one reaches myriai myriad units of the myriai myriadth order of the myriai myriadth.

"The number of grains of sand that could be contained in the sphere of the fixed stars, not that it matters, works out to less than one thousand myriad units of the eighth octad. This figure is equivalent to ten multiplied by itself sixty-three times."

V

Extract from the Notes of the Comedian Lallos

Fortune had turned her back upon the coppersmith Kimon. To his great grief and that of his adopted daughter, Claudia, Eratho had succumbed to a minor epidemic that swept of a summer through the town. Soon thereafter, a customer was severely injured when a carthorse, drawing a load of the smithy's wares, was frightened and ran from the shop; the driver was adjudged at fault, and there were heavy damages to pay. A fire completed his ruin — fighting it, the smith was so badly burned that after months of enforced idleness and medical treatment his right arm and hand were permanently useless.

He was left with no wife, no shop, no trade, and a crushing load of debt.

It was small wonder, therefore, that he accepted all too readily when some old friends invited him to an evening of wine-swilling in the taverns. And when, a few days later, his body was found in the harbor, it made little difference whether he had fallen from a wharf or a befuddled despair had pushed him over.

To Claudia's grief was added the great anxiety about her future. She knew that she was an adopted child; what she did not know was that she was legally still a slave. It was therefore a shock that passes the comprehension of most of us when, immediately after the modest funeral, Kimon's creditors got a judgement, and the slave dealer's Scythian suddenly appeared and unceremoniously bound her wrists and dragged her off to his master's barracoon. It was, as it happened, the establishment of that same Adeimantos who had sold her as an infant.

The girl was in black despair. The dreams that every girl fashions — of marriage, of a home, of living a happy life in the

88

secure love of husband and children — had been swept away in a moment. What she faced was a set of alternatives each worse that the others. She wept while she had tears to weep, and contemplated the darkness of her future.

What happened was something better, apparently, than she had dared to hope.

Lysander, the fifteen-year-old son of the wealthy Phaedrus, was beginning to take notice of girls; and to guard against the perils, medical and criminal, of the stews of Syracuse, Phaedrus and his wife had decided to buy him a bedfellow of his own. Claudia was shown them — she was pretty, apparently healthy, of the same age as the boy, and of a wholesome background. They bought her, and the girl perforce accepted her fate.

The fate presented itself as a kindly one. The lad was prepossessing, well mannered, and considerate. She was the most delightful thing that had ever happened to him, and he appreciated her accordingly. His bearing toward her was less that of the master than that of the wooer; he was thoughtful and understanding. Within days they were deeply in love.

The rest of the household, too, behaved toward her as though she were one of the family. In fact, in their circle people prided themselves on their behavior toward their slaves; the same forms of address were used as to their friends. The man whom Claudia thought of as her father-in-law, except for a tendency to make jokes and word-plays which even to the girl's budding intelligence were banal, was always pleasant; his wife was understanding.

And so, happiness came back to Claudia.

In fact, with it came an advantage that freeborn women did not usually enjoy. The girl had a lively intelligence; and when tutors were engaged with Lysander and his younger brother, she obtained the privilege of attending. So by day she fed her body at the table of her master, and her mind at the lore of his teachers, as by night she fed her heart with his caresses.

So she prospered and counted herself blessed.

Claudia had long known about her origin, but even now, when her natural father was winning a name for himself as one of the more doughty soldiers of Rome, she did not repine. The coppersmith and his wife were the only parents she remembered, and she remembered them with such affection that she could not regret having become their daughter. Had she fallen upon more evil days upon their demise, it might, of course, have been a different matter. As it was, glowing in the affection of her youthful consort, she could envisage no better lot. Furthermore, she had heard about her Roman father's rejection of her, which would have reinforced her feeling of present contentment, had such reinforcement been needed. In my opinion, and in Oppia's too, she was living in a fool's paradise, but there was nothing to be gained by telling her so.

Lysander continued ardent and indulgent. He spoke vaguely about interest in politics, and some ambitions in that direction; but if his mother offered an excursion, or Claudia had some suggestion for the day, he allowed his attendance at court or office as observer and learner to be put off for another occasion.

Livia, as I have written, had despairingly accepted a way of life she detested for the sake of her daughter. When the girl was nine years old, that happened which she had been dreading.

They lived on a narrow street off the agora. When one day, for some reason, Livia wanted some of the particularly pure and sweet water of the spring Arethusa, the girl begged so hard to go along that the mother gave in. They crossed the agora — it was late afternoon, and the market stalls were all dismantled or empty — and walked to and across the causeway to the island Ortygia, and half way along its western shore, looking idly at the press of ships moored in the great harbor and at the marble-faced temples of Apollo and Athene. Arrived at the spring house, they entered, and among the chattering slave women and house-wives of the humbler citizens Livia quickly filled her amphora, set it on her head, and the two of them started home. The little one looked with delight at the delicately colored chitons on the women who were out on similar errands.

As they approached the agora, Livia encountered a recent customer. The fellow was in drink.

With a "So you're raising a daughter for your trade! How much for the little one?" and a guffaw, he attempted an indecent caress on the child. Livia gave him a blow that sent him reeling, and fled with the girl.

A new kind of desperation drove her as a suppliant to the elder son, now grown to manhood, of her erstwhile mistress and persecutor.

Fortunately, she was wise enough to refrain from recriminations directed at the young man's mother. He proved more sympathetic and understanding than she had dared to hope. He placed her as nurse-companion with a pair of aged and helpless retainers, and undertook to provide his half-sister with a modest dowry when she should arrive at an age to wed.

The heavens have fallen upon Claudia.

Lydiades owned one of the greatest estates in the kingdom, and part of it adjoined the lands of the father of Lysander. He also had an only child, a daughter. The two families had long had an understanding, to which the boy, I believe, was not privy — not that it mattered. At any rate, Lydiades, who had become a father rather late in life, had recently been experiencing certain symptoms which, the Asclepiads warned him, gave sign that it would be well if he set his affairs in order. They had not planned to marry the children quite so young, but this, of course, put another face on the matter.

His parents told Lysander that Claudia would have to go.

Her presence would not have mattered, of course, to a well established marriage; but as it was, her mere being in the house would seriously interfere with the development of a happy relationship between the bridal pair.

Lysander raged — or exhibited what in the feeble-spirited youth was the nearest thing to rage. He pleaded. He wept. All was to no avail. He came to take his farewell of Claudia.

"But Lysander!" she exclaimed incredulously. "We cannot part! We love each other!"

"What can I do?" he asked. "My parents control everything!"

"Not quite! Have you not told me that an aunt left you a little freehold of which you have complete disposal? We can make do with that!"

"And be poor?" The words, the look of amazement, told her the whole wretched tale of his weakness, to which she had been willfully blind till now.

There was a bitter scene in which she stormed at his parents. They were rather decent people, after all; they did not have her whipped. But they would not keep her. Neither did they want to send her back to the chances of the barracoons and the auction block of Adeimantos. They even considered freeing her, but were deterred by the fear lest she make a nuisance of herself about their son's new household. In the end, they directed a reliable old slave to take her to the estate of a guest-friend in the city of Naxos, with a deed of gift and a letter asking him to treat her well. They let her keep the jewelry that Lysander had given her.

Broken-hearted, she took the road to the north.

Agenor, a young captain in the light infantry of Messana, was on his way home by chariot from Katana (the season was too advanced for a sea voyage). He had been on the staff of an envoy, and had full gear and panoply. Rounding a bend in the road, he became aware of a knot of struggling figures about a screaming woman. A touch of the whip quickly brought him alongside, and he saw an elderly man — a slave, by appearance — bleeding on the ground, and five ruffians, having torn away practically all of a girl's clothing, about to ravish her.

As Agenor put it, "I had but two choices — try to rescue the girl, come what might, or for the rest of my life, whenever I tried to cozen a woman into surrender, remember the time I had not dared to prevent an outrage." Which reminds me, of course, of Socrates — the brave man is he who knows what things he should be afraid of.

Fortunately, he had his complement of two javelins in the chariot. With each he transfixed one of the villains (they had gotten the girl down, so there was small danger from a misdi-rected cast). One he ran down with his horses; the other two succumbed to a first-class professional armed with a better sword than either of them had set hand to.

It seems that for some reason the girl had been lost in misery of some private sort, and that the attempted assault had represented the last stages of ignominy and despair. And when he found himself quite captivated by her obvious goodness and beauty, she began, although doubtingly and painfully at first, to live again.

For Agenor swept her up into his chariot in masterful fashion. The old servant he carried to a village where his wounds would be cared for; and learning that he had rescued a slave girl of a Syracusan house, bade the old man return and report that Agenor of Messana was buying the slave Claudia at whatever price they cared to fix, but that in any case, have her he would.

Let it be said to the credit of Claudia's former owners that when she added (by letter) her request to Agenor's they made her over to him as a free gift.

It was over a year after the separation of Claudia from Lysander that she came once more into our ken. I was choosing a cast for the production of my Diprosopis. This satire on the hypocrisy of some of our governmental personages struck so closely to home that they prevented any subsequent performance of it. It has been read and highly praised in Aetolia and Athens; naturally, none of the monarchies or oligarchies enjoy having their shortcomings so brilliantly exposed. In this state, it was not Hiero himself, nor his son Gelon, who were disturbed by it; Hiero, in fact, was a beneficent ruler. His tax, so far from the oppressive seventh or even fifth of the farmer's crop, prevailing in so many countries, was a mere tenth, and that payable in kind, not cash, so that the farmer need not have the additional hazard of having to deal in futures; in addition, its levying was carefully controlled to prevent fraud and extortion. Hiero was well loved, accordingly, by both aristocracy and peasantry, although the latter circles were well aware of how heavy might be the hand of Rome, and his pro-Roman policies were disliked by them.

At any rate, my play did not do well. These are bad times for the playwright who wishes to do any serious writing, whether

comic or tragic. In the great days, an Aristophanes could prop-
agandize against skepticism or the radical movement in the
vehicle of a comic play, flavored with a little Attic salt just a bit
on the bawdy side, or even scatological, if you will. And not only
did he win a hearing, but his message was rewarded with honor.
But today a writer of comedies, in particular, cannot even be
listened to unless he offers a new twist on the technique of
seduction of male or female or a more explicit presentation, if
possible, of what takes place in a sexual encounter.

An actor of Messana was applying for a role. He had some
kinship with one Agenor, a captain of light infantry, and the
captain's favorite had given him a message for Oppia, through
me. He recounted her history since leaving Syracuse....
Claudia's coming to Agenor was like the transition from day-
dreaming to waking. Where before, in her helplessness and
inexperience, she had given her love to a weak boy, who, after
accepting the gift had discarded it, she now had as lover a
dashing, glamorous, young but mature man who so swept her off
her feet that in a surprisingly short time her heart was his as
much as her person. And he on his side found himself entranced
by this seventeen-year-old girl as never before.
Agenor was not the man to neglect his duties in uxorious
self-indulgence, and his rise in the service of his city continued
as before. His was one of its best and oldest families. Few of the
ancient lines had survived the rule of the Mamertines, from fifty
to thirty years earlier, and almost all of those that did were, like
his, impoverished. Thus, Claudia had to share the hard and
menial work of the household with their single, not very able
slave in order to make ends meet and to keep up the appear-
ances necessary to the prestige of a rising young officer in the
army. She had no complaints; she had become a woman, living
and working shoulder to shoulder with her man among men.
She loved it.
The actor from Messana proved to be lacking in fire. An adequate supporting role, however, was not beyond his powers; and
there was a certain advantage in having someone who would not

try (vainly, of course) to take the play away from me. I employed him.

Terentia, who had been sold as a wife to the son of a farmer, was happily marrying off her daughter. (It was at the wedding feast that I conceived the theme of my "Geophagoi". The "Land-Eaters" was to be a satire on those land-owners whose insatiable desire for larger and larger estates threatened the ruination of so many sturdy yeomanries of Hellas.)

The girl was fifteen, and well developed for her age. She was being married to the son of another farmer of the vicinity; the young man's interest ran to livestock, and his father's land, which would one day be his, was very well adapted to this purpose. Terentia's son was, of course, the prospective heir to his father's farm, and a herd of cattle and some goats were his sister's marriage portion.

I made good use subsequently of some of the broad humor of the type that one hears at rural weddings. In this setting, it was not unnaturally very earthy. My tablets were in constant use.

Such aids to the composition of a play are, of course, always welcome. Or any others. I find a tremendous variation in the facility in which I work. Some passages almost write themselves, and my pen races to keep up with my inspiration; elsewhere I run into blocks, and return day after day to the manuscript in vain, until finally I gather my strength and bull it through. The former passages are likely to be the better.

No piece of writing is ever completed. One gets idea after idea for its improvement; a time comes when one must simply declare it finished.

Not even the editing is ever done. No matter how many times I go over my work, long afterwards I find minor errors of syntax, needless repetitions of words, infelicitous expressions, etc., in numbers that astonish and depress me.

Claudia is back in Syracuse!

I have recounted her blossoming forth in the sun of her Agenor. After three years, the blossom yielded its fruit.

It was early spring when the girl began joyfully to think that she had conceived, but delayed telling Agenor lest she be mistaken. Agenor meanwhile decided, rather suddenly, to go off on a season's campaign as a mercenary with the Achaeans, and before she knew it, he was gone.

Claudia went through the desperate worry that women know so well, wondering from day to day whether she still had a mate and her developing child a father.

It was in the fall, when her time was upon her, that she received word that in a few days her beloved would be with her once more. She had just time to sacrifice a pair of doves in gratitude to Zeus the Savior before she went into labor.

Her first baby was a long time coming, and mother and midwife wrestled desperately with death. Only after a night and the better part of a day of agony did she bear a perfectly formed son.

It was just at this juncture that Agenor arrived home. He looked at the child, gave his orders, left word for her of his love and devotion, and went to report to the commanding general.

A long night's sleep, coupled with a vigorous constitution and the resiliency of youth, went far toward restoring Claudia's strength. She awoke. Her breasts were full, and she called for her baby in joy and triumph. "The baby is sleeping in the next room," said the woman in attendance, "and he should not be disturbed."

An hour or two later she repeated her request. "It would be better to wait," the attendant repeated.

"Wait? Why? Surely the baby should be hungry by now!"

"He did not seem so."

"Something is wrong here. Is he deformed or impossibly ugly?"

"By no means — I have never seen a more beautiful child."

"Bring me my baby at once!"

"I cannot now. I must hurry to buy some fruit," and the attendant rushed out.

Her heart cold with terror, Claudia gained her feet and struggled into the next room. It was empty. She dragged herself out of the house and screamed for help. None of the neighbors seemed to hear. Soon her attendant came running with Claudia's maid, and they forced her into bed. Finally, further postponement being pointless, they told her that the child had been left in the hills to die.

It was evening when Agenor returned with a Corinthian necklace of northern amber in his hand to find a half-crazed woman in their chamber. When he would have kissed her, she repulsed him and struck the gift aside.

"Where is my baby?" she screamed.

He assumed a deprecatory tone. "I'm sorry, dearest. Don't take on so. In time you'll forget. Just get well, as fast as you can, and it will be you and I together, just as in the old days."

"But this was your baby — yours!"

"I know. And I'm truly sad about it."

"But why — why?"

She was being difficult. "Why? But you should know why. I am a poor man. You should understand that it's out of the question for us to have a family — I can't afford it."

"Do you mean that you don't intend ever to have children — that you'll let your line die out?"

He was becoming irritated. What had she expected? "No, of course that is not my intention."

"Then, why? Why?"

He saw that there was to be no side-stepping the issue. He would have to let her have it right in the face.

"Did you really think that I would raise your half-Roman bastard as my son and heir?"

He did not return for several weeks. Then, again on her feet, she said to him, "I have one request to make, and only one. Sell me."

He saw that she was not to be dissuaded.

He had the grace to free her.

To Claudia the very stones of Messana had become unendurable.

Where else would she flee but to Syracuse, where she had known at least a happy childhood? She found a mercantile shipment with an armed escort for the road — the season was again too advanced for sea travel — and with a trifle of her jewelry obtained the privilege of its protection. Arrived here, she sought Oppia, and at her request I put her friend up for the time being.

We left her alone, naturally, in the absence of sign that she wanted consoling. Not till about the fifth day did she enter into conversation, and then, naturally, it was about her future.

"I cannot earn my living as a hired unskilled worker," she said. "Slaves furnish a cheap competition that I cannot meet."

"That is true," I answered. "And you have, of course, no saleable skills."

"None."

"You might open a little shop of some kind," was Oppia's suggestion.

"I know nothing of business. I'd lose what little capital I have."

"Perhaps," Oppia answered again, "a marriage with some freedman could be arranged."

"And live happily with him, and love him? I've had my bellyful of that."

"But there's nothing else," I objected, "except a brothel or the streets."

"And if that should become my way, who would dare blame me?"

I shrugged. "You're not far wrong."

"No. But I have a much better plan. As you may remember, my parents paid for schooling for me, and my teachers said I did very well. In the home of Lysander, I took advantage of the presence of tutors to the young ones, and continued my instruction. I studied the manners and bearing of his family. And when Agenor" — a spasm of pain passed over her face — "was away on maneuvers or fighting, which was often, I read continually in books that he borrowed for me. I am probably one of the best educated women in Syracuse. And some of the efforts of Agenor's supposed friends gave ample evidence that I am not bad looking."

"So?"

"I have some good jewelry. I can turn it in to a jeweler for imitations, and with the proceeds I can outfit myself with a few good clothes. I can hire the services of a maid until I can buy one. In short, I shall be a hetaira."

We were dumbfounded. This was the one possibility we had never considered. We had to consider it now.

I no longer believe that these notes will ever be the base for a comedy by my friend Thesetidion, in Rome. In fact, I do not know what I shall do with them, if anything. Nevertheless, it interests me to go on recording the fates of these girls; and it makes it a little more worthwhile — or apparently so — if I write with Thesetidion in mind.

He would have, at this point, to make clear to the Romans exactly what a hetaira is, and how she is regarded in Greek society.

A hetaira sells her body, true. But between her and the harlot is a world of difference — and not merely in price. More important than physical love, a hetaira furnishes intelligent companionship — a kindred though female soul which can meet a man's needs to have someone enjoy with him a poem, an epigram, a statue, a philosophical concept, a political discussion. She is a woman he can introduce to his friends and not be ashamed of. She represents a union not, it is true, as permanent as marriage, but equally not as evanescent as a tumble in a disreputable establishment or a furtive hole-and-closet affair that can besmirch the honor of a decent house. And on her side, a hetaira is above the quickie sex deals of her more meretricious sisters, and is in a position to say "no" to any man not of her choice. She represents a welcome contrast to the bovine ignorance that characterizes the dame in the mansion and the slut in the gutter. And she has the acceptance and respect of the community, in consequence.

It was not as though Claudia were a dewey-eyed innocent dreaming of the husband who would cherish her. Even were some such man to appear — a most unlikely eventuality — she would not again risk disillusion and heartbreak. Twice betrayed, Claudia was finished with love and romance. And motherhood.

It occurred to me to wonder amusedly how this intention of hers would strike her father, Marcus Claudius. His had become a name to reckon with in Rome — in fact he was beginning to be called Marcellus, by reason of his prowess in the fields of Mars. The daughter of a Roman Praetor, a hetaira in Syracuse!

VI

Extracts From the Correspondence
of Marcus Claudius Marcellus

Decius Manilius to Publius Tullius. At Rome, on the 14th day before the Kalends of August, in the Year after the founding of the City the 516th.

The latest bit of news is something to be discussed both here and in the provinces for many a day.

You heard, I am sure, but may have forgotten, that a dozen years ago there was a piratical descent upon Liternum. The raiders captured the wives and daughters of some of the first families of Rome — a Fulvius, an Aemilius, a Julius, a Livius, a Cornelius, an Oppius, a Terentius, and a Claudius were all bereft.

Very recently, for the first time, word of their fate has come to Rome. It seems that they were taken first to Sardinia (one might have guessed it!), then sold in Sicily. Some of the girls, a Greek shipmaster informs us, are still in Syracuse alive, and one of them sent this word hoping for ransom.

Arrangements were being made when it came to the ears of the curule aedile, Marcus Claudius. He made his way to the forum and mounted the rostrum.

"As aedile of Rome," he proclaimed, "charged with the prosecution of violators of public morals, I forbid this ransom!

"A Roman woman," he pronounced in the manner of a judge giving a verdict, "captured and facing disgrace, knows her duty. If she chooses to live and accept violation and shame, Rome will know her no more. We will not have her back."

"A woman may be violated against her will," suggested the Greek, who was present and awaiting an answer. "But shame can come to her only as a result of her voluntary action."

The aedile's lip curled. "Greeks may hold that notion. A Roman will have none of it."

"That there are women of Rome, as of other lands," the captain objected, "who will not live except on their own terms, I do

101

not doubt. That all, or even most, Roman women are made of such iron, I do not believe. In any case, I condemn your attitude. Among both men and women, one may admire those who will not compromise with their ideals, even in the face of certain death; but one has not the right to demand it of them."

"My own daughter is among the captives," Claudius replied, "and was a mere babe when she became one. But I will not have her back. No one shall say that a Roman magistrate is swayed by personal feelings from the way he points out to others."

You can imagine the sensation that resulted. It has become a nine days' wonder. I think that some of the interested families would have found a way to overrule him; but one of the tribunes of the plebeians took it up, and made it an issue of morals and propriety versus privilege.

They say that Claudius had a terrible scene with his wife. She ran to the Censor Licinius, threw herself at his feet and demanded her daughter. Naturally, it did her no good. The scandal is sure to set tongues wagging the length and breadth of Italy.

You had better do something about your son. Gossip has it that he has lost his heart to a sister of Lucius Marcius. The girl hasn't a portion, and Lucius has no future.

I am returning to my farm at Tusculum. Why don't you visit me? There's a lot of gossip that I don't care to put down on the tablets.

If you are well, then so am I.

Thesetidion to Tibullus. At Rome, on the second day before the Ides of September, in the Year after the founding of the City the 518th.

In your letter you ask me my explanation of the stand taken by the curule aedile recently in the matter of the Roman girls in Syracuse.

To anyone else I should reply that I do not know, and do not attempt to understand, matters of statecraft. But you have been interested in the divine drink of philosophy, and I shall risk somewhat in this reply.

As a dramatist, I know that there is in human life far more acting than appears upon the stage. Men who have achieved positions of standing, in the eyes of themselves or of others, do it almost universally. By doing so, those who enjoy only their own regard merely make themselves ridiculous. In men of prominence, however, the role-playing is accepted and indeed usually undetected. One who looks closely can nevertheless perceive that a man prominent in government, a sea-captain, a military leader is always acting the part of This One, the great statesman; That One, the fearless seaman; Such a One, the unconquerable general. The mannerisms have been so completely incorporated into the role that it is hard to say which came first. And people expect them, and therefore accept them.

There are nations whose pride, well- or ill-founded, affects every citizen in this fashion, making him feel that merely by virtue of nationality he is superior to any foreigner. That is true of us Hellenes, and the feeling attains almost or perhaps quite to arrogance in Athens and Sparta.

It is particularly true here. (Please do not be offended.) The mystique of the city on the Tiber is such that every citizen, no matter how wretched his state, thinks that his "Romanus cives sum" puts him high above all other beings.

The quality most admired among aristocrats is "gravitas", a stern dignity of bearing. Its results are predictable. Add to that a reputation for prowess in battle, in this city which rivals Sparta in its worship of the military ideal, and you can see the inevitable mould into which not only the actions but even the appearance of a rising officer in the army are cast. Hence, the dehumanization of a Coriolanus, or of a Horatius, who slew his sister. Or of a Marcus Claudius.

What inner agonies it costs them I can only surmise. In youth, I believe, they suffer greatly. And it makes them the more merciless to their foes, because if they exhibit human pity for these, some of it might spill over onto themselves. And this they dare not risk, lest all be lost.

In exercising his authority as aedile on the recent occasion, therefore, I believe that Marcus Claudius was three men. The one grieved over his long-lost babe and his tormented wife. The second, stronger than the first, looked to the honor of Rome. And the third, of whom the other two were but dimly aware, looked on in admiration and thought, "How grand am I!"

Before I condemn him, there are two reflections which give me pause. The former is that there is something of this poser in all of us. The second, more important, is that a Roman goes to great lengths to be "pius", deeply mindful of his obligations — to the gods, to the state, to his family and friends. There are often conflicts between these. The Roman decides according to his lights....

Marcus Claudius to Otacillius. At Ariminium, on the 4th day before the Nones of November, in the Year after the founding of the City the 520th.

We have gone into winter quarters here. Having been elected praetor this year by so large a majority, I confess to some disappointment at first over the size of my command. Now I am quite reconciled to it. In fact, encountering so many new problems, I am glad not to have my difficulties complicated by a larger number of troops.

I am learning rapidly. I have already discovered, for instance, that in the matter of logistics one can count on nothing that is not actually in hand. Promises — solemn engagements, even — are not worthless, but are considerably less than performance. And intelligence must be checked and rechecked and compared with other items similarly checked and rechecked, and then doubted. And a commander has no friends.

For all that this is such an out of the way place, I welcome the opportunity to learn the local terrain and population. We shall have to fight the Gauls again, I am sure, and this is a probable battlefield. In any event, we shall certainly, sooner or later, have to put a stop to the Illyrian depredations on our shipping to the east, and this is a likely naval base for such a war.

Greet my father for me.

If you are well, then so am I.

There have been some more outrages on the Adriatic. Three Italian merchants, one Roman and the other two of this city, have memorialized the Senate, seeking redress for wrongs. King Agron's Illyrian pirates seized their ships and cargoes and they themselves were lucky to be released.

I think that the Senate will take no action, as hitherto. Preoccupation with a possible attack by the Gauls, and with the progress of the Carthaginians in Spain, has made the Fathers very reluctant to have our forces engaged in the East.

In my opinion, it is foolish and dangerous to let a bad state of affairs go to worse. It is, I think, axiomatic that if wrong-doers are suffered, for whatever reason, to go unpunished, they will carry their depradations further and further, to the detriment of the state, until an intolerable situation compels the latter to adopt corrective measures infinitely harder and more costly than those that could have resolved the matter in the first place.

We have had a small feast on the occasion of my eldest grandson discarding the toga praetexta for the toga virilis. He now has the responsibilities of Roman manhood.

If you are well, then so am I.

Marcus Claudius to Otacilius. At Rome, on the 12th day before the Kalends of October, in the Year after the founding of the City the 522nd.

My good wishes on the betrothal of your daughter to young Sp. Caecilius. May he be rejoiced by her, and may the marriage be fruitful!

Queen Teuta and her Illyrians have subdued Epirus and Acarnania, and the Epirotes have surrendered Atintania with its passes into central Greece. Her pirates have made several descents upon the shores of Italy, and are pushing southward. The shipping from our eastern shores has become a trickle, and will soon be at an end. Corcyra is under siege.

Even as I write this, comes word that the Senate is at last sending an embassy to Illyria, to demand an end of her piracy!

VII

Extracts from Pyrrhon's Voyages

I became conversant with ships of war in the following wise.

In the unsettled state of central Greece and Peloponnesus, food, never raised too easily in this mountainous area, had almost all to be imported. The war of Illyria, backed by Demetrius of Macedon, against the Achaean and Aetolian leagues, was in full swing. It was in the confident expectation of good trading, therefore, that, having aboard a load of our Sicilian wheat, I set Harmonia's course for the Ambracian Gulf. The enterprise was wholly mine — I had bought out the former owner.

The voyage was uneventful. Unfortunately, two of Ptolemy's grain ships had forestalled me. Egypt had had a good season; even had I been earlier, I could not have met their price. I was sitting somewhat dejectedly on deck at Idomene considering which way to direct my course, when I noticed a gentleman slightly older than myself, well dressed and attended by a slave, approaching along the wharf.

"May I have a word with you, Captain?" he hailed me.

"Come aboard!" I invited him. "I am Pyrrhon of Syracuse. Who is doing my ship the honor?"

"Margos of Caryneia. I understand, Captain, that you have a cargo of wheat for sale."

"Of prime quality. Fresh from the fields of Sicily — all of it this year's crop."

"What are you asking?"

I quoted the standard rate in silver. "Of course, the price will be higher if it is to be delivered more than five day's sail to the east, and still higher if I have to venture into waters infested by pirates."

"I will buy your whole cargo, Captain, at three times your price, on condition that you deliver it promptly to Toryne in Epirus."

As I raised my eyebrows he continued. "There has been a

108

rising against the tyrant, and the town is under siege. There are five thousand of his Illyrians before it, and they have a fleet of two quadriremes, three hemiolas — the one-and-a-half bankers — and some dozen of the open lembi. The wharves and some little distance beyond are controlled by the city walls with their missiles — if you once can get so far, you are safe."

"And how does a merchantman fight her way through such a fleet?"

"I cannot tell you."

"And if she does get in, how does she get out again?"

"I cannot tell you that either."

"You cannot get ships to convoy me?"

"There are only two ships in the harbor — old quadriremes. The city will not spare them. They must assist in defense in case Demetrius' Illyrian allies get this far."

"I can see four from here."

"Two of them, triremes, are no longer seaworthy."

I laughed. "I should like right well to earn that triple price, Margos," I said, "and I have a score of my own to settle with the Illyrians. But I cannot fight a fleet of men-of-war with a single merchantman."

After his departure, however, I could not stop thinking about his offer. It was, of course, sheer insanity. Nevertheless, I found myself unrolling the periplus to study the harbor directions for Toryne.

It opened to the south, and the entrance, except at the sides, seemed free of dangers, if you didn't consider the hostile fleet a danger. From a point on the west, a mole made out across the harbor mouth, narrowing it to some three hundred feet. The eastern side of the harbor was a chain of rocks and islets, extending right out to the south from the shore.

I had always rather prided myself on what I was pleased to consider my ingenuity, and if I could get some of my own back from King Agron's rascals — they had cost me a shipload of salt, and several weeks of time lost in consequence — so much the better. My arrangement of the lumber rafts for Egypt, though risky, had paid off. Too bad that the war galleys were not available for escort, and were not a larger force. But two, he had said, were worthless.

I strolled around the harbor and made a quick survey of the triremes.

Their sides were no longer quite smooth; some of the planks stood out a little further than others — evidence that their fastenings were no longer any good. The explanation was disclosed by brownish stains. In their building, for reasons of either economy or haste, the shipwrights had used iron fastenings instead of bronze, and they were far gone with rust. Nor, as my knife told me, could the fastenings be renewed; the planking, and probably the timbers, were rotted to a point at which they would not take any. These ships were quite worthless. They would float — the caulking, surprisingly, was still good — but they would take no strain; the shock of battle, hard sailing, even hard rowing, would deform them, open the seams, and cause them to fill with water.

I thought again about my lumber rafts, and had my idea.

The Ambracians were more than willing to give me the worn-out ships for use against a common enemy. With them they were willing to include, at very little cost, lumber enough for a raft. Rigging came higher, but Margos was willing to pay for it. That the triremes should work as little as possible in the seas, I divided sheets and braces into half a dozen leads each, distributed as widely as possible through the length of the ships.

When all was ready, we gave each trireme and the raft a very light load of hay, moistened with oil lest it be wetted with water, and some pitch. Early on the first day of a southerly, assisted by a tow from the serviceable quadriremes and some harbor craft, we got under way and made the mouth of the bay. The local craft cast off with good luck wishes and under sail we stood to the northward along the coast.

Harmonia held the center of the flotilla. Close aboard on either side was a trireme; the raft, likewise under sail, followed my ship at the end of a tow-line. Each of the three was handled by a two-man crew.

Of course, I had gotten men at Idomene. Many of my own

ship's company had not cared for a voyage of this kind. Margos, with a smiling, "I wouldn't send a man where I dared not go myself", had joined the ship.

It was two hundred eighty stadia to Toryne—just about thirty Roman miles. The triremes were leaking, of course, but there was not much of a sea. They were burdened with no cargo and our distribution of the stresses of the rigging had been successful enough so that they had only a minimal strain to resist, and made not too much water. The fine weather held, and toward evening we arrived off Toryne.

And there, sure enough, was the Macedonian-Illyrian fleet, waiting for us. Seeing only a merchantman and two triremes, they came up confidently for the capture.

We passed a towline of two ship-lengths to each trireme, which fastened us together, but not closely, by the bows. Their helmsmen lashed the rudders so as to give each trireme a strong sheer away from Harmonia. Then on each of the two and on the raft, the crews set the oily hay and pitch ablaze. At the ends of life-lines, the men then leaped overboard and were hauled to Harmonia. In a moment we were surrounded by a wall of flame.

The enemy lay on their oars in futile rage. Their catapult bolts cost me a few men, but the assailants dared not close. We sailed past them, cut away our fiery escorts at the mouth of the harbor, and tied up at the seawall amid the cheers of the inhabitants.

During the next two days, while the sirocco swelled to fury outside, as such southerlies usually do on that coast, we ate and drank well as guests of the citizens of Toryne. They paid me my triple price, as agreed, and a handsome bonus besides.

There comes a time, however, when one wearies both of giving and of receiving praise. I was a merchant seaman and a Syracusan, and had no desire to share with the people of Toryne the chances of the siege. We made ready for sailing.

When I awoke one morning to see dark, thick storm clouds about the mountain peaks, I ordered my crew aboard. Very soon there was an air from the north, which very quickly became a screaming gale whipping down through the gullies and valleys. We put to sea.

Under ordinary conditions, of course, a merchantman is help-less when a man-of-war is around. In a storm, however, this is not true. In the construction of a war galley, everything must be sacrificed to speed; she has neither the strength nor the free-board to stand up to a gale, and she is frequently undecked into the bargain. If one has the courage, therefore, to brave a storm in a stout roundship, no fighting ship dare challenge the seas — she would be swamped or broken.

So while our enemies lay helplessly on the beach, we stood out under a trisail and headed south. The seas were not too heavy, but the gale tore off their crests and hurled them downwind in a spray so thick we could not see our way. Further off shore, I had heard, as a peculiarity of this coast, that the wind would mod-erate, but the seas, paradoxically, would be more dangerous. To hug the shore, on the other hand, might mean running onto an off-lying reef, blinded as we were by the flying spume. The wind was no guide; even if it blew steadily from the same quarter, its direction near the harbor we had quitted might have been greatly modified by the contours of the land.

At this point the bow lookout sang out for a large whale close aboard! Such a creature is seldom seen in our seas. I accepted the omen and vowed an ox to Poseidon. A whale would hardly be making for the beach, so we set a course trending a little more to the westward than his lest, as we would have to steer by the wind, it should haul, and set us ashore.

By the time we were off the Ambracian Gulf again, the storm seemed to be moderating. Visibility was good, at any rate, and we could set more canvas. We stood in.

There was a second round of festivities. The people of the Aetolian League were only too delighted at my having made possible a setback for the allies of Macedon, and what they were so complimentary as to call both my boldness and my cleverness called forth endless praise.

Actually it was not, I think, that brilliant an idea. It was in the first place dependent on having available ships which could be sacrificed, which is seldom the case. One had also to have a harbor as destination which one could sail straight into, without any twists or turnings of the channel. One needed also a steady favoring wind strong enough to give a good turn of speed, but not so strong as to raise the sort of sea that would have overstrained those poor wracked vessels. And even so, a miscalculation by me or a flaw of wind might easily have resulted in my own ship catching fire as well. Finally, an unusually resolute or quick-witted commander would have found a way to overpower me despite my fireships — I can think of two or three possible means myself. However, I had gambled on the dismay caused by a totally unfamiliar tactic, and won. I would not, however, do it again.

In the same way, a more protected waterway outside the harbor would have permitted the enemy to interdict my escape.

This was not the end of the enterprise. While I had been in Toryne, five hundred Achaean heavy infantrymen had arrived in Idomene to take part in the defense of the northern city, and I was offered the command of the flotilla to put them into the town. It was a challenge which my pride would not let me refuse.

This time they were willing to entrust to me the two still-operative quadriremes. Accordingly, I distributed the men between those ships and my own, having previously loaded as much wheat as I could carry in addition. We had also built another raft, and equipped it like the former.

In the same formation, when the wind blew fair, Margos and I set a course for Toryne.

As we approached the bay, the Illyrians came out to meet us as before. The raft could be set ablaze as previously. On the galleys, one on either beam, I had instructed the soldiers to lie in concealment behind low canvas dodgers. We had provided a number of pots, in each of which a fire could burn harmlessly. Seeing the burning raft astern and the smoking galleys on either side of Harmonia, most of the pirate craft shied off in fear, thinking that they were again dealing with fireships.

One of the enemy quadriremes, however, had a skipper who was more resolute and ingenious than most. With a long spar extending from his bow, he set a collision course for one of my ships, intending to push her in upon me so that Harmonia should fall victim to the flames that we had prepared for him. There was, however, a small catapult in the bow of each of my warships; the men began to lob firepots at the pirate; most, of course, went astray, but a few landed aboard, and distracted him briefly but long enough. We arrived safe in harbor.

Our reception can be imagined.

This time my triumph was not to be without cost.

The enemy controlled the mole that made out from the western side of the bay. While we were in harbor, they prepared a boom made of logs chained end to end; they fastened one end of it to the extremity of the mole and the other to the rocks forming the eastern side of the harbor. They had us in a trap.

The quadriremes, I felt, could break out of it. But Harmonia was another matter.

The tubby old cargo-carrier had served for my apprenticeship. In her I had learned the ways of the sea, had risen to seaman, boatswain, mate, skipper, and owner. It was with a heavy heart that I set about selling her.

It was not too difficult. If Toryne survived the siege, her new owner could profit from the vessel, just as I had. If not, all of his treasure would be forfeit to the enemy in any case.

And so it befell that I entered Harmonia's cramped little cabin for the last time, and transferred my personal effects to one of the quadriremes.

We waited for another norther. As it was blowing itself out, we took aboard each ship sixty young men of the town — all good swimmers. They crowded as far aft as they could get. This sank the sterns lower than usual, and raised the bows out of the water. We then drove at full speed for the boom.

As I had hoped, each bow slipped up and over the log. As this passed under the middle of the keel, my sixty swimmers dashed forward, depressed the bow, and let the ship slide easily off and into the water. Thereupon, the swimmers jumped overside and made their way back to the quays.

With the moderating of the breeze, the enemy ships had left the beach for the blockade. But the sea was still lively, and the weather gauge a great advantage. With hoisted sail we evaded them without too much difficulty and started on the journey to Idomene. They tried to pursue, but a stern chase is a long chase, and they dared not put themselves too far downwind of their station.

I received another hero's welcome in Idomene. The allies were delighted. They offered me a commission as trierarch to command the next war galley to be built and fitted out. (The citizen at whose expense this was to be done was too old to exercise even nominal command in his own person.)

Margos of Caryneia had a share in their gratitude and my friendship.

"Tell me," I asked him one day, "what has been happening in Sparta?"

He laughed. "You ask the wrong person. I am a man of the League; Sparta is no friend of ours. But I'll tell you what I know. You may have heard of King Agis, and his attempt to restore the golden age of Sparta."

I nodded.

"It was, of course, foredoomed to failure. One cannot bathe twice in the same river. But more than that, there never was a Sparta of Agis' dream. Oh, she had that reputation, of course, and certainly she has fallen on sadly degenerate days; but the old uniform rugged simplicity is a myth. There were always richer and poorer men in Sparta, and the Spartiates never objected to the color of money. Be that as it may, Agis left behind him a young widow, immensely wealthy in her own right. Leonidas, king again (and solely, which was unconstitutional) wanted to get his hands on her fortune. Accordingly, he married her to his son, Cleomenes, very much against the wishes of both."

"So that's why he did not assassinate her along with the other women of Agis' family. I wondered, when I heard about it in Alexandria."

"No doubt. At any rate, Cleomenes succeeded to the throne four years ago."

There was no point in my remaining there inactive to wait for my galley. I returned home in a merchantman of Rhegium.

News of my activities had preceded me, and I found that I was being much spoken of in Syracuse.

I have often speculated on the problem: what is courage? On the basis of observation and report, I think that the Spartan King Cleomenes, of whom I shall write hereafter, was the most completely fearless human being I have ever known. Such I am not. In the actual physical presence of danger, I am in great misery of spirit, and am hard put to it to take the required risks, and to conceal my feeling from my men. I am not the stuff of which great poets sing.

On the other hand, I have never hesitated to put myself in harm's way. And once in peril, I acquit myself well enough. I think there is something to be said for me, even though I am no lover of danger for its own sake.

Beyond the personal factor, the hostilities in which I had just participated are an example, I am afraid, of the futility of one-sided pacific intentions. Toryne, and beyond her the cities of the Gulf of Corinth, had just two choices—submit to the tender mercies of the pirates of Illyria, or cultivate the arts of war and resist. Were I the head of a family in that part of the world exposed to the ravages of Queen Teuta and her savage allies, I know what I should urge.

While I was casting about for an interim occupation, pending service on the mainland of Greece, I spent much time with my brother. One day, I came upon him in the company of a stranger, Eudoxus of Tauromenion. "You come in good time, Pyrrhon," my brother remarked after the introduction. "This morning I heard that Saul ben Menasseh has acquired a ship, for which he will need a captain."

"Saul ben Menasseh?" remarked the stranger. "That sounds like a name of Judea."

"That's right," my brother replied. "His grandfather came here, I have heard, as a result of his too vigorous resentment of some outrage or other by a Carian mercenary in Judea. His further residence there became incompatible with the possibility of dying in bed. Soon thereafter, he distinguished himself here in the suppression of the oligarchy, and was rewarded with citizenship. Saul is one of our merchants."

"I'm sure you're joking," laughed Eudoxus. "A Jewish businessman! I spent some time in Judea in the service of Ptolemy, and I know the Jews very well. They make good farmers and stockmen, and they're great on theological discussion — but trade? The Jewish genius does not run that way at all. I simply can't see one as a man of business."

"Be that as it may, Saul is in trade, and now wants a skipper."

I lost no time in presenting myself before my prospective owner.

"By the horn of Gideon," he exclaimed. "I am glad to see you. Join me at dinner."

While we ate, he told me about the Dolphin. We quickly agreed on my command. Afterwards, we went to view the ship. She was a holkas — an oarless, fat-bellied merchantman with a capacity of some five thousand amphorae, not too old, and in fairly good condition, with a reasonably complete inventory of equipment.

The Euxine that year had its worst season in the memory of living men. There was drought, then excessive rain, then drought again. The grain harvest there was sure to be a failure. Egypt too, it was reported, was likely to have a smaller crop than usual. In the spring we loaded with wheat for Athens.

With a failing wind we glided under the promontory of Sunion, its marble-pillared temple to Poseidon welcoming us from the height. Slowly we stood westward along the numerous tiny bays and capes of the Attic shore until, halfway to our goal, the wind deserted us altogether. A harbor penteconter, looking for business, approached and hailed.

"Want a tow, Captain?"

We made our bargain, accepted her towing hawser, and resumed way on the muscle of her fifty rowers. Leaving the so-called Thieves' Harbor to our starboard, we made for the entrance between the twin moles that sheltered the Peiraios. As we entered, a small boat drew alongside and the customs officer boarded the Dolphin.

"Welcome to Athens, Captain! I don't think I know the ship, though I seem to remember you."

"Yes, I've been here before, though not in the same vessel. I am Pyrrhon, and this is the Dolphin, Saul ben Menasseh owner, all of Syracuse."

"Have a good passage?"

"A quick one, thank you. Off Cape Malea we were threatened by some pirates, but a ship of Rhodes drove them off."

"We all thank the gods for Rhodes. And now, captain, what is your cargo?"

"I am carrying a full load of wheat — 3,300 medimni."

"Your duty will be our usual 2%. You may, if you wish, pay it in kind. Here comes the port captain's representative, to collect the fee for use of the port facilities."

When they had left, we turned to starboard and tied up at the Long Colonnade, in the emporion. A dozen wholesalers in grain came aboard, crying their offers, with a supervising port official. I closed the deal with the highest bidders (to prevent a corner in wheat, no one might lawfully buy over 50 measures) and unloading began.

An exception to the 50-measure rule was made in the case of Charikleides, who, like other wealthy men, bought grain in time of scarcity to be distributed gratis. He took 1/3 of my cargo.

Having asked the way to the office of Kritias, the shippers' agent who handled the local enterprises of my owner, I made my way through the noise and bustle of the Deigma. In this colonnade I saw the booths with the wares of the dealers in Attic ceramics, honey, and olive oil; Cretan hides; Macedonian pitch and lumber; white lead from Smyrna; dried fish from the Black Sea; wine of Ionia and the islands; Carthaginian fabrics; Egyptian line and papyrus; slaves from many nations; and nuts, cheeses, and dried meats of our own Sicily. The moneychangers' tables exhibited all the coinages of the world. Greek in all dialects, Latin, Phoenician, Lybian, Syrian, and half a dozen languages that I could not recognize mingled in my ears.

"I'm glad you've made it so early in the season, Captain," Kritias said to me. "I have a pair of partners who want to import a shipload of wheat from Egypt. Clearidas and Laches, my principals, have lined up their financing at the bank of Eurymedon and Perdiccas, resident aliens from Cos. They are looking for a sound bottom. Are you authorized to charter your ship?"

"My owner entrusted the ship's business to me for the duration of the voyage, without any specified restriction."

"Excellent! Now let us talk price and sailing date."

I knew, of course, about prices at both ends, and about interest rates on such ventures — 25%, give or take a little — and was accordingly able to get as good a charter price as possible for my owner. Naturally, I wanted to pick up a cargo for the outward journey. Kritias helped me there, and I loaded with pitch and ceramic hollow ware for Crete, and olive oil, honey, wine, and bronze for Egypt.

With the two shippers aboard, we set sail a week after our arrival. I could have acted as their purchasing agent at Alexandria, and so offered; but they declined my services, for reasons which only later were disclosed.

On the dependable Etesian wind we made a rapid run to Heraklion, on the northern side of Crete, where we discharged our cargo for that island. Nearby was the traditional location of Knossos and the Labyrinth of Minos, where Theseus of Athens slew the Minotaur. I wandered through the wood to the location indicated to me by the local antiquarians, of whom there were few — the area was altogether on the crude side, with little evidence of cultural interests. I saw broken and scattered fragments of dressed stone, but as to its age I could make no intelligent guess. As can be imagined, however, I let my musings run untrammeled. There is a unique wildness about the Cretan woods.

Our further progress to the mouth of the Nile was likewise uneventful. I got rid of the rest of my cargo at a good price, but then received a surprise bordering on shock. My two shippers bought only some seven hundred medimni of wheat — less than a quarter of my capacity! To my protests they replied sharply that they had chartered my ship, and that how efficiently they used it was no business of mine. This, of course, was true.

Obviously, there was some sort of skulduggery afoot, but it was not up to me to ferret it out. Unknown to them, I got a written statement of the facts of the sale from the Controller of the port, countersealed by the president of the grain wholesalers' association and the treasurer of the city. A month after our departure from the Peiraios, we slipped our moorings for the return.

It is always a long, weary struggle from Egypt to the northward, except, of course, in winter, when southerly winds prevail; but in winter one cannot safely voyage north of Crete. The breezes we encountered off the Egyptian coast were mostly the usual moderate northwesterlies, on which we stood diagonally across the sea in the direction of Syria. There the expected southerly airs made their appearance often enough for us to work up the coast, round Cyprus and stand to the westward toward the Aegean.

It was on a balmy evening, as we were passing along the southern side of Rhodes, that the villainy of Clearidas and Laches became apparent. The former was singing loudly on deck, accompanying himself on a lyre, when some of my crew became aware, above the sound of the music, of a sound of a different sort coming from below. Investigation revealed Laches in the act of sawing through the ship's bottom!

He was haled to the deck to face me. But he pulled out a knife and thrust at those who held him; as they fell back in the shock of surprise, he wrenched free and leaped overside. We saw him no more.

He had obviously tried for the ship's boat towing astern, but missed it. We shed no tears over his drowning.

It was now clear. The wretched pair had intended to scuttle the ship and escape in the longboat to Rhodes. The rest of us were to perish with the foundering vessel, and they would enjoy three quarters of their purchase money at the expense of the bank that had loaned them the funds.

When we arrived at Athens, Clearidas retained a lawyer who

fought desperately for a delay. But Athens, so dependent upon shipping for her existence, provided in her laws for its protection. Any action involving ships or seamen was to be tried within a month of the instigation of the proceedings, and any such offense was punishable expressly by imprisonment, not by a mere fine. Clearidas went to prison for a long term.

By the time that all of this had been accomplished, the season was too far advanced for our return to Sicily. I had, of course, written to Saul ben Menassah about the delay. I paid the crew off, and settled down in Athens for the winter.

It proved to be an interesting time. As a military power — even as an independent state — Athens was finished; but as the heart and cultural center of Greece she was still the queen of cities (despite Alexandria's library and preeminence in the sciences). The beauty of the agora, all marble, to say nothing of the acropolis, quite put our boasted Syracuse to shame. I attended all of the plays in the Great and the Lesser Dionysia; I haunted the stoae and heard the philosophers; I used the gymnasium. Nor was I lonesome; by courtesy of Kritias (who, of course, was quite innocent of complicity in the attempted swindle) and a shipmaster or two whom I had known here and there in the ports of the world, I lacked not for company; and I found a girl who saw to it that I did not perish nights of the cold.

At a certain banquet I was asked to contribute to the symposium, and gave them some impressions of the vicinity of Heraklion in Crete as follows:

> *Sprawled beneath the Cretan sky*
> *Roofless court and castle lie.*
> *Fallen column, splintered plinth*
> *Mark the ruined Labyrinth.*
>
> *Minos, lord of doom, is dead.*
> *Empty is the sea-queen's bed.*
> *And the man-bull's reeking throat*
> *Bellows not in dreadful note.*

On a fine spring day we set sail for home. We had loaded with fine Attic ceramic ware, Macedonian pitch, colored marble of Asia Minor, Lesbian, Lemnian and Ionian wool and Phoenician glass. It was not without regret that I saw first the entrance to the Peiraios, then the Acropolis, and finally Sunion with its lovely temple to Poseidon vanish in the distance.

It was a season of calms, very worrisome to the merchant seaman not merely on the basis of time lost, but because of the perfect opportunity presented to sea rovers, who can swoop down in their light, many-oared fighting ships while their immobilized prey can neither fight nor flee. Luck was with us, however, and on my return I devoted a silver chain to Tyche on her rolling ball.

It was a good profit that I handed over to my owner — the proceeds of the sale of his cargo of grain at Athens, my trafficking at Crete and Alexandria, the charter price which the Athenian court had adjudged me at the expense of the survivor of those two rogues, and finally the gain on the homeward voyage.

There were both my salary and a bonus waiting for me at the hands of Saul ben Menassah. "By the horn of Gideon," he exclaimed, "you have done well!"

"You have said that several times in my hearing," I remarked. "Who was Gideon? And what about his horn?"

Saul smiled. "Gideon was a hero of my people." He sang:

Darkness encompassed him, black of night begirt him.
On the hill of Moreh was Gideon with his band.
The Lord hath delivered the foe into our hand!
"Arise, My servant Gideon! Gideon, go forth!"
Every man a pitcher pick, to hide his burning brand,
And every man his trumpet and his spear!
"Fear not, My servant Gideon! The Lord will be thy shield!"

The godless lay unguarded in their folly and their pride.
Thrice a hundred trumpet blasts burst into the night!
The shattered jugs of clay loosed every one its light!
"Arise, My servant Gideon! Gideon, go forth!"
Midian and Amalek woke to terror and to flight,
And friend turned his sword upon friend.
"Fear not, My servant Gideon! The Lord will be thy shield!"

Like other ship owners, Saul frequently sailed with his cargo; but he owned more ships than one, and had interests ashore besides. He sailed in the Dolphin that summer to Rome with grain, nuts, fruit, and hides — all our own Sicilian produce. We traded for some wine, dried boar meat and venison, and a little oil, but most of our payment was in silver. There was also some amber that had come from the north by way of Massalia. We picked up some dried fish and timber at Sardinia, ran down to Melita where we discharged some of the meat and timber, and picked up quite a bit of ivory from a ship of Carthage that had suffered in a stranding. We returned home in time to lay up for the stormy season.

Almost the last ship to arrive from the east that year brought me the letter I had been waiting for. The synod of the Achaean League, meeting at Aigion, had voted to offer me the command of the quadrireme Arete, then building at Patrai on the Gulf of Corinth.

Saul made me a nice offer to continue with him, but I declined. "Wish me good luck," I told him, "I'm off to the wars!"

The gales of winter safely past, I took passage on a ship bound for the Gulf of Corinth. On the eve of my sailing, my friend Archimedes procured for me the honor of an audience with King Hiero.

"We wish you every success," the ruler was kind enough to say. "The Achaean and Aetolian Leagues are making a brave resistance to the encroaching power of Queen Teuta and Demetrius of Macedon. Syracuse, like every other commercial city, has a great interest in the suppression of the pirates of Illyria. Those rulers, too, are the enemies of Rome, with whom we have a treaty of friendship. We will be not unmindful that in any operations you undertake in behalf of the leagues, you will be advancing the interests of Syracuse."

Archimedes, a member of his council, took the opportunity to speak. "Let me urge you again, on this relevant occasion, King Hiero, to consider once again in what peril, undefended, Syracuse may find herself in a warring world. I beg Your Majesty to look further to your defenses before it be too late."

Nicodemos made answer. "Against whom are we to arm? Carthage is overawed by Rome. Rome is our friend, and so is Ptolemy. Demetrius has more than enough trouble in Greece, and even if he should be able to put down all opposition there, Attalus is on his border giving him enough to worry about, and beyond Attalus, Seleucus in Syria plots mischief. Against whom are we to arm?"

Archimedes tossed his head impatiently. "I don't know against whom. What difference does it make? No land is ever permitted to remain long at peace, and it is too late to build a navy when a battering ram is thundering against the city gate!"

Nicodemos laughed. "Terror tales to frighten children! I am sure that the shipyard proprietors and the arms factories will be delighted to absorb the wealth that should go to the further prosperity of Your Majesty's city!"

The king sighed. "He is right, Archimedes. I will not seek trouble. It is my earnest desire to live in peace with all men and nations. So will Syracuse become richer and more glorious in the ways of peace."

Some weeks later, in the unimpressive little city of Patrai, I presented myself to Admiral Philetairos as prospective commanding officer of the quadrireme Arete. He made me heartily welcome. Before arranging for quarters, I wanted to see my ship.

Virtue was of the same size as a trireme — that is to say, 150 feet long, twenty in beam, but slightly deeper, and of about a foot more draft. She had the three tiers of oarsmen of a trireme — beamer, yokeman, and holdsman; but above and slightly aft of each of the first sat two topsiders pulling together an oar longer than those of the rowers below them, and pivoted on the same outrigger as the oars of the beamers. There were then a total of 236 oars, pulled by 298 rowers.

Above them was a deck with a catapult and a raised fighting castle fore and aft. In these were a commander's cabin and a few tiny staterooms for the ranking officers of my command.

The keel and the knees were, of course, oaken, and so was the ram under its brazen sheath. The ribs were cypress, the planking and the deck pine. The bottom, later to be leaded, was thick with pitch, the topsides handsomely painted in white and green. She was fastened with tree nails and bronze, except for the ram, where iron had been used, on the supposition that the life of the ram was in any case likely to be briefer than that of the ship. Two waling-pieces ran along the hull as strengtheners on either side, and above them it was girdled by a hemp cable.

Although his first command is the one which a sea captain assumes with the greatest feeling of pride, never have I been so moved as by the beauty of this ship. Except in the realm of art — and perhaps we need not except even that — the most beautiful creation of man is a well-designed ship, and among ships the man-o'-war is the loveliest. Even when she rides quietly at anchor, long, lean, and low, there is a sense of power inherent in the hull; when she runs under sail, the inexpressibly lovely curves give life to the rolling, plunging body, flinging crystals and rainbows from the rising bow and sending long waves to attend upon her like the outriders of a king gorgeous in shining armor; but when her rowers send her driving through the advancing seas, shattering each one as she meets it and sending its fragments high in a shower of spray, the long lines of oars flashing at each stroke in the sun, there is nothing on earth that can compare with her.

I wonder whether it is not her very deadliness that gives her beauty. Nimble as he is, can you compare a rabbit to the lean-flanked hound? Or an ox, mighty-thewed though he be, to the lion that drags him down? A gull glides with inexpressible grace, and the plumage of a dove shines with beguiling iridescence in the sun; but is it not the circling hawk that attracts the eye?

When a sailor puts out to sea, or a huntsman takes up his boar-spear, is it not the wine of danger whose scent fills their eager nostrils? Perhaps it was a not wholly reluctant Proserpine who mounted the chariot of divine Hades.

Implicit in the very menace of the slim, grim ships, I believe, is the secret of much of their beauty.

Menander of Rhypai was my executive officer, a wiry, alert man of about my own age, and, as subsequently appeared, a competent seaman, though, like myself, without much experience in actual warfare. The first lieutenant and bow officer was Ephippus, a lean, saturnine man of middle age, formerly of Megalopolis, but reckoned as an Achaean by sympolity. The rowmaster was a short, muscular, merry youngster of Sicyon. The junior lieutenant had not yet reported in.

Of the petty officers, the boatswain, still vigorous although his head was quite white, was a hard-driving old salt of local residence; Timaios, the ship's carpenter, who much resembled him, was his brother; the oiler, charged with the preservation of iron, leather, and other materials likely to deteriorate under marine conditions, the surgeon's mate, and the oar keeper made up the list.

The rowers, ten seamen, and twenty-eight marines (including three archers and five artillerymen who manned the catapult) made up the number of the crew.

Most of these, of course, had not yet been assembled, nor could I have used them at this time. But when, early in the summer, Arete was launched, the complement was complete.

For all of my impatience, there was no action that year. We spent the summer and the early autumn in badly needed training. The first concern of a galley captain is, of course, the quality and condition of his ship, the second the calibre of the rowers. On both these counts I had fared well.

There was, of course, some grumbling at the kind of discipline I enforced. A new ship is always a "hot" ship. But I persisted, and the officers, despite the disagreements which I sensed, gave me loyal backing. All of this, I knew, was routine for a naval vessel in our condition, and by early summer we had become a crew.

We then proceeded along the shore of the gulf to Aigion. There behind the breakwater we encountered the nine other ships of the League, with the Admiral. He proceeded to train us in squadron evolutions. By autumn we had become a fleet.

We wintered there. There is a greater expansiveness to life in the west. In mainland Hellas even the temples are smaller, although richer in marble. After Syracuse this was like prison. Fortune keep me from ending up in such a hole! I had to endure it and I did. The food was fair, the water exceptionally good and abundant. I lived just over the harbor in a tiny rented cottage. An import from Corinth named Phila helped to make it bearable.

Even more important, I found there my old acquaintance, Margos of Caryneia, who had recruited me to go to the aid of Toryne a few years earlier. We spent much time together, and became close friends. That is, up to a point. I have never gone in for the sort of intimacies with men that I enjoyed with Phila, nor did Margos attempt anything of the sort.

He had devoted his life to the service of the Achaean League. "The Leagues," he told me, "are the great hope of Hellas. The city states, even the most powerful, cannot stand against the tyrants. As things were going, it would only have been a question of time before the monstrous tyranny of the Great King would exist here, as formerly in Persia."

"The cities combined and beat him," I countered.

"And look what happened thereafter!"

"Would it be any better if one League set out to conquer?"

"Why speak of conquest? There has been a free alliance between the Achaean and Aetolian Leagues. It is only a question of time, again, until the sympolity that exists within each becomes reciprocal as between the two. All citizens have an equal voice."

"All citizens over thirty."

"True — on this side of the Gulf of Corinth. But in the Aetolian League all men of military age form the general assembly."

"Does not the host city, then, consistently outvote the others? The citizens of Sicyon, for instance, cannot come *en masse* to Aigion to protect their interests."

"No need — the voting is by cities, and each must have a quorum. Some day, I hope, there will be a League embracing the whole of mainland Greece — perhaps even the whole of Hellas!"

We talked much of sports, as well — Margos had been a good man with the discus in his youth, and had once brought home to his city the laurel wreath from the Isthmian games.

He introduced me one day to Aratus of Sicyon, guiding spirit of the Achaean League, whose life work, to evict Macedon from the Peloponnesus, had met with the full success which is denied to most men.

So, one way and another, the winter went by.

It was spring once more. We refurbished the gear, stepped up our training activities, and set about filling the vacancies in our crews that several months had created.

A celetes, larger than most, came out of the west, her ten oars whitening the sea with the urgency of her mission. She made the shore, and three men, carrying the fillets of ambassadors, proceeded to the temple of Zeus Amarios, the Capitol of the League. The Synod was not in session but this was in any case a matter for the Assembly, which was convoked forthwith.

Queen Teuta was really on the march. Apollonia, up the Epirote coast, was under siege. There had been a landing of her Illyrian pirates on the island of Corcyra and the town was under attack. Others of them had rowed into the harbor at Epidamnos, ostensibly for water and supplies; some had landed lightly clad and apparently unarmed; once within the gates, they had drawn out swords from within their water jars, killed the guards at the city gate and received their fellows, who had followed and mastered the walls.

The city seemed lost. But they are brave men, those of Epidamnos; and after a long, desperate fight through the city streets they drove out the invaders. These thereupon put to sea again and joined their fellows at Corcyra. The odds against the city were hopeless.

In their extremity, the citizens of Corcyra and of the other two towns, which could not hope to withstand the combined forces once Corcyra had been overwhelmed, had sent this embassy to the two Leagues, with a desperate appeal for aid. If Corcyra and the coastal cities fell, and if the Illyrians pressed on the Leagues from the west, the Macedonian too would certainly come down upon us.

Two days later our entire force of ten decked vessels put out for the relief of Corcyra. We were ten sail of quinqueremes and quadriremes. We cleared the Gulf of Corinth and stood north for the island. Given a favorable wind, it would have been an easy day's sail from where we were; but the winds were northerly, and the Admiral had no intention of joining battle with wearied rowers. The Epirote shores, under the domination of the Queen, must be reckoned as hostile, and there was always the chance of a surprise by the enemy fleet (we had seen their scouts watching us at a distance); so we moored nights where a promontory would shelter us from the prevailing norther, and slept aboard.

We met the enemy fleet on the third day, with the hills of the Paxos Islands some twenty stades to the west. Further off, to the northwest, was the rugged form of Corcyra. A gentle northerly wind permitted a smooth, even beat of the oars.

The Illyrians came in their lembi — long, low, heavily manned open craft; with them was the fleet of their ally, Acarnania — seven decked ships like ours on their left wing. As they came closer, it appeared that the lembi were lashed together in fours, which made these usually swift and handy vessels slow and unmaneuverable — perfect victims for the catapult or the ram.

Our right wing closed with the Acarnanian galleys, our left

drove in for the all but immobilized lembi. Arete was in the center, so we had a choice of antagonists. My second-in-command was jumping with eagerness at the chance to do fearful execution among the light Illyrian craft, and many of the crew looked at me eagerly for the order.

Perhaps it was my place of origin that made me smell a trap. We of the west, unlike those great sea-fighters the Athenians and the Rhodians, have never favored the ram; we use it of course on occasion, but prefer to grapple and carry a ship by boarding. It is true that when circumstances are favorable, one can dispose of an enemy in a minute by smashing in his side; but for this one needs perfect coordination and instant obedience to command among the rowers. And even the best disciplined rowing team can be thrown into momentary and fatal confusion if a very few oarsmen are disabled and let their oars foul those of their neighbors. Granted that our modern cataphract ships offer protection against javalins and arrows, but the ships of today carry catapults and their bolts go right through the flimsy guards.

I made for the Acarnanians.

For some minutes we were in a confusion of darting and circling ships, trying to hole one another and evade the enemy bows while arrows, spears and catapult bolts whistled through the air. Men fell. Sometimes the twenty-foot boarding lance would find a victim. Once my quartermaster managed to shear off most of the oars from one side of an enemy, but before we could turn and deliver the death blow one of his fellows counterattacked, and we had to lose the chance. The rest of our right wing was similarly active. We were about to close and board, when we became aware of what was happening on the left.

The lembi, lashed in fours, had been unable to avoid our comrades' rams. Nor did they try. But as each bow of a League ship smashed in, the pirates gave it no chance to disengage, but swarmed aboard in irresistible numbers. Four of our quadriremes were taken in this fashion.

The rest of us broke off the action lest we be surrounded and overwhelmed. We set our boat sails, and fled to the south.

Not all of us. A quinquereme, as she lay entangled with a lembus she had rammed, had been struck in turn by an Acarnanian galley and sunk with all hands.

In her perished Margos of Caryneia, selfless patriot, idealist, dreamer of unity and freedom for all Greece, and a tireless worker for the Achaean League

Of course there was a board of inquiry at Aigai. Some of the members of the assembly, in their shock, were looking for a scapegoat on whom to load the onus of the defeat. Perhaps it was better for him that Philetairos, our admiral, had not survived the disaster. I came in for some sharp examination. Luckily, there was ample testimony that I had not hung back, but had fully committed my ship to the action; and as to my tactics, both my own officers and those of the surviving vessels agreed that had I closed with the lembi (other than the single isolated one which I had engaged), it would have made no difference in the result except the loss of one more ship and her company to the League.

But at the trial conducted in my own conscience, I failed to win so complete an acquittal. My old comrade in arms, Margos, was dead, and here was I alive and well. I could tell myself a hundred times, and truly, that to have fought my ship otherwise would have ended in her loss. But was the field to be surrendered to the Illyrians because something looked suspicious? What if every commander avoided an action of which he did not like the looks? The loss of all of those ships was a reproach to me, a captain in the fleet. This was ridiculous — all I could do was direct my own crew as best I knew how. Yet I could not wholly master the feeling. The burden of defeat is a heavy one. And Margos was dead.

For a time I thought of tendering my resignation. Only the fact that this would be a last disloyalty to Margos kept me from it.

Would I never get over this feeling of guilt when another suffered misfortune, not of my doing, and I escaped or profited?

VIII

Extract from the Correspondence
of Marcus Claudius Marcellus

*Marcus Claudius to Otacilius. At Rome, on the first day of the Nones of
November, in the Year after the founding of the City the 522nd.*

Now Queen Teuta has gone too far.

Our ambassadors, Caius and Lucius Coruncanius, had an
audience with her (King Agron, you remember, died last year).
They made their representations. Her manner is said to have
been quite haughty. She replied to the effect that under Illyrian
law she could not and would not restrain her subjects in their
private expeditions for plunder. Lucius replied that "the
Romans would find means to compel her to reform the Illyrian
laws."

Monarchs don't like to hear words like "compel". She had him
assassinated.

This means war, and high time.

The Illyrians, taken as men, are doughty fighters; but their
organization — or lack of it — will not let them stand up to the
legions in open field. Their lembi are long, narrow, shallow-
draft, very light craft, with sharp bows but no ram, driven by a
single bank of oars. Each ship carries some eighty to a hundred
men. She can give a formidable account of herself even against
war galleys of conventional type.

Marcus Claudius to Marcus Claudius maior. At Nutria, in Illyria, on the 14th day before the Kalends of October, in the Year after the founding of the City the 523rd.

I am writing this, Father, to catch what may be the last sailing of the year, barring special dispatches. The arrow wound in my leg, about which I believe Lentulus wrote you, was festering but is now doing well.

As prefect under the consul Gnaeus Fulvius, I sailed with my twenty ships for Corcyra, where we were hoping to raise the siege. At Crotona we learned that the city had surrendered on terms, and that the Illyrians had garrisoned the city and left to besiege Epidamnos. There were however intimations that Demetrius of Phaleron, the Queen's commander at Corcyra, was not too happy with his ruler, and might be willing to make a deal. We proceeded to Corcyra accordingly.

Our advices proved correct. Demetrius came over to us, to the great relief of the townsmen. We then joined the army of consul Postumius at Apollonia, which was likewise glad to put itself under Roman protection, and sailed together to Epidamnos. News of our coming prededed us; the besiegers fled, and we received the willing submission of that city, as of several other cities, including Issa, and the tribes of the hinterland.

At Nutria it was another story. There was sharp fighting with the Illyrians, and there fell Sextus Minucius the quaestor, and several tribunes.

It was there too that after a severe struggle in the siege-works, in the course of which I put some of the enemy troops, one of them an officer, out of action, the arrow forced an interruption of my military career. We are fortunate; it was one of the days of ill omen, but we had to fight nevertheless. The gods were kind.

At about the time this reaches you, Fulvius should be arriving home. I shall go to Epidamnos, now that I am convalescent, and winter there with the army of Postumius.

Queen Teuta will have to sue for peace. Our terms should be stiff.

We have installed Demetrios as our eastern administrator.

Elsewhere, too, fortune this year has favored Rome. Demetrios of Macedonia is dead, and his son and heir, Philip, is a boy of nine. Antigonos, the late king's kinsman, has taken the throne; he had been named by Demetrios after promising to ensure the succession of Philip. The sceptical Greeks have nicknamed him Doson, the promiser. He is marrying the queen, Philip's stepmother, and adopting the young prince; perhaps he means to keep his promise. In any case, there will be a period of readjustment and enfeeblement, which can only work to our advantage. Macedon is still no friend to Rome.

I hope that your rheumatism gets no worse this winter. I have been favorably impressed by the Greek physicians and surgeons — they have done excellent work among our sick and wounded. If you become ill again, I urge you to consult one of the Greek physicians in Rome.

Please greet my son for me.

If you are well, then so am I.

Aratus, General of the Achaean League, to Marcellus, Ambassador of the Senate and the Roman people. At Aigion, on the 26th of Elaphebolion, in the second year of the 138th Olympiad.

It is now known that the ship by which I sent you the former dispatches foundered or otherwise came to grief. I therefore repeat my former news, and add what has happened since.

No doubt you have heard from other sources of the unhappy action at Ladoceia, late last year. My forces were considerably outnumbered by those of Cleomenes of Sparta. Nevertheless, the initial success was ours; we held a strong position, and I had every reason to anticipate a victorious outcome.

Unfortunately, Lydiades of Megalopolis, who commanded my cavalry, made a charge strictly against orders. His horses were thrown back, he himself being killed; his fleeing troops broke into and disordered my formation, and the rout became general. I unjustly bore the brunt of the blame.

Cleomenes thereupon made with all speed for Sparta with the foreign contingent of his army, where he abolished the ephorate, killing some of the incumbents, and making himself dictator. He has voided all debts, increased the number of Spartiates to four thousand by the enrollment of neighboring Laconians and resident aliens, confiscated the land for general distribution, and restored the old common meals and state control of education.

It will, I am certain, be apparent to the Senate that Cleomenes is a dangerous radical whose suppression is necessary for the health of all countries. That he is, and keeps his army, strong, frugal, hardy, and free of those forces of dissipation that corrupt most armies, makes him all the more dangerous.

To the rabble he is the great liberator. In Arcadia, in Argolis, even in Boeotia they acclaim him. Because of him, Cercidas of Megalopolis is preaching even more abhorrent doctrines.

I shall fight him to the end.

IX

Extract from Heraclides' Life of Archimedes

Hiero was one of the few rulers who even while they occupied the throne loved to take part in the life of the intellect. He followed with eager fascination the discoveries of his friend and kinsman Archimedes, taking, to the happiness of his people, more pleasure in the other's conquests in the realms of thought than he might in the conquest of cities and lands by his armies. Wealth and wisdom multiplied in the land; and had the gods granted him immortality, or granted the city successors of his own ability and virtue, the glories of Minoan Knossos and of Periclean Athens would have paled beside the brilliance of the age of Hiero in our beloved Syracuse.

Archimedes was, for a time, very much engrossed in the law of the lever, as exemplified in the steelyard balance. "It may easily be demonstrated, Hiero," he observed to the dictator, "that weights balance at inverse distances from the fulcrum of the beam."

"All weights, regardless of magnitude?"

"All. That is why a workman on a lever can raise a weight which would otherwise be far beyond his strength. Of course, there is a penalty. If he moves a weight five times the force he applies, he moves it through only one fifth the distance. This law applies in many ways. One can, for instance, use pulleys of two or more sheaves each, one pulley fixed, the other attached to the object to be moved. The effort applied to the rope will be multiplied by the number of sections of line paying to and from the object to be moved. By the same token, one must pull the rope through that many times the distance which the object is to be moved."

"What is the limit of the application of this law?"

"Hiero, there is no limit. That is to say, there is no limit to the validity of my law; there will be limits to the efficiency of a pulley as constructed, or to the strength and weight of an available lever."

136

"Then your law is not really a true one."

"It is true." And then Archimedes added the grandest words ever spoken by man. "Give me whereon I may stand, and I will move the world."

Hiero laughed, and dismissed the matter from his mind.

A few days later, the king was at the royal shipyards to witness the launching of a ship of greater size than usual, and of somewhat different design. He climbed over the ship, inspected her inside and out, congratulated the builder and the naval architect, and seated himself for the launching. The ways were greased, the stopping block knocked out of place, the flutists began a lively air — and nothing happened. Gangs of workmen pushed and hauled, but in vain. The ship refused to budge.

There was present a certain rascally fellow by the name of Archias, who had once been a prosperous goldsmith but had been ruined by greed in an attempt to cheat the ruler some years before, and had never been able to recoup his fortunes. Archimedes had been instrumental in exposing the rogue's dishonesty, and the fellow, like most evildoers, had refused to accept the responsibility for his own misdeeds, but had laid his misfortunes at the door of Archimedes. He had conceived accordingly the most virulent hatred for the master; and not so much hoping, as I suppose, for any result but just as an expression of his pent-up feeling, sent up a shout (from well back in the crowd, naturally) of "Send for Archimedes!"

This, of course, reminded the dictator of his recent conversation with his kinsman, and send for Archimedes he did.

The latter arrived and the difficulty was explained to him. "Well, cousin," remarked the ruler, "this is not the world, but a very small piece of it. I will give you a place to stand. Can you move it?"

The scientist surveyed the situation without hurry. Finally he made answer. "Give me ten days to prepare."

The forges worked long hours in the workshop of Archimedes; and at the rope walk cables were laid with care. Then his carpenters descended upon the shipyard. When on the appointed day Hiero returned to the yard, he saw a cradle about the ship's stern built so that several huge levers could bear upon it. The stone bollards served as fulcra, and to the long ends of the levers triple pulleys were attached whose lines led to other triple pulleys made fast to bollards nearer the bow.

"Well, cousin," was Hiero's greeting, "are you prepared to keep your word?"

"I am."

"I have brought all of the palace slaves to assist you, and there are the yard workmen as well; and I can call upon an army unit if you desire. So you see I leave you no excuse for failure."

"Ready and eager."

Archimedes' workmen led their lines to windlasses and began to turn. Around went the spokes and the lines grew taut and tauter; the levers bent; the workmen strained at the now motionless windlasses, and strained again, and again; there came a great groan from under the ship, she stirred, and slid majestically down the ways.

There was a great outburst of cheering. The yardmaster was pounding Archimedes on the back, and Hiero went to him and wrung his hand. "That was a marvelous demonstration, cousin! Marvelous! I think that there is nothing that is beyond you!" And Archimedes repeated the proudest words ever spoken by man, "There is nothing that is beyond science. Give me whereon I may stand, and I will move the world!"

"I am very glad, cousin," said Hiero, "that there is no such place!"

"Some day," replied Archimedes, "there may be."

Hiero was jesting, but Archimedes was not.

This is what really happened, and to any person of sense, what Archimedes accomplished is marvelous enough. But, of course, fools have had to embellish the tale. I have heard, for instance, that he did not launch the vessel, but drew her ashore, that she was of a size far greater than had ever been built hitherto, that she had aboard an enormous cargo, as well as her full crew and complete inventory of equipment, and that he handled the apparatus alone and unaided. Such tales are ridiculous. The royal dockyard, of course, did not build ships far beyond existing sizes and of a new type — such ships evolve slowly if at all, and no one who knows the first thing about ship construction, and not even some of us who don't, would dream of subjecting one to the unnatural and unintended strain of a large cargo while on the beach.

Archimedes, however, was the sort of man who inevitably turns into a figure of legend and about whom all sorts of extravagant tales accrete, and the consideration of what has happened to his reputation already in this short span of years has given me a new perspective on history such that I no longer reject out of hand even the wildest tales told about our ancestors, but look for the core of truth, however distorted, in each one.

One would naturally think that Archimedes would take a legitimate pride in so notable an achievement as the launching of the ship, and would have written out for the use if not the admiration of the public the principles and details of his device. Not so.

It was only his attainments in pure science that gave the master pleasure, and that he delighted in sharing with the world of savants. When it came to applied science, he did not value it; he would turn his hand to it now and again, superbly, but only as an obliging fellow-man, and to all practical intents forgot the matter on each occasion as soon as he had performed that which he had undertaken. Even his later devices in military engineering, the wonder of the profession of arms, seemed to afford him no gratification except that of doing his citizen's duty; and once he had finished their construction, he apparently put them completely out of his mind.

When I got to know him well enough, I once commented on what to most of the world seemed a singular peculiarity.

"I suppose it is the result of the influence of my father, Phidias," he said thoughtfully. "He was a man of little fortune, and at times my mother was hard pressed to run the household decently. Nevertheless, he could not interest himself in what are usually considered practical matters; he was wrapped up, heart and soul, in his astronomy. Probably nothing else in his life gave him as much satisfaction as his estimation of the diameters of the sun and the moon.

"It was from him that I learned mathematics; and for this gift I revere his memory more than for the simple fact that he sired me, or even for my raising. (Indeed, my mother deserves far more gratitude for that.) When he felt that he had little more to offer me in his field, he sent me for further study to the Museum at Alexandria.

"He could not have done this but for the assistance of my cousin King Hiero. It was Hiero's further generosity, by the way, that put me in this comfortable financial position. Hiero and I were very close companions in boyhood, and the love between us, as you know, has never grown less."

"I know. Some day I too hope to study in Alexandria."

"You should. It is a marvelous milieu for a student. When I first took lodgings in the Museum, I could hardly sleep for the thrill of occupying the quarters where Euclid had lived and worked. It was there that I made the great friendships that have so expanded my life — Eratosthenes and particularly Conon. I still send Conon everything I write for his reaction."

"I have been told that the cochlias is the product of your Egyptian days."

"That's right. You know, of course, that the Egyptians farm by the use of Nile water, which has to be laboriously raised to the level of the fields. I felt sorry for the poor peasants, and devised the cochlias to help them at their task.

"But," he returned to my original question, "Euclid especially was known for his indifference to what are called practical concerns. The story is told that a student, compelled, I suppose, by his father to attend the great man's sessions, asked how he would profit by studying geometry. The geometer turned to his personal slave and said contemptuously, 'Give him an obol — he has to make a profit.'

"The scholarship of a man, Heraclides, like the beauty of a woman, is debased if it is offered in the marketplace to the highest bidder."

Illustrative of the kindliness of Archimedes was the time, at a meeting of his club, when he remarked that he had just received a request from Krateros, a wealthy citizen of some sixty years. Krateros was proposing to build a circular bath of thirty feet in diameter, to be filled to a depth of four and a half feet from a water heater which was rectangular and measured four feet by three by two. He wanted to know how many times it would have to heat its capacity of water in order to fill the bath.

There were suppressed chuckles; it was the talk of the town that Vanessa, a saucy wench from Miletos, was making a fool of the old man.

"It is a foolish question, of course," Archimedes remarked. "The first of the water would cool long before the last was ready. Krateros must either install a much larger heater, or build a system of heating the water right in the bath."

"How would you calculate the volume of the bath?" asked Segovesus, the Gallic freedman.

If the questioner had been a Syracusan of good family, the master would have been justifiably sarcastic at his ignorance.

But Segovesus, by reason of his origin a man of no education, had been slave to a potter. His master was a humane man, and Segovesus had the sort of constitution that required a minimum of rest; he was permitted to hire himself out for a few hours a day, and save toward the purchase of his freedom. He achieved it by being the butt of what was intended as a vicious jest, but redounded to the good fortune of the intended victim.

A ship loaded with amphorae of wine of Samos had been wrecked close off-shore. Its owner had attempted salvage operations, but the depth was a little too great. One of Segovesus' fellow slaves, without the capacity of working toward his freedom, and therefore jealous of Segovesus, had overheard a conversation of his betters, and decided to thwart his fellow's hopes of liberty.

"Segovesus," he said. "I hear that Medon is ready to abandon hope of salvaging his cargo."

"So I hear too."

"He is a fool. He will probably sell his rights for less than the price of an able slave. If he only knew, Aristotle has described a huge kettle which can be lowered, full of air, into the water, and under which a man can live and work."

"Is that true?"

"Indeed. Alexander of Macedon, using such a device, descended to the bottom of the sea."

"How do you know such things?"

"I carried some of the master's pots to the house of a wise man, and overheard him and his guests tell of it."

To make a long story short, Segovesus inquired, and made the attempt. As he told me, he had not a great deal to lose. True, he had almost enough to purchase his freedom, and stood to forfeit it; but even a free man, landless, penniless, and a foreigner, is in no enviable case; and the possibility of acquiring at a stroke both freedom and a modest capital was not to be passed by.

As every man of education knows, the story that Segovesus' fellow bondman dismissed as a ridiculous fable is in fact correct; and while he struggled with suppressed laughter, the other used his pitiful hoard to buy some free time from his master, make a huge sheet-copper bowl, invert it, weight its edge, and sink it over the wreck.

Technically, he was not too successful. But he did manage to recover a little of the sunken cargo; this gained him a very little money, but increasing local fame which reached the ears of the king and won him a royal reward, and thereby his freedom and something to invest in the pottery. He was thenceforth a partner. It also won him the interest and friendship of Archimedes.

"To calculate the volume of the bath," the master answered him, "one multiplies the area by the altitude. The latter we are given. There are several methods of calculating the area. Perhaps the simplest, in theory at least, is to inscribe a regular polygon — triangle, square, or hexagon — in a circle, its angles just touching the circle. Let us use the square. Its area is readily calculable, is it not?"

"It is."

Try as I might, I could not refrain from imagining the red-haired, milky-skinned Vanessa swimming in her bath.

"Now from the middle of the top of the square, let us draw a perpendicular line to the circle. We can thus construct two equal triangles, which are likewise in the circle. It is easy, also, to calculate the area of a triangle, is it not?"

"Certainly."

I was trying not to visualize a triangle that was less of a purely mathematical abstraction. Well, perhaps I was not trying too hard. I was a young man then.

"Then we double this area, because there are two triangles, and quadruple the product, because our square has four sides. We now have an octagon inscribed within our circle. The length of each side is readily ascertainable, either by direct measurement or by calculation (a triangle of which one side and all three angles are known)."

I imagined myself forming triangles by swimming from the center to intersect the course of the voluptuous Vanessa.

"The area is thus available. This process is repeated as many times as seems worthwhile, the perimeter approaching closer and closer to that of the circle itself, the area likewise. Then we summate these areas."

I was seeing two, then four, then eight, then a writhing press of seductive white figures in the pool.

"Or," he went on, oblivious to the crowded condition of the bath, "it can be proven that the area of a circle is equal to that of a right-angled triangle of which one of the legs equals the radius, the other the circumference, of the circle. (The circumference equals 22/7 of the diameter; this can be demonstrated by the method of exhaustion, analogously to what we have just done.)

"Let K be the area of a circle, T the area of the triangle just described, and I and C the areas of polygons of n sides inscribed within and circumscribed about the circle, respectively.

"If K is greater than T, according to the postulate of Eudoxus, n can so be determined that $K - I$ is less than $K - T$, whence I is greater than T. But I equals the area of a right triangle whose legs equal the apothem and the perimeter, respectively (those legs again!), of the regular inscribed polygon; these are less, respectively, than the radius and the circumference of the circle, that is to say, less than the corresponding sides of triangle T. From this it follows that I is less than T, which is contrary to the proposition.

"If, on the other hand, K is less than T, one can, as I shall show in my work on Sphere and Cylinder, determine a number n such that $C - K$ is less than $T - K$. Whence C is less than T."

I had by now laboriously dragged myself out of the pool, exhausted by my efforts.

"In this case, C equals the area of a right triangle whose legs equal respectively the radius of the circle and the perimeter of the regular circumscribed polygon of n sides, that is to say, respectively equal to and greater than the corresponding sides of triangle T. From this it follows that C is greater than T, which is contrary to the proposition.

"The only remaining possibility is that K equals T."

He was wrong — for once the master was wrong. There was another possibility. But it would have needed Vanessa's cooperation to realize it.

Euphranor showed up at our group meeting one day accompanied by a young woman. She was very attractive; although her looks fell short of what one would call beauty, she was at the same time dignified, modest in manner, but not a bit what one would call bashful. She was well dressed; over her pale pink chiton a deep blue himation, worked with gold designs, was draped about her waist; she wore a moderate amount of jewelry and a fine coiffure — all in the best of taste. The make-up on her face was adequate, but not excessive. It was not hard to guess from her adornments that she was a hetaira.

A follower of Zeno cannot but feel somewhat uncomfortable in the presence of a member of her profession. The principle of homonoia applies to people as to states, and no one can be shut out of our fellow feeling, and while we do not hold the calling as a disgraceful one, it is forbidden to the daughters of citizens, especially of us Gamoroi. And if we landed gentry ban it for our daughters, that is proof enough that we regard it at the least as a misfortune. It is self-evident that a girl must live, and if she has no provider there are few roads open to her, and of those few some are considerably more opprobrious than this; it is also the stoic doctrine that any man, even a slave, can be free in his soul; nevertheless, the lot of the hetaira, like that of the slave, is one that we do not gladly dwell upon because of the equivocation in our own minds.

Archimedes, of course, received her with the same exquisite courtesy which he tendered to all. She accompanied Euphranor on many occasions, academic and social. She had a knack for figures, so was less out of place at our discussions than might have been expected.

This was the time when the master went off in a totally new direction of investigation, the equilibrium of planes, which introduced an interrelation between what had been pure mathematics and mechanics. Much of this had been inherent in his famous tour de force in the shipyard, but this formal foundation of mechanics on the basis of postulates gave it a new and more vigorous life.

One day the topic under discussion was the master's proposition 13, "In any triangle the center of gravity lies on the straight line joining any vertex to the middle point of the base." Archimedes had turned over to Hesychios the demonstration of the proof which begins by joining a supposed center of gravity to the three angles of the triangle.

Hesychios, although a brilliant student and a fine mathematician, left as a lecturer not much, but everything, to be desired. He droned on in so monotonous a mumble that on this warm day, with the songs of birds, men and bees in the air, it seemed impossible to keep our attention fixed on the presentation; and one after one we turned to our day dreams.

When he had finished, he wanted to see how well he had made his points, and started to quiz us.

"Katreus," he asked, "on what basis rests the identification of points K and L as the centers of gravity of triangles EBL and ZGD, respectively?"

"I don't know," Katreus had to respond.

"Agamedes?"

"I don't know."
"Heraclides?"
I shook my head.
"Thyoneios?"
"Sorry."
"Doesn't anyone know?"

There was an embarrassing silence. Then, in a womanly treble, "By reason of proposition 11. If two triangles be similar to each other and within these triangles two points be similarly situated with respect to the triangles, and one point be the center of gravity of the triangle in which it is situated, the other point will also be the center of gravity of the triangle in which it is situated."

I tell you, that produced a sensation. We all stared in amazement. Hesychios smiled in relieved gratification — he had been talking sense, after all, as even a woman could see if she put her mind to it. Archimedes himself was delighted, and complimented her fulsomely, and ever after to his usual courtesy to her was added real respect.

Later on, Claudia confessed. She too had been nodding almost throughout the whole period, but she had recovered consciousness briefly to hear Hesychios make that very point, and thereafter she had relapsed into the same coma as the rest of us. If he had asked about anything else, she would have been as ignorant as we; but that one fact, she knew.

It was still, of course, a remarkable achievement. This girl — for she was hardly more — without our educational advantages (despite what we later learned about her scanty opportunities and how well she had used them) measured up to our standard. It gives one to think. Perhaps the Spartans are right in educating boys and girls together without regard to sex.

Although the Master corresponded and debated with the greatest minds in the civilized world, he was never unwilling to meet even a beginner on his own terms. I well recall an occasion when, in response to an invitation, Pyrrhon, a young shipmaster, paid a call. Few were present, so Archimedes was the more willing to present his subject in the most elementary manner.

After some general preliminary conversation, in the course of which I took occasion to congratulate our guest on a very exceptional feat of shiphandling which had caused the waterfront and beyond to laud his ingenuity, the talk turned to mathematics (as indeed it always did, and generally sooner rather than later), and our host unbent far enough to expound some of the most elementary concepts — too elementary, really, because I could see that the young man was prepared for meatier fare. I recount the conversation nevertheless as an example of Archimedes' willingness to put himself out for anyone whom he regards as worthy.

(I am, of course, aware that there are people who regard mathematics as a bore or worse. I run the risk, I realize, of losing their interest when I introduce this sort of matter into my account. Yet how, I ask you, could I write about the life of a general and not go into the art of war? How could I write of the life of a statesman and not mention his laws? How, then, could I write of a mathematician and ignore completely his mathematics? The cognoscenti, therefore, will appreciate what minimum of calculation I present in this work, and the rest, I hope, will simply skip it and pass on to what they regard as more interesting matter.)

"We must begin," said the Master, "with some fundamental concepts in the theory of proportions. Let us thus establish the ratio A:B::B:C. Then we call A:C the duplicate ratio of A:B. It follows furthermore that A:C:: the square of A: the square of B, or A:C :: the area of the square whose side is A: the area of the square whose side is B. The triplicate ratio can similarly be stated for their cubes. We can consider some of the lemmas that are derivable. For instance, if of two series of the same number of magnitudes those similarly placed are proportional to one another, and of the magnitudes of the first series all or some bear to other magnitudes any ratios and the corresponding magnitudes of the second series bear the same ratios to other magnitudes, all the magnitudes of the first series will be to all those of the third as all the magnitudes of the second series to all those of the fourth."

Pyrrhon was frowning.

"Difficulty? Well, let's be a little less abstract. Suppose that an architect was designing a temple in whose sanctuary was not a statue, but a wall with paintings of episodes in the story of a god. Not every part of the representation was to be given the same emphasis; a differential illumination was required. The wall opposite the mural accordingly has windows of different sizes in a row, as I shall illustrate here, and outside the wall and its windows is a portico whose columns are of these proportional heights and intervals, in feet.

"Now examine my drawing. Do the figures meet the ratio postulated?"

Pyrrhon made some rapid mental calculations. Yes, 6 was to 4 as 3 was to 2. 6 was to 18 as 3 was to 9. "They do," he admitted.

The Master verified his thesis in a rapid calculation.

"Were not some of these ratios implicit in the harmonic numbers of Pythagoras?" Pyrrhon asked.

"To an extent," the master replied. "Unfortunately, however, the mathematics of Pythagoras, despite his genius, are largely vitiated by the mystique of his numerology. It beclouds the whole science of numbers to maintain that 1 is the symbol — nay, more, the essence — of reason, that 2 signifies opinion, and 4, justice; that there is maleness in odd numbers and femaleness in even, etc. This it was that made some stumble over the concept of irrational numbers, such as the (to them) infamous attempted calculations of the legs of a right triangle from the length of its hypotenuse.

"Here is another lemma," Archimedes went on in his enthusiasm. "Given a series of magnitudes, each of which is equal to four times the next in order, all the magnitudes and one-third of the least added together will exceed the greatest by one-third," and he proceeded with the proof. This, as is well known, is in his "Quadrature of the Parabola." (Euclid gives a different method of proof, that of Eudoxus.)

They proceeded in this fashion for a time, and Archimedes, I could see, was well pleased with his guest.

Meanwhile, a few more of the Master's disciples had come.

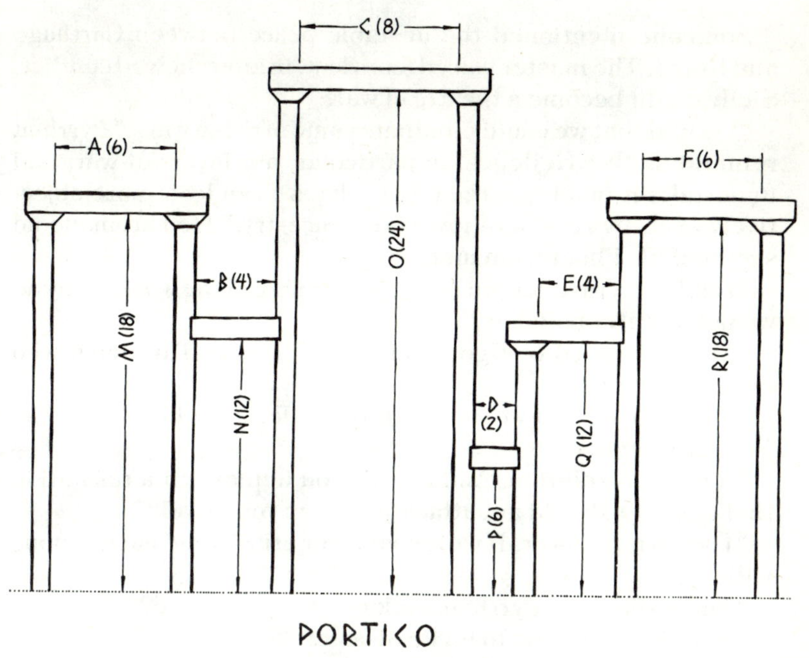

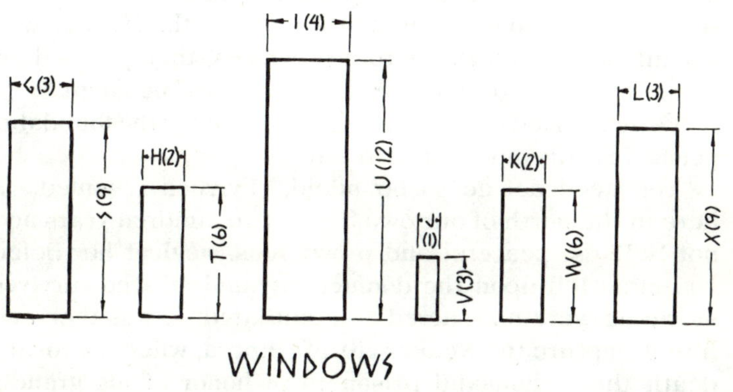

A (6)
C (8)
F (6)
M (18)
B (4)
O (24)
E (4)
N (12)
D (2)
R (18)
P (6)
Q (12)
PORTICO

I (4)
G (3)
L (3)
S (9)
H (2)
U (12)
K (2)
T (6)
J (3)
V (3)
W (6)
X (9)
WINDOWS

149

Someone mentioned the unstable peace between Carthage and Rome. The master voiced fears lest, in any renewed conflict, Sicily might become a theatre of war.

"I would that we could eliminate some of these wars," Pyrrhon remarked. "We Hellenes, in particular, are lovers of war, and undertake it much too readily. Perhaps I can look more objectively at it, by reason of my mixed ancestry." He had made no secret of his Phoenician mother.

"Yes," the Traveller put in. "It is the curse of the world. Why do we not simply abolish it?"

"And how does one go about that?" It was Thyoneios who challenged them.

"By resolving that we will settle our differences in debate," the Traveller replied.

"A noble resolution. And how do you implement a resolution that a bandit should not attack you when you travel?"

"That is no answer. If we disband our armies and navies, none will fear us."

"And do you too, Pyrrhon, endorse this procedure?"

"No. That would be to invite disaster."

"Have you ever tried?" the Traveller wanted to know.

"When I was in Egypt," Archimedes contributed, "I heard a tale that Pharaoh Amenhotep the Fourth did something of the sort. But instead of imitating the gesture, the Hittites wrought fearful carnage on the border provinces, then pressed on and came very close to conquering and annihilating Egypt."

"Pericles tried to assemble the cities to lay the foundation for peace," Scyllis put in, "but in vain."

"You need not go so far afield," Pyrrhon resumed. "Right here in the north of our own Sicily, two hundred years ago, did not Selinus, peaceful and prosperous, neglect her defenses? Hannibal fell upon the doomed city and all who survived the storming were massacred and mutilated. It was then easy for him to capture the weaker city of Himera, where he tortured to death three thousand prisoners in honor of his grandfather Hamilcar. I should like to see fewer wars, but not at such a price."

"Either you are for the killing of your fellow-men, or you are against it," the Traveller protested. "You cannot have it both ways."

"I am against it. But — and here, I think, is the crux of the matter — I have tried never to believe that something was so merely because it would please me to have it so."

"There has never been a war that was justified."

"Would you say that the war by which mainland Hellas threw back the Persian army of conquest was not a just war? Or that the war by which, at the same time, we in Sicily successfully resisted conquest by Carthage, was not a just war?"

"I still say that it would have been better to settle our differences without fighting one another."

"And so say I, and so says every reasonable man. And there are certainly times when the spear can be turned aside with words. But there are other times when it can not."

Afterwards, the talk shifted to the theatre (Ctesiphon had just given an outstanding performance in the Bacchai) and we had some refreshment. When Pyrrhon was about to leave, our host suggested, "We enjoyed the verses on Lesbos. Perhaps our guest will favor us with something else of his composition?" Pyrrhon hesitated a moment, then accepted the proferred lyre, and chanted (he wrote down the words for me subsequently),

> *"Sage of the Argives! Aged Nelean Nestor!*
> *Counsellor of the kings in the crested helmets!*
> *Say, was it malice of man or a god's devising*
> *That we know of you only the drivel of dotage?*
>
> *Once you were valiant and young, a wooer of women,*
> *Smasher of shield-arms, bearer of brunt of the battle;*
> *But when the captains tore down the towers of Troia*
> *Feebly you bent by the brazier and muttered of exploits*
> *Tarnished by time and sea-distance. Gone was the glory.*
>
> *You too, Priam, sire of children of sorrow!*
> *You, Laertes, whose get was the wily Ulysses!*

I showed the verses to the comic dramatist Lallos, who was a member of Archimedes' club. To my surprise, he did not laugh at them. Neither did he praise them overmuch.

Archimedes was now to experience the great recurrent tragedy of all mankind. His wife, with whom he had lived in harmony for almost thirty four years, had been complaining of increasing pain in the chest. The local Asclepiads confessed their complete inability to help her, so he sent her by sea to the Akragas Clinic.

She slept in the temple, but the god sent no dream to guide her cure. She took the prescribed baths, made the sacrifices, and attended a play glorifying Apollo the healer; but all in vain. She was an intelligent woman, not given to self-deception; and when the fever laid hold of her, she returned to die in her own place, and within a week thereafter was no more.

The kings Hiero and Gelon attended her funeral.

The master was deeply affected. He continued his meetings with his students, but for a long time the merry humor which customarily cropped up in his speech and bearing were absent. He made the prescribed offerings at her grave on the third, sixth, ninth and thirteenth days.

She had borne him a son and two daughters; but the former had died in early childhood and the other two were married and had family responsibilities of their own, which made it impossible for them to be physically present for very long to comfort their father.

XI

Extract from Pyrrhon's Voyages

Wintry Orion flees from the skies; and the storms are o'er.
The zephyrs gentle the sea, and the ships fare forth once more.
You stand no more by the rowers who beat the bitter brine,
Nor when the rovers storm aboard will you lap your shield with mine.

If now from your shattered leaguers, Margos, the life runs red,
May it trouble not your resting in the dark abode of the dead.

Last year saw the shattered fleet of the Achaean League, half of its ships lost to Macedon's piratical allies, fleeing defeated to its base, where the Assembly considered despairingly what defense might be improvised against the ravenous Illyrians.

This year, thanks to the intervention of Rome, the power of Queen Teuta is utterly broken, and she is little better than a fugitive in Rhizon.

Aratus, the League's General, recaptured Caphyae and presided over the voluntary accession of Argos. It was the full flood tide of fortune; the League now controlled practically all of the Peloponnesus but Sparta, and the island Aigina as well.

From the consul Postumius, who had wintered in Illyria, came an ambassador — none other than Marcus Claudius Marcellus, whom I had met in Sardinia years ago. He was now a man of forty, rugged, confident, thoughtful, and one of the most influential men of Rome. His mission was to open diplomatic relations with the League, and to explain the causes and accomplishments of Rome's war in Illyria.

The Assembly heard him with mixed emotions. Certainly we had needed rescue, and there was great relief that we no longer had to suffer the terror and the actual presence of the pirates. On the other hand, there was no little humiliation in having to thank a foreigner for our protection. He was at any rate well received, and my ship was detailed to escort him on the return, as a mark of honor.

153

We had been lying at Sicyon, a short day's sail up the Gulf. We arrived at Aigai on the eve of his departure. I had to see about replacing two of my rowers who had fallen sick at Sicyon (one of them, I am sure, was a victim of nothing else but the overblown charms of a tavern tart); to find the fleet revictualing officer and complain about some rancid olive oil; to have a supply officer certify a dozen or so oars and a couple of water butts as unserviceable due to fair wear and tear; and to collect my pay. I did not see the ambassador before we sailed.

Perhaps to avoid an endless round of receptions for which he had no taste, Marcus Claudius had ordered his captain to make no more landings, but to pass the nights at anchor. And, since the Roman quinquireme remained afloat every night instead of beaching, I had perforce to do the same, and make my crew, like the Romans, sleep aboard.

I did, however, pay my respects to Junius Sempronius, commanding officer of the quinquereme in which the ambassador was taking passage.

It was when we were only a day's sail from Epidamnus, our destination, that we received the first inkling that our troubles were not wholly over. We had rounded the Acrokeraunian Promontory in the straits at the entrance to the Adriatic; when just north of the isle of Sason we saw a fleet of the accursed lembi in the act of overhauling six merchantmen.

There was a mild northerly wind. Seeing us, the fugitives steered directly toward us, and the lembi followed suit.

There were about twenty of them, full of fighting men from up the coast beyond the domains of Teuta, and therefore not involved in her surrender. I closed with the Roman.

"Sir," I shouted across, "there are about 1,800 men in those ships." We had, together, about 800. "I have fought these ships before. They are light, swift, and too many and too hard to ram. They have no rams themselves. Their tactic is to carry a ship by boarding with sheer weight of men. I respectfully suggest that we lash our two ships side by side. The sea is fairly calm. That will cut in two the length of deck each of us will have to defend, and we can reinforce one another as necessary."

He hesitated a moment, then, "Very good. Come alongside."

Each of us was able to get off a few bolts from our catapults — which did great execution among the packed pirate hulls — before they were upon us.

They came like a swarm of bees. Our archers and javelin men were launching their missiles from the fighting castles fore and aft, and the enemy were replying in kind. Men were falling. Our rowers were protected from any aerial weapon except catapult bolts, which the pirates did not have; but as they stormed at the rails their swords, spears, and boarding axes reached the upper level of rowers, who had in any case relinquished the oars for weapons of their own. And as the oarsmen of the lower tiers, likewise armed, came rushing on deck to join the fray, the boarders were held at our gunwales.

It was hot work in the melee. I was in the stern castle with three archers — two more were down — and a marine wielding a twenty-foot boarding spear. I was out of reach, of course, of the swarming swordsmen, but was a target for I know not how many arrows. While keeping an eye on the action generally, I was hurling spear after spear into the packed Illyrians. I am not much of a hand with the javelin, but at that range it was impossible to miss.

The quinquereme was faring in the same way.

It was, I think, our greater height of deck that decided the issue. The pirates were magnificent fighters. Man for man, I should say that they outclassed my seamen (though not the marines, and not, probably, our infantry ashore). But they could not scale those few feet of ship's side against a determined resistance, and suffered fearfully from the sweeping downward blows that our crews were able to deliver.

A lembus drove into the space between the two sterns, hoping to find an undefended few feet of ship's sides; but the Romans, with their larger crew, were waiting for just such a maneuver. The men climbing over our gunwale they easily speared in the back, and their swords went into the throats of those who attempted their own side.

Suddenly, our assailants had had enough. The outermost vessels began to pull away. Before those alongside could do so, my men leaped into them in turn, to carry the battle to the enemy. I shouted at them to come back, but they did not hear me in the din of yells, screams, clash of weapons, and tramp of feet. This might have been our undoing. A few of the nearest pirate ships, in the act of cutting loose, paused, and their men turned again to the attack. It was thus that I sustained my heaviest losses. But Sempronius had seen, and half a century — he had almost a hundred more men than I — came charging across, and the battle was ended.

At Sempronius' direction, both ships, although hardly in condition to do so, got under way and rammed and sank four Illyrians whose losses did not permit them to evade our rams. We had captured two of their craft at the end of the engagement, the Romans three.

We had suffered heavily. Sixty-three of my crew were dead, a like number likely to be corpses or cripples; half a hundred were more lightly wounded, myself among them (an arrow in the shoulder). The Romans had lost proportionately. But there were, as well as we could estimate, close to four hundred Illyrians who would never plunder a ship or a town again.

Marcus Claudius came aboard to thank me. It had been nine years since Sardinia, but we knew one another at once.

"Well, Pyrrhon, we meet for the second time. Again to fight as allies against pirates."

"And again to render one another needed assistance."

He expressed concern over my wound.

When we reached Epidamnos, he turned over a few captives for the extortion of what useful information they might have; after which, more dead than alive, they were crucified after what was coming to be the custom in Rome, as in Carthage. I thank the gods that I do not live among barbarians — in saying which I mean no slight to the memory of my mother. Nevertheless, the word gives me an uncomfortable feeling on her account.

We lay at Epidamnos for three weeks, while some of my wounded mended — myself included — and some died. Menander, my exec, was among the latter. He had been transfixed by a javelin at his post on the fore castle, and had lingered unaccountably for four pain-wracked days. We held a joint funeral service for all, at which the consul Postumius attended with a detachment of troops.

I engaged some new rowers and returned to Aigai.

In the Aegean on convoy duty later that summer, I had occasion to put in at Athens. There was excitement in the air. Athens had after long subjection just thrown off the yoke of Macedonia, and her people were bursting with pride in their new-found freedom. True, it had been attained not by military action, but by bribing the garrison commander; but at any rate they had done it, and one must bear in mind that freedom must not merely be won, but preserved thereafter, which may take more doing.

And indeed the temporary weakness of Macedonia due to the death of Demetrios was already giving place to a renewed burst of vigor under Antigonos Doson.

I was sufficiently inspired by the air of adventure to dash off the following for a drinking party at the military boat sheds.

> *How stands our shining city,*
> *Her lofty citadel,*
> *Her pleasant walks and waysides,*
> *Her hearthfires? Stands she well?*
>
> *Lie down, Oh men of Marathon!*
> *So well you kept the strand,*
> *Tiptoe above the beaches*
> *The reaching towers stand.*
>
> *What of the youth of Athens?*
> *What of our grandsons' get?*
> *High hearts in hardy bodies,*
> *Hold they the spear-line yet?*

Lie down, Oh men of Marathon!
Beneath Hymettus hill
The well loved wives of Athens
Give suck to heroes still.

What of the high gods' temples,
The priesthood's chant and cry?
Do smokes of laden altars
Seek yet the clement sky?

Lie down, Oh men of Marathon!
The Attic people pray
To the high gods undying
Who keep their folk to-day.

Yet looms the Persian peril,
The lances of the dawn?
The Great King's countless legions,
Do they come marching on?

Rise up, Oh men of Marathon!
Stand for the Attic plain!
The gale that hurled you earthward
Sweeps from the north again!

I was becoming somewhat disenchanted with my service. The alliance between the Aetolian and the Achaean Leagues was giving place to hostility. A mercenary warrior, in theory, fights only for pay; and that if my salary had suddenly come to an end, my services would have ended with it, is certainly true. I owed no allegiance in that quarter. While I could fight wholeheartedly against those enemies of the human race, the pirates of Illyria, or to free Hellenic soil from the oppression of an alien northern king, I had no interest whatsoever in shedding my blood so that Aratus of Sicyon might dominate the Peloponnesus. Still less was I interested in frustrating the noble project of idealistic young Lacedaemonians who sought to revive the pristine virtues of their people.

In this frame of mind and while still in Athens I was surprised to encounter Sphaeros of Sparta, former tutor of Agis, Cleombrotos, and Cleomenes.

"I hope that we do not meet as enemies," was his smiling greeting (there had already been border clashes between Lacedaemonia and the Achaeans).

"That would be a sad day. What has happened in Sparta? How is the queen? What brings you to Athens?"

"One question at a time, please," with a laugh. Then, serious, "You probably know something about the projects and the tragic death of King Agis."

I nodded.

"You probably know, also, that soon thereafter his widow Agiatis was married by King Leonidas to his son, Cleomenes, to secure her wealth? Good. Well, the marriage was very much against both of their wills. She was a grieving widow, naturally bitter against Leonidas and all his house. Cleomenes too was angry and ashamed, and not the man to force himself upon a grief-striken woman."

He smiled again.

"The unexpected result bids fair to surpass any of the love tales that have begun to circulate in Hellas. Their very common resentment of the marriage, paradoxically, first drew them together. Mutual sympathy passed to tenderness, and then — she is a very beautiful woman, you remember — "

"I remember."

"Well, nature took its course. He fell utterly, devotedly in love with her; and soon thereafter, she with him. If that were all, it would be tale enough. But she, recognizing in him the same lofty character and sympathies as in her first husband, continued to plant the same ideas in his breast, and found fertile soil. Fortunate woman, to wed two such men!"

"Fortunate men, to wed such a woman!"

"Ah — yes. Yes, indeed. Oh, thank you — I am a bit dry. But as I was saying, Cleomenes is not another Agis. Noble of mind and high of purpose he is; but he is tougher, more ambitious. He too would restore the strong, virile Sparta of olden time, and put an end to the misery of landless men and the greed of the mortgage holders; but he has profited by the experience of Agis, and knows that to a Spartan king there is only one road to power — war. And he is a great leader of men."

"And what will he do now?"

"That brings me to your third question, what do I here. A leader of men needs men to lead, and especially such as are leaders of men themselves. The Spartiates are few; we seek mercenaries. Pyrrhon, there will be war between Cleomenes and Aratus. You are on the wrong side. You too are of the Doric speech and parenthood. Earn gold and glory fighting for Cleomenes and Agiatis. You can still change sides without discredit, but next year it may be too late. Your quinquereme is waiting for you at Troezen. What say you, captain?"

To make a long story short, I agreed. Arete I turned over to the admiralty at Aigion. How I felt about it, any old ship captain will know. I resigned my commission, and after a decent interval took the road to Troezen.

"I am Pyrrhon of Syracuse," I introduced myself.

"Welcome, Captain!" the port captain of Troezen replied. "We have been expecting you."

Nikis was a little larger than Arete, but her lines were similar. There were the usual fighting castles at bow and stern, a catapult forward, and a bronze-sheathed ram. In her side I saw two levels of oar ports. The upper ports were spaced in threes, sloping downward aft, about a foot apart and about two feet between groups, so that I knew that she had the zenzile arrangement — rowing benches extending diagonally inboard from the ship's side and slightly aft, seating three men, each pulling his own oar. The lower ports were in groups of twos, similarly spaced and with the same intervals, for paired oars and oarsmen in the same arrangement. In calm weather, all of the rowers together should be able to develop a good turn of speed; in a seaway, the lower line of ports would be closed.

She was, as I discovered, well found and manned, so far as the crew had been recruited; Cleomenes' agents were still hiring rowers. My officers were almost all on board, and good, competent seamen they seemed to be.

Nikis had harder bilges than most; perhaps for this reason she was an exceptionally good sailer with a beam wind, making astonishingly little leeway; she could in fact with new canvas hold almost six points off the wind.

It was not long before I was presented to King Cleomenes. He was tall, strong, and not so much handsome as with bearing of vitality, as though he had the vigor of several men, and with an air of self-confidence such that you found yourself instinctively trusting and relying upon him — which I suppose is another way of describing the quality of leadership.

Somewhat later I met, for the second time, Agiatis his queen. I had long since, of course, gotten over that silly infatuation of youth. Except in the unrealistic love stories that are beginning to flood the libraries, we Hellenes do not wear our hearts upon our sleeves. Only the callowest of youths would lose his head over a woman, however beautiful, who moved in a world so remote that she could be neither wife nor lover — nor do we choose either thus. I was a maturer man, now, and past all that.

I was...until I heard the sound of a remembered voice, and then into the audience chamber walked a woman who might have posed for Phidias or the painter Apelles. And I knew why I joined the Spartan cause.

She remembered me, or was so gracious as to say she did. She thanked me for supporting the king, and added, "And you will keep him safe for Sparta and for me, will you not, Pyrrhon?" And I knew that when he was embarked in my ship, I would give my life for him.

Near Gytheion, the port of Sparta, stands a stone sacred to Zeus Kappotas. Thither came the king and the queen to worship the god.

Ostensibly, at least. After making their devotions, the royal pair boarded my Nikis for the passage of a few hours across the bay to Cyparissia. That a general in the midst of a campaign, and a king who is rebuilding his state despite enemies eager to pounce, could make an expedition of five or six days for worship at an obscure shrine and then an idle sail, let him believe who will. My own opinion, in the light of a few hints and of what later transpired, is that he was going to confer with a messenger of Aristomachos of Argos. Be that as it may, the queen soon asked me to take the helm myself and send all other ship's personnel forward out of earshot. I did so. They could afford to trust me, rather than a Spartan who might be an enemy agent or a sympathizer with one of the men of recently nationalized fortunes.

"Cleomenes," she said to him, "hear my thoughts. You have accomplished in Sparta what you set out to do. Aratus and Achaea have been humbled. The plutarchy here has had to bow to your will. Let it be enough. You will have work till the end of your days to consolidate the revolution right here in Sparta, and make it again the city of Lykurgos' dream. Do not risk everything by further ventures abroad."

He laughed. "I have only begun. I am a king of Sparta, and my business is war. Fortune is smiling upon me. Why should I stop now? Why should Spartans be concerned forever with that miserable Achaean League? Let me make my frontiers unassailable."

She did not smile in turn. "You fill me with dread. Do not push your good fortune too far! Tyche has a way of turning upon those who do."

"Shall I tell my army on the borders of Arcadia that my wife says it is time to go home?"

"Aratus is willing to make peace."

"I am not."

"There is frenzy upon you."

"Then let my enemies beware it — not you, not I."

"If you are a king of Sparta, I am her queen. I would not quail at little perils — I am no cow-woman of the north. We women of Sparta have always walked proud and free."

"Walk prouder. I will make you Queen of Hellas!"

"My love, unsay the word! This is hubris!"

"Let come what may, the phalanx marches on!"

"My love! Oh, my love! Beware of Nemesis!"

The hairs rose at the back of my neck, but he answered, "Let Nemesis and the Fates decree what they will. Sparta's strength has come again, and she goes grandly on!"

Through the Peloponnesus ran a whisper among the poor: "The shackles of debt are breaking! The land is lying open for the plow!"

Mantineia. I saw it myself; Nikis had convoyed a supply ship to Thyrea, on the Gulf of Argos; and in consequence of a sudden slight epidemic, I had to take command of the train up the Tanus valley to the army (and it was strange to hear the antique, Homeric Greek of the Arcadian mountaineers!). Rebels in the city hurled the hated League garrison from the walls, opened the gates to our storming party, and wreaked bloody vengeance on the Achaean interlopers.

Lasion. Our spearmen found it an Achaean outpost; they stormed it and left it in the hands of the men of Elis once again.

Hecatombaion, in far west Achaea. I lay at Dyme with the supply ships while Cleomenes' men broke the Achaean power in pitched battle. Aratus, he who had spent his youth driving Macedonia out of the Peloponnesus, in desperation sent to her King Antigonos for aid; but the price was Corinth, and the price was too high.

Argos. Aristomachos led the rising, and the town was Spartan without spitting a man.

Corinth. The Corinthians rose, and welcomed the Spartans in. Cleomenes laid the Achaean garrison of the high Acrocorinthos under siege.

Pellene, Philus, Troezen, Epidauros, by scores they went over to him; and everywhere ran the whisper, "Land! An end to debt! Land!"

From Pylos to the Isthmus he held the land, all but Megalopolis and a few small towns. But only to Sparta had he brought the longed-for reforms.

Cleomenes besieged Aratus' city of Sicyon. Within months, all of southern Greece would be in his hand.

It was when reduced to control of a dozen or so towns, that Aratus and the Achaeans betrayed their lifework. They called in Macedon. King Antigonos appeared at Corinth and launched his Macedonians against the isthmian wall. The Spartans hurled them back. The spearpoint could not breach that battle line.

But a whisper could. A whisper that became a rumble, and then a swelling outraged cry: "No land! No debt relief! No freedom!" Argos in the Spartan rear summoned Aratus, and by sea and land it was seized by the troops of Antigonos and the League. Cleomenes came raging down, and stormed the walls; but Antigonos came implacably after, and the Spartans had to fall back and cover their city. Town defected after town, and the Argolid was lost. Antigonos turned west, and joined with the followers of Aratus; Sicionia fell away.

But worse, far worse for Cleomenes, was his loss in Sparta. Suddenly, tragically, Agiatis was dead.

He gave no sign of his grief. Grimly he fought at bay. But I knew how it was with him. It felt like a rock from a ballista in my belly. Between her and me there had been nothing; I could hardly even call myself a friend. But there was a great darkness where there had been light.

Cleomenes sent me to Egypt, to Macedonia's old enemy Ptolemy. Ptolemy sent gold, and Cleomenes rearmed his troops and raised fresh levies. He sent me to raid the shipping of his foes, and I took the fat grain ships, put prize crews aboard, and sent them home to Gytheion. Meanwhile Antigonos stormed Mantinea and let the Achaeans have their surfeit of slaughter in revenge for the killings of three years before; the surviving population was sold as slaves. Arcadia fell. Antigonos sat down in Argos with an army of hirelings, and sent his Macedonians home for the coming winter. Cleomenes struck hard and fast and took Megalopolis in Arcadia by storm; it was razed and plundered.

Risking the last of the winter storms, I sailed again to Egypt; but the ambassadors of Macedonia had been before me, and Sparta was abandoned. Cleomenes heard my report.

"Then I must stand and fight. There is no more money for the mercenaries. If I win, I drive Antigonos from the Peloponnesus and crush the traitor Aratus forever. If I lose —."

I looked into his eyes. Spartan kings died with their troops.

He knew my thought and negated it with his head. "No. If I perish, so does the revolution. But if I can reach Egypt, Ptolemy will yet learn that the Antigonids are his implacable foes, and must be driven back to the north. Therefore, Pyrrhon, you will lie at Gytheion with your ship ready for sea, till you receive news of the battle."

I heard later about the fighting.

Sparta's 20,000 bestrode the Oionos valley; Cleomenes on a hill on the right, his brother Eucleidas on another on the left, their center in the valley between. Antigonos came on with half as many more — Macedonians, Achaeans, Megalopolitans, Acarnanians, and the accursed Illyrians. He made a frontal attack on his right; the Spartan center met it and counterattacked, to be driven back in turn by Philipoemen's horse.

The Illyrian column, unseen, was climbing the hill on Eucleidas' left.

Now Cleomenes gave the word; the fierce Lacedaemonian war cry filled the valley, shields across breasts, a thicket of gleaming spearpoints blossoming on its front, the line moved. The Spartan heavy infantry, the terror of Greece for thrice a hundred years, charged down the hill upon the hosts of Macedon; and they drove the men of Macedon before them.

On suitable ground, with its flanks protected (it does not change front easily), the Spartan phalanx is irresistible.

But the Illyrians, too late perceived, topped and cleared their hill. Then they swept murderously down on the exposed left of the Spartans. Antigonos reformed his own phalanx and charged back in.

Death mowed the Spartan grain.

It was almost dawn of the second day following. I was awakened by the sound of pounding hooves. I left my cabin to see two horsemen ride up, fling themselves off their steeds, and shout, "Make ready to put to sea. Order of the King!"

I needed to ask no questions. My crew was already awake. Soon there were more horsemen, and then chariots with frightened, weeping women and children who hurried aboard. Last of all came Cleomenes.

"Alexandria!"

I nodded, and we got under way. Throughout the voyage he sat in the bow, silent, eating and sleeping little, gazing ahead.

And so, for the first time in history, the streets of Sparta knew the tread of a conqueror.

At Alexandria, before going ashore, Cleomenes said to me, "For your loyalty, thanks. I have nothing more to offer you. But when I return, to conquer once more, I should like you by my side. If you will, take service with Ptolemy till then. Charter the ship to him, if he will have her, on those terms — otherwise, find some king who will. And if I die, I have no children, and Spartan power is no more. Take the ship in lieu of pay."

It almost broke Cleomenes' spirit when the news came from Greece. Almost immediately after the battle, the Dardanians had invaded Macedon, and Antigonos had had to hurry home with his troops. If only Cleomenes had refused battle and had held behind the walls of Sparta, he would have won!

XII

Extract from Heraclides' Life of Archimedes

Archimedes now reached what he considered the pinnacle of success in his career. He had long been tantalized by the difficulty of inscribing a sphere within a cylinder. It was a marvel to him that the relationships in which his geometry dealt were not sooner understood, for in his own words, "These properties were all along naturally inherent in the figures referred to, but they were unknown to those who before our time were engaged in the study of geometry, because none of them realized that

symmetry exists between these figures." It was the more un-
satisfactory to him, therefore, that he should long be unable to
derive the formula to express the relationship between the two
forms mentioned above.

The greater, therefore, were his joy and satisfaction when he
had finally penetrated the secret. He and his friends signalized
their gratification by providing a feast for the city, while they
dined in private together and admired the now completed book,
"On the Sphere and the Cylinder". It was dedicated to his friend
and correspondent Dositheus. The master expressed the desire
that this achievement be memorialized upon his tombstone.

The dinner was a notable one. The bread was especially fine.
We ate eels in olive oil, lentils, cabbage, onions, pork dressed
with garlic, figs, and nuts. There was a dessert of two kinds of
cheesecake. There were wines of Crotona and Chios, cooled by
snow from a cold-cellar. We drank them undiluted.

A Thracian girl did an amazing dance in and out between
clashing swords held by two who were blind-folded. It was a
thrilling and frightening thing to watch. Some mimes played the
story of Persephone and Hades, after which we heard some
delightfully rendered Theocritos.

From what I have written hitherto, it should be evident that
the interests of Archimedes were as wide as they were deep. All
of the arts were within his ken.

His construction of the hydraulic organ furnishes an interesting example of how he could make one discipline serve another.
The instrument, in case any of my readers is unfamiliar with it,
was devised by Ktesibios of Alexandria around the middle of the
present century. Water is admitted from below to compress the
air in a large chamber; as the player manipulates the keys, they
permit the escape of the air through this pipe or that, producing
the desired tune.

The master's construction was considerably more complex
than any of the few known hitherto, and its musical quality was
by much superior.

I have mentioned the fact that although Archimedes' mechanical achievements were responsible for much the greater part of his reputation, at least among laymen, his own attitude toward them was decidedly deprecatory. In general, he valued and prided himself only on his abstruse, purely intellectual discoveries in mathematics and astronomy, as indeed did the fellowship of scholars with whom he corresponded so assiduously, for whom he wrote and who held him in such universal admiration.

To this attitude he manifested one curious exception.

He took great pride in the planetarium which he had constructed, which he fully described in his book, "On Sphere-making", in which he gave directions and specifications to anyone who might wish to duplicate the work.

The less important item was a celestial globe of extraordinary accuracy and beauty, on which were depicted all of the stars in their constellations.

Much as this was admired, it was as nothing compared to his working representation of the sun, moon, planets, and earth, which were arranged at their relative distances from one another; and were activated by a hydraulic engine in such fashion as to reproduce faithfully their diurnal and annual movements relative to one another, and relative to the constellations, indicated on a large hollow globe about the moving bodies. The mechanism also showed the phases of the moon and its eclipses.

Men of learning were loud in his praises, and some of them made far journeys to see and study it.

Hiero too paid tribute to his kinsman's inventiveness, but his further reaction was, to the master, disconcerting.

"Cousin," he said, "with the skill you have demonstrated in the shipyard, and now with this hydraulic apparatus, I am sure that you could solve any mechanical problem to which you put your mind.

"I have been giving thought to the defensibility of the city in case of war. We have experienced two notable sieges. Our walls are thick, high and strong; but as you know, it takes more than walls and more than courage to stop a strong and determined enemy. If a sea power, by the way, such as Athens or Carthage, should attack again, it may well be at the sea wall. Give thought to it, cousin, and see what you can devise."

It was a sober and preoccupied Archimedes whom we found later that day. There were long silences in his speech. At times he seemed not to hear. His reply to questions, and even his expositions, were frequently off the mark. We looked uneasily at one another. Finally I ventured to ask him whether he were ill. He raised his head in denial.

"Forgive me, kaloikagathoi! I had not meant to inflict my problem upon you. No, fair sirs, not a problem really, in the sense of a decision to be made. Rather a feeling of deepest awe."

He remained silent a moment, and I said, "I did not mean to pry, sir. I apologize."

He had, when he wanted it, one of the warmest smiles I have known, and we saw it now. "There is no secret, Heraclides. King Hiero has asked me to devise some weapons to defend our city in case she is ever again subjected to siege."

This was interesting news. Still, "I'm sure you'll come up with something, sir" — this was Hesychios.

He waved his hand impatiently. "I'll do my best, which is all anyone can do. It's not that."

"You will have to divert time and attention from your studies," said someone, I forget who.

"Doesn't any one of you see that this is one of the momentous events in the history of mankind?" the master asked.

We simply stared.

"When, in the course of the quarrels of our earliest fathers, some man, angrier or more ingenious than the rest, thought to raise a club against his enemy instead of relying on fists or teeth, weapons were born — a portentous moment. Now, the first time in history, a scientist is to put his knowledge at the service of weaponry. The results are incalculable, and will go down through the ages in shapes we cannot guess. The world today has been fundamentally changed. It will never be the same again."

The Traveller spoke up. "Sir, why do you not refuse? you are a scientist — a contributor to human knowledge and human progress, not to death. And in any case, there are things that are better not known."

"Neither a scientist nor any other should hold himself above his duty to his people. As to the latter thought, there is really no choice. All things that the mind of man can discover will be known — if not through me, through others. Nothing can halt that march, whether to good or to ill. What things I do not find out, some other will bring to light. If Odysseus had not sailed to Ogygia and the Isle of the Cyclops, think you that no other man would ever have made that voyage?"

The Traveller spoke again. "Sir, war has been the curse of Greece. Hellenes have gone blithely and irresponsibly to war from the time of Homer on. Is a man like you to be drawn into the service of this horror? Is it not time that men began to think of peace instead?"

Saul ben Menassah took a part. "Do not think, Traveller, that the idea of peace, even of permanent, universal peace, is a new one. Half a millenium ago the prophets of my people dreamed that great dream. 'They shall beat their swords into ploughshares, and their spears into pruning hooks; nation shall not lift up sword against nation, and they shall not learn war any more.' But a dream it remains, and the cry of the peoples rises to the heavens."

"The choice is a simple one," the Traveller replied, "and man can make it. It is peace and happiness, or war and misery. We need merely to say a resounding 'No!' to war. 'You shall not again lead us forth to kill and maim our brothers.' "

The master sighed. "The choice is not a simple one. It may be war and happiness, or peace and misery. When the Athenians discovered that rich vein of silver at Laurion, there were those who would have devoted the money to the uses of peace. Fortunately, Themistocles was wiser. He fanned the flames of the desultory war with Aigina, and persuaded his fellow citizens to let him use the silver to build fighting ships. He knew, as they were unwilling to believe, that the Persians would come again. Too late then to build triremes and train rowers! And the event proved his wisdom. But for him, there would have been no fleet and no Salamis, and Hellas would have groaned under the tyranny of the Great King."

"And would that have been worse than the wickedness of war? The man of integrity, under any regime, does what is right and refuses to do what is wrong, come what may. To refuse to condone a war is not necessarily to be afraid to die."

"You are visualizing a band of heroes standing against a wall, calmly and proudly, to receive in their breasts the arrows of the tyrant's archers. But it is not like that, and not all men are heroes. One of the noblemen of Persia was so rash as to remark that most of the credit for an exploit of the king's was rightfully his. For this he was twelve days dying in the boats! Subjugation means massacre — not once, but again and again. Witness the Helots. Subjugation means fear — not the passing, honorable fear of a man facing the enemy's heavy infantry, but the endless, creeping fear of a people with the spies of a conqueror everywhere among them. Subjugation means shame — the broken manhood of a man who obeys because he does not know from day to day whether his farm will be left to him, or he to it. Subjugation means dishonor for the women, first by force, then, even more disgraceful, voluntarily. Worst of all, subjugation means treachery — the betrayal of one's own fellow citizen — one's friend — yes, one's brother — for the purchase of profit or safety. Subjugation means our children dying for want of food, and men dying for want of the fruits of their labor."

"And against what enemy, pray, are we to arm?"

Archimedes spoke impatiently. "What's the difference? I don't know whether he will be Macedonian, Roman, Carthaginian, Gallic, or another."

"And if this imaginary enemy never materializes?"

"Then so much the better."

"Are you saying that it is useless to work for peace? That it is forever unattainable?"

Saul broke in again. "I do not know whether peace is attainable. But I am sure that it is useless to work for it. Peace, I believe, can never be approached directly. It must be a by-product, the result of a change in the character of man. If you can free man of selfishness, of hatred, of aggressiveness, of love of combat, more importantly perhaps, of unwillingness to be critical of his own reasoning and desires — and lastly, make him willing to accept and abide by a situation that he considers unjust, and even dangerous to his survival, rather than try what he is sure will be a successful resort to arms to attain to his rights — then, perhaps, we can have a rational world in which disputes will be settled by debate and reason."

"What is it, grandfather? You seem ready to burst! No, don't be afraid — tell us what is on your mind!" Aristotle had noticed an aged slave moving in and out of the room on his duties.

"Sirs, my mother was a Theban. She often told me about how her countrymen watched the rise of Philip of Macedon and did nothing about it. He conquered king after king; but what business, they said, have we in Thrace, or in Illyria, or even in Thessaly? And the Athenians said the same. When they finally realized their peril and went to war, it was too late.

"My mother was a girl when Thebes made a last attempt to regain her freedom on King Philip's death. It ended with the razing of Thebes after her soldiers had been killed. My father was among them. Eight thousand citizens were sold into slavery.

"My mother was one. She never saw her family again. She fell into the hands of a speculator, who bred her for profit. Each baby was torn from her as soon as weaned. I was the last; her master died while she was carrying me, and her new one was sorry for her and let her raise me.

"The curse of Ares on all who refuse to act upon their danger before the chance is gone!"

The Traveller objected. "Could not Thebes have accepted Macedonian rule without destroying herself?"

The old man drew himself up. "Even a slave knows that a man should be master in his own house!"

"I too," Hesychios interposed, "stand aghast at the enormous amount of blood that has been shed, thanks to an obstinate refusal to face unpleasant facts, and to prepare men and material against a potential aggressor. In fact, I abhor an ill-considered pacifism as much as a brutal militarism. Both are alike the enemy of well-meaning men who wish only to tend to their own business without interference."

"And meanwhile you will support war?" The Traveller was still obdurate.

"Meanwhile I will support my city in a war," the Master replied.

"Even an unjust war?"

Archimedes resumed. "Justice and injustice — right and wrong — are almost always a matter of opinion. Therefore, we have laws, which attempt to codify these things, and are objectively so or not so; or if they're not, we have courts to decide the matter. I think that in almost every war, one can find those who will maintain that it is morally wrong. If, therefore, the state is not to be reduced to helplessness, we must let the decision rest with those who are duly appointed to make it."

"Then you will take part in any war, no matter how vicious and evil?"

"Almost any. Before I will hold aloof from my country's cause, she must have stated explicitly, and not merely by someone's interpretation, that she has renounced the code of righteousness of gods and men. That would have applied to the fifty sons of Aegyptos, as told us in the 'Suppliants'. Or to the expedition of Polynices, who defied the gods of Greece and their laws. Or, coming down to modern time, the conquest of Melos by the Athenians, who justified their action on the grounds that 'The strong do what they can, and the weak suffer what they must.' Otherwise, when my country is at war, my place is with my country."

"You reject, then, Archimedes, the rule of Socrates, who never went counter to what his Daimon whispered into his heart?"

"By no means. His Daimon bade him always uphold the sanctity of the laws."

"You feel, then, that law is more important than right or justice?"

"So complex is our living, and so various our natures, that

there can not be a man who is perceptive and sensitive without being disapproving — nay, more, outraged — at some of the things his city is doing, at home or abroad. If, therefore, each man obeys only those laws which he considers just, we come to a condition in which each does what is right in his own eyes; we have first chaos and then savagery. If men wish to live lives of civilization and order, each must subordinate his action to the decision of the state. Only when the state will not tolerate attempts under its own laws to change its ways, will the righteous man refuse his submission."

The Traveller spoke once more. "It is for men to resolve that they will simply not kill — not for any reason."

"Will man do that?" Hesychios asked him.

The other nodded. "In my own country, the land of Hind, far to the east, there arose two teachers, centuries ago. Both preached the ideal of universal love and brotherhood. They taught the principle of Ahimsa — refusal to harm any living being. Their converts were numbered in the hundreds of thousands. One was Gautama Buddha. The other was Mahavira the Jain. But the greater of the two was the Buddha."

"And did it bring his people peace?"

"Peace of soul, yes."

"I asked, did it bring them peace? Were they left undisturbed in their homes and farms?"

The Traveller hesitated before answering. Then, "When Buddha died, his own people, the Sakyans, had all been massacred, and his royal protectors had met miserable deaths."

"So I should have imagined," the other responded. "I would not choose such a path for my own people."

The Traveller had nothing more to say. After a minute or so, Euphranor remarked, "Surely, since the invention of the catapult, only minor improvements in arms remain to be made!"

Archimedes answered with the most prophetic words ever spoken by man: "Give me whereon I may stand, and I will move the world!"

I have recounted this conversation for the sake of yet another light which it throws on the character of that many-sided man.

It is very revealing, too, of the Traveller. He is not like a Hellene. He is dark of skin, and has large, lustrous eyes. None of us has seen a man of Hind before.

Gradually, Archimedes turned his efforts to the walls of Syracuse.

The effectiveness of the catapults, scorpions, and ballistae was limited by the size and weight of the missile, the range and the accuracy. They were vulnerable to storming by infantry, of course, and to hits by the enemy's artillery.

He determined that for the defense of Syracuse, range was less important than weight of missile. For the most part, the walls crowned a slope; an attacker would be slowed by this, giving the defenders more time to hurl their rocks and darts during the last part of the approach. It would therefore be wise to sacrifice the ability to begin striking while the foe was still relatively distant, in order to deliver more devastating blows when he came within range. Part of the wall faced the sea; here only ships could attack. It certainly seemed worthwhile to sacrifice range in order to hurl rocks which would crash through deck and bottom, and sink the target ship.

The construction of engines which could hurl such weight had not hitherto been practicable. For smaller catapults, the launching force derived from the further twisting, with a windlass, of a bundle of already twisted cords. To throw arrows, with the specialized pieces of artillery called scorpions or ballistae, there was a simple construction formula — the diameter of the cord bundle was 1/9 the length of the arrow or dart. But the stone-throwers required a cord bundle whose diameter, in standardized lengths of a finger between joints, was 1.1 times the cube root of the weight in minas of one hundred projectiles.

The latter result could be approximated by earlier designers for small weapons. But the derivation of cube roots had been beyond the mathematics until Archimedes' friend, Eratosthenes of Alexandria, and Archimedes himself, attacked the problem. As a result of their calculations, Syracuse soon boasted of engines which could loft a rock whose weight equalled that of a man!

It seems quite fitting that the greatest of the catapults was designed in the same city that saw their invention under the great Dionysius, over a hundred fifty years ago.

The dart-throwing scorpions he set mostly on the land defenses. He lowered them below the top of the wall, and cut holes in the wall for their missiles. The rock-throwing ballistae he set on the walls both by land and by sea. Their size and capacity were increased. He then marked off land and sea in imaginary squares, and for each square he determined the weight of the missile and the elevation of the catapult to land its rock in the area. The variation due to changes in tension of wood and hemp or fiber at different times he could not of course control.

He also did many other things, the character of which I shall not go into at this time.

To the credit of Hiero and the joy of his people, there was no prospective need for these engines during his lifetime. He sent some of them as a gift to his friends, the Rhodians, and wrote his treatise on agriculture.

A remarkable phase of the great man's personality was the fashion in which, occasionally, he would combine whimsy with his mathematics.

He was human enough to be annoyed with Apollonius, whose calculation of the ratio of the circumference of a circle to its diameter was, let it be said frankly, somewhat more accurate than Archimedes' own in his "Measurement of a Circle", and who had been guilty of something approaching plagiarism of the master's "Sand-reckoner" in his treatise on the notation of large numbers.

It was for that reason, I think, that he sent to Eratosthenes his Cattle Problem, which has already become famous in scientific circles, with the injunction that he submit it to the mathematicians of Alexandria. For the benefit of those who are not initiates of the mystery, it goes as follows.

In Sicily graze four herds of the cattle of Helios — white, black, dappled, and yellow. Let the numbers of the bulls in these respective herds be represented as W, Z, P, and B; and let the numbers of the corresponding cows be represented as w, z, p, and b.

Between the numbers are these relations:

$$W = (1/2 + 1/3)\,Z+B \qquad w = (1/3 + 1/4)\,(Z+z)$$
$$Z = (1/4 + 1/5)\,P+B \qquad z = (1/4 + 1/5)\,(P+p)$$
$$P = (1/6 + 1/7)\,W+B \qquad p = (1/5 + 1/6)\,(B+b)$$
$$b = (1/6 + 1/7)\,(W+w)$$

Furthermore:

$W+Z$ equals the square of a positive integer.

$P+B$ equals a triangular number, one of the form $\dfrac{m(m+1)}{2}$, m likewise being a positive integer.

I have never been able to solve the problem. When I have asked Archimedes about it, he has always put me off.

I suspect that he was having some fun at the expense of some of his colleagues in Alexandria.

The master habitually worked in a rather heavy abacus; it measured about a cubit and a half on each side, about a digit and a half deep, and presented a smooth surface of powdered glass in which fine diagrams could be made with compass, straight-edge and stylus. The distinct definition of such drawings was indeed needful when he tackled the problem of finding a sphere equal to a given cylinder or cone — one of the most beautiful instances of the problem of two mean proportionals. He attacked the Proposition analytically, constructing the sphere between two cylinders, one of them with altitude and diameter equal to the diameter of the sphere, the other with broader base and height inversely proportional.

I think I had never been made so thrillingly aware of the beautiful system of detailed relationship which exists between the quantities of the critical properties and diameters, chords, diagonals, arcs, etc., as though some god had patterned the shapes of this world after a perfectly balanced choral dance. Archimedes' mind went striding like a giant along a logical pattern, but taking two and three steps at a stride.

This was during that period of his life when he was still absorbed in the subject of the sphere and the cylinder, which he then and thereafter considered of such importance that he held the circumscription of the sphere by the cylinder, and the formulation of their relative volumes, to be his most notable work (although in this I believe that he was deceived), and the one by which he wished chiefly to be remembered and to be memorialized thereby upon his tombstone, as was in fact done.

The peace between Rome and Carthage was an uneasy one. Everyone, in both private and public life, was by now aware that war clouds were gathering in the west. King Hiero called a meeting of all his advisors, Archimedes being included. It seemed certain that Spain would be the theatre of a great and perhaps decisive war between Rome and Carthage; the position of Syracuse was up for discussion.

The debate, the master told us, was less one-sided than might have been expected. The King and much the greater part of the Gamoroi were strong partisans of Rome; whereas among the commoners there was much pro-Carthaginian sentiment. This was difficult to understand; certainly the Punic constitution had little in common with those of such democracies as Athens or the Aetolian League; nevertheless, such was the fact.

It was decided that Syracuse would refrain from belligerency, but in lesser respects would be, as hitherto, friendly to Rome.

When, at the conclusion of one of our daily sessions on mathematics, we turned to the news of the day, the Traveller resumed his favorite topic. "There is nothing worse than war," he said again.

"Look at Lacedaimonia," I argued. "Since the beginning of history the Helots have been slaves. Their men are massacred periodically without even the allegation of any offense. Their women are ravished at will by masters who come at night. When a woman bears a child, she cannot look at it with happy imaginings of a bright future. Would it not be better for them if their ancestors had resisted to the end, even if that end had been death?"

Timaios, recently from Athens, gave my opponent some support. "It is being said now in the stoa that war could be abolished, and that one should not fight in a wrongful war.

"In defiance of the polis?"

"In defiance of the polis, especially if it be a war of aggression."

"And dissidents are to be relieved of the duty of defending the city?"

"Yes, if they feel in their hearts that it is not truly a defense."

The master fell into the Socratic dialogue. It was a century since Plato had been in Syracuse, but his influence was still strong among the philosophers. "Is each individual to make that determination on his own, and to act upon it?"

"The virtuous man will always act according to his conscience."

"The law prescribes, does it not, that any person accused of crime has a right to a fair trial?"

"It does."

"Citizen or foreigner?"

"Yes."

"Do you approve of this?"

"Of course."

"And if you had evidence in favor of a foreigner who was on trial you would give it, would you not?"

"Certainly."

"Even if it incriminated a citizen?"

"Even so."

"You are aware, are you not, that there are barbarian countries where this is not so, and it is considered wrong to take the part of a stranger against a citizen?"

"I know."

"Perhaps there was a time when that was true of us also. At any rate, when such unjust customs were made illegal, there would have been those who disapproved of the change, would there not?"

"No doubt."

"Who felt in their hearts that it was wrong to give truthful testimony in behalf of a stranger and against a citizen?"

"I suppose so."

"Should they obey the law, or heed the voice of conscience?"

"That is a special and rare case."

"Not so special and rare — I daresay there are those still who would feel the same way when it is a question of a loved one's welfare."

"Do you feel then that law is more important than right or justice?"

"As I have said on another occasion, when my city admittedly controverts her own code of right, I will then and only then forsake her cause."

The position of Claudia in the household of Archimedes was an anomalous one. She was legally a slave, and as a former hetaira one who was particularly desirable to men. And there was no wife to inhibit, to whatever degree, the owner's enjoyment of his property. Granted that the owner was an old man (but a vigorous one), his Stoic ethic was more effective in keeping them apart than any other barrier could have been.

It took a brush with death to break the old philosopher down. He was visiting his farm, and had taken Claudia along to see the source of some elements in her accounts at first hand. They had almost finished cutting across a field when the bull saw them.

The first intimation of danger was when Archimedes was suddenly knocked off his feet. (How he escaped being gored, no one can understand.) As the animal went in to finish him off, he shouted for Claudia to climb the fence.

She had other ideas. She swung the cloak she was carrying at the beast, and for a moment it caught on a horn and obstructed his vision; as she started to drag Archimedes away, a few of his men jumped over the fence to the rescue, and that was that.

Later, in safety, he threw his arms around her in affection and gratitude; and found that they stayed around her for other reasons.

On her part, it seems to have been such tenderness as gratitude for his kindness evoked; on his, the half proud, half ashamed display of a belated virility, with the added piquancy of a measure of intellectual companionship; a gratification in which, thanks to her resolute hostility to the idea of a youthful romance, he could indulge himself, stoic though he was, without a sense of guilt.

It was thus that they became lovers.

It is difficult for the young to understand either love or lust in old age. But neither body nor spirit submits willingly to the loss of the good things of the world; eternity is long enough to forego all that makes life sweet, without advancing their fading more than must be; and if in my old age the gods are so kind as to permit me still to enjoy their blessings, I shall accept the gift with becoming gratitude.

I have seen both men and women, in advanced age, loving with all the ardor of their youth, even though not able to give it as much expression as in the halcyon days of life.

There is no period to the age of Eros.

XIII

Extract from Pyrrhon's Voyages

Having sold Nikis to King Hiero's procurement officers and paid off my crew, I found Admiral Gylippos in a well appointed office whose windows offered a beautiful view of the Great Harbor of Syracuse.

"Welcome home, Pyrrhon!" he greeted me. "You have been long away."

I uttered appropriate sounds. He had sent for me, and I waited for him to ask his questions.

"Tell me, how did you find things in Egypt?"

"For our purposes, sir, very ill. Ptolemy — the Third, that was — it was almost three years ago — was quite willing to charter my ship and retain me in command. But he was a sick man, and it quickly became evident that there was nothing to be hoped for from him. I sailed on this errand or that one, or drilled with the fleet under Ptolemy's admirals. Maintenance, I am bound to say, was good, and pay was always prompt; there was little difficulty in keeping good rowers and seamen. Once I convoyed some ships to Pergamon. Once I carried an embassy to Rhodes. It was pitiful to see the once beautiful Colossus of Apollo prone beside the harbor, overthrown by the earthquake of four years before.”

“If you will pardon my curiosity, I am wondering why you remained so long in Egypt.”

I had often asked myself why I lingered in this alien land, in a service without a future. Yet such was the spell of Cleomenes — yes, and of dead Agiatis — that I could not bring myself to leave him. But this, of course, was none of his business.

“While in Alexandria, I made good use of the library. I was also fascinated by the bankers’ tables. Here men grew wealthy without toil or peril; and the fates of kingdoms, I could see, were being decided. But more important, I could see that the king would not live long; and under his successor I might have made a new career.

“In fact, Ptolemy Philopator succeeded to the throne in the following year. Cleomenes for a time had hopes of firing his ambition. But he could not have had poorer material to work on. The young king, it appeared, was interested only in pleasure and self-indulgence; he was as little concerned about Greece and Macedon as about the welfare of groaning Egypt.”

“How was Cleomenes treated?”

“Cleomenes and his entourage were treated with honor; but they might not step beyond the gates of Alexandria. Only I as a Syracusan was free. For three years they ate their hearts out in a golden prison.

“Then there was a plot afoot — there are always conspiracies in these eastern kingdoms. The Spartans joined it.

“On the day they rose. Nikis lay ready for flight, as before, this time to the Seleucid kingdom in Asia. When I saw three of the wives running for the ship, with their children, there was no need for me to ask what had happened. Not one of them lived to make it.

“As the troops of the Harbor Guard raced toward us, I cast off and put to sea.”

"We have heard many fine things about you, Pyrrhon. Even before you left you of course enjoyed considerable reputation in naval circles. How would you feel about entering the service of King Hiero, as commander of Nikis again?" As I remained silent, he added, "I can assure you that it would not be long before you commanded a squadron!"

Although both earlier and later I should have jumped at the chance, I declined the offer.

I found myself for the time being unable to take any decisive action. I was in a prolonged fit of black depression. I shunned all company, and sat and brooded away my days. For again, as several times before — the last time after the death of my friend Margos — I was the survivor of events that had taken the life of some one close to me. Perhaps if I had advised Cleomenes against it he would not have undertaken his ill-starred revolt; or perhaps it would have been better planned, and either succeeded or permitted him to escape with his life.

As hitherto, my common sense told me that this was all nonsense. He would not have wanted to survive the possibility of his return to power, and there had been no chance of success. His rebellion had been a gesture of desperation. Besides, he was the king, and it was for me to follow his orders.

But was he? He was a barely tolerated exile in Egypt; the only legitimate authority was Ptolemy's. To the extent that I did not accept the latter, I was a free agent, and could have spoken my mind. Was there perhaps an uglier reason? Did I perhaps hold some unconfessed lingering jealousy on account of Agiatis; the worse, knowing as I did that Cleomenes was the better man?

All these, of course, were sick imaginings, and really I knew that they were so; but for weeks I was powerless to regain my customary vigor.

I have known several of the great men of my time, in many nations — Hiero, Archimedes, Aratus, Marcus Claudius Marcellus. Than Cleomenes none has been loftier in ambition. None has been more daring. None has been more indefatigable in his selected toil. And none has been more ill-starred. His story has all the attributes of classic drama — a great and noble man who makes a fatal error because of hubris, that arrogant pride which is dreadfully punished by the gods.

The tale requires, alas! a greater pen than mine.

Not the least of his mistakes was that he did not die in battle among his men. Evil it is to die before one's time. But worse is the fate of him who lives too long.

Archimedes drew closer to the brazier. "Chilly," he said. "Well, the days will soon be lengthening again."

I shivered. "The Sicilian winter takes some getting used to, after three years in Egypt."

"I daresay. Well, that's quite a tale. I don't think I've ever known anyone just like your Cleomenes."

"I don't think there is anyone just like him."

"Perhaps not. But now to your plans. Having sold your ship to the king, what are you going to do? Buy another merchantman?"

"Possibly. But I've been playing with another idea. I should like to remain here in Syracuse for a while. I've been talking to my brother, and I have him half persuaded to put up some capital. With that, plus what I have of my own, I might be able to buy into a banking firm, in a small way."

"Really! Well, yes, there's quite a bit of money in mortgages. And it has occurred to me that one could encounter some very interesting problems in the mathematics of it."

"One could, sir. But I wasn't thinking of mortgages. I was thinking of marine finance. There has never been a Syracusan bank that handled it satisfactorily. There is a branch of an Athenian firm that does, but why not keep the profits here?"

Segovesus the Gaul had come in while we were speaking. Encouraged to join in, he said, "Tell me more. I'm ashamed to let you know how ignorant I am in the world of business." His knowledge of it was restricted to the pottery works.

"Suppose a merchant wants to import a shipload of copper from Cyprus. First, he has to charter a ship — or, in the case of a smaller quantity, he pays for space in a ship that is making that voyage, if he can find one. Then he must provide the money to buy the copper in Cyprus. Usually he doesn't put up his own money — often he doesn't have that much. So, he goes to a banker and borrows it, with the freight itself as security. When the copper arrives, he pays back the loan, plus interest (interest rates on such loans run from 20% — a very low figure — to 30%) for the period of the voyage."

"That seems high — let me see, 70 to 90% per year," from Archimedes.

"Well, in the first place, the money doesn't work for you all year, unless you find an immediate and profitable reinvestment; the voyage takes four or five months, which means that you can usually make only one in as much of the year as offers safe sailing weather."

"Of course."

"In the second place, what with piracy and shipwreck, the risk is high."

"I thought that piracy had been pretty well suppressed, between Rome in the west and the Rhodians in the east."

"Far from it — they have done well to reduce it to a tolerable level."

"Go on."

"At the same time, the merchant is gambling on futures. By the time he receives his shipment, the price may have dropped. Contrariwise, of course, it may have risen."

"Go on."

"Furthermore, there are various kinds of skullduggery that may be practiced." I told him about my experience with the rascals who had tried to scuttle my ship.

"And, some cargoes are subject to deterioration. Finally, he may find nobody who wants his cargo when it arrives. Although he can guard against that possibility by contracting with a wholesaler for his merchandise in advance. Or by bringing in something for which a permanent market is assured — like wheat to Rome or Greece, or marine supplies to an island."

"Yes, of course."

"My experience as a merchant seaman should reduce the risks. I know many of the shippers and shipmasters — who is honest, who is prudent, who is skillful. I am competent to assess the seaworthiness of the ships. I know something about admiralty law in all countries. I know which routes are inherently more dangerous, and what, if anything, to do to minimize the danger. And when I do not know any of these things, I am in a better position than a landsman to find them out."

"Do you know," said Archimedes, "you interest me. I have just sold some land at the importunity of the king, who wished to connect two of his estates. I have been wondering how to invest the money. And I can lay my hands on more."

The details of how we came to an arrangement, like its terms, do not matter. Suffice it to say that Archimedes and I became partners in a venture in marine banking.

We did well. At times, in fact, it seemed that we did almost too well, as the volume of business increased to an amount, what with finances, correspondence, surveying and inspection, occasional foreclosures, etc., which I found difficult to handle. Archimedes, of course, paid little attention (he was not supposed to). But he supplied an office in his villa and he had a slave woman who had received a good education and was gifted with arithmetical dexterity, and she helped out. In fact, there were times when I would find it necessary to spend much time on the waterfront, and then Claudia would take over much of the paper work. She was a rather good looking young woman, who was pleasant to be with and work with; not as much so as my current mistress, but pleasant enough.

At the end of a year we were already as far ahead as I had expected to be in twice the time. Archimedes gave a dinner to his club by way of celebration. Among the guests was the actor and comic dramatist Lallos.

Someone asked me a question about getting a ship under way. If Lallos had already favored us with a selection, I should not have ventured to reply as I did; but since he had not yet done so, I sang in his honor a little thing I had once composed.

> *The morning came, a tidy housewife; first*
> *She flung the shadows from her house, then swept*
> *The cobweb-mists from off the summer sea.*

She scented all the air; upon the waves
She laid a mantle of the deepest blue,
And last the golden sun uncasketed
And hung him overhead for ornament.
She shook awake the ship and all the crew,
Who tumbled up to get her under way.
They hoisted canvas to the stirring air
That loafed from off the island for the sound.
Three lined along the anchor cable, hove
The vessel forward, paying down the line
Into the locker, till the cable led
Sheer; then the sudden ease proclaimed her free.
The yard was braced, the sail was sheeted full,
The bow swung round to point the harbor-mouth,
And as the dripping anchor came aboard
The ship with started sheets went running free.

Lallos was quite gracious in his praise. Those who had commented on my un-Hellenic style had done so to sneer, more or less covertly, and those who had found merit in my work ignored as a shameful blemish my stylistic differences from the prevailing mode. Lallos quite frankly took note of it, pointing out virtues and defects as only a professional poet or critic could do, but without any air of patronage and without overdoing his praise, which of course made it all the more acceptable. I was naturally delighted.

XV

Extracts from the Correspondence
of Marcus Claudius Marcellus

*Gnaeus Manlius to Marcus Claudius. At Lanuvium, the 14th day before
the Kalends of February, in the Year after the founding of the City the 526th.*

With deep grief I learned of the death of your father. I loved
him well. He was a true Roman. Valeto!

Public clouds are added to private griefs. The Gauls are restless. It is, I think, inevitable that we must fight them. The
Senate has done well to secure our rear by crushing the Illyrians
first. Apparently they have decided to temporize with the Carthaginians in Spain. There is no doubt, I think, that we shall
have to fight them too; but our great danger now is in the north.
The only enemy that has ever breached the gates of Rome!

I can only say what your father would have had me say — good
fortune attend you!

The Gauls are on the march!

The Insubres are marching on Etruria. They have been reinforced by the Gaesates from beyond the Alps, and 50,000 infantry and 20,000 cavalry and charioteers are in the field.

There is terror in Rome. People flock to the temples with
lavish sacrifices. Never have so many Romans been called to
arms. Yesterday, in accordance with an oracle in the Sibylline
books, we buried alive two Gauls and two Greeks, a man and a
women of each, in the Forum Boarium — be the gods propi-
tiated!

The consul Lucius Aemilius has been sent with an army to
protect Ariminum; a praetor has been sent with an army to
Etruria. The consul Caius Atilius is unfortunately in Sardinia
with his legions.

May the gods save Rome!

Sextus Lutatius to Marcus Claudius. At Rome, on the 12th day before the Kalends of July, in the Year after the founding of the City the 528th.

Guard yourself well.

The Picenum River has run blood red. Three moons have been seen at Ariminum. The augurs state that the omens at the announcement of the election of Flaminius and Furius to the consulship were unfavorable.

The Senate therefore by letter has ordered the consuls not to join battle, but to return to Rome, to lay down their offices and their arms.

The gods preserve you!

Otacilius to Marcus. At Genua, the 7th day before the Ides of August, in the Year after the founding of the City the 530th.

I send you both my condolence and my congratulations on the wound you suffered in the recent victory of the consul Flaminius. There is much talk of your bravery. I think that the Gauls are finished.

Despite the victory, there is great indignation in Rome because the consuls did not obey the senate's order to return without a battle. Flaminius will probably be granted the honor of a triumph, but he will certainly be deprived of his command.

I consider it very probable that the next consulship will fall to you.

If you are well, then so am I.

Gnaeus Fulvius to Marcus Claudius. At Rome, on the 3rd day before the Kalends of March, in the Year after the founding of the City the 531st.

My best wishes on your consulship! I have followed your career with interest and pleasure. You have now completed the cursus honorum. Vale!

*Marcus Claudius to the Senate. At Acerrae, on the 4th day before the
Nones of July, in the Year after the founding of the City the 531st.*

I urge that the Senate reject the peace overtures of the Gauls.
Let us smash them once and for all, and end this menace forever!

Carthage is aggressive in Spain. We shall certainly have to
fight her again. At our backs is the hostile power of Macedon.
Let us not leave an enemy in the north!

No peace without total, crushing victory for Rome!

Gnaeus Cornelius, Consul, to the Senate. At Mediolanum, on the 2nd day before the Kalends of September, in the Year after the founding of the City the 531st.

My colleague has already sent the tidings of victory. I give you the particulars herewith.

While at Acerrae, we received word that King Britomartus with ten thousand Gaesatae was ravaging the valley of the Padus. Marcellus, with the cavalry and six hundred picked men of the light infantry, made forced marches and caught up with the enemy at Clastidium.

He was given no time to rest his troops. The Gauls, seeing the small number of the Romans, and priding themselves on their own valor and their great excellence as cavalry, advanced upon them.

Marcellus, in the forefront, vowed to Jupiter Feretrius the finest suit of armor that he should capture from the enemy. At that moment, the Gallic King Virdumarus recognized him by his insignia as commander, and riding out in front of his men challenged him to single combat.

Marcellus, although past the strength of his first youth, accepted. He charged the king with his lance, pierced his breast-plate and quickly despatched him. The King's armor was the finest that he had seen; so he laid his hands upon it, looked toward heaven and prayed, "Jupiter Feretrius, who judgest the feats of generals and captains on fields of war, behold! I, a general and a consul of Rome, have slain with my own hand a general and a king, the third Roman commander to perform this. To thee I dedicate this first and best of the spoils. I pray thee to grant us the like good fortune through the fighting of this war."

The Romans then charged upon the foe, horse and foot, and after hot fighting won the victory. Most of the enemy were killed, and their arms and baggage were taken.

In point of the odds engaged, this was the most notable cavalry victory in history.

In the meanwhile, I had laid siege to Mediolanum; but the

arrival of an army of the Gaesatae had made me the beseiged in turn. When however, Marcellus arrived with his force and the news of his victory, the Gaesatae retired to their own country. This led to the capture of Mediolanum and of the rest of the cities of the Gauls.

It is a pity that you could not come to Rome to see the triumph of Marcellus. Such a spectacle has seldom been seen in Rome.

You have surely heard how the consul vowed to Jupiter Feretrius the suit of armor of the King of the Gauls, whom he had slain in single combat. For the occasion he cut the trunk of a young oak tree; upon this he arranged the armor, and, thus displaying it, rode resplendent in his four-horse chariot. His men wore their finest armor, and as they marched sang odes to the general and hymns of victory to the gods. The gigantic size of the prisoners and the quantity and richness of the plunder were amazing.

A golden bowl is being sent as a thank-offering from the Senate and the Roman people to the Pythian Apollo at Delphi. A share of the booty is being sent to King Hiero of Syracuse and other friendly cities.

If you are well, then so am I.

Decius Manlius to Marcus Claudius. At New Carthage, in Spain, on the 2nd day before the Ides of July, in the Year after the founding of the City the 533rd.

I write this unofficially but with the knowledge and permission of the ambassadors, whose secretary I am.

Hannibal, the local Carthaginian commander, has not responded well to our warning against interference with the city of Saguntum. He has made countercharges to the effect that Rome has been guilty of executing innocent Saguntine citizens. That this is a trumped-up charge, and that we are here at the urgent request of the Saguntines themselves, you know.

The embassy is about to proceed to Carthage itself.

XV

Extract from Pyrrhon's Voyages

As a result of the capture of Saguntum in Spain by Hannibal this year, war broke out between Rome and Carthage.

I immediately cancelled all loans currently being negotiated for voyages to the west, and doubled the interest rates on those to Italy, Carthage, Gaul, and Spain. As far as Greece, Egypt and the east were concerned, I was not greatly worried. I felt that both powers would be too desperately engaged in their own and Spanish waters to spare ships to raid one another's commerce in the eastern half of the sea.

At about this time I had some minor annoyance as the result of rumors impugning our state of solvency. The matter was quickly set straight. It seemed to be the work of a crank; investigation revealed that the stories were attributable to one Archias, a down-and-out waterfront wastrel.

When I mentioned it to Archimedes, he recognized the name at once. The man had been exposed as an embezzler through the instrumentality of Archimedes, and had cherished an insane hatred for him ever since. When word came that the Carthaginian general Hannibal was ravaging Gaul, Archias tried to give the impression in certain quarters that most of our liquid assets were tied up in Massalia. The story, of course, was ridiculous, and its source did nothing to increase its credibility.

To the amazement of all, the march of Hannibal turned out to be not merely into Gaul, but across the Alps into Italy itself! In a great battle at Lake Trasimenus Hannibal, with little loss to himself, annihilated a Roman army of twenty-five thousand men — one-fourth of all the Romans under arms! The consul Flaminius was among those who perished.

Hiero was deeply grieved by the calamity which had befallen his friend and ally, Rome. He resolved to send her a large gift as tangible evidence of friendship. The banking firm of Archimedes and Pyrrhon was entrusted with a part of its preparation. We accordingly set about purchasing in advance some of the

198

winter wheat which would become available in the spring of the following year. Gold was gathered in the amount of 330 Roman pounds (twice the weight of a man!) for a statue of Victory.

Even Archimedes helped. Claudia and I worked many hours at the production of this truly princely gift. When assembled, it was to amount to 300,000 measures of wheat and 200,000 of barley, with as much to follow, besides the gold. With them went 1,000 slingers and bowmen.

When the grain had been reaped and threshed in the spring, all was ready.

The wheat and barley had been loaded aboard the ships and the thousand troops were about to embark. I was to sail as supercargo, although on an errand of this sort the office seemed almost superfluous. I was going over some last minute details at lunch with Archimedes and Claudia. As we finished, she dropped a knife. It was very sharp, and gashed her ankle.

"King Hiero will be expecting me — I must be off," he said. "Send for a surgeon."

"No need," she replied. "Pyrrhon, I'm sure, has dressed hundreds of such wounds on his ships."

I nodded. "I'll have to take some stitches," I said, and sent for what I needed. Archimedes left.

She put her foot on a stool and I sat down before her. I picked up my instrument, casually, and poised it over her foot.

And then my hand would move no further. I felt myself grow weak. I looked up and my eyes met hers.

And then I knew.

And I knew that she knew.

I could not tell how many minutes we sat there, grave and silent, living only in our eyes, before the messenger came.

"On the King's orders. The time of sailing is advanced. You are to go aboard at once."

I voyaged to and from Rome in a fever of impatience. Under other circumstances the gratitude of the Romans in their dark hour would have given me, or anyone, pleasure; as it was, I could think only of Claudia, and my love.

Could she be persuaded to give up the greatest man in Sicily — perhaps in the world — for me? I would buy her from Archimedes; he would certainly let me have her; he was not the man to stand in the way of another's happiness without reason. She was merely a slave girl to him. I would marry her; the anomaly of my own origin would probably remove any legal barrier. And, if the gods were propitious, she would bear my children.

Did it matter to me that she had almost certainly shared the beds of men whom I knew, and who knew me? Yes, it did. But I was not the man to blame her for what was no fault of hers. At any rate, I would rather have her, such as she was, than any other woman in Hellas.

I would dissolve the partnership with Archimedes. Perhaps I could find another partner; perhaps I would become a merchant; I might buy a couple of ships and establish my own shipping firm. As long as I had Claudia, nothing else would greatly matter.

Back in Syracuse at last, I went to the house of Archimedes.

"Pyrrhon!" His delight was evident. "How are you? Did you have a good voyage?"

"Yes, thank you. And you seem well. Sir, I want to discuss —"

"Later, later. My friend, I have the most wonderful news. It concerns Claudia. She is with child!"

I could only stare wordlessly.

"Pyrrhon, she has given me back my youth. I love her. Yes, I know that it sounds strange to the young — sometimes even grotesque — when an older man or woman falls under the sway of Aphrodite. But — I can speak to you about this, because you, more than any other of my friends, know and appreciate her for what she is — I love her with all the ardor, all the rapture, of fifty years ago. I shall do everything I can to make her happy."

Still I was dumb.

"She is my life, Pyrrhon. I know that I must one day leave her bereft though young, but she is a strange girl, and perhaps there was no other pathway for her. And she loves me. Oh, not in this same divine frenzy — I do not deceive myself — but more gently, as a dear friend. I have never been so happy. If I should lose her, I should want to die. And perhaps the child will replace my poor dead son! Wish me happiness!"

I managed some sort of croak.

"Oh, forgive me, there was something you wanted to say to me?"

"Yes, sir. We shall have to dissolve the bank. I have decided to go back to the sea!"

In time of war, ships are in short supply. I was in any case eager to put distance between myself and Syracuse. I took passage to Crete, where I just managed to make a late season sailing to Athens. It would have been much quicker and more direct to go by way of the Gulf of Corinth; but I doubted the wisdom of showing my face in that area again.

And so for the second time I wintered in that city, so rich in poetry and thought, while the unbearable anguish subsided to an ache that I knew would never leave me, but with which I could live.

Here I found a kerkouros, one of that class of ships which supposedly was developed on Cyprus, beamier than a quadrireme, so that she could carry freight, but narrower than the usual round ship, which made the type useful in war as in peace. She could be propelled by oars or sail. In short, she represented a compromise, and had the faults of one, being less than perfect for either function. But then all marine architecture is a compromise, reflecting the designer's estimate of the mathematical probability of his ship's encountering one set of exigencies or another.

In the troubled conditions which I expected on the seas for some years to come, it seemed worthwhile to accept marginal freight capacity for the sake of the turn of speed that might just possibly get me into haven before a raider could pounce.

Her owner had just died, and his widow wanted cash. The price was right, so I bought her.

My brother died that winter, although of course I did not learn of it until my return home. We had grown somewhat apart; we had little in common but my father's blood. I had never forgotten, however, that but for his generosity I might have led a miserable life, if indeed I had not succumbed in childhood. I had loved him, and I mourned him. His widow was well provided for, his children grown and with young ones of their own.

With the coming of spring I engaged a crew, loaded up with a cargo of wax and dried fish from the Euxine, Macedonian pitch, and Attic earthenware and bronzes and set sail (with very mixed feelings!) for home. The season was still early and the weather unsettled; I elected therefore not to sail through the stormy seas south of the Peloponnesus. In fact, many among my crew had joined with this express understanding.

We stood up the Saronic Gulf on the Etesian wind. The passage was rapid and smooth, thanks to the lee of the Attic coast, and a day's sail brought us to Lechaion, the port of Corinth. Having made all secure, the men took their way up between the long walls to seek wine and more particularly, the sort of entertainment for which Corinth is especially famous. I let them go; had I attempted to keep them aboard, I should have had a mutiny on my hands. In fact, the attraction of Corinth may have had as much to do with the insistence of the men on this route as fear of the storms of Cape Malea. The mate was a lusty young blood, so I gave him too leave to go for the night. The middle-aged boatswain and I remained aboard for security. Besides, I was not eager to be recognized hereabouts.

In the morning, the local stevedores unloaded the kerkouros and packed my cargo in wagons, which were started in a convoy across the isthmus. By evening the emptied ship had been hauled ashore at the beginning of the Diolkos. This was smooth and wide enough so that on the next day she was dragged on the rollers to Cenchreai on the Gulf of Corinth. Slaves did much of the work. I have often wondered why more use is not made of draught animals; they are usually cheaper to buy and maintain than human beings. If one buys by opportunity after the sack of a city, however, and if one is not too particular about decent treatment of his men, the latter may be more economical.

As I was reloading, my crew straggled in. We got under way with the oars, and with the Acrocorinthos high over the port quarter, the ship headed west down the gulf toward Syracuse.

I have never liked the westward passage down the Gulf of Corinth. The wind is usually adverse, and the sea rough, so that one loses time in the bays of the north shore (the south has little shelter) waiting for the wind to change. On this occasion, however, luck was with us; one of the easterlies of winter, much belated, blew us steadily along between Mount Parnassus with Delphi half guessed on its shoulder, to the right, and the peaks of Arcadia to the left. Once through the narrows, of course, one picks up the northeasterly "Gulf Wind" off Patrai in any case, and so we issued onto the Ionian Sea.

I arrived home as King Hiero, ninety-three years old, lay on his death bed. His son Gelon had preceded him by a few months, and Hiero's grandson, the fifteen-year-old Hieronymos, assumed the crown.

Upon hearing of the death of King Hiero, I went immediately to condole with Archimedes.

"I can imagine, sir, how deeply grieved you must be," I said. "You have lost at once your king, your kinsman, and your old friend."

"It's more than that," he replied.

"I know. All of us think of you both — thought, I must say now — as gentlemen of the old order; men who stood for decency, stability, honor, and all the rest of the outmoded virtues. In all the fifty-five years of his reign, not once did Hiero slay a man in anger."

He shook his head. "When a young man experiences the death of someone he loves, Pyrrhon, he loses that person; he is distressed over the great emptinesses in his life that will ensue. And he grieves also for the sake of the other, who may have lost untimely the sweet sun and earth, and can know the joys of the beautiful world no more. But when an old man is bereaved, it is himself whom he sees on the funeral pyre; partly, of course, because it reminds him of how soon he too must come to this, but even more for a subtler reason.

"Hiero is the last of the friends and kinsmen who knew me as a lad. With his passing snaps the golden thread that bound me to my childhood. Who can now testify to me with his every breath that I was indeed that boy that I remember so well, who ran so effortlessly and carelessly about the town and fields of home, who was loved by that shadowy mother that drank the waters of Lethe so long ago, who wrestled and told tales with his companions, who dreamed the spacious dreams of youth when world and time stretched endlessly before him! But now the vision of that boy is fading, and I fear lest I shall know him no more. There is none to say that in very truth he was, and that I am he; none save an aged man whose unsupported memory begins already to doubt itself! Remember this, Pyrrhon, and when you see an old man mourn, know that it is for himself that he weeps!"

Despite the old king's strong partisanship for Rome, there had not been wanting a pro-Carthaginian faction, particularly after the serious Roman reverses. This group was soon in the ascendant.

When Archimedes visited the new monarch to offer his services and to express his continued devotion to the crown, he was received without warmth.

The council, which had deliberated regularly during the regime of Hiero, met no more. Where Hiero had been prudent, unassuming, and generous, his grandson soon proved to be cruel, headstrong, and tyrannical. Syracusans are not prudes, but his sexual proclivities they found revolting. As his anti-Roman inclination became more and more evident, Archimedes visited him again to urge the wisdom of standing by the old king's policy of friendship for the city of the Tiber, but Hieronymus rudely bade him look to the devices for the defense of the city walls which he had constructed several years ago, and leave high policy to those who understood it better than he. Gloomily, the aged scientist tore himself away from his beloved mathematics to resume his activity as a military engineer, in the fear that his engines might be only too sorely needed.

To lose no time in implementing his Carthaginian alliance,

the King marched at the head of his armies to reduce those cities which were held by Roman garrisons; unfortunately for himself, he also lost no time in demonstrating to his troops that he was rash, imprudent, and overbearing, with the result that disaffection soon made its appearance; as much to avert disaster through his ill-advised leadership as to be free of his capricious severity, some of his troops assassinated him as he marched into Leontini.

The Roman faction at once made common cause with the conspirators. Archimedes, despite his distaste for politics, would have associated himself with them, but was revolted by the savagery with which they murdered the head of the Carthaginian party and all of the women of the royal house. His feeling was general, and the chance to reverse the flow of events was lost. Hippocrates and Epicydes, the two agents of Hannibal, were elected generals; the public temper was further inflamed when Appius Claudius, his fleet reinforced to a hundred Roman sail, rowed provocatively past the Syracusan harbor, and the news of the arrival of a Punic fleet off the southern point of Sicily naturally strengthened the inclination of the mob for a break with Rome. Archimedes set himself more grimly to work on the walls.

My ship was loaded with wheat for New Carthage in Spain. Shortly before departure, I received a visit by Saul ben Menassa and one Apameios, a functionary of the court.

After greeting me, Saul spoke very briefly. "I am here for only two purposes — to vouch to each of you for the reliability of the other. What this is about, I do not know, nor do I wish to." With these mysterious words, he took his leave.

"I have come to you," my other visitor began, "Because you have a reputation for resourcefulness and daring. The government wishes to enter into talks with Hannibal. I am here to request your aid."

"I must tell you frankly that I do not approve of this rapprochement."

"We know. But approving or no, will you serve your city as she requires?"

I sighed. "Yes."

"This will be dangerous."

"The answer is still yes."

"Good. You will take your cargo, not to Spain, but to Tarentum in Italy. Almost immediately thereafter, you will find it necessary to seek the shore. Have you ever been to the temple of the Lacinian Juno?"

"I have been to Croton."

"You know something about the cove, then. You will beach your ship there for repairs. Two men will approach you, and commiserate with you upon the misadventure. You will say, 'She was caulked with the best Macedonian pitch.' The answer will be, 'There should have been some northern linen to give it body.' You will reply, 'Why not wool?' as though in jest. When one of the strangers thereupon asks whether you need a couple of rowers, you will engage them, and bring them to Syracuse. Will you do that?"

Of course, I had committed myself in advance. If I refused, it would be unsafe for them to let me go free. Equally of course, I did not feel at liberty to refuse.

Before leaving, I paid my respects to Archimedes; he had always been my friend, and had never knowingly done me an injury. I even saw Claudia, in his presence, with a mixture of delight and anguish.

On the voyage, as I was studying the sailing directions for Croton and for the haven under Cape Lacinium, I called to my boatswain, "Take a look at the halliard. I thought I saw some chafe."

He reported that he could find none.

On the last night of the voyage, while the moon was down, I expressed dissatisfaction with the set of the mast slings. A couple of sleepy men of the watch lowered sail while I busied myself with the gear. What I was doing was working in the darkness with a rough stone at the bight of the halliard on the sling of the yard.

We entered harbor under sail. With the wind just forward of the beam we were passing rocks close aboard. I was at the helm.

"That halliard is too slack!" I called. "Sway it up!"

Two men threw their weight on it.

"Get the lead out!" I roared. "Look alive!"

Another joined them.

"Boatswain, kick some life into those damned sleepers!"

The halliard parted; the yard and sail fell.

"Oars! Get the oars out!" I screamed.

Too late. We drifted upon the rocks.

"Too bad, captain," said the harbor master a little later. "What caused it?"

"Halliard parted," I told him.

"Maybe a disgruntled seaman cut it," he suggested. "I've known that to happen."

"No — see? It's worn. I told my boatswain only yesterday to renew it in harbor."

"How badly do you think you've damaged your hull? There's a pretty good shipyard here."

"Oh, I don't think there's much damage. I'll wait and see."

They were of course very glad of my wheat. We unloaded and started home in ballast. Outside of the harbor, I went below and opened the seaplug for a few minutes.

"I think we've strained her after all," I said to my mate. "She's making a little water."

He verified it.

By the time we had passed Cape Lacinium the situation demanded attention. We put in at the temple of the Lacinian Juno and beached her. Sure enough, I found an area where the caulking had been displaced.

The time was not wholly lost. I was able to engage a couple of seamen.

This is how Hannibal's emissaries came to Syracuse. The half Carthaginian, half Greek pair were called Epicydes and Hippocrates. They were made generals in our army.

The news I received on my return was grave. Our troops had stormed a small Roman outpost and killed its defenders. The Roman consul Marcellus had pronounced this an act of war (as of course it was) and had demanded the expulsion of the two

Carthaginian generals from Sicily. Clearly, Syracuse would refuse.

The bronze foundries of Syracuse had a rapacious appetite for copper. Storm clouds were lowering over the city, which had now, incidentally, become at least nominally a republic. I was asked to risk a winter voyage to Cyprus; by the next summer the harbor might be blockaded. I consented, with much trepidation. The crew agreed to sail on promise of a generous bonus.

The run east to Cyprus would under ordinary occasions have been considered unpromising at this late date; we made a rapid passage on the prevailing westerlies, however, a bit rough though it was.

While we were loading, three of the crew deserted. I had rather expected some losses, and had signed on a large complement; nevertheless, I set about trying to replace them, and was able to engage two seamen of Smyrna.

I was very cautious on the homeward voyage. We made harbor for the night whenever possible, as it frequently was. Whenever the wind was unfavorable, even if light, I remained in harbor; I wanted rapid passages, and a crew unwearied by fighting to windward with the oars. It should be needless to say that any indication of the approach of bad weather likewise kept me harbor bound.

It was a boisterous passage nevertheless. I took advantage of a southerly slant to run for a day and a night across open sea to the Kalidonia Islands, close to the shore of Pisidia, and then worked westward along the Lycian coast to Rhodes. We put in next at Khalkia Island, then at Karpathos, and rode out a north-westerly blow for a day at the Kaso Islets.

There was of course no difficulty in finding nightly shelter on the northern coast of Crete. The Cretans have always been one of the wildest, most primitive peoples of Hellas; I slept with one eye open, ready to cut the anchor cable and flee on the approach of thieves. Rhodian cruisers keep the high seas pretty well clear of pirates in this part of the world, but no naval establishment can prevent cutting-out parties from infesting the coasts.

It was in broad daylight, however, that the peril came. We

were approaching the Cretan Khersonese when a dark, sausage-shaped cloud appeared to the south. We knew what that betided, and so, although it was still the forenoon, we turned to put into the capacious harbor of Aptera, and lowered sail.

When I ordered the men to begin rowing, some god put it into my mind not to lower the mast. As we closed the shore, two light boats, crowded with men, put out toward us. It required no more to tell us that these were the dreaded Cretan freebooters. We put about in frantic haste, drew in the oars, hoisted sail and made for the open sea.

It was largely against such an emergency that I had always preferred hired men to slaves in my ships. In the true round-ship, of course, it made no difference; the ships were too slow to flee, and the crew of a pure sailing vessel too small to fight. But a kerkouros was faster, and carried a full complement of free oarsmen and sailors, who would take any risk to avoid capture and enslavement. So my men, poor archers though they were, harassed the approaching rowers enough to make men miss the beat and occasionally need replacement on account of wounds; as the range closed, javelins were cast with some effect, and then long spears were brought into play.

It could of course have had only one ending. We were hopelessly outnumbered. But the rising southeast wind and the growing waves with their lengthening fetch from shore were endangering more and more the fragile craft that pursued us. They decided that they had had enough. Defeated by the weather, rather than by us, they broke off the attack and made for shore.

In summer we should have fared worse. But this was past the season when merchantmen might be expected, and neither the larger, more seaworthy boats nor, probably, a full complement of men was available.

In a rising wind and sea, then, we doubled the cape. We should have been glad of the imperfect shelter of one of the harbors on its western side, but could not work to windward. There was nothing for it but to run.

All night we ran to the north. A westward course would naturally have suited me better, but on a dark night I could not be sure of steering safely through the channel between Mount Tityrus, which with its out-reaching cape marks the northeasternmost point of Crete, and the island of Anticythera to the north of it. We towed drags, to keep our stern into the wind and prevent broaching to (we hoped), as well as to slow our progress lest we run onto one of the outlying islets of the Cyclades. The ship tossed, rolled, and pitched. Although she flew only a rag of sail to give steerageway, the sheets and braces were lance-stiff. The wind howled eerily through them and the shrouds; the ship creaked and groaned at the straining of her timbers and fastenings. The steersmen toiled mightily.

She took on water, and there was continuous labor with the bailing buckets. A deputation of the crew approached me around midnight.

"Sir," said one, "she's making water as fast as we can bail. We ask you to jettison the cargo."

"We're not in that bad a way yet," I replied. "She's holding her own bravely. We'll make port with her."

At dawn they came again. Daylight with the sight of the size of the seas was even more terrifying than darkness. "Captain, we'll never make port alive. The cargo will be lost in any case; we want to save our lives. The water is gaining on the bailers."

I was still not willing. "We're not lost yet, by any means," I told them. "The gale may soon moderate, or we may make some harbor by nightfall. Syracuse desperately needs this copper for bronze weapons, in addition to iron. You knew when you joined that this was to be a winter voyage. I call on the Syracusans among you" — about half my crew were fellow-countrymen —"to stand firm. You are fighting for your city, just as though you carried a spear and shield. Would you surrender at the first sight of danger?"

I was not nearly so confident as I hoped I sounded. Because I too was afraid. Despite my deep unhappiness over Claudia, I found that I was far from ready to take danger lightly. As more than once before, I asked myself what strange quirk drove me again and again onto the bitter sea, knowing that I would find discomfort becoming misery, worry, loneliness, fear, and perhaps worse?

About an hour later it was mutiny. The two rascals from Smyrna, I believe, were the ringleaders. The mate had given a man an order; the man gave him some lip; as the mate hauled off, one of the two standing behind him swung a large fid and the mate went down. In a moment the deck was a profusion of knives and clubs.

Fighting is never a parlor game, but on this wet, reeling deck it was nightmarish. You would try for a blow, but stand by helplessly; then as the ship rolled or pitched the other way, you would overshoot the mark. You would see a man being killed and be unable to move to his assistance until too late. You would slip and strike the wrong man!

I saw the mate get up again, hold his head for a brief moment, then join in the fighting. At that moment, I got a knife in the chest, and went down and out of the fight.

The mate and the loyal hands gained the day. The mutineers, knowing what fate awaited them ashore, fought till they were all cut down.

By afternoon the hold was half full of water. But the weather was moderating, and there was high land to port. The mate took the ship into the land-locked harbor of Hierax in Laconia. By this time I was in a desperate way. He engaged a coaster to take me across the Bay of Argolis and so to Epidauros, where if anywhere I could be healed.

I was, obviously. And the mate repaired and refitted the ship. Lastly, he engaged men to replace those who were no longer with us.

By this time the winter was at an end. We put to sea again, rounded Cape Malea and stood westward across the open sea for Sicily. Twice we lay for days to a sea-anchor while the westerlies blew. After twelve days we raised the Promontory of Hercules at the tip of Italy and turned southward, hoping that we had not been seen.

We had not. But as we pulled toward our harbor entrance, a blockading Roman fleet moved to intercept us!

They were men-of-war — faster than we. And to fight would be equally useless.

I had not gone through so much to lose my cargo — and ship — and probably freedom — at the last. Desperately I racked my brains. I remembered my strategem at Toryne. But I could not fake burning ships here.

But why fake it? My ship was lost, in any case. Syracuse should have her precious cargo.

The wind was westerly and gentle. I sent all personnel forward, to double-man the bow half of the oars. I poured some oil on clothing aft and deliberately set my ship afire.

The flames leaped up. The approaching Romans sheered off in consternation, as well they might. But since the wind blew the flames over the stern, my men in the bow could still row. We steered with the sculls themselves.

Under the eyes of the frustrated Romans, we entered the harbor, beached the ship, and made our escape ashore. When the fire burned out, the precious copper was recovered.

This was the most difficult voyage of my life. I found myself briefly the hero of Syracuse. The generals awarded me a laurel wreath and a handsome bonus; nor were the mate and the loyal seamen forgotten. The actor and dramatist Lallos composed a panegyric in my honor, which he sang in the theatre.

All who have ever loved will know that during all my adventures and difficulties, there had not been a day on which I did not dream achingly of Claudia. And now in my glory, most deeply felt was the bittersweet of the warmth in her eyes when she came with Archimedes to congratulate me.

XVI

Extract from the Correspondence of Marcus Claudius Marcellus

Marcus Claudius to Appius Claudius. At Ostia, on the 3rd day before the Kalends of May, in the Year after the founding of the City the 537th.

One important lesson Hannibal has already taught me.

Our horse cannot stand up to his. The Numidians are the finest cavalry that the world has seen since the army of Alexander of Macedon.

Let no praetor risk his mounted troops in open field against the enemy. They should be restricted to pursuit or to fighting infantry who have lost formation.

The Numidian training and tactics should be very carefully studied and imitated.

Caius Flavius to Marcus Claudius. At Rome, on the 2nd day before the Nones of August, in the Year after the founding of the City the 537th.

There has been a great battle at Cannae. We have lost 50,000 men, the enemy scarcely a seventh of that figure. The consul Lucius Aemilius Paullus has fallen. Not a family in Rome but mourns its dead.

To public disasters in the field are added those at home. Two of the Vestal Virgins have violated their vows of chastity. Floronia's lover, Lucius Cantilius, was publicly beaten to death by the Pontifex Maximus; Opimia's is unknown. The one girl was buried alive, as the law prescribes. The other killed herself.

Representatives of some of our troops who surrendered have come by Hannibal's permission to seek ransom. The Senate has refused it.

A slave gave information on the presence of an agent of Carthage in the city; and a cabal among others of the slaves. He was given his freedom and a generous reward. Twenty-five of the guilty were crucified; the hands of the Carthaginian were cut off, and he was driven away.

May the gods save Rome!

I learned with joy of your election to the consulate for the third time. Between you and your colleague, Quintus Fabius Maximus, Rome should finally be able to reverse her ill fortune in the war. You have been able to win victories over Hannibal. You or Fabius will have to win them here.

For Syracuse, and with her much of Sicily, is defecting to the Punic cause. The young king's uncles managed to eliminate from his regency cabinet all friends of Rome. Hannibal sent two half Greek, half Carthaginian agents, Hippocrates and Epicydes, who persuaded the regency to rebuff the Roman envoys. I am informed that Hieronymos concluded an alliance with Carthage, the price being the whole of Sicily. He was a fool — even if Carthage wins, she'll never keep her word. He has since been assassinated, and Hannibal's envoys control the city.

I have of course kept the Senate informed of developments. No doubt much of this is known to you.

I hope that you or Fabius will be sent here with a consular army. Nothing less will avert disaster.

If you are well, then so am I.

Marcus Claudius, Consul, to all praetors, prefects, and tribunes of the first class in the consular army. At Rome, on the 4th day before the Ides of October, in the Year after the founding of the City the 539th.

Advice to Officers Exercising Command

The unprecedented extent of the present day theatre of war, and the accompanying magnitude of our operations, make advisable a reconsideration of many of the principles of command in their new setting.

Echelons of Command.

It is axiomatic that in any military organization the chain of authority is well defined, and clearly understood by all concerned. Neither of these conditions can any longer be assumed. The writer has seen a situation in which three opposite numbers in their respective interlocking commands had each a separate false idea of the command relationships. Every officer therefore must make certain not only that he understands the chain of authority, but also that those with whom he may have to deal have the same understanding.

Geography of Command.

Our sea is vast, the lands about it even more so. Size and irregularity of contour induce brevities of expression; an area or island command may include dependent areas which are not ordinarily thought of as appanages of the primary territories. A newly assigned officer cannot expect his commander to take time to brief him on such details. He must investigate the spatial limits of his responsibilities for himself.

Relationships.

The ultimate reason for the existence of every officer is to facilitate the work of the common soldier; his true responsibility is to this man. It may therefore become necessary for him to fight for his ideas against those even of higher rank. This is unpleasant, but must be done, despite the risk of incurring resentment and prejudicing the possibility of working harmoniously in the future. Naturally, utmost tact is to be used. Circumstances arise in which one can receive — or give — the most unexpected aid, even otherwise than on the field. This sort of interchange is less likely in the absence of liking, or at least good will.

Information.

The basis of all action is information. It cannot be too strongly emphasized that all material presented as factual must be checked and rechecked and cross-checked; and this applies not only to intelligence of the enemy, but almost equally to data from friendly forces, and even one's own. The amount of misinformation which is passed around is all but incredible, and the prudent officer, cynical as it sounds, must early learn never to believe anybody about anything. The difficulty, of course, is not deliberate lying. But one must be on guard against half-conscious slanting or emphasis of facts in the direction of the informant's honest opinion as to what ought to be done; his own wrong belief about facts; his ignorance and desire to conceal it; his misunderstanding of what seems to be the plainest of questions; his opinion as to what the questioner should have meant to ask, and answer according thereto; his assumption of partial knowledge on the questioner's part, and submission of the additional information only; and last, but strangely by no means least, the lack of mastery of his own language, a widespread phenomenon, which makes it impossible for some persons to make an intelligible and unequivocal statement. GET THE FACTS!

Personnel and Materiel.

The wise officer will be aware of far more than is called for in the organizational plan. If there is some cut lumber, for instance, in his territory, he will be aware of its quantity and character; if there are men, in the service or out of it, who possess special skills, especially as artificers, he will be aware of their names, reputation, and availability.

In military as in civilian life, there are the play-it-safe and the stick-your-neck-out schools. This consul adheres to the latter.

The Senate and the Roman People to Marcus Claudius Marcellus. At Rome, on the 12th day before the Kalends of September, in the Year after the founding of the City the 539th.

It is our wish that you repair immediately to Sicily as commander in chief.

You will take with you the Twelfth Legion.

You will seek out and destroy all armies that may take the field against Rome. You will reduce all cities that declare for Carthage or that assist her.

You will completely pacify Sicily.

XVII

Extract from the Notes of the Comedian Lallos

I have been working on a satire to be called "Antaeus". When, in his fight with Herakles, Antaeus lost contact with his mother Earth, he lost his strength and was overpowered. The present day Antaeus, Hannibal, without contact with his mother land Carthage seems on the contrary to grow stronger. Only Marcus Claudius has had any success in the field against the Carthaginian invader, and this has not been such as even to begin to compensate for the enormous Roman losses. This year Rome has suffered a further disaster, in Gaul; the Boii have destroyed a consular army of 25,000 men, two legions and their allies.

Only in Spain has fortune favored Rome and her arms.

The progress of the war and the changing sympathies in Syracuse encourage me to think that the play might be well received.

At the beginning of the winter, Claudia gave birth to Archimedes' son. The old man is said to be beside himself with happiness and love. It would appear that her ship has finally found haven. He will certainly make provision for her. I have seen the child; it is a fine looking baby, and is growing nicely.

My dramatist's instinct had told me that there was more to the sudden severance of business relations between Archimedes and Pyrrhon than met the eye; and when I asked her point blank Claudia made no bones about it.

Archimedes alone understood nothing of the drama that had played under his nose, and Claudia's loyalty to him has of course been reinforced by her maternity. At the same time she has been genuinely distressed at being the cause of unhappiness to Pyrrhon, whom she liked well enough. More than well enough now, in fact; because for the first time in her life, here is a relatively young man whose romantic interest in her has not been a selfish one, and who has been moved to change the entire pattern of his life because of her. He is futhermore twelve years her senior, old enough to escape her unhappy associations with youthful lovers, and to qualify in part for the paternal role that apparently she now finds so essential.

Nor is that all. Here I am guessing. After a period of abstinence, Claudia was reintroduced by Archimedes to the role of man as male. She is now thirty-five — in the full bloom and vigor of womanhood. Her lover on the other hand is a man of seventy-one, and the flicker of sensuality has been largely spent. No, this is not wholly a surmise; a man who concerns himself primarily with the emotions of men and women can usually look at a couple and make a pretty shrewd guess at the character of their relations. And so I have a strong suspicion that there are times when our Claudia rests uneasily in her bed.

The question of the attitude of Syracuse in the war between Rome and Carthage seemed several times to have been decided, only to be reopened. There were intrigues, fighting, debates, and a continuation of the negotiations with the Roman consul. In the midst of these, in the spring of the year, the Romans took Leontini. They behaved, as they claim, with considerable restraint; according to other reports there was a massacre. I have not yet heard convincing evidence either way. Certain it is that two thousand Roman deserters who were captured in the city were scourged in the Roman fashion; that is to say, the legionaries armed themselves with clubs and stones and fell upon the doomed men and beat them — most of them to death. All, living and dead, were then beheaded.

Our two generals propagated a report that the Romans had subjected Leontini to all the horrors of sack and massacre, with the inference that the fate of Syracuse would be even worse. The vilest elements of the mob at once launched upon a mass hunt for all who were known to be sympathetic to Rome or even suspected of such sympathy. The unfortunate victims were despatched without mercy.

Livia was at her door when a man, streaming blood, turned a corner, dashed along the street and fell exhausted at her doorstep. His appearance and the shouts of the approaching mob told her what was afoot. Without reflecting, she dragged the fugitive within doors and returned to her former station, and the mob found her staring down the street as though after some fugitive; and indeed when questioned she gave them that sort of answer.

"Who are you?" she asked him while dressing his hurts. He was a well developed man, with poor clothing but no air of poverty, and like herself of middle age.

"A Roman."

"I see." A pause. "I'll fix you up and keep you till dark; then you'd better leave town and seek shelter with your countrymen."

It was his turn to pause. "I can't. They'll kill me, and not quickly."

"Why?"

"You might as well know. I'm a deserter. Two years ago, while in the army, I was in desperate need — it doesn't matter any more why — and I stole. I was caught. A thief in the army is scourged in Roman fashion. Do you know what that is?" She nodded. "Now I daren't show my face among Romans, nor, it seems, among Syracusans." Then, bitterly, "A few more months, and I should have been out of the army."

"You might settle in some small town."

"The Romans will be all through Sicily."

"It is unlikely that the ones who see you will know you."

"They will. I was in the Twelfth Legion. I had been decorated for valor — everyone saw me, and will recognize me."

"Another walled city."

"The Romans will take every city in Sicily. Including this one, if it decides on war." Another pause. "My only chance is to take ship to some place far away."

She looked at him pityingly. "Today a Roman fleet set up a blockade of the harbor."

His shoulders slumped in despair.

"Don't give up hope. There are always ships that run blockades. For the time being, you can hide here. Then we'll see what can be done."

"Would you help me, a thief and a Roman?"

"I am, or was, a Roman too. And it ill befits me to look with contempt upon a thief."

"Who are you?"

She told him.

It was months before the opportunity came. By day he remained indoors, only venturing out (against her remonstrances, of course) at night for change and exercise. He saw no woman but her, and she, though her charges had long since died, likewise went abroad but little. They found consolation in their common lowliness — the thief took pity on the harlot, as she on him. Because of his crime, he was alone in the world. Because of the war, her son-in-law's business had vanished, and he had departed with his wife for Rhodes. If all went well with him, Livia was to follow, but for the time being, she too was alone.

He was forty-six years old; she was fifty, but her still surviving beauty took years from her age. So these two, each of them an outcast in both Rome and Syracuse, found comfort in one another, while war raged over their heads (for war by now it was, with the Romans at the city walls). And of each the pitiful, broken pride in self began to mend and bloom again in the warmth of the regard of the other; and each looked on the other and saw worth and dignity once more. So, at least, I believe.

What I know is that Livia inquired of Oppia whether I might know of any projected sailing. As it happened, I did. A successful actor and dramatist has many ears. I learned that the generals found it necessary to send a message to Carthage, and I learned before the messenger did who was to carry it.

They tapped Pyrrhon for the mission.

At Oppia's request I arranged an interview between Livia's Roman and Pyrrhon. The latter agreed to enroll the fugitive, ostensibly as a member of his crew.

"I can carry you to Carthage," he said. "Do you speak Phoenician?"

"No. And in any case, only a Roman who will fight for Carthage will be welcome in Carthage now. A criminal I am. A traitor I am not."

"There is traffic between Carthage and Greece," Pyrrhon suggested. "You could work your way in a ship. I have a commercial representative in Athens. Go there. I'll give you a letter to him.

He will find work for you. You'd better take a Greek name, and call yourself a Greek."

"With my Roman accent?"

"Say that you were born of a Roman mother," Livia suggested. "Take the name 'Skopas'."

"Then it's all settled," Pyrrhon said as he rose.

"Not quite all. Will there be room for Livia too in your ship?" He turned to her. "There is nothing to keep you in Syracuse. I want you with me — for the rest of my life. What that life will be, and what I can offer you, I do not know. Will you come?"

"I have a daughter. Might we possibly go to Rhodes?"

"Why not?"

There was a look of happiness in her face. "Whatever my life with you may be, it will be better than being known as a former harlot. I will come with joy."

"Wait a bit," warned Pyrrhon. "A man can sleep in a Carthaginian field, and go anywhere and do anything for food while he waits for a ship to Greece, and then he can work his passage, as I said before. A woman can do none of these things."

Oppia stripped off bracelets, earrings, and pendant. "May I?" I nodded. "These are not cheap. They will keep Livia while she waits with you in Carthage."

"And I have saved enough out of what the son of my former master has given me to pay for my passage," Livia said. She fell into Oppia's arms and sobbed her gratitude.

And so it was arranged, and so it befell.

Of course Pyrrhon might have been letting himself in for some trouble, carrying passengers on an official trip. So Claudia remarked when she heard about it. She said no more, but her eyes shone.

I forbore to tell her that she was rarely distinguished in having two such men in love with her. I was sure she knew it.

It must be admitted that the Roman consul Marcellus made every effort to induce the rulers of Syracuse to return to the Roman alliance and avert hostilities; Rome had difficulties enough already. But in vain. He invested the city, therefore, with his army.

223

I might describe the shape of the city of Syracuse for Thesetidion or some other foreigner. The city is situated on a broad, blunt peninsula measuring some twenty-two stadia or three Roman miles wide. At its southernmost point is the island Ortygia, one fourth as long, connected by a very short bridge with the mainland, and within the city wall. Sheltered by this is the Great Harbor. From Ortygia the massive, century-old wall of Dionysios extends northward along the coast, then westward and inland along the high ground for some thirty stadia or four Roman miles, and then back to the Great Harbor on the southwest side of the city. To the north is a more open harbor. The important Hexapylon gate is in the north wall. The Fortress Euryalos is the inland anchor of defense. With its height, its back-up walls, its complex of tunnels, passages, and storehouses, it is the greatest piece of military engineering in the world.

I was very glad that my daughter was at Akragas. Claudia's son was still a babe; mine too was much too young to man the walls, to his disgust and his mother's delight. Terentia's son and family were in the countryside, and Livia's, as I mentioned above, had recently departed for Rhodes.

Many of us were very apprehensive about the course that the state had taken. While the mass of the people were for Carthage, the better educated among the townsmen had a much more vivid picture of Roman might. Despite Hannibal's successes in Italy, we feared that the Republic had still vast powers of recuperation and would be a tough, relentless antagonist. Anyway, the prospect of a victorious Carthage dominant in Sicily was not one in which to rejoice.

For the time being, however, the mass of the people appeared to have no misgivings. The generals were cheered whenever they appeared, and accounts of Hannibal's victories were on every tongue. Bets were even being placed on the date on which the Romans would sue for peace.

When the decision for war had become irrevocable, there was a spirit of gloom among the Gamoroi. The commoners, as noted above, at first exulted. But when the tramp of the legions was heard, and the Roman camp was established in full view of the city, and when the gleaming front of the maniples drew up against the walls, and above all when huge siege engines took shape, it was the turn of the man in the street to panic, whereas the Gamoroi became more resolute and calm in the face of the peril they had tried in vain to avoid. The great temple of Zeus Olympios south of the city and the temple of Athene on Ortygia were thronged with suppliants, and their altars sent incessant columns of smoke to the sky.

As I have indicated, my erstwhile friend, Archias, had gone from bad to worse; now he added blackmail to his sins.

He presented himself at the offices of the Carthaginian masters of the city to denounce the son of Xenocrates, long since grown to manhood, for a serious violation of the food regulations. As witness he named Julia, once the nursemaid of the orphans, now a middle-aged retainer in the household. She was arrested, examined, and ordered to the torture for further questioning.

What happened was exactly as Archias had planned. Rather than see their beloved old nurse tormented, the children of Xenocrates would have paid still more than the considerable fine which was the penalty of the alleged offense. I am certain that the charge was false, but the fine was paid, Julia was saved from the horror, and Archias pocketed the informer's fee.

XVIII

Extract from Pyrrhon's Voyages

In anticipation of a prolonged siege, the generals wished to arrange for seaborne supplies from Carthage. I was selected to carry the letter.

We controlled part of the waterfront within the harbor. Ships of various types were available. I considered a merchantman, in which I could run past the Roman fleet when it was beached for a storm, as I had done before, but there would be the problem of getting back in again — after a long traverse across open sea, one cannot pick one's weather. I decided to rely on speed and my detailed knowledge, from boyhood up, of the local waters.

Accordingly, I selected a quinquereme of the type that has five banks of oars, with two men on each oar of the upper two banks. That gives seven rowers for each three feet of the ship's length; the shorter, lower three oars being pulled by one man each, he sits at the point of maximal effectiveness; the longer upper oars, pulled by two men apiece, permit each man to sit only half a man's width away from that point. Given a smooth sea, and a crew of strong, superbly trained rowers, such a ship can show her heels to anything afloat.

The drawbacks are that in a seaway five banks of oars are unmanageable and poor oarsmen are certain to foul one another. Well, I could choose my weather for departure — on very many days there is at least a short period of calm — and with most of our shipping idle, I had my pick of the finest oarsmen in Syracuse.

For all-weather purposes, under ordinary circumstances, I would pick a ship with all rowers pulling on one bank of oars; in which case a smaller number of expert rowers, only one to an oar if necessary, could give the beat to their less skilled companions. But, as stated, there was now no dearth of fine oarsmen, and in general fighting is done only in fine weather. There are of course exceptions.

As a compromise ship for most conditions, I would pick a three- or four-banker with one man each on the oars of the two lower tiers, and two on each of the oars above them.

Both further to increase my speed and to reduce my draft, I set out with almost no ballast and a minimum of supplies; in smooth water I could dispense with ballast, and a fast ship consumes only a small amount of food and water. On the other hand, I had to carry the usual mast, yard, and sail, as the Romans, who were not going anywhere, did not.

I closed my house once more, bought wine and a few delicacies for my own table, made a handsome present to the woman who had tried unsuccessfully to distract me, and went on board.

When, at the chosen time, I made for open sea, the Romans massed to oppose my passage. With my local knowledge and my abnormally shallow draft, I emerged from the shallows where they did not expect me and did not dare venture; and when they realized what was up and attempted to close, my rowers, pulling a beautiful stroke, easily left them astern.

Down the coast, we beached and took on some rock for ballast.

Now came our greatest danger. Cape Pachynum and environs were, we knew, in Roman hands, so we had to give it a wide berth. That meant at least four days of blue-water sailing, given exceptionally favorable conditions. We dared not touch at the islands of Melita or Kossura for fear of encountering a Roman fleet. And this type of ship is ill adapted to dirty weather.

Aeolus and Poseidon treated us not too well, nor too badly either.

We soon felt the customary northwest wind of summer, and ran easily southward, keeping the mountains of the island within view, but not closing the shore lest we be seen. Once south of Cape Pachynum, however, we found the westerly no longer our friend. We pulled against it when it was light, and lay to a sea anchor when it blew more strongly. It did not approach gale force, thanks perhaps to the bull that I had vowed to Poseidon.

We had two days of calm, the gods be thanked! During this time I drove the rowers to the limit of their strength; they rowed in shifts, a third of the crew at a time. The lower banks of oars were almost impossible to manage in a sea, and we did not use them. There is an easterly current in the strait between Sicily and Africa, and in the calm I hugged the large island as closely as I dared, especially at night, to get the benefit of a slight countercurrent that is sometimes found along the shore. With the return of the west wind, we stood further out.

Once the agitation of the sea led me to use the lead, and I

found bottom at six fathoms (there are several shoals in these waters, not dangerous in most weathers). We hove the anchor, dropped astern on a long cable to a slight lee offered by the bank, and lay so for a night.

A southeaster, blowing a little harder than I liked, gave the rowers a day and a half of rest.

After eight days at sea we made our port. I set my passengers ashore, went into the city and delivered my letter.

The return voyage, with the answer of the Carthaginian Suffetes, was easier. It was all downwind to Cape Pachynum, and then with wind abeam we reached northward along the coast. I re-entered the harbor as I had left it, to the chagrin of the Romans. The invaders lived largely off the rich Sicilian fields, so there were no massive grain convoys to intercept.

Nevertheless I was sent out to raid Roman supply lines and other shipping. I found some lone merchantmen and sent them to the bottom. Once I ran into a Roman war squadron, but with my large crew of crack rowers had no difficulty in leaving it astern.

My most notable achievement on this cruise was raising havoc off Mylae with a convoy of fourteen roundships escorted by two Roman quinqueremes. One galley I would have tried to ram, trusting in my fighters to hold off the Roman marines until their ship should have sunk under them; but since there was a second, she would come to the aid of the first, and between them I might be overwhelmed.

Instead, I made a feint at the foremost merchantman, and as the men-of-war came up I changed course and maneuvered about them, relying on my greater speed to avoid contact, until I inveigled them into a position in which the three of us were on a collision course, myself in the middle. At the last moment, I struck a loud gong. My men stopped rowing, stepped right over their oars, and at a second sound of the gong pulled hard on the reverse course.

My ship stopped almost as though she had rammed a mole, then made rapid way astern even as each Roman captain ordered his helm over in triumph, to close and board.

They saw the trick too late. One Roman rammed the other; before he could work clear I had reversed again, rammed him, and backed off in the confusion. Both ships sank.

It was, of course, a chancy maneuver. I might have been caught in a mouse trap of my own making. Had they been Greeks I should never have risked it. But the Romans, although they understand sea power, do not understand ships. Conversely, the Carthaginians understand ships but not sea power. But you cannot fight a war and be safe.

After that I raged through the scattered merchant fleet like a wolf in a sheepfold. Some of course escaped.

When we slipped into Syracuse in the fall, I became the idol of the city — second only to Archimedes. As far as I was concerned, the war was a pathway to adventure and honor. But I would gladly have given up all that, could I have been assured of the eventual safety of Claudia.

Nor was I uneasy on her account alone. Like the Gamoroi, with whom, landless though I was, I felt myself akin, I had a realistic idea of the resources and tenacity of Rome; I was by no means certain that for all his genius and devotion Hannibal would bring her stubborn citizens to their knees, and even if eventually he did so, it might well be too late to save his allies.

There are those who are skeptical when someone has told them about my adventures. They claim that only superhuman courage, skill, and luck could account for them. Of courage, to speak plainly, I suppose that I have my share; although I am frank to admit that I have known more than a few men who were braver than I. And I pride myself on my competency in my trade, although in this of course I am far from unique. As to the luck, it is quite true that Tyche has favored me.

Seamen who are lacking in courage have no exploits to write of. There are of course many men who are willing to take the ordinary risks of the seafarer's life — and they are great enough — but do not go looking for trouble. Nor do I blame them. Courage is in part a matter of circumstances. There are many men, I believe, among those who suffer the name of coward, who are simply slow in their thinking and reaction, waste irretrievable time in looking for a safe way out which does not exist, and then are forced willy-nilly into inglorious acts; who, given warning, and time enough to assess the situation, may well have played a hero's role. Besides which, I think that most of us, once in a great while, step out of character, and do things that are unworthy of us, as well as the converse. If this aberration coincides with a crisis, the ordinary man finds himself branded thereafter as a coward, and accepts the designation in his own heart, not realizing what has happened to him. Or, the quite ordinary man suddenly finds himself a hero.

Seamen of no more than average competence may do well enough in the coastal trade, but do not last long enough at blue-water sailing to have much of note happen to them.

Of those who are left, and it should be obvious that they constitute a minority, in the natural order of things there would be many whose luck would give out sooner or later, and the very few who are almost uniformly fortunate.

Unlucky men do not survive to write their memoirs.

XIX

Extract from the Correspondence of
Marcus Claudius Marcellus

Marcus Claudius, Consul, to the Roman Senate. Before Leontini, on the 2nd day before the Kalends of November, in the Year after the founding of the City the 539th.

I have been approached by approximately 1,500 — the number is stated thus indefinitely because more appear daily — of those Romans who fled at the battle of Cannae, and were sent out of Italy in disgrace. They wish to redeem themselves by serving under the eagles again.

It is my opinion that their wish should be granted. It has often happened that men who did not lack courage have nevertheless panicked and fled, sometimes with less excuse than these. I must point out, furthermore, our severe shortage of manpower.

I therefore request authority to enlist these Roman soldiers.

To Marcus Claudius, Consul. At Rome, on the 4th day before the Ides of January, in the Year after the founding of the City the 540th.

Decree of the Senate

The Senate has considered the request of the consul touching the re-enrollment in the legions of the soldiers who fled at Cannae.

It is the opinion of the Senate that Rome does not desire the services of cowards.

The Consul, however, may, if he sees fit, make use of the men in question. Under no circumstances, however, are honors of any sort to be paid them.

It now appears that my letter to you was overly optimistic. The reduction of the fortifications of Syracuse will not be a one-two-three operation.

As I wrote you, we had assumed that it would be no more difficult to take this city by storm that any one of the many others that have succumbed to Roman arms. Upon investing it, Marcellus made a survey of the walls. So widely extended are the defenses that it seemed there should be no difficulty in carrying them.

The consul determined that the city was most susceptible to an amphibious assault. There is a section of the wall just north of the island Ortygia that runs right along the sea, in an area that is ordinarily protected from waves. Apparently thinking that the sea gave it immunity to attack, the Syracusans did not build their wall as high and strong there as elsewhere. This, the consul resolved, should be their undoing. We spent some twenty days in preparation.

And so, six days ago, we confidently advanced to the assault. Marcellus had constructed a huge platform supported by eight ships. On it was a great tower, with a bridge at the top to reach to the top of the wall. In it were picked men to seize and hold the wall while their fellows followed in sufficient numbers to overwhelm the defenders at that point and descend and force a gate. Behind this were ships carrying small pieces of artillery, archers, slingers, and javelin men — the last equipped with the new type of javelin that cannot be hurled without practice, so that the enemy cannot throw it back at us again. Their function of course was to clear the wall of defenders.

To our amazement, there were no — or almost no — defenders to clear. But long before we were within our range, or any range, as we thought, from over the wall came rocks — and such rocks! More than half the weight of a man in armor! — flying through the air. When they struck, men went down; but of course we had expected casualties. What we had not expected was artillery that could demolish our huge siege engine at a distance.

But missiles came crashing down upon it, and ladder and platform were battered into shapeless ruin. And before we were able to reverse and get everything out of there, the rocks were breaking through into the hulls, and it was all we could do, with luck and nerve, to get the eight galleys back to safety — one of them completely ruined, two in need of extensive repairs. The miserable condition of their crews you can imagine. It was a crushing defeat. And not a single Syracusan paid with his life!

The state of gloom in the camp you can imagine. Never have Roman arms known a more one-sided reverse.

There is only one man who could have accomplished this. One name is cursed on all lips. Archimedes!

Appius Claudius, Praetor, to Marcus Claudius, Consul. Before Syracuse, on the 7th day before the Kalends of July, in the Year after the founding of the City the 540th.

Although you have already been notified concerning the action of yesterday, I send you this preliminary report in writing.

According to your orders, I prepared a general assault against the north wall of Syracuse.

At two places where the wall was on relatively low ground and easier of access, there were gates. We accordingly made ready battering rams with strongly built housings to protect their working parties. These were being moved up into position, accompanied by the storming party and archers and slingers to harass the defenders. This of course was a feint to draw the enemy to these sectors. The real assault was made where the wall ran along the summit of steep slopes. One might expect to find a less concentrated defense in the less accessible area. It seemed that it might be just possible to reach the top of the wall with ladders. Some of these were therefore prepared, and were carried up the slopes with no little difficulty; the bearers were accompanied by a larger number of missile troops than the others, with the main body of heavy infantry behind them.

The feint was a complete failure.

As our storming party reached the walls, large numbers of huge boulders were dropped upon them. Such was the steepness of the slope that the boulders after doing severe execution at that point rolled downhill, crushing the columns of men in a most horrible manner; some soldiers, perhaps the luckier ones, were killed outright, while others had one or both legs, less frequently arms, reduced to bloody jelly, while others again who received a glancing blow on their middles lay moaning with internal injuries. Where the terrain deflected the boulders, and we might have hoped to hold our ground, the foresight of Archimedes (it is said) had pierced the wall for the bolts of the scorpions.

Worse was to follow. The troops on the hill panicked and fled, but in the cases of many this was unavailing. More boulders followed, overtaking and felling the men as they ran; their course was naturally determined by the unevennesses of the ground and was therefore quite unpredictable, so that even if a man saw one approach he did not know which way to turn to dodge it. And even at the foot of the slope their momentum carried the rocks onto the level ground, seeking their prey like things alive, until it was exhausted. I saw a boulder making for a group of soldiers; they separated into two groups, to let it pass harmlessly between them, it struck an outcropping of rock, split in two, and one half of it crushed each knot of men.

Losses were heavy — the tally has not yet been made. Most of the wounded (they could not be recovered until after dark) are not expected to live.

The army is completely demoralized; I have never seen Roman troops so overcome by terror. We will get them over it, of course, but it will take some days.

I recommend that such an assault not be repeated.

Asinius Siro of Neapolis to Publius Lollius. Before Syracuse, on the 4th day before the Nones of July, in the Year after the founding of the City the 540th.

I write to you in sadness about the death of your son and my friend, Quintus, killed in action yesterday. Never in all the history of siege warfare can there have been a siege like this one!

The legion of the Praetor Appius Claudius was defeated some time ago in an attempt to storm the northern wall of Syracuse where, on the ridge, it was low enough for the use of scaling ladders. Yesterday, under the prefect Junius Scipio, the twenty-first was ordered to attack the Hexapylon gate.

Our maniple marched along the road to the gate of the city where the relatively low country gives the road easiest access. We had a covered battering ram, which was drawn along on wheels toward the gate. As we approached it, we looked for the defenders on the wall who were to be picked off by our missiles. To our surprise, there were none to be seen.

Our van was within fifty paces or less when that sector of the city wall exploded into life. Men suddenly began to fall around me. Through embrasures in the wall arrows flew at the foremost men in the column, and almost immediately thereafter slingers and javelin men appeared above and added to the casualties at its head.

Our own slingers and archers tried to counter, but now from other embrasures scorpions sent their bolts into the middle distance, where Quintus and I were placed. They came in great numbers. I saw Flaccus fall, and young Piso, and the Tiberius brothers.

But worse was happening further in the rear. Over the wall huge rocks came flying, cutting deep swathes through the maniple. We were being rapidly decimated — too rapidly for our men to make any effective reply.

In a few minutes there was general flight. As those in front got out of range of the arrows and slung stones and spears, they came under fire of the scorpions; and the bolts cut down man after man. It was horrible! And beyond this point came the

terrible boulders of the ballistae! It was here that the centurion
Licinius, the one we called old "Give-me-another" from his habit
of breaking so many staves over our shoulders, died trying to
stop the flight — still laying about him with his staff. It was
hopeless. There was nothing we could have accomplished.

Quintus was running by my side when one of the last of the
huge boulders hit him. He went down without a sound. I believe
that when he touched the earth he was already dead.

I have wept over him and given him decent burial. He was a
good friend and a brave soldier. The consul Marcellus has been
here and made the rounds of the graves.

We have learned through a deserter that all of these engines
are the works of one man, Archimedes, a mathematician. I
should like to get my hands on him. Marcellus, oddly enough, is
said to admire the fellow, and speaks of him almost affection-
ately.

This siege has become a duel between the two. Only Marcellus
could keep men at such unheard-of combat; only Archimedes
could resist him.

May the gods favor our arms!

I am sending you your son's effects. I am sore at heart, but
your grief, I know, is far greater. May better fortune attend your
younger son!

Gladly, cousin, would I write you a letter that would give you pleasure and encouragement in your troubles. But the news I have is bad.

Your family, to set your mind at rest, are well, and your son accumulates honors in Spain.

In the Senate there has been much dissatisfaction and re-crimination over your last report. That your third sea-borne assault on the city was delayed pending construction of the steeply angled roofs over your ships to deflect falling objects, most of the Senators could understand; although even at this there was some cavilling by the few who are badly disposed toward you — I am sure I need not mention names.

But your description of the monstrous engines of this man Archimedes challenges belief. You write of "Huge iron jaws which, let down from the wall, grasp the bows of the ships and draw them up (I am changing only the tense), spilling out men and equipment into the sea as they do so, until the ships hang vertically, after which they are let drop and either crush them-selves upon the rocks or swamp and sink as they fall into the sea."

There was some speculation as to — forgive me, cousin, but you should know — your sanity, and even as to your truthfulness. Some of us suggested the pointlessness of deception when the truth must necessarily out, but to no purpose. Even your friends, while convinced that you reported truthfully what you thought you saw, incline to the belief that you must be deceived. To believe otherwise would be to assign to this Archimedes a de-gree of genius which would make him one of the greatest men of all time!

All this comes on top of the repeated failures of the siege. Some of the Senators are asking whether you have forgotten how to storm a town in the simple, bold, forthright, old-fashioned Roman manner, sword to sword and spear to shield!

*The Senate and the Roman People to Marcus Claudius. At Rome, on the
10th day before the Kalends of September, in the Year after the founding of
the City the 540th.*

We bid you take note of the tragic losses that Rome has
sustained at the hands of the Carthaginian Hannibal, at the
battles of Lake Trasimenus and Cannae, as well as before and
since. We bid you further consider the great need for manpower
in Italy to continue the struggle, the drain upon our human
resources occasioned by the campaigns in Spain, Sardinia,
Illyria, and elsewhere.

We therefore urge that you delay no longer in storming the city
of Syracuse to release men for service in other theatres of war.
Even if this should necessitate a greater expenditure of lives
than would a long drawn out siege, it would almost certainly be
more economical of them in the long run. Your troops are badly
needed elsewhere.

Marcus Claudius to Lucius Claudius. Before Syracuse, on the 5th day before the Nones of September, in the Year after the founding of the City the 540th.

It is a source of continual amazement to me, cousin, what a wealth of military genius the gods have bestowed upon Rome! I have received all kinds of advice, both officially and otherwise, about the conduct of the siege. It matters not that many of my unsought correspondents have had little experience in war or none. It matters still less that the siege of a great seaport city is the sort of exploit that Rome has seldom undertaken.

I have read all of the pertinent military history that was available to me, as my critics have obviously not. It took the Spartans almost a generation to reduce Athens. Alexander was held up for months at Tyre, and so were we at Lilybaeum. Demetrios, with overwhelming force at his disposal, never did succeed in getting through the walls of Rhodes. Hannibal, the victor of Cannae and Lake Trasimenus, has not yet been able to take Ariminum. Neither Carthage nor Athens was able to capture this city of Syracuse!

If the Senate wishes me to resign my command to someone who in its opinion has more understanding of my trade, I shall gladly do so. If any private citizen has anything really pertinent to say about the taking of Syracuse, I shall listen to him most humbly, and surrender to him the place of honor at the triumph, if there be one. If not, then let those who are ignorant alike of military science and the particular conditions of this siege preserve a becoming silence.

Marcus Claudius to Lucius Claudius. Before Syracuse, on the 4th day before the Kalends of October in the Year after the founding of the City the 540th.

There is one ally, who, if a commander can enlist him on his side, is worth many maniples. I refer to the stupidity of the average soldier.

Five days since, a new assault was being launched against the walls in the Lesser Harbor of Syracuse, when we observed a number of burnished, mirror-like shields being mounted on the battlements.

That much is certain. The rest of the genesis of the catastrophe, after all my cross-examinations and surveys, is conjecture.

Archimedes, as I suppose, was trying to harass our operations by dazzling the eyes of our helmsmen with reflections into them of the rays of the sun. I say Archimedes, so far at least in agreement with the men, because I doubt whether anyone else would have thought of it.

He was eminently successful.

On one ship they had a fire in a large copper pan to melt colored wax for painting exposed bulkheads. This of course should be done ashore, but there was to be an inspection on the next day, and they had had no opportunity to paint for some time. A seaman passing close by was blinded by the mirrors and tripped over a maul lying on the deck. (You may be sure that the man who left it there has been thrashed.) The wax was upset, caught fire, ignited a painted sail into which it flowed, and the ship was ablaze.

Of course everything went wrong. The sand buckets were empty. The smoke blew right into the eye of the helmsman, who veered into the next ship (with a reef close aboard she could not take evasive action), and the accursed mirrors blinded the helmsman of still another ship. One of those perfectly incredible summations of things going wrong. In no time three ships were ablaze.

Now for the truly disastrous aspect. Within minutes panic

swept the fleet. The storming party was convinced that Archimedes had managed to focus the sun's rays on my ships with his mirrors in such intensity as to set them on fire, and there was a general rout.

By the next day the ridiculous story had spread through the whole army. The men were in a state of terror. They looked on this Archimedes as sort of a demigod. He had destroyed a fleet of ships. He had caused the waters of the harbors to burst into flame. A squadron of cavalry had had their clothing set ablaze, and the fire had consumed them completely, horses and all!

Naturally I relieved of his command the captain of the ship on which petty irregularities had set the whole business in motion.

It will be at least a week, maybe longer, before the troops are an army again.

XX

Extract from Heraclides' Life of Archimedes

It had occurred to Archimedes that by the use of a battery of mirrors he might be able to reflect enough of the sun's rays into the eyes of helmsmen of the Roman ships to interfere somewhat with their steering. With this in mind he one day assembled some well burnished shields and had them deployed and directed accordingly.

Before he could determine the effectiveness of this maneuver, something caused a few of the ships to catch fire. There followed a short spell of cloudy weather, so that he could not immediately repeat the experiment.

About a week later a female Roman slave who was busying herself in the council house during a meeting was sent to the kitchen on an errand. While she was there, a coal leaped out of the fire onto her foot. Not unnaturally, it provoked an oath. "Edepol!" she exclaimed.

At once an attendant ripped the chiton from her body. She stood revealed as an adolescent youth. The other dragged his victim before an officer. "A Roman spy!" he exulted.

"Good work!" said his superior. "How did you know?"

"I spent several years in Rome in my youth," replied the attendant. "I know Roman customs pretty well. Only men swear by Pollux. A Roman woman always swears by Castor."

"Well, young man," said the officer grimly to the captive. "I can tell you that you're in for a pretty bad time, unless you can make it worth our while to kill you quickly. You'd better start talking." And talk he did, as a result of which the following conversation took place.

One of the generals, in my presence, told the master of a report that had reached us from the Roman spy. "It seems that the enemy believes that it was your mirrors, Archimedes, which set fire to their ships."

The Master laughed. "Absurd," he said. "I was merely trying to dazzle the helmsmen."

"The story is that you focused together so much of the rays of the sun that the heat was sufficient to ignite the wood. There are further rumors that you caused other blazes in the same way. There is great terror in the Roman fleet and army lest you repeat on a larger scale."

"Utter nonsense."

"Nonsense it may be, but to us it is valuable nonsense. You have at least temporarily demoralized the enemy forces."

The master shrugged. "If that is the case, I will bring my mirrors into play again."

"And disprove the whole business? On the contrary, let them alone, and let the Romans worry. And do not deny the accomplishment in public — a report might reach the Romans through a deserter or a spy. And by the same token, it will be good for the confidence of our people to have them believe that they have such a wonder-worker among them."

In Archimedes' own circle, of course, there was no such credulity. It was at a gathering a few days later that Thyoneios mentioned the report that was running through the town. There was general laughter.

"Tell me, Archimedes," Agamedes asked, "might it be possible actually to perform such a feat?"

"Certainly there is sufficient heat in the sun, and in its rays," the master replied thoughtfully. "The practical problems involved in their utilization are something else again." He pondered the matter for a moment. "I daresay that given a heap of dry wood and tinder, I might be able to set it ablaze from a distance. But to focus even one mirror, and keep it focused for a sufficiently long time, on a moving ship — even a ship at anchor, which responds, however slightly, to every wavelet, and swings continually about her mooring to every slight shift in direction of the breeze, would be excessively difficult. To do this with many mirrors would verge on the impossible."

" 'Verge,' you said?"

"That is what I said, Agamedes. To the scientist, nothing which does not violate natural law is absolutely impossible."

"One could set fire to a forest, perhaps?"

"Undoubtedly, it could be done."

"Or a prairie?"

"I suppose so. If it were dry."

"Could not the heat dry it?"

"I would have to say yes, in theory; which ultimately means yes in practice."

"So that your mirrors could conceivably destroy a hostile army?"

"Conceivably, yes. But many years of experimentation would first be needed. Many lifetimes, more likely — if not centuries. But to determined men, it is only a question of time."

"How about bare rocks and soil?"

"I do not know whether they are combustible even in the greatest heat. If they are, it could be done."

"And you could do it?"

"If I lived through enough lifetimes for the necessary experimentation, yes, I could do it."

"Hail," cried Euphranor, "to the new Phaethon, who builds a sun-chariot with his own genius!"

"He who truly understands the Law of the Lever is gifted with awesome power. He can wax mightier than the Titans," said the master. "He can burrow deep into the earth and tap the fires of Hephaistos. He can ascend Olympus, and snatch and hurl the thunderbolts of Zeus himself." And then Archimedes pronounced the most terrible words ever spoken by man. "Give me whereon I may stand, and I will move the world!"

There was a moment of silence. Familiar as we were with the statement just repeated, it had never before presented itself to us — even, I am sure, to Archimedes — in so dread an aspect. Then Hesychios voiced our thought.

"Master," he said, "you have discovered the ultimate weapon, against which there can be no defense."

The Traveller burst forth. "It would be monstrous to use such a weapon. It would be inhuman!"

Katreus challenged him. "Why so? Because it can kill men? What are our swords and javelins for, if not to kill?"

"But this would kill so many!"

"And do you kill fewer otherwise, in the course of a war?"

"But this would kill them in an hour!"

"Is it kinder to draw out the agony over months and years?"

"The deaths would be painful."

"It is to be doubted. In such intense heat, death might well be instantaneous. In any case, have you watched a man die slowly and agonizingly of a belly thrust? Or for that matter, of some cancers or other diseases?"

"Do you realize that this will mean the end of every good on earth? Why should a young man strive to accomplish anything, knowing that he may die?"

"Nonsense." I put my oar in. "Every man has always known that he was going to die."

"Yes, but now there is the prospect of complete extermination. There will be no future for the young. They will abandon every effort."

"Nonsense again. Man has always faced peril."

"Of extermination?"

"Certainly."

"How so?"

"In many a besieged city, the defenders have known that only death awaited them. Do you suppose that they hugged to themselves in delight the thought that at least their slayers would live on? As far as they were concerned, it was extermination. And the same dread must have been in cities that feared they were next. When a mother sees her only child at the point of death, for her it is the end of the world. We ourselves may be in the same fix, if the Romans take Syracuse. They have never been a humane people."

"It will be pointless for a nation to resist, if war is threatened and such a weapon is available to the enemy. Better Rome than doom!"

"To reason so would mean that any tyrant could at will gain lasting sway over the world. We would all reject that fate. There have always been brave men and women who thought that there were things — many things — worse than death. There are such people still. One can meet a far worse end than death in battle."

"Would you be so inhuman as to use such a weapon if you had it, on the Roman army?"

"War is killing. Would Rome think twice about using it on us?"

"Archimedes, I implore you! Forget your words. Do not pursue this line of search. Do not hurl the world into catastrophe!"

"I do not intend to," slowly answered Archimedes. "But not for the reasons you have cited. As I said before, it would take more time than is left me to accomplish such a project."

"But that does not make any difference," he went on. "If it is not I, it will be another. The mind of man is on the march, and nothing can stop it. And if death lies at the end of the march, why, man has died before, as Katreus remarked. But for man to shrink from the challenge, and to cast behind him his intellect, the most glorious gift of the gods, would be to surrender the one thing that divides him from the beasts. And that would be so shameful that he were far better dead."

"Nations have lost wars, or surrendered without fighting; yet later have become strong and prosperous."

"Not this time. For the weapon would always be at hand, ready for use in any subsequent dispute."

"What we are dealing with is the survival or death of mankind. Is not that more important than any other possible consideration?"

"I have been speaking not of death, but of the danger of death, which is a very different thing. Men and women are often willing to face the latter, and accept its fatal possibility, who would not make a simple sacrifice of their lives, with no possibility of escape."

"But I will accept your theoretical implication, and try to answer.

"No, I do not think that life or death is the most important consideration. Life is not of such surpassing sweetness that we should pay any price for bare survival. If life must be endless terror or degradation, if man may not build him wings to soar like Daedalus close to the very gods, if a Socrates cannot stand in the might of his intellect and the purity of his virtue fearless before mob or tyrant, then let come the fire, and the end."

The Traveller spoke more softly. "And if it comes to that, and if mankind perishes in a holocaust of your making, and if this beautiful world is left only a lifeless and blackened cinder, then what, Archimedes, will you say when at dark Acheron the thronging spirits of the unburied dead call you to account for their children's children who can never be born?"

The master was silent for a longer time before he spoke.

"When inadvertently we breed a line of weak or sickly cattle, we let it die for its own sake, as well as for our own. Perhaps the gods are no less provident. If mankind cannot sufficiently master its cruelties and greeds to avert the final catastrophe, then I shall say that it carried within itself, like a cancer, its own doom.

XXI

Extract from Notes of the Comedian Lallos

In that terrible year the great hero of Syracuse was Archimedes. He in Sicily, as Hannibal in Italy, was the bane of Rome. A white-bearded old Herakles, almost single-handed he took upon his aged shoulders the burden of the war; three Roman legions were thundering at the gates, and they were held at bay by the genius and determination of this one man! It made more credible the storied exploits of old time —

"There mid the hard-pressed prows, where battle rolled
    Its drowning wave on godlike Diomede."

Marcellus was sufficiently taken aback to march off temporarily with a third of his army for the reduction of the rest of Sicily. We could mark the diminution in numbers before us. The Carthaginians landed an army to the westward and there was fighting. We hoped, of course, for relief.

The cities of Helorus and Herbesus went over to Marcellus; Megara he stormed and sacked. Murgantia, on the other hand, despite its Roman garrison, took up for Carthage. Enna, supposedly, was about to do the same, but the Roman detachment in it fell suddenly upon the unarmed citizenry and perpetrated an atrocious massacre and then sacked the town; Marcellus, when he heard of it, gave his approval. Where he captured deserters who had taken up with the enemy, he crucified them.

This cruelty, especially in Enna, sacred to Proserpine, did much to estrange the people of Sicily from the Roman cause.

It became known to the Romans that some of the enemy had infiltrated their camp. These men were rounded up; the Romans cut off their hands, and sent them away.

It was Thucydides who wrote, "The thing that has been is the thing that will be."

The Carthaginian army, with troops of our Sicilian allies, was encamped on the wet soil of the Anapos banks, on the Great Harbor south of the city wall, precisely where the besieging Athenian forces had established themselves two hundred years ago. It was now late in the summer, the weather still hot; and just as in that earlier time, the marshes bred pestilence. Men began to fall sick.

They were lethargic, irregularly feverish, constipated; they did not bother to line up for meals, and complained of headaches. Most developed a cough. After some days the fever became worse, and so did the weakness and dullness. A flux, often bloody, ran through the camp. The surgeons were powerless to help. They noted belly tenderness, rosy spots in the skin, distention; there would be sudden severe pain in the belly, after which its wall became hard as a board. The draughts and powders had no effect. A delirium appeared, which passed into coma and death.

Even those who had apparently recovered were frequently subject to a relapse, which might be fatal; if not, a second such episode might occur.

From sporadic cases the incidence leaped in mighty increments. The death rate was frightful. Those attending the sick were themselves stricken; then the disease appeared in all directions, even among men who had had no contact with patients. Funerals and graves multiplied. By early fall, the victims were being buried in mass pits; thereafter they were left unburied, and the stench reached us even in the city. The horror was beyond telling, both for the wretched sufferers and for those who still lived and moved among the dead. Patients were by now ignored, and left to perish unattended in their own filth. Some there were who in their terror slew themselves. The survivors among the Sicilian allies marched a short distance inland, and established healthier camps at two strong points.

Among the victims were the generals Himilco of Carthage and Hippocrates of Syracuse.

Nor were the Romans exempt. The disorder attacked their camp too, on the other side of the city; but it was in an area not quite so unhealthy, and in any case Marcellus took his sick into houses outside the city, where they did very much better than the wretched men in the marsh. Far fewer Romans perished, therefore, than their enemies. Among the townsmen the attack rate was lighter still.

By the time the epidemic had run its course, the Carthaginian force had ceased to exist as an army; and the associated Sicilian troops had left.

Oppia too was stricken, though not mortally. When I went to inform Claudia (they were in fairly close touch) I encountered Archimedes with the seaman Pyrrhon, who had come to confer with him on some business or other. At the glance that was exchanged between him and Claudia, my dramatist's instinct told me that she was warmer toward him than she had been.

At her insistence, I moved Oppia into Archimedes' house for her better nursing; and they were so kind as to make room for me too.

With the loss of the Sicilian troops and the Carthaginian force, alarm has spread through the town — or through as much of it as remains in our hands. The situation is grave. Unless another army can be found to come to our aid and lift the siege, I fear the worst.

The reality of our situation is finally coming through to the citizenry. Naturally, each tries to convince himself and others that he was of the peace party all along. The mothers of children begin to weep.

Oddly enough, there is at the same time something of a festal mood. Some of the youth are forever drinking and dancing. Girls of good families, who would otherwise be quite circumspect in their conduct, are out by day and even by night, clad in the scantiest and costliest of garb.

The Carthaginian admiral Bomilcar landed an army of 25,000 foot, 3,000 horse, and 13 elephants. Later, with fifty Carthaginian sail, he put in at Syracuse, a few local craft with them. It was for the purpose of making a demonstration; not to use up our food (they said), they soon left.

The fall and then the winter passed with no essential change in our situation. Except that there was less food in the granary than there had been. People began to grow weary of the siege, and of the rather stringent rationing of food. The bitterness with which the Romans behave is daunting to some of those who a few months ago lightheartedly opted for war.

The new Roman consuls are Appius Claudius and Quintus Fabius Maximus, the younger.

The First Roman Legion has been landed, making four here in all. We can repulse attacks, but the Romans cannot possibly abandon this enterprise; if they do, the encouragement it will give to those persons and cities of undecided loyalties will be incalculable. It will be difficult for us to control the harbor mouth well enough not to suffer increasingly from interdiction of our food supply; especially since, in general, Rome controls the sea. It will be on the water, not on the land, that the fate of Syracuse will be decided.

Several of the pro-Roman aristocratic families had left when the city went over to Carthage, and the men were in touch with the Roman general. It occurred to him that, through these Syracusans, it might be possible to find those who could be induced to open the gates of the city to his troops. He gave them his solemn undertaking, in such an event, to respect the lives and liberty of the people of Syracuse.

Such was the degree of suspicion and alertness on the part of the city authorities that a conference between the exiles and their possible sympathizers in town was not practicable. They did, however, take a slave into their confidence, and he entered the city in the character of a deserter. Once there, he broached his business to the proper people, some of whom hid under the nets of a fishing boat and had themselves rowed around to a landing from which they could contact the partisans of Marcellus.

The plot was developed, and a number of people were involved, when the whole conspiracy was betrayed to Epicydes. There were wholesale arrests.

All of the conspirators in town were tortured and executed. This act reflects rather the desperation of the Carthaginian authorities than their justice.

We are hungry much of the time — not starving, but hungry — and the trend is definitely downward. There will be riots soon if no larger grain shipments get through the blockade.

The mood of the commoners had been gravely dampened by the spectacle of the Roman war machine. When they beheld preparations for assault, apprehension gave way to fear, and vows were made to the gods if only the city might escape capture. When the enemy actually advanced to the attack, one sensed panic among the unstable, and the temples filled with frantically pleading worshippers.

When, however, by the genius of the great man who lived among us, our assailants were sent reeling back, the mercurial masses at once swung to the opposite extreme. There were boastful shouts and laughter directed at the discomfited foe. The generals rose in popularity again, and Archimedes could not venture out of his house without the formation of a ragged guard of honor. The supplies of food were wastefully depleted at victory feasts.

During the Great Festival the comic dramatist Lallos tried to steady the commons with his "Riders on the Breeze", a reference to those insects and spiders that float on bits of silk, yielding themselves unselectively to every chance shift of wind that blows them they know not whither. I thought it very pertinent and well done.

XXII

Extract from Pyrrhon's Voyages

We had information that the enemy were engaged in some new modifications of their ships. Their fleet was beached in the Bay of Thapsus, on the north side of the city; and they were on a promontory that forms the northern side of the bay. We decided to have a hand in the execution of their plans.

As a preliminary we made a series of raids by ship from the Great Harbor on coastal points to the north. We made a point of passing close by the mouth of the Bay at dusk, to accustom the enemy to our proximity at that hour. We knew that they would suspect what we were up to, but counted on the difficulty of maintaining a tense readiness in the face of no incidents over a period of time.

There was one possibility that worried us. If the Romans had concentrated artillery for the defense of the camp against sea-borne attack, our losses could be serious. But we could only tell by trying.

Accordingly, one evening, instead of passing harmlessly by, fourteen ships of us suddenly altered course and, rowers making their best possible speed, dashed for the shore. Trumpets blew, calling men to arms. But it would take some minutes for an effective fighting force to appear — we hoped — and in that time much destruction might be effected.

Bow catapults working, we dashed in. There was light opposition as our men leaped ashore, but it increased rapidly. We formed a line of battle between their beached ships, with the elaborate, developing superstructures, to hold the Romans at bay while our demolition party placed combustibles.

Meanwhile a second party was landing on the other side of the promontory where our intelligence had reported a lumber depot, and was similarly active.

We set our fires and withdrew. The destruction of the ships and timber was great. Of course we lost some men.

In Syracuse this was hailed as a great victory.

We in the fleet knew better. It had been a success, yes. But it had after all been only a raid — a very good raid, of course, to be sure, well conceived and, if I may say so, well carried out; and it had done the Romans a deal of damage. Nevertheless, it had still been only a raid, and raids, even masterly ones, do not win wars.

There is a penalty attached to a reputation. You are selected for every difficult and dangerous assignment that the powers that be can dream up.

Things were not good in Syracuse. It was impossible for the Roman fleet to maintain a tight blockade. Supplies came in. But, swollen as the population was by refugees from the countryside, our demand was great; and Roman interference with shipping was sufficient that our stores were being depleted.

We knew that Philip of Macedon had renewed his activity on the Adriatic coast, hoping to profit by Roman preoccupation with their war with Hannibal; and that he had suffered defeat, with the loss of his ships. There was some hope, however, that with a large subsidy (and of gold Syracuse had plenty) he might be induced to take up the struggle again and relieve the pressure on our city.

To put off Roman intelligence, the generals decided to send an ambassador who was not a Syracusan. They selected a resident alien, Damippus of Lacedaemon, whose accent would proclaim to any knowledgeable listener that he was a mainland Hellene. With him would go Saul ben Menasseh, who could pose as a Judean at need (he could speak his ancestral tongue).

I was to command the ship. With the Carthaginian allies encamped south of the city, we controlled the Great Harbor.

We selected a roundship, as less likely to arouse attention away from Sicily.

I slipped out in bad weather, as so many times before. I don't like dirty weather any more than the next seaman; but there are times when it must be accepted. When the blow was over (I knew that it would not last), we reached northeastward across the Ionian Sea to Palaiste, in the extreme northwestern part of

Epirus. This was as close to the Roman-dominated Adriatic as I cared to risk my ship.

The two-man embassy made its way overland to the court of Philip.

I might of course have sailed to Corinth, far off the patrol area of Roman men-of-war, and from there the ambassadors could have taken a ship for Therme in the northern Aegean; but too many eyes would have seen, and there might be speculation and investigation, and in the cockpit of Hellenic politics one could not tell who might be an agent for whom.

The mission, as it turned out, was a failure. In vain our spokesmen pointed out that if Rome were victorious over Carthage and Sicily, it would be only a question of time before she swallowed Macedonia. Philip had had his bellyful. He was not to be moved.

Despite our precautions, someone talked. When we left harbor, a Roman quinquereme materialized. There was a good norther blowing (I vowed a white bull to Poseidon), and we just beat her into Panormus, a little further down that inhospitable coast.

The Roman captain was unwilling to invade the wharves of the Epirote town, but anchored for a death-watch in the harbor. Days went by, but he did not leave. He obviously knew his prey.

I racked my brains, but in vain. Finally, I proposed to my passengers that we sell the ship, travel overland to the Ambracian Gulf, and buy another ship for our return.

"I don't like the prospect at all," said Damippus. "Some one will seize us and sell us to Rome."

"By the horn of Gideon, neither do I!" was Saul's reaction.

I looked at him in delight. The horn of Gideon! There was my solution!

I despatched most of my crew overland to Chimaira, an hour and a half by road to the north, their pockets well (but not too well) supplied with money, with instructions to buy fishing boats and large row boats, large jars and trumpets.

Two nights later, his watch roused the Roman captain to report a dozen lights suddenly appearing at sea. Trumpets sounded; I answered with trumpet and signal light blazing suddenly.

I daresay the Roman had his suspicions. But he could not afford to chance it. He would never be able to explain in Rome why he had remained and let himself be captured by a hostile fleet. He cut his cable and fled.

I put out from the wharf, picked up my boat crews, and set sail for home.

It was an easy passage — until the end. About to enter the harbor of Syracuse, we were caught by a fierce, too early south-easterly blow. There was no sea room. Wind and wave cast my ship ashore, and her people, except for a few who were drowned, were made prisoners by the Roman army.

Having been in my small way something of a thorn in the side of Rome, I was not eager to identify myself. I deliberately gashed my cheek on a rock as we made the shore, which gave me the excuse for covering part of my face with an improvised dressing. I took the identity of a seaman, and announced that the captain had been lost. It was then that I reaped my reward for having, on the whole, given my crews pretty decent treat-ment. None of them gave me away.

Damippus and Saul, however, were identified by the Syracu-san exiles. Among them, to my surprise, was one who was not a Syracusan — Eudoxus of Tauromenion, the former officer of Ptolemy, to whom my brother had introduced me several years ago. He was now, obviously, in the service of Rome.

Marcellus too knew our errand (some deserter from the city must have informed him), and lost no time in letting Syracuse know about our shipwreck and capture. An officer of ransom came promptly.

The Roman was quite willing to discuss the ransom of Damip-pus. As he explained quite frankly, he was not loathe to gain some goodwill in Damippus' home state of Lacedaemon, since it was allied to Aetolia, whose friendship, as a counterpoise to King Philip, he wished to cultivate. Damippus requested that I (still under an assumed name) be sent as his negotiator, to which the praetor readily assented. For Saul, however, he had other plans. I heard about them much later from Saul's attendant, who was present at the interview. It was Eudoxus who conducted it.

"I am approaching you, ben Menassa, for two reasons. In the first place, we are both men of the world, with a wider outlook than some of our associates — the Romans in my case, and the Syracusans in yours. In the second place, we are in analogous positions, both of us foreigners among a haughty and overbearing people.

"The praetor offers you a great opportunity for life and even wealth. We know that there are those in Syracuse who want no part of this war. We will let you be ransomed; once inside the walls, contact these people and arrange to open one of the gates to our troops. You will be doing Syracuse a great service — ridding her of an unpopular war, and sparing your friends and neighbors from the horror of the inevitable final attack.

"We are not children, you and I. We have looked long and hard at such mummeries as honor, loyalty, and patriotism, and know exactly what they are worth. What is the going rate for the corpse of a hero?

"What say you, ben Menassa?"

"I say that I am a citizen of Syracuse."

"Are you, really? Hark you, Saul, I have travelled widely, and you cannot put me off with such nonsense. I know that you will never be accepted, completely, in any country outside of Judea; and I daresay that that is true for every other variant. I have been in Judea, remember, and I have learned the history of your people. What happened to you in Egypt, after your forefathers had been received there with honor? Do you not have a terrible story about your perils in Persia? And did not your countrymen groan under Ptolemy? And if I know Antiochus, worse is in store for your nation at his hands — or the hands of his dynasty."

"I am not here as one of a conquered people, or as a member of a state within a state," Saul replied. "I share in the privileges and responsibilities of Syracusan citizenship, like my father and grandfather before me."

"Do you indeed? Almost any other Syracusan could, given the

right circumstances, attain the highest power in the state. Could you, do you think? Are there not circles that are closed to you? Do you not know the hate that hides in men's hearts? You are very much aware that you walk with danger, and so do your children."

"I have loyal friends whom I love, and who love me. I do not believe that they are false."

"No more do I, Saul; no more do I. But such good will is never enough. Do you think that there was no sincere friendship in Egypt? Your real peril does not come from those sick souls who distrust you and hate you, and continually plot your destruction. It comes in part from the great mass of men who are aware of their ill will as an evil thing, and struggle against it — successfully, until a time of public crisis, when they lose their reason. Still worse is the refusal of the truly good men to believe in the extent of the machination of the lovers of evil; when it bursts forth, some of them go bravely down with their honesty unsullied, but can that save you? Tell me, Saul, have you not heard insults that were not even known for insults by those who uttered them? Do you not hesitate to be the first to offer friendship, lest it be rebuffed? Do you not — be truthful, now — do you not feel that you walk as a man apart? When you are denied what you think is your due, do you not forever wonder whether the cause is not too ugly for the light of day?"

"I think," said Saul slowly, "that you have resorted to witchcraft to steal the secrets of men's souls."

"Aha! Then you admit that all I have said is so!"

"Yes. It is so."

"Then why do you feel that you owe Syracuse loyalty?"

"I could say 'patriotism', and it would be true, but that would not really be the answer. I could say 'duty', and that would be true too, but that would not really be the answer either. I could say that I would not have my name be a stench in men's nostrils, and that would come closer to it, but there would still be much unsaid. I could say that I would not leave such a heritage to my children, which is perhaps more important than any of the other words I have uttered, but that is still not the real answer.

"No, the essential reason is all of these, and something more. A parent should love all of his children equally. Many, we know, do not. There are parents who hate some of their children, and treat them with cruelty. Such children owe their parents no love. This was our condition in the land of Egypt. But there are many parents who have favorites, and love some children more than others. The less favored offspring know this well, and resent it deeply, and never forget it. But these parents are not so unnatural as not to have given even these children much love and nurture, who know this too, and never forget it either, and despite their resentment love the parent in return — sometimes even more than their more cherished brethren.

"Such is Syracuse to me, and I will never betray her."

"Even though you know that Syracuse might someday betray you?"

"Even though I know that she might."

"And are you not afraid, Saul ben Menassa, of the wrath of Marcellus?"

"I am very much afraid. But I have said my say, and I take my stand upon it."

Damippus was ransomed, and I, his supposed attendant, went with him into the city. It made my heart ache to see how thin and pale Claudia was becoming under the shortages of the siege. I tried to ransom my crew, but they had been sold to a slaver. His family wanted to ransom Saul, but Marcellus kept him, because of his ambassadorial rank, to march in chains in his Triumph if he should have one, and to be strangled thereafter.

A report somehow got around that Saul had been approached by the Romans. A good-for-nothing ex-jeweler named Archias smeared paint on Saul's house one night in company with a band of ruffians. Some of the women spat at his wife at the market, and his schoolfellows threw stones at his grandson. But there was no hard evidence that he had held conversations with the Romans, still less that they had been treasonable, and all decent people disapproved of such goings-on.

It was Saul's attendant who, having somehow escaped, later told me the whole story.

It is somewhat surprising that I got away with my masquerade. The Romans should have been sharper than that, and perhaps they were. The possibility has occurred to me that despite all the iron in his soul, Marcellus may have been reluctant to see an old comrade-in-arms pass so hopelessly into captivity.

I took hard having lost my crew to Rome and slavery. Most of them had been free men, and by reason of their trust in me they were free no more. And there was Saul ben Menassa, a friend, also lost to the enemy. It weighed heavily upon me. I could not see what I might have done to save them. Nevertheless, the fact was that they had come to grief, and through me.

I felt physically ill. But I could not allow myself, in this desperate time, the luxury of a long recuperation. For added to my private misery was public calamity — as the result of inexcusable negligence on the part of the defenders, the Romans got over the wall and possessed themselves of a great part of the city!

So I pulled myself together. It was at this time that I began to have severe pains in the stomach. They were to plague me as long as I remained in Syracuse.

XXIII

Extract from the Correspondence of
Marcus Claudius Marcellus

Marcus Claudius to the Roman Senate. At Syracuse, on the 10th day before the Kalends of August, in the Year after the founding of the City the 541st.

I have the pleasure of informing you, Conscript Fathers, that one-half of the city of Syracuse is in the Roman hands. It came about in the following wise.

The negotiations leading to the ransom of the Lacedaemonian Damippus (concerning which I have reported to you before) were conducted before Galeagra tower in the northern wall which overlooks the Trogylos Harbor in the Bay of Thapsus. In the course of these talks Gnaeus Atilius noticed that at this point the wall was lower than had been realized. He counted the courses of masonry in it, estimated the height of each, and discovered that the wall here was not too high for a scaling ladder.

Careful examination of deserters and prisoners revealed the fact that the enemy too were aware of this, and maintained an especially strong guard at that point in consequence. We also learned, however, that a three-day-long festival of Artemis was soon to be held. This was customarily observed with feasting. On account, however, of the shortness of supplies, and the circumstances, as one of our informants very positively reported, that there was no lack of wine, it seemed likely that extra rations of this would be issued and drunk.

Such indeed proved to be the case. Well after dark on the first day of the festival, when it seemed likely that the somnolence following drink would be upon the defenders, a storming party of chosen men was sent forward under the command of the tribune Titus Veturius Philo. A century brought up the ladders; after them a thousand men marched silently.

First on the wall was the decurion Lucius Pomonius Matho. No defenders were seen, and the entire detachment entered the city undetected. They passed through deserted streets to the great Hexapylon gate, broke open a postern, and admitted the main body of troops.

Stealth was now abandoned. Trumpets were sounded from the wall, to terrify the enemy. Severe fighting broke out in the streets, especially toward the Epipolae, the well fortified western and highest quarter of the city. So vast is Syracuse that most of the population was still unaware of the occupation. When they finally roused themselves it was too late to save the larger part of the town. The Epipolae too had fallen; as well as the two central districts of Neapolis and Tyche. Walled Achradina, built on a ridge above the sea, the island of Ortygia and Euryalus, a fortress at the westernmost part of the town, still held out.

I accepted the submission of the population of the occupied areas. Their lives were to be spared, but their property was given over to plunder by the troops.

After the sack, Philodemos the Argive, commander of the Euryalus fortress, surrendered on terms of a safe conduct for his garrison to Achradina.

Such is the present situation. There is now no doubt about the ultimate fall of the rest of the city. I cannot, however, estimate how much time will be required to bring it about.

By now you will have heard about our recent successes.

It is impossible even for a Roman to contemplate unmoved
the prospective despoilment of this, the most beautiful of the
Greek cities. As I stood on the high point of Epipolae and looked
over the town, I found myself unexpectedly moved by the prospect. This was the city that had resisted an Athenian and a
Carthaginian siege; it had for so long been a faithful friend and
ally of Rome; its commerce had spread its fame throughout the
world; it was the center of Greek culture in the West. Now,
perhaps, was its end.

Bomilcar, the Carthaginian admiral, had left with thirty-five
ships. It blew too hard one night for our blockade to be maintained, so he took the opportunity to return, as I suppose, to
Carthage. He left fifty-five ships behind him. He returned today
with a fleet of one hundred sail bringing reinforcing Carthaginian troops.

This makes even more doubtful the date of our final victory.
That it will come, I am certain.

I was of course most pleased to receive your account of my
son's exploits in Spain, although deeply grieved at the death
there of Gnaeus Scipio. He was a good friend and a fine soldier.
Valeto!

When you are next in Rome, please greet my daughter and my
grandsons for me. Be well!

XXIV

Extracts from Pyrrhon's Voyages

Our situation was desperate. We still held a strong position in the Achradina and the island of Ortygia, the Roman blockade was still far from complete (though by no means wholly ineffective), and allied Sicilian troops were still in existence and in fact held two strong points in the immediate vicinity of the town. But wars are not won by defense alone, and unless we could obtain more help and pass over to a counteroffensive, everyone who understood anything of warfare knew that we were lost.

The cheer that swept through the city when that help was at hand therefore can be imagined. Bomilcar had again returned from Carthage! The word ran overland by swift courier from the south, and then around the Roman lines by a fishing boat, that 130 ships of war and 700 transports had arrived! This was a large enough expedition to turn the tables on Marcellus, and make the besiegers into besieged!

The fleet had made an easy passage from Carthage to the southern tip of Sicily, and now lay windbound by a prolonged easterly behind Cape Pachynum. Our commanding general, Epicydes, fearing lest the resolution of this ally might falter under continued unfavorable weather, put out with a small convoy to join him. I had just bought a new roundship; nevertheless, for this expedition I accepted command of a quinquereme.

Marcellus was quite aware of his danger. He had no intention of being trapped by a reinforced Sicilian and Carthaginian army in his rear, and a hostile fleet off the harbor. With commendable resolution he despatched his own ships, outmatched though they were, to oppose the passage of Bomilcar's squadron. The two fleets lay on the opposite sides of the Cape, waiting for the lively sea to subside that they might engage. It grew calmer. The Syracusans and the Carthaginians stood toward the enemy. The encumbering sailing gear had been sent ashore, the fighting ships stripped; the marines stood some in bow and stern castles with ample supplies of arrows and javelins, some on the decks, spears at the ready to board or to repel; and the rowers, well rested, were making the oars bend to the stroke. The whole sea was covered with the panoply of war. The smaller Roman fleet advanced gallantly to meet us.

Clearchos, my second in command, stood beside me. "It seems possible to me, sir, that when we have won this day, the Roman siege will have to be raised."

"It is possible," I agreed, and so I thought it was, though one would have had to be very guarded in such a hope.

"Despatch boats leaving the flag, sir!" the lookout reported.

"They're going through the fleet!" Clearchos exclaimed, and in a few minutes a boat pulled up alongside. "Orders from the admiral! The transports to return to Carthage! Carthaginian men-of-war to follow the admiral to Tarentum!"

Clearchos dashed his shield to the deck in helpless fury. "Bomilcar has turned craven! Damn him! Damn him! Damn him!"

A great cry of rage and despair went up from the Syracusan squadron as the Carthaginian fleet divided and fled. Gladly, I think, would most of us have joined with the Romans to annihilate those faithless allies!

But more shame was to follow. "Sir!" from the lookout. "The admiral has hoisted signal to follow him!" And a moment later, "He is standing toward Akragas!"

Epicydes, our commander-in-chief, who with Hippocrates, now dead, had led us into this war, had no stomach for its end. Hoisting a signal for us to follow, he turned tail to seek refuge in Akragas.

I addressed my crew. "Men, the Commander has deserted the city and us. All that I love, all that I treasure, is in Syracuse. I am going back to share my city's fortunes. Whoever wishes to seek safety will be landed somewhere on the coast, to fare as he may. This ship returns to Syracuse. Who goes with me?"

I had not a single deserter.

Now indeed hope was lost, and the war drew sickeningly toward its end. Madness entered the town. Epicydes' three generals were murdered. A delegation was sent to Marcellus to ask for terms. The Roman deserters in the city, who knew well that there was no hope for them, persuaded the allied Sicilians among us that they were in like case; these flew to arms, assassinated the magistrates, and raged through the streets, killing and looting as they went. And when, clearer-sighted, they perceived their folly, the worst happened. The Spaniard Moericus, in charge of a sector of Ortygia's defenses, made an accomodation with Marcellus and admitted Roman troops. Then all was over.

XXV

Extract from Heraclides' Life of Archimedes

Marcellus fully realized the value of the busy seaport, the Hellenic metropolis of the West, that was falling into his hands. If only for practical and economic reasons, therefore, I think that he would have prevented the random killings if he could. But after the long siege, the plague, and especially the bloody repulses that they had suffered at our hands, not even he could restrain the Roman soldiery from its revenge.

He did, however, as we later found out, give orders that Archimdedes and his family were to be delivered unharmed into his hands. To that end he sent sentries to the master's house; if any of its people were abroad, it was nip and tuck whether they would be encountered first by friend or foe.

Marcellus had undertaken that none of the citizens would be enslaved; and this undertaking he kept. He did not consider that his promise covered resident aliens as well. Our Gallic friend Segovesus was among those who were led to the market in chains. In accordance with Roman discipline, one half of the army scattered for plunder, one half stood guard. The loot would later be fairly divided by the officers.

Archimedes was of course one of the first to be notified of the desperate turn of events. He hurried to the agora, myself and an attendant accompanying him, to be available for whatever council might be held at this late date; but already all was in confusion. We started back toward his home.

I have had occasion ere now to mention a villain by the name of Archias; through the agency of Archimedes he had been exposed in some rascality a number of years back, and had developed in consequence a deathless hatred for the master. Spying him on this occasion, as I later learned, he sent some worthless fellow to inform Archimedes that his beloved Claudia and his son had both been killed.

For all his stoicism, it was as though the full effects of his age fell suddenly upon him. His back bent, the lines of his face deepened, his features seemed to lose their firmness and his head drooped. Presently in a tired voice, "There is no need for me to return home now, Heraclides," he said. "There is nothing at home that concerns me. Live, if you can, and rejoice in a better time, if one comes. I am now seventy-five years old, and have already lived too long. This is as good a place as any for me to meet — whatever I shall meet."

I urged him frantically to try to flee, but he only smiled sadly. "Go, Heraclides," he said. "I have loved you best of all my friends. I choose to spend my last hours in communion with my beloved mathematics." And with his staff he drew a circle and an included triangle in the earth.

It was at that hour that Fate in the form of a Roman soldier came upon him.

My Latin is poor, but obviously the sight of two well dressed men meant plunder, and he was ordering us to move — probably to lead him to our homes. I started to obey; but Archimedes said, "Out of my way, fellow! You are disturbing my diagram!"

The Roman sword leaped. Archimedes went down without a sound.

Thus fell the greatest man of his time — brought low by that wretched Archias, a lion fatally stung by an adder.

I led the soldier to my home. Unfortunately, my sister had sought refuge there with her children. One of the Roman's first acts was to cut their throats. He then, with a tender smile, put my niece's ivory doll into his pack — obviously for his own little girl.

The world seems strangely empty without Archimedes.

One can say of him that he died swiftly without long pain or loss of dignity; it is true that in this the gods were kind. One can say that he had reached an age which is vouchsafed to few men. This too is true; yet one is only partly consoled thereby. For at the end the Master was still vigorous in mind and, for his age, in body. One additional year of his beloved studies would have been more fruitful than a century for a lesser man.

From the memories of Hellas we have stories of Great Ones who, like noble monuments gilded above the mists of dawn by the rays of the rising sun, stand out from the dimness of antiquity. Even so stands the figure of Archimedes, no less a hero. With whom shall I compare him, among the paragons of modern times? With Pythagoras, perhaps, who first understood the magic of numbers; with Euclid, who established the science of geometry, for which the Master did so much; with Aristotle, that lord of all learning? No other is worthy.

Is not then the Master as truly a hero as the Lord of Men, Agamemnon? Or as fleet-footed Achilles?

The Master's gift to the world of mathematics and geometry will exist for all time. And is not his defense of the walls of Syracuse as great a feat of arms as ever Ajax or Hector performed? Is not his invention of the cochlias a greater boon to mankind than all the works of Daedalus?

Rest, great soul, with the noble and the fair of the ages, in the Islands of the Blest so far away!

XXVI

Extracts from the Notes of the Comedian Lallos

The sounds of a city being sacked became unmistakable.

Oppia and I and our son were in the house of Archimedes with her friend Claudia. It was a miracle that we were not at once attacked; we heard the screams of women being ravished or seeing their loved ones put to the sword (frequently both), men and children crying out in terror and agony, and more and more the crackle of flames.

Archimedes' body servant came with terrible news. His master was dead. He had seen him slain. Tears came to Claudia's eyes.

Shortly afterward Pyrrhon, the sea captain, arrived. Resistance having collapsed, he had made his way hither to do what he could in defense of the household. The major-domo told him of the death of Archimedes. He shook his head sadly. Then he looked questioningly at Claudia and started to speak, but she fell weeping into his arms. I had not been mistaken. My dramatist's eye even then marked their reactions for future reference.

When the first Roman soldiers arrived, to our surprise they assumed guard at the door of the house, directing looters elsewhere.

The most I had hoped for was the unlikely chance of being ignored by our conquerors; but the undaunted Pyrrhon had other ideas.

"I have a ship ready for sea," he said. "With the aid of one person I can handle her in a pinch. Most of the Roman fleet is beached at the Trogylos Harbor. When darkness falls, if we're still unhurt, Claudia and I will try to sneak aboard with Claudia's son and get away. With luck we'll win clear of the harbor. Any of you who want to come along, may."

Oppia and I and our son resolved to be among the number. So did several of the house staff.

Late in the day came Marcellus.

"I had hoped to see Archimedes in his house," he said to us. "Although he was an enemy, I honored him. But a body has been identified as his. I suppose you knew that?"

"We knew it," said Pyrrhon.

"Pyrrhon! We meet for the third time."

"This time, unhappily for me."

"Who are these?"

"This lady was the companion of Archimedes. The little boy is his son and hers."

"They are under my protection."

"This man is the comic dramatist and actor, Lallos, with his slave of many years and their son. The rest are members of Archimedes' house staff."

"None of his relatives?"

"No. He has two married daughters."

"Decurion!"

"Sir?"

"Send men, with a pair of house slaves for guides, as sentries to protect the homes of Archimedes' daughters."

"Yes, Praetor."

There was a small commotion, and a soldier came in with my former friend Archias. "Praetor, this man says he has information for you."

"Well, fellow?"

"Praetor, it was I who brought about the death of your enemy Archimedes," and he recounted his deception with evident pride. "Furthermore, I have been hanging around the house to see what else I could do to merit your good will, and I learned from a servant of a plot that is being hatched. This man — " pointing at Pyrrhon — "is planning to steal down to the waterfront after dark, seize a ship and with these companions flee from your judgment. And this woman — " pointing to Claudia — "is a Roman renegade."

"Are you?"

"I have been told that I was born in Rome. I was brought here as an infant."

"In which year?"

She told him.

"Her real name is Claudia," Archias spat out. "She was the slave and mistress of Archimedes. Therefore she and his brat should die together."

"Come here, boy," said the praetor. He laid his hands on the child's shoulders and looked long and searchingly into his face, then into his mother's. Father and daughter regarded one another silently, still without a word of claim on her part, or of acknowledgement on his. Then, "About this escape. Is it true?"

"Yes, Praetor," said Pyrrhon.

Marcellus turned to Archias. "Whom else have you told about all this?"

"No one, Praetor. I came directly to you with my information."

"Well done. You shall be rewarded fittingly. Decurion!"

The soldier came to attention.

"Take this man outside and kill him!"

He looked long at Claudia again, and then at the boy. "Were I other than a Claudius, I should adopt him. Because I honored his father — and for other reasons. But the Claudian tribe has ever set its face against adoption, and I will not violate old custom. Were you going to flee with this man Pyrrhon?"

"Yes."

"Are you lovers?"

"Not yet."

"What do you intend to do with this woman and child?" to Pyrrhon.

"I have wanted her for my wife. Her son I wanted to raise in the memory of my friend Archimedes."

"Is that your desire?"

"Yes," from Claudia.

"Then be it so. This will be a Roman city henceforward; I cannot have you living here. You saved my life twice, Pyrrhon. For the first time I repaid you with your freedom; for the second time I repay you now in the same coin. I do this for you and for —" he paused and looked directly at Claudia — "for the son of a great and noble enemy. Where will you go?"

"I have a house and a warehouse in Massalia."

"Have you money?"

"I had. It has probably been plundered by now."

"Take everything of value from this house in compensation — and for Archimedes' son. Decurion!"

The soldier ran in and saluted.

"This is Pyrrhon. He will take this party and up to ten men

besides, if he wishes to select them, with their families if they have any, and he will take a ship and depart. See that he has a safe conduct."

"Yes, Praetor."

"Cleanthes!"

"Praetor?"

"See to a suitable burial for Archimedes. I understand that he desired a gravestone on which should be represented a sphere circumscribed by a cylinder. Let it be done!"

It had been my purpose to flee the stricken city. But now I had second thoughts. Having come to the notice of the conqueror in favorable company, I had excellent hopes that he might see to my survival, and that of my family. All the more, in her ruin, Syracuse might need comedy, to relieve an unbearable present; and if she did not, there were other Greek cities in Italy, as well as Sicily; some of them, like Tauromenion, allies of Rome, therefore relatively prosperous. It would go hard but I would be able to make a living. And I was old now, 65; I might fare worse where I was less well known. I decided to remain.

Of course, I have had many bitter reflections on the folly of this war that ruined the finest city of modern Greece. And yet, I am not so sure that those responsible for it were wholly wrong. When giants struggle, it is difficult to take no role, but to remain safely aloof. And those who felt that Rome was already lost at that time certainly had good arguments on their side. If we had continued to be allied with Rome, and the Carthaginians had won the war, that would certainly have been the end of Syracusan independence, and perhaps of most of the Syracusans. A choice had to be made; unfortunately, the wrong course was followed.

This brings to a close my history of the nine Roman girls who were captured by the pirate so long ago. Three are dead —Fulvia by her own hand in the brothel, Cornelia in the mine, and Terentia, as I learned, at the hands of a Roman foraging party on her farm. Aemilia and the younger Livia have vanished in the underworld where life is cheap and death an expected occurrence. Livia is presumably happy with her Roman on Rhodes, and Julia is still with the grown children whose orphaned childhood she solaced. Claudia sailed away with Pyrrhon, and my Oppia is still my treasure.

XXVII

Extract from the Correspondence of Marcus Claudius Marcellus

Marcus Claudius, Praetor, to the Roman Senate. Syracuse, on the 3rd day before the Kalends of November, in the Year after the founding of the City the 541st.

I am happy to report that the city of Syracuse is in our hands. All resistance has ceased. I shall forward what is left of the royal treasure.

I am proceeding with the pacification of the rest of Sicily.

XXVIII

Extracts from Pyrrhon's Voyages

As we were leaving, I said to Claudia, "I am grateful, of course, on my own account; and yet I think the Roman has dealt most unkindly with you. He should have acknowledged you and taken you home with the honors of a conqueror's daughter. In fact, he should have done it years ago."

"But then, darling, I should never have had you! There would have been no Pyrrhon for me, ever!"

"What did you say?"

She repeated it. But the voice I heard was the voice of my long-dead mother, uttering those very words; and the face that rose in my mind was my mother's face; and I had on a sudden such a sense of bitter loss that I sobbed aloud. But then realization came upon me, and I knew why I had tormented myself so uselessly and so often; and I said, "I am free!"

"Yes, darling," she said, not understanding, "you are free, and so am I, and my son!"

There would be time enough to tell her, during the rest of our lives. For now it was enough that I knew that the old ghosts of guilt and shame had been laid forever. I was as free as any man to succeed or fail, to live with my fellows or without them, to face a good or evil lot as one who bore only his own burden, and was not answerable for the fate of any other. At long last I was whole.

The gales of winter were by now well established in the Ligurian Sea that washes the shores about Massalia. I had no intention of subjecting myself to such weather, still less Claudia and her child; so I worked southwest to the lesser Melita, in Kerkina, an island well south of Carthage and too insignificant to attract a Roman fleet. We wintered there.

So, after a somewhat stormy voyage, I landed here in Massalia, five years ago. Lallos and his family elected to remain in Syracuse under the protection of Marcellus. It is a city sadly reduced. The Roman had an eye for beauty, and all of its wealth and the best of its art went to Rome. But the spoken or written word cannot be looted, and Lallos, I hear, still carries on in the theatre. Of other old friends and acquaintances I know little.

Marcus Claudius Marcellus fell in battle last year, at the age of sixty.

Claudia and I live comfortably in the house I bought unwillingly so long ago and my daughter and son are the pride of their half-brother. My shipping business flourishes; I conduct an active tin trade, in particular, with Rome and Greece. Seldom now do I command the ship that carries my goods; and I think I shall not again have occasion to set foot, except perhaps as a visitor, on the deck of a man-of-war. But I look back with satisfaction and pride on my days in the service of Syracuse, and even of that ill-starred, self-defeated dreamer, Cleomenes, and his surpassingly lovely Agiatis.

When I tread that last deck under the orders of grim Charon, I shall have known many beautiful ships. I have been fellow to men of many far off lands. In my life there have been women to be loved — the fair unattainable Agiatis and my infinitely dear Claudia, who has borne me my children. I have played my part in great affairs, sometimes in pain and peril; but I account the life of him who of his own accord has shunned the flash and fire of the age comparable to the dim, shadowy existence of the impotent wraiths in Hades. Above all, I have shared in a struggle to the death between two giants not merely of this but of all time. I think that such a duel will not be seen again.

Author's Note

It is difficult even for some of us who should know better not to have our notions of history colored by historical novels. I hold therefore that the writer of such fiction is obligated to present only such incidents as, on the basis of our knowledge, either happened or might reasonably have happened. I owe it to my readers accordingly to defend certain apparent divagations from published accounts.

It is, I think, generally conceded that a bireme had two banks of oars, the one above the other. But concerning the rowing arrangement of a trireme, and still more a quinquereme, there is much hot dispute and no agreement whatsoever. In the latter case, most theories fall into one of the following categories:

(a) There were actually tiers of oars, five high.

(b) There was a single bank of oars on each side, each oar pulled by five rowers.

(c) There was a single bank on each side, each oar pulled by one man, the oars being clustered in groups of five.

(d) There were successive units of five rowers pulling two or three tiered oars.

I see no reason for assuming that resourceful men, such as we know the ancients to have been, would not have explored the possibilities to the full. Just as we design different ship styles for different functions and conditions, and build experimental types, the classical peoples would certainly have done the same. It is no doubt true that five or even three banks of oars would have made heavy weather of it in a seaway; but the seamen of those times expected to do, and did, most of their fighting when the sea was relatively calm. In even a moderate disturbance, they probably unshipped the oars of the lower banks.

In any case, it seems to me that those (the majority, be it admitted) who assert the impossibility of hypothesis (a) above, are hard put to it to explain away the clear words of Livy, XXVIII, 30, describing a battle in the tidal eddies of the straits of Gibraltar:

"Chance ruled; but while the triremes were engaged in

this indecisive manner, the Roman quinquereme — perhaps
because her size steadied her, or because her *more numerous banks
of oars (pluribus remorum ordinibus)* made her easier to control in the
tide-rip — sank two triremes and sheared off the oars from one
side of a third." — de Selincourt's translation. Moore is one of
the few students of ancient marine architecture who assign this
passage its full significance.

So far at least as the trireme is concerned, the following from
Thucydides should dispose of the three-man-to-an-oar theory:
"The men were to take each his oar, cushion, and rowlock thong,
and going overland from Corinth to the sea," etc. The Peloponnesian War, II, 93. Or Aristophanes' earthy jest about the oarsmen above making wind in the face of the thalamite. Frogs,
1071-1074.

Orosius tells us that Antony's fleet at Actium had ships (de-
ciremes, it is true, but that would make no difference as far as
refuting those who are committed to a maximum of two banks)
with a ten-foot freeboard.

Why so high, if not to accomodate several tiers of oars? The
windage alone of such high ships would otherwise set them at a
serious disadvantage. To say nothing of the extra weight en-
tailed; in galleys, every pound counted. Nor could it have been
for defense; the boarding nettings of the eighteenth and early
nineteenth century ships would have served far better — defenders could thrust through at random against men whose
hands were needed to climb, and who had in any case no firm
base under their feet from which to thrust or strike in return.

About the rowing of hexaremes and upward, I have nothing to
say.

There is much scepticism concerning the more spectacular
achievements of Archimedes — achievements of which in any
case he himself thought little. I have suggested what might have
happened.

The contemporary historians state unequivocally that after
his first repulse, Marcellus did not again venture on an assault
against the walls of Syracuse. For one with any experience of
warfare, this is hard to believe.

In view of the frightful losses inflicted by Hannibal upon Roman manpower in two battles alone — Cannae and Lake Trasimenus, its further attrition at his hands, and the need for men in so many theatres of war, it is impossible but that the Senate sent Marcellus peremptory orders to try again to storm the city, rather than tie up so much manpower so long in a static operation.

Furthermore, Archimedes reportedly devised several types of defensive engines — the improved ballistae and scorpions, better launchers of missiles than had been known before; mechanically controlled beams which dropped weights further from the walls than the enemy could have expected; huge grapples which seized and drew to destruction whole ships. But a general does not display his entire bag of tricks to an enemy at first encounter; he rather uses the first as long as it is effective, and only when the enemy has devised an effective counter does he shift to the next.

It is also hard to credit Marcellus' use of the 8-ship storming tower, and the 2-ship scaling ladders, in a single action. I have reconstructed the siege as well as possible, in consideration of the rest of the reports of Polybius and of Livy.

There is some disagreement between Plutarch and Livy on the order of events. I have had to be arbitrary. The Cambridge Ancient History gives the date of the fall of Syracuse as 211 B.C.; all other historians I have consulted give 212 B.C.; I have accepted the latter date.

Archimedes, like all others of the great Greek thinkers, was called a philosopher — etymologically, a lover of wisdom. If I style him a scientist (Latin scio, know) I do not think that I have done great violence to language.

In rendition of proper nouns I plead guilty of inconsistency. I favor, in theory, trasliteration as close to the original as possible, with k rather than c for Greek names, and the Greek o rather than the Roman u in the terminal syllable. Nevertheless, it would be unreasonably stubborn not to keep well established forms such as Syracuse. And in some cases, I might vary the form of expression according to whether Greek or Roman uses it.

It will be noted that in republican Rome until very late, women had no given names, but were known by their tribal nomina, as in my examples.

For equivalent place names I have relied heavily upon Long's Classical Atlas.

One wonders about the nature of the epidemic that destroyed a Carthaginian army. We are given neither diagnosis nor symptoms. The troops were encamped on low, marshy ground; that suggests malaria. But in such case the report would have been of "the" plague, not "a" plague; the affliction was obviously something not well known in Syracuse. Furthermore, mosquitoes would have had plenty of attention to spare for the townsmen, as well. And the epidemic would have begun before late summer or early fall.

But on wet ground, the equinoctial rain would carry night soil into the Anapos River, or wells if there were any. A typhoid patient or a carrier on the upper edge of the camp could easily have contaminated the water supply; the results would inevitably have snow-balled. The flying radius of flies would have accounted for the relatively slight infection in town and in the Roman camp.

I have described symptoms on this supposition.

Archimedes' romance and the account of his boyhood are my inventions.

There are those who affect to find the "forcing" of past events into modern implications objectionable. I reply in the words of Ecclesiastes — "There is nothing new under the sun." For a strong presentation of this point of view, see the histories of the Durants. Let me close with another quotation —"To write about the past; to mean the present; to affect the future."

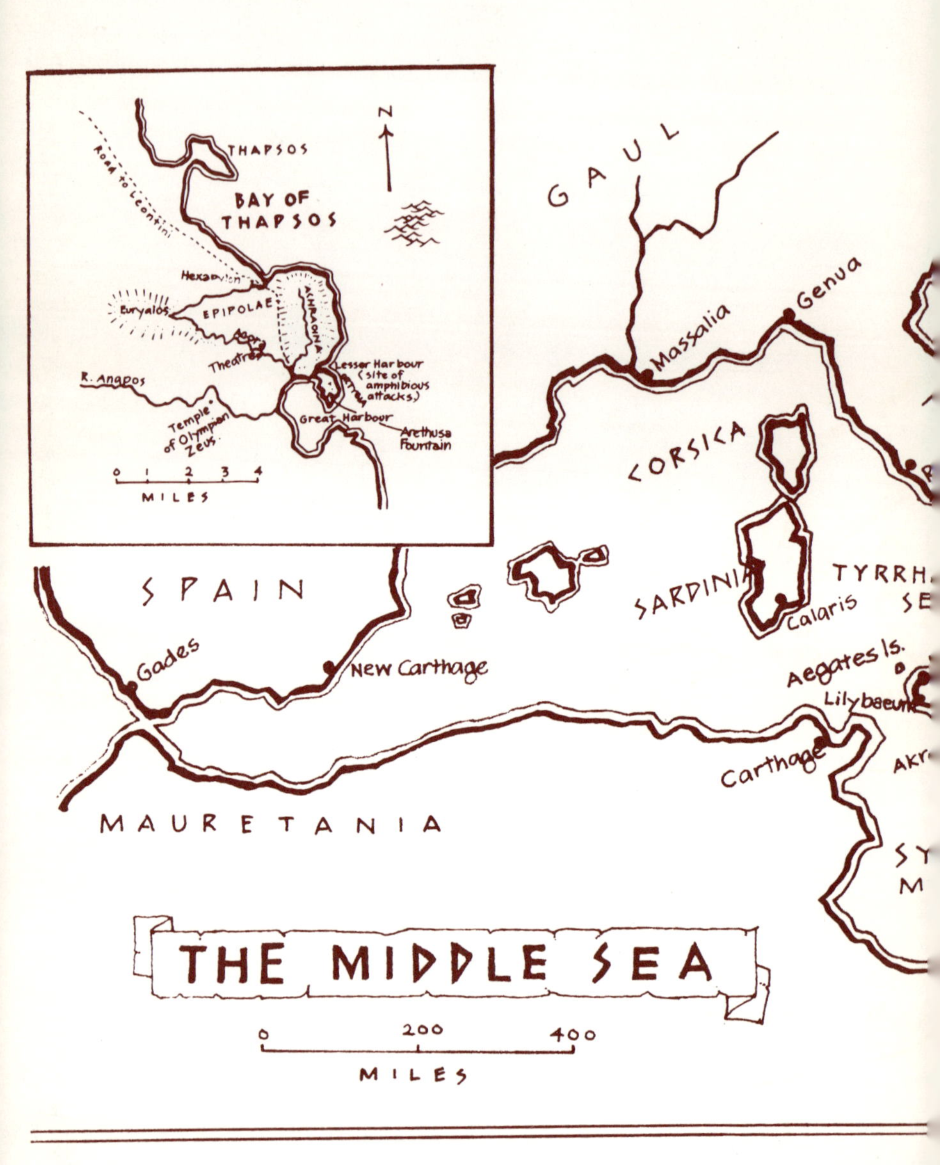
THAPSOS
BAY OF THAPSOS
N
Road to Leontini
Hexapylon
Euryalos
EPIPOLAE
ACHRADINA
Agora
Theatre
R. Anapos
Temple of Olympian Zeus
Great Harbour
Lesser Harbour (site of amphibious attacks)
Arethusa Fountain
0 1 2 3 4
MILES
GAUL
Massalia
Genua
CORSICA
SARDINIA
Calaris
TYRRH. SE.
Aegates Is.
Lilybaeum
SPAIN
Gades
New Carthage
Carthage
AKR
SY M
MAURETANIA
THE MIDDLE SEA
0 200 400
MILES